Helen Black grew up in Pontefract, West Yorkshire. At eighteen she went to Hull University and left three years later with a tattoo on her shoulder and a law degree. She became a lawyer in Peckham and soon had a loyal following of teenagers needing legal advice and bus fares. She ended up working in Luton, working predominantly for children going through the care system. Helen is married to a long-suffering lawyer and is the mother of young twins.

DARK SPACES

HELEN BLACK

Constable & Robinson Ltd
55–56 Russell Square
London WC1B 4HP
www.constablerobinson.com

First published in the UK by C&R Crime,
an imprint of Constable & Robinson Ltd., 2013

A copy of the British Library Cataloguing in
Publication data is available from the British Library

ISBN: 978-1-84901-474-8 (paperback)
ISBN: 978-1-47210-460-1 (ebook)

Printed and bound in the EU

1 3 5 7 9 10 8 6 4 2

BBC News. Tuesday 11 June 2004. 18.45 GMT
'Cruel and Despicable'

A man and two women have been convicted of abusing and assaulting seven children in their care.

George Talbot, 47, his wife Sinead Talbot, 35, and her sister Mary-Ann Yates, 34, were guilty of acts so cruel and despicable they would stay with him forever, said Judge Patrick Wilkes at Luton Crown Court this morning.

Members of the jury wept openly as all three defendants were found guilty of abuse towards the children aged between eight months and sixteen years.

George Talbot, the court heard, had routinely starved all the victims, often forcing them to beg or fight one another for morsels of food. One child told the police that the defendant would invite other adults to come to the house and watch. Sometimes the children would be filmed.

The victims were almost never allowed to leave the house and the youngest three had never been outside, even into the garden.

Doctors confirmed that all the children had been physically and sexually assaulted.

A senior detective described the house in Luton as 'the most evil place' he had ever encountered.

In court, Judge Wilkes said, 'These offences are some of the worst to have come before me.'

The three defendants were between them convicted of cruelty, administering noxious substances, unlawful wounding, sexual assault and grievous bodily harm.

HELEN BLACK

His Honour Judge Wilkes said there would be no option but to sentence them to substantial prison sentences and ordered reports to be prepared.

In the meantime the victims have been placed into the care of the Local Authority.

'My only hope,' said the judge, 'is that these children can now find the families they truly deserve.'

Chapter One

'How is your health, Miss Valentine?'

Dr Kendrick leaned on his desk and gave a small smile that didn't reveal his teeth.

'Me? Fit as a fiddle,' Lilly replied. 'I mean the veins on the back of my legs look like a relief map of Africa and if I sneeze twice in a row I need a clean pair of knickers, but you know, not bad for my age.'

Dr Kendrick laughed politely. 'And your mental health? Any issues there?'

'Depends who you ask,' Lilly said. 'I think my ex-husband might say I was away with the fairies.'

Kendrick nodded and made a slow deliberate note on his A4 pad. 'What about Alice's father? Health-wise I mean.'

'Oh my ex-husband isn't Alice's father,' said Lilly. 'That's the ex-boyfriend.'

Kendrick continued making notes.

'Which makes it sound much worse than it is.' Lilly gulped. 'Much more exciting than real life.'

'It's not my business, Miss Valentine.'

'All the same, I wouldn't want you to think I had a new man every night of the week.' She was gabbling now. 'Chance would be a fine thing, but a wild night chez nous consists of a DVD of *Downtown Abbey* and a family bag of Maltesers—'

Kendrick interrupted with a soft cough. 'And the health of Alice's father?'

'Fine,' Lilly squeaked.

While Kendrick went back to his pad, Lilly puffed out her cheeks and scanned the artwork behind him. There was a black and white photograph of a clown, a thick smile painted around a thin frown.

'Why are you asking me all this, Doctor?' she said. 'I came to discuss Alice.'

She gestured to the car seat at her feet, and the baby in it, sucking a pink fist.

Kendrick put down his pen. 'With babies as young as Alice it's very difficult to make a diagnosis.'

'Maybe there's nothing to diagnose,' said Lilly.

'Indeed,' said Kendrick. 'Her hearing and sight tests came back perfectly fine.'

'There you go then.'

Dr Kendrick managed another smile, but again there was no sign of his teeth. 'And yet your health visitor and GP both confirmed that she failed to meet any of her six-month milestones.'

Lilly shrugged. Tick-box culture pissed her off. Some kids developed later than others. It had always been that way. If Elsa, Lilly's mother, were here now she'd regale this form-filling moron with tales of Candy Cooper from number seven who didn't say a word until she was four.

'And from that moment on they couldn't bloody shut her up. Drove her father to drink.'

Then there was Christopher Quigley who everyone said was backward, but it didn't stop him making a fortune selling knickers on the market did it?

'Listen, Doc,' said Lilly. 'I know you have to do this. A referral's been made and you've got your job to do. I'm a solicitor, so I know how all this works, but I really don't think there's anything wrong with my little girl.'

She scooped Alice out of her car seat and kissed the top of her head. As she ran her chin through the messy curls she could smell sugar and flowers and sky.

'You're probably right,' said Kendrick. 'A mother's instinct usually is, but as you correctly pointed out, I must do my job.' He scribbled something on a second pad and tore off the page. 'Let's meet again in one month and in the meantime, blood tests.'

'Blood tests?'

Kendrick waved his hand. 'A pinprick, nothing more.'

Lilly threw back her head, opened her mouth wide and let out a bark of laughter.

'This'll be interesting.'

Alice's screams rang through the hospital and she batted away the nurse brandishing a needle. In different circumstances Lilly would have been impressed by her daughter's force of will. In her working life she'd met every kind of nutter wailing for their freedom, and every kind of junkie begging for a fix, but no one could scream as loud as Alice.

'I blame the parents.'

Lilly spun on her heels, a retort at the ready for the interfering cow behind her. She was sick to the back teeth of strangers tutting at her in supermarket checkout queues. If they thought they could do better with Alice, they could be Lilly's bloody guest.

When she saw who had spoken, the sharpness fell from her tongue. 'Sheba!'

Lilly's friend gave a deep curtsey. Or as deep as a woman who looked like she was about to give birth any second could manage. Sheba and Lilly both opened their mouths to speak but another one of Alice's determined screeches pierced the air.

'What's wrong with the ankle biter?' asked Sheba. 'I think we can safely assume it's not her lungs.'

'She failed her six-month check-up. Didn't meet her milestones.' Lilly made quotation marks with her fingers around the last word.

Alice screamed again with the melodrama any B-movie actress would be proud of.

'Hey you.' Sheba held up a finger at Alice. 'Shush.'

The baby seemed entranced by the perfectly rounded scarlet nail and her jaw slackened. Peace fell.

'Thank you,' said Sheba and turned to Lilly. 'So she failed to reach her milestones? Which ones?'

'I'm not sure,' said Lilly.

'Supporting herself? Motor skills?'

'Like I said, I'm not sure.' Sheba was lovely but doctors were all the same. Even those who specialized in matters of the mind. 'What about you? What are you here for?'

Sheba ran a hand over her bump. 'I am now officially overdue and whilst I agree that it's never fashionable to be early, keeping people waiting is simply poor manners.'

'They say raspberry leaf tea brings on labour,' said Lilly.

'I've tried it.' Sheba wrinkled her nose. 'Tastes like shit.'

'And sex,' said Lilly. 'That can get things moving.'

Sheba gave a gritty chuckle. If giving up vodka tonic, espresso and Marlboro lights had been good for her unborn baby, it had had no effect on her vocal cords. Even at nine months pregnant she was like the naughtiest girl in the dorm. Lilly sighed. When she'd been carrying Alice her feet had swollen to three times their size and she'd spent most of her days chugging on a bottle of Gaviscon. Sheba, as stylish and saucy as ever, looked as though she might just throw on some black lace undies and enjoy the challenge. Her partner, whoever he was, probably considered himself the luckiest man alive.

'Actually, I've been meaning to call you,' said Sheba. 'I need a favour.'

'Don't tell me,' said Lilly. 'You want to borrow the Alexander McQueen ball gown again.'

Sheba rolled her eyes. 'I need help. Professional help.'

'Go on.'

'I have a patient. A fifteen-year-old girl and she's been charged with stealing a car and driving under the influence,' said Sheba. 'The family instructed their solicitor, but he's from a big commercial practice in London and I don't get the sense he knows his way around the criminal courts.'

Lilly clicked a tongue. Too many lawyers thought crime was an easy ticket. But it was specialized and could be tricky, particularly where children were concerned. You had to know what you were doing.

'Let me grab a pen.' She held out Alice to Sheba, who looked shocked and appalled in equal measure.

'I don't really do babies,' she said.

Lilly nodded at Sheba's belly, hard as a basketball. 'I'd say it was time to start.'

Sheba sniffed and took the little girl, a hand under each armpit. She held her out in front of her, Alice's legs dangling in mid-air. Alice blew a spit bubble.

'Charming,' said Sheba.

Lilly grabbed a biro loitering in the bottom of her bag and flicked a piece of orange plasticine from the nib. It pirouetted through the air and landed on the sleeve of Sheba's elegant jacket.

'I can see where you get your impeccable personal hygiene,' she told Alice.

Lilly stuck out her tongue. 'Fire away.'

'Lydia Morton-Daley. Like I say, she's fifteen. Came to us about two weeks ago after the police caught her driving home from a party. Apparently she came this close to wrapping the car round

7

a tree.' Sheba tried to demonstrate a tiny distance between her fingers, but with Alice still held at arm's length like a smelly nappy, she could do little more than jiggle her wrists. 'Can't I put her in the car seat?'

'If you're prepared to shout above the din, go for it,' answered Lilly.

Sheba pouted, but kept Alice in her grip. 'When the cops breathalysed Lydia she was three times over the limit.'

Lilly whistled, which made Alice laugh and pedal her feet.

'If you don't want me to drop you onto the hard floor, I suggest you keep still,' Sheba told her. 'When the parents brought her to the Grove, I thought they might be trying to pull a fast one. Another middle-class brat avoiding her punishment by blaming it all on depression.'

Lilly might have called her a sceptic but experience told her that Lydia's parents wouldn't be the first to use their power and money to escape justice.

'And now?' she asked.

Sheba frowned. 'Now I'm not sure. Whatever the reason for Lydia's admission, she does seem to be exhibiting symptoms of mental illness. One thing I do know is that I need her in hospital for assessment, not in custody, which is where she might end up if Mr Pinstriped Suit puts his size tens where they're not needed.'

Lilly finished writing down the details, slung the paper and pen back into her bag and appraised Sheba, who was now trying to rock Alice from side to side in what was probably meant to be a soothing manner. Alice swung like a flag in the wind, snorting and drooling.

'Will you help me, Lilly?'

It wasn't clear if Sheba's request was for help with the case or the removal of Alice.

Lilly held out her arms. ''Course I will.'

★ ★ ★

The ground was hard under Jack's trainers, each ridge of earth frozen solid, as he pounded up the hill. Even at midday the sun couldn't summon enough strength to melt the January frosts.

'Mary, Mother of God.' He wiped the sweat that was running down his face with his sleeve. 'This is a tough one.'

Kate didn't break her stride and laughed at him. Christ, the woman wasn't even panting.

'You're getting old, McNally,' she told him and upped her pace so that she was a few feet ahead, her pert arse-cheeks waving at him through skintight Lycra. 'Ready for the knacker's yard.'

He shook his head, found a spurt of energy and propelled himself upwards, slapping her backside as he passed her. There was life in the old dog yet.

At the summit the view was spectacular, the valley below sparkling and white, as if the fields were covered in glass beads. Jack slowed to a stop. He loved it up here on the Downs, where it was always deserted.

'Lightweight,' said Kate and took her place by his side. Unlike Jack she kept moving, swaying from side to side.

'I need to make a call,' said Jack.

'You need a breather more like.'

Jack pulled out his mobile. He did need to make a call, but in truth he did need a second's rest before he keeled over. He ran regularly and considered himself pretty fit but Kate was something else. She extended her right leg in front of her and bent forward from the waist to pull up the toe of her trainer and stretch out her hamstrings. She looked up at him, her face flushed pink, her lips slightly apart.

'Who're you calling?' she asked.

Jack went into his contacts. 'Lilly.'

'Right.' Kate stood upright.

'She took Alice to the hospital and I want to know how they got on,' he said.

Kate nodded and took a couple of steps away, cupping her hand over her eyes to look out at the scenery while Jack waited for Lilly to pick up.

'Hey, Jack,' said Lilly.

'How did you get on?' he asked.

'Fine. The doctor agreed that there's very unlikely to be anything wrong with Alice. All they did was take a bit of blood.'

'Blood!'

'A pinprick, Jack, they didn't drain pints of the stuff from her.'

Jack felt anxiety wash through him. 'I should have come with you.'

'We talked about it, Jack,' she said. 'There was no point us both having time off work.'

He was about to point out that Lilly stating something as fact and them talking it through were not one and the same thing, but Kate tapped her watch with her finger. They needed to get back to the nick.

'Can I come and see her tonight?' he asked.

'There's no need Jack, she's fine,' said Lilly.

'It's not about need.'

'You're coming over tomorrow morning to collect her,' said Lilly. 'You'll see for yourself that she's on top form.'

Jack hung up and took a deep breath. He hated having to make an appointment to see his daughter. It wasn't how it was supposed to be.

'Okay?' Kate put a hand on Jack's arm.

He shrugged. It wasn't okay was it? But what was the point in going over it? When he and Lilly had been together they had spent fecking hours chewing stuff over and where had it got them? Barely speaking and Jack only allowed to spend time with his flesh and blood if it was on Lilly's pre-agreed schedule.

'Let's go,' said Kate and set off.

★ ★ ★

DARK SPACES

Lilly held Alice in the crook of one arm and wiped the brass name-plate fixed to the wall outside her office with a spit-moistened tissue. A bird had shit from on high, obliterating the '& co' after 'Valentine'. Frankly, the sparrow had known what he was doing. There was no '& co'. Lilly had had a brief spell of assistance from a young Muslim woman called Taslima who had brought with her a steely calm that was much appreciated. Unfortunately, she had ended up embroiled in one of Lilly's cases, getting kidnapped and having to leap from a burning building. It had not been a great shock when she had decided to retrain as a barrister. Then there'd been Karol: a refugee, who had a knack for fixing technology, was a dab hand at filing and sported a six-pack Justin Timberlake would be proud of. But he'd left to open a bar in Brighton called Dorothy's with his boyfriend.

As Lilly unlocked the door and stepped over the post, she vowed to get some proper, permanent help.

She ignored the answer machine, winking its accusations at her, and picked up the phone. She dialled the number Sheba had given her and laid Alice on a play mat she kept in the reception.

'Brady Moore and Lodge.' The response was instantaneous.

'Blimey,' said Lilly. 'Were you waiting for the phone to ring?'

'Yes,' said the receptionist, as if that were obvious. 'Can I help you?'

Lilly checked her notes. Her biro had been running out and it was difficult to make out the name. 'Can I speak to a Paul Sara . . . sorry I can't read my own writing.' Lilly squinted. 'It's definitely Sara-something.'

Lilly heard nails tapping a keyboard.

'There's no one here of that name. Could it be Paul Santana?' asked the receptionist.

Lilly rechecked the piece of paper. In all honesty it could say anything. 'Let's give him a twirl,' she said and gave her name.

The hold music was *The Planets* by Holst, a deep resonant cello rising and falling. Lilly pressed the squawk box button and the music filled her own office. Alice looked up and pointed a chubby finger towards the sound. As the crash of a cymbal resonated, Lilly bent over her baby and began conducting. Alice gave her best smile, the stubby ends of front teeth erupting through her gums. The music lifted towards a crescendo and Lilly waved her arms and head madly, her long curls flying. Alice squealed in delight.

The music stopped abruptly. 'Paul Santana.'

'Right.' Lilly straightened. 'Hello there.'

'Miss Valentine?'

Lilly blew a stray tendril from her mouth. 'That's me.'

'I'm sure the error is mine,' he said. 'But I can't place you momentarily.'

Ooh, he was slick.

'No error at all,' said Lilly. 'We've never met.'

'An unfortunate circumstance, I'm sure.'

A bit too slick.

'Your name was passed on to me by Lydia Morton-Daley's therapist. I understand you're the family's solicitor.'

'Indeed,' he said. 'I deal with all the Morton-Daleys' legal affairs.'

'The difficulty, as I understand it, is that you specialize in commercial work and that Lydia requires criminal advice.'

'Oh, I think my knowledge will be enough to cover the small matter of a teenager drinking too much,' he said. 'I may not be Rumpole but this isn't serious enough to cause concern.'

Lilly sighed. When would some lawyers learn to stick to what they were good at? She wouldn't pull up a chair, stick her feet on his desk and advise his clients on their tax bills, would she?

'She was three times over the limit and crashed a Merc she'd hot-wired. When the police pulled her out she was still holding a bottle of vodka. With her history it doesn't look great.'

'History?'

'She's been nicked four times in the past couple of years. Once for criminal damage, twice for shoplifting and recently for disorderly conduct. Each time she got off with a caution but that's most definitely not going to happen this time,' said Lilly. 'It's not beyond the realms of possibility that Lydia could spend some time in custody. And, if that happens, her family aren't going to be best pleased, are they?'

Lilly let the question hang in the air, her meaning as clear as a mountain stream.

He coughed. 'Perhaps on further reflection it would be better to transfer the file to a solicitor with more time to spend on it. These cases can get very time-consuming.'

The oil slick oozed out.

'Why don't I give you my email address?' said Lilly. 'And you can send the papers over.'

When Gem wakes up it's nearly one o'clock and the telly and the lights are off. The leccy must have run out. Her cheek is stuck to the settee and when she pushes herself up it peels away like a plaster coming off in the bath. It feels like some of her skin got left behind. She even checks there're no bits of it on the PVC.

Gem didn't go to school this morning. Mum was on the missing list and she couldn't leave Tyler on his own could she? But it's gonna get well boring if they can't watch anything.

Tyler opens his eyes and looks at his sister. He's been asleep too, cuddled up with Marley on the floor.

'I hungry,' he says.

Gem nods at him. She's hungry as well but she doubts there'll be anything in the fridge.

She pats Marley on the head and he wags his tail. The dog must be starving too. When Mum gets back she'd better have been to the shops.

She picks up Tyler. His nappy is massive and his trousers feel damp around the bum. Mum thinks he should be dry by now, but he ain't, so Gem don't know why she even says it.

She takes him through to the kitchen and opens the fridge. It don't work so they just keep stuff in there away from Marley. Like she thought, it's virtually empty. There's a tin of chicken soup but she can't even heat it up, can she?

'I hungry,' Tyler says again.

'All right,' Gem says and reaches for the tin opener. They'll have to eat it cold. It ain't like it's the first time.

She's spooning it straight from the tin, one for Tyler, one for Marley, then one for herself, when Mum walks in.

'That's not clean, Gem,' she says and flops into the chair opposite.

Gem shrugs and carries on. 'We need money for the meter.' She notices Mum ain't carrying no shopping bags. 'And food.'

'Why didn't you go over to Mary's and borrow a couple of quid?'

'We already owe her a fiver,' Gem replies.

Mum sighs and pats herself down. Right in the bottom of her jacket pocket she finds a single battered ciggie and lights it. Gem watches the end glow red and the smoke stream out of Mum's nose.

'Give us a puff,' she says.

'You shouldn't even be smoking at your age,' Mum says. But she hands it out to Gem. 'You should be in school.'

Gem hands the spoon to Tyler so he can lick off the cold soup and takes the fag. Marley jumps up at the baby, trying to get the spoon.

'Get down.' Mum bats Marley away.

'He's hungry,' Gem tells her.

'We're all fucking hungry.' Mum holds out her fingers in a V shape to take her ciggie back.

Gem steals another quick drag and puts Tyler on the floor. Marley leaps at him and steals the spoon, making a run for it into the other room. She can't be bothered to chase him.

'I'll go out then, shall I?' she asks.

Mum nods and drops her dog-end into the empty soup tin.

It was dark by the time Lilly got back to her cottage and she made straight for the kitchen, ditching Alice in a high chair alongside. She flicked on the kettle and when the water boiled she poured it over a large saucepan of spaghetti. Then she added a fistful of salt crystals. Her mother had always told her that the water for cooking pasta should be as salty as the Mediteranean; a rather exotic pronouncement, given she had never been further than Blackpool.

When the pan was bubbling Lilly pulled eggs, bacon, cream and parmesan from the fridge.

'Is that Carbonara?'

Lilly almost jumped out of her skin. 'Bloody hell, Sam.'

Her teenaged son dropped his school bag on the floor at his feet. Not far behind was his dad.

'Is that what I think it is?' his dad asked.

Spaghetti Carbonara was her ex-husband's desert island meal. When they'd first got together Lilly had made a huge vat of the stuff which they took back to bed with them. She'd cooked it at least once a week during their marriage.

'I think you have a sixth sense about it,' she said. 'Isn't Cara expecting you back home for dinner?'

David shrugged. His new wife didn't really cook. Instead she followed a macrobiotic lifestyle that featured a profusion of raw vegetables and pulses. Lilly laughed and slung more spaghetti into the pan.

When they'd all had seconds, Sam slunk out of the room mumbling something about geography revision and Lilly poured herself a generous glass of wine. David did the same.

'You're driving,' she told him.

'Actually, Lil . . .' He took a gulp. 'I was hoping I could stay here tonight.'

Lilly almost choked. 'What?'

When she and David had separated she'd been bereft. Gnawed bare like a dog's bone, even her marrow sucked away. It had taken her years to get past the corrosive anger to a place where they could be friends for Sam's sake. Surely he couldn't be suggesting what she thought he was suggesting?

'I meant on the sofa of course,' he said.

Relief washed over Lilly but that was quickly eclipsed by the piquing of her temper.

'Why?' she asked. 'What's happened?'

David didn't look up from the rim of his glass, but the pink glow seeping up from his collar to his ears told her everything.

'Cara's thrown you out,' she shouted. 'She has, hasn't she?'

'Shush,' he said and pointed to the ceiling, indicating where Sam's bedroom was situated.

'Bloody hell, David,' Lilly stage-whispered. 'What did you do?'

'Nothing.' David put down his wine and coughed. 'But Cara has got it into her head that I'm seeing someone else.'

Lilly slammed her own drink onto the table, sloshing its contents over the wood.

'Christ Almighty, David, when will you ever learn to keep it in your trousers?'

Lilly was furious. God knows she was no fan of Botox Belle but she and David had a life together, a child together. Lilly thought he'd finally grown up.

'It's not how it looks,' he said. 'Cara has got it all wrong.'

'That's what you told me,' Lilly spat.

'Well this is nice.' Sam leaned against the door frame. 'Just like the good old days.'

David looked up. 'Sorry, Sam, your mother and I were just discussing a few things.'

Sam rolled his eyes and lifted his shirt to scratch his stomach. His muscles were washboard tight, each ab clearly delineated. Lilly knew he'd started to use the gym at school but the transformation was incredible. She had to stop herself staring.

'Your dad's staying here tonight,' she said. 'He's had a bit of a row with Cara, but nothing to worry about.'

'So you thought you'd come over here and row with Mum instead?' Sam shook his head. 'Sucker.'

'Sam!' Lilly and David shouted as one.

He put up his hands in mock surrender. 'Whatever. Just keep it down, would you, some of us have work to do.'

With that, he sloped away and David mouthed his thanks to Lilly.

It's hours before Gem has anything worth taking to Ali.

First she tried Superdrug but it was completely on top. Some old cow of an assistant followed her around. Even when Gem pretended to check out the rows of nail varnish, she stood about a foot away, her arms folded. Bitch.

Boots was no better.

And it ain't like Gem's green. She's been shoplifting since she was about ten or eleven. Definitely ten. She started when she went into care the first time. Mum got sent away and Gem got sent to a foster family. Ronnie and Sandra Fitzpatrick. They were all right as it goes. Treated her like one of their own kids. The oldest was called Chris, only Sandra insisted everyone call him Christopher, which is a bit wanky really, but then she gave the name to him, so it was up to her. Anyway, it was Chris who first took her out on the rob. He showed her all the best places and how to get the stuff from the shelves to her pockets. Gem was a natural and they were soon at it every day.

'I have taught you well, young Padawan,' he used to say.

He tried to teach her some other things as well, but Gem weren't having none of that.

In the end she got even better at it than Chris and they only ended up getting caught 'cos he got all competitive and tried to nick a bike from Halfords.

Chris blamed it all on Gem of course, and Ronnie and Sandra believed him. After that she got sent to a children's home.

When she gets to the end of Ali's road, she counts up what she's got. Four packs of batteries, a jar of coffee and a half-bottle of Jim Beam. It should earn her at least a tenner.

The house next door to Ali's has been closed up, wooden boards nailed across every window. He'll be glad about that 'cos the place had got taken over by junkies and they were always setting fire to stuff and leaving dirty needles in the garden.

When Gem rings the bell, it's Ali's wife who comes to the door. Her name's Herika and she don't speak much English.

'Is Ali in?' Gem asks.

Herika nods and points to the kitchen at the end of the hallway. Gem wipes her feet on the mat. The house is always spotless and she don't want to trail any mud indoors. Ali is sat at the kitchen table chatting to two other men. He once told her he was from Turkey so he must be talking in whatever language they speak there 'cos Gem can't understand a word. Herika skirts behind them to the cooker where she's frying slices of them big shiny purple things. Gem don't know what they're called but they smell lovely.

Ali looks up at Gem and smiles.

'Hello, my precious stone.' He always calls her that. 'What have you got for me today?'

Gem lays the gear on the table and waits as Ali inspects it, turning the batteries over in his hands as if he's never seen any before.

'It's all good stuff,' Gem tells him. 'None of that own brand shit.'

Herika slides a plate of food onto the plastic tablecloth and the men each take a piece. Gem's stomach growls.

Ali swallows and sighs. 'I can see that, my precious, but it's getting very hard to shift anything these days. There's a recession on, you know.'

Ali turns to his mates who all nod in agreement, their lips and fingers greasy.

That's the trouble with Ali. He makes out he's all nice and friendly but he'll still try to rip you off. Sometimes, if he won't give her enough, she'll try Fred the Shred over in Ring Farm, but that's miles away and she's got to get back with some tea for Tyler and Mum.

'I'll give you a fiver,' says Ali.

Bastard. If she buys fish fingers, chips and beans from the Spar, another bunch of robbing bastards, then there won't be anything left for the meter.

'It's easily worth a tenner,' says Gem.

Ali shakes his head. 'Sorry, my precious, no can do.'

Tears sting Gem's eyes. She's really cold, really tired and really hungry. 'Eight.'

Ali shakes his head and slips another piece of food into his mouth. Gem watches him chew and tries not to scream. In the end Herika puts a hand on his shoulder and whispers something in his ear. Her lips are all pink and smooth. Gem runs a finger over her own chapped mouth, the dry skin catching on her nail.

'My wife will be the death of me,' Ali laughs and reaches behind him to a tin box. He takes out a five-pound note and three one-pound coins, then holds them out to Gem. 'Spend it wisely, my precious stone.'

Gem grabs the cash, hurries down the hallway and heads off to the Spar.

Lilly snuggled under her duvet, Alice asleep on her chest, laptop balanced on her knees, family-sized bag of Revels on her bedside table.

She smiled at the thought of David downstairs on the sofa, trying to get comfortable in an old sleeping bag that hadn't been washed since Sam's last camping trip with school. She'd chucked a folded towel at him for a pillow and told him to sleep tight, an edge of cruel enjoyment in her voice. There was a spare on her bed, but she was buggered if she was going to give it to the two-timing rat.

She logged on and accessed the file Santana had sent her. It was made up entirely of police documents. Mr Slick hadn't made any notes of his own, hadn't even been to see his client in the Grove by the looks of it.

Lilly popped a Revel into her mouth and opened the arresting officers' notes. PC Rashid and WPC Knight had been called to attend a party in Great Markham. The neighbours had reported an argument breaking out among a group of youths in the country lane outside the house where the party was taking place. But before the police officers arrived at the scene they were forced off the road by a blue Mercedes SLK careering wildly up the lane at speed.

My colleague, PC Rashid, who was driving the squad car, quickly made a U-turn and we set off in pursuit of the Mercedes.

The temperature that night had fallen well below zero and the roads were icy. It soon became obvious that the driver of the vehicle was making no concessions to the conditions, travelling at speeds of over seventy miles an hour.

Both our siren and lights were functioning, but the driver made no attempt to slow down. As the Mercedes approached a particularly sharp bend it slid over a metre to its left, scraping a tree.

My colleague and I were very concerned that if another car approached from the opposite direction there would be a head-on collision. We took the decision that at the first opportunity we needed to overtake and force the Mercedes to a standstill.

We followed the car for a further mile, during which period it hit more trees, bushes and even a low wall. At all times the speed did not fall below sixty miles per hour.

When the road opened out PC Rashid accelerated. As we came alongside the Mercedes I looked inside. The driver was a young female aged 14–18. She was white with short dark hair. She glanced in our direction and I gestured her to pull over. Instead she began to increase her speed.

'Mum.'

Sam slouched in the landing outside Lilly's bedroom, a toothbrush lodged in the side of his mouth.

'You should be asleep,' she said.

He pulled out the brush and waggled it, his lips ringed with white froth. 'Why did you and Dad split up?'

Lilly opened her mouth to give a platitude about no longer being able to live together.

'And don't give me any of that shit about not being able to live together,' said Sam.

Lilly let her lips fall shut. What could she say? Did Sam really need to know that his Dad had got bored of Lilly? That he'd started an affair?

'Dad says it's because you didn't trust him. He says that's why you split up with Jack too. He says you have issues.'

Lilly felt a strong urge to tell Sam a few home truths but she kept it in check. 'He's quite the amateur psychologist isn't he?'

Sam pointed the brush at her. 'He says it's because your dad took off when you were a kid.'

'All very interesting,' said Lilly. 'But let me refer you to the evidence here: our resident relationship expert is currently having to sleep on our sofa.' She closed the lid of her laptop. 'The truth is, big man, marriages end for all sorts of complicated reasons and things are never as straightforward as he did this or she did that. What's important here is that your dad and I get on better than ever.'

'It didn't sound like that downstairs,' said Sam.

'Once again can I refer you to the evidence. Dad is sleeping on our sofa. '

Sam pouted. The toothpaste had dried to chalky scabs that flaked down his chin.

'Now go to bed for God's sake,' she said. 'As much as I love these light-hearted little chats it's ten o'clock on a Monday night.'

She listened to the sound of the tap running, then the creak of his bed as he made himself comfortable before she allowed herself to return to her work. Trust issues indeed. She'd give David a royal bollocking tomorrow morning.

PC Rashid put his foot to the floor and we managed to overtake the Mercedes.

I turned around, looked at the driver through our rear window and made another gesture for the driver to pull over. Once again she did not do as requested and as PC Rashid began to slow, she hit the back of our car.

We continued to slow and the driver of the Mercedes attempted to get round us several times, leaving PC Rashid with no alternative than to place the squad car in its way. It hit us a further three times.

In this way, we forced the Mercedes to slow and I assumed the driver would eventually stop. However, when we reached approximately twenty miles per hour, the Mercedes veered off the road to its left, crashing through trees and undergrowth, landing with force in a ditch.

PC Rashid brought the squad car to a halt and I ran towards the Mercedes, which was badly damaged from the accident. I opened the driver's door and found the female driver slumped over the steering wheel. Her hair was covered in shattered glass from the windscreen. Her left hand was outstretched onto the passenger seat and she was still holding a bottle of Smirnoff vodka.

I asked her repeatedly if she was all right, but did not want to move her in case of injury. After a few seconds the female appeared to come round and she turned her face to me. At this point I could see that she was younger than eighteen and that her mouth was covered in blood.

She mumbled something to me that I could not make out so I knelt down and put my ear to her lips. I could smell alcohol strongly on her breath.

'You shouldn't have stopped me,' she said.

I pointed out that she was driving in a reckless manner endangering not only her own life but the lives of others.

'You shouldn't have stopped me,' she repeated.

At that point the ambulance arrived and I handed the scene to the paramedics who took the female away on a stretcher.

As gently as she could manage, Lilly lifted Alice from the nesting place on her chest and placed the baby in the cot beside her bed. Lilly held her breath as Alice's eyes fluttered open. When she cranked herself up, Alice could scream into the small hours and, having just read the shocking statement of WPC Knight, Lilly knew that she was going to need a good night's sleep before her appointment at the Grove in the morning.

Tyler has fallen asleep on the settee so Gem puts her coat over him. He needs a clean nappy but there wasn't enough money left after she'd bought food, fags and saved a couple of quid for the meter.

Mum looks up from the telly. 'He'll get a sore bum.'

Gem don't say nothing. Nothing she can say. There weren't enough left.

'We don't want the social on our backs again,' Mum says.

Their caseworker, Maria, is a proper cow. One time she checked the baby and he had rotten nappy rash so she put him on the child protection register. Being honest, it were pretty bad, the skin peeling off and bleeding and that, but all it needed was some cream from the doctor's.

'That bitch is just waiting for me to slip up,' says Mum. 'Then they'll put Tyler up for adoption and we'll never see him again.'

She don't worry so much about Gem. If they put her in care again, there's not much can happen at her age. They might find a foster family, but probably not. Wherever they place her she'll just get on the next bus home.

Mum opens the packet of Bensons, counts them up to make sure she's got two left for the morning, and lights one. Gem fishes in the ashtray and finds one she nipped earlier then she flicks through the channels to find something to watch.

'I hate that one,' says Mum, when Gem settles on a programme about traffic police.

'There ain't nothing else on,' says Gem.

Gem laughs as some boy on a dirt bike gets chased through an estate, 'til he hits the kerb and it flies from under him. The copper jumps out of his car and tears after him. But he's a fat bastard and the kid gets away on his toes. He thinks he's escaped when another police car pulls up right in front of him.

'He's fucked now,' says Mum.

The boy spins around, trying to work out which way to run, but there's filth on all sides of him. The first copper, the fat one, is on him now and looks like he wants to give him a right clump. Gem cringes, waiting for the fist to strike.

Instead, the telly goes dead and they're plunged into darkness.

'Shit,' says Gem.

The money in the meter has run out.

They sit there for a few seconds, their fag ends glowing red in the black, 'til their eyes get used to it. Then Gem stabs out her dog-end and picks up the baby. Maria says he should be sleeping in his own bed now, but the sheets ain't been changed. And anyway he prefers it in with Gem.

'Might as well go to bed,' she says.

'Might as well,' says Mum, but she don't move.

Chapter Two

**In the Central Criminal Court
Case number 1374**

Regina

v.

Talbot, Talbot and Yates

On 11 June 2004, His Honour Judge Wilkes ordered reports to be prepared on the convicted defendants George and Sinead Talbot and Mary-Ann Yates in order to assist with their sentencing.

In my capacity as a probation officer, I was tasked with the report on Sinead Talbot and scheduled three appointments with her at HMP Highpoint where she was in custody.

During the first meeting on 18 June, Mrs Talbot remained extremely taciturn for much of our time together.

She spoke only to confirm that she had been born Sinead Yates on 9 May 1969 in Liverpool and that she had spent her childhood living with her parents who were immigrants from County Cork in Eire, though she spent extensive periods in the care of the local authority.

Mrs Talbot would not comment on why she had been taken into care and unfortunately there is scant documentation on the Social Services file. There is an indication that on at least two separate occasions her mother voluntarily placed her daughter into the hands of social workers.

The record does however show that at fifteen, Mrs Talbot ran away from the children's home where she was then residing and became pregnant to and engaged with George Talbot, the first defendant. He was twenty-seven at the time.

Mrs Talbot confirmed by nod only that she miscarried that child, but married her husband two days after her sixteenth birthday.

When I asked Mrs Talbot to describe her marriage she did not reply, eventually placing her hands over her face. She did not acknowledge any further questions and did not provide any explanation as to why she, her husband and her sister abused their victims. She did not, in fact, move.

As the end of our appointment drew close and I stood to leave, Mrs Talbot finally looked up at me and asked if I had seen her 'babies'. I informed her that I had not met the children. She told me that was a great shame and that they had 'lovely manners'.

Lilly poured boiling water over instant coffee, the steam swirling around the kitchen.

'Milk no sugar,' David called from inside his sleeping bag.

'Get it yourself,' Lilly shouted back. 'This isn't a bloody bed and breakfast.'

All the same, she pulled another mug from the cupboard and shovelled in a spoonful of granules. When David ambled into the room in his boxer shorts, she thrust the drink into his hands. 'Sleep well?'

He frowned his answer.

'I'd jump in the shower before Sam if I were you,' said Lilly. 'Or there'll be no hot water left.'

'Haven't you had the boiler fixed yet?' David asked.

'My ex-husband insists on sending his son to private school,' said Lilly. 'After the fees we can barely afford to eat.'

David slapped Lilly on her ample backside. 'You don't look starving to me.'

She laughed. He wasn't being rude. He'd always had quite a thing for curves. Or so she thought before he took up with the bag of bones that was Botox Belle.

'Towels are in the airing cupboard,' she said, ushering him upstairs. 'And whatever you do, don't come down while Jack's here.'

'Why not?'

Lilly sighed. 'You know how prickly he gets. He's already on the warpath about not coming to the hospital with me yesterday. If he finds out you're staying here, it'll just make things even more difficult than they already are.'

David shrugged and headed into the bathroom. Lilly knew she was being daft about what Jack might think. First, David was just crashing on the sofa, and second, it really was none of Jack's business. But there didn't seem any point in troubling trouble.

When the doorbell rang, she scooped up Alice and opened the door. Alice beamed at the sight of her daddy.

'Hello, angel.' Jack took the baby from Lilly. 'I hear you were a very brave girl for the doctors.'

Lilly laughed. 'She screamed the bloody place down.'

Jack's smile fell. 'You said she was fine.'

'Relax, Jack. I'm joking. She was fine. She was just being Alice.'

Jack looked from Alice to Lilly and back again, clearly unsure where the truth lay. Lilly knew there was nothing else she could say and bent down for Alice's changing bag.

'Everything's in there.' She handed it to Jack. Their conversation was at an end.

'I'll be off then,' he said.

'Yes.'

Lilly kissed Alice's head and was grateful when she shut the door behind them.

'You don't have to be so rude.' Sam was chewing a piece of toast.

'How was I rude?'

'You couldn't wait to get rid of him.'

'It's tricky at the moment.' Lilly's stomach rumbled. She was starving. 'Jack's being tricky at the moment.'

'Whereas you . . .' Sam let it hang in the air.

Lilly marched to the kitchen and rammed a slice of bread into the toaster. 'Whereas I am just trying to do my bloody best.'

She waited for it to pop and then smeared it thickly with butter and lime marmalade.

'Any going spare?' David appeared with a towel wrapped around his waist, water dripping down his bare chest.

'Not a chance,' Lilly told him.

'Oh go on.'

Lilly waved him away, but he stood there opening and closing his mouth like baby chick.

'Jesus,' Lilly laughed and shoved the toast into his mouth as if she were posting a letter, vaguely registering the doorbell ringing again.

The next moment Jack was stood in the kitchen with Sam behind him mouthing an apology. Jack's face darkened at the sight of Lilly and her ex-husband frolicking half-naked in her kitchen.

'Hello, David,' he said.

David ripped the toast from his mouth and swallowed what was left. 'Hi, Jack.'

'David's staying here for a few days,' Lilly said. 'On the sofa.'

Jack nodded coldly. 'I just wondered if you'd got any antiseptic. Alice's arm looks a bit inflamed where the needle went in.'

Lilly rummaged in the drawer where she kept her first aid kit. Among the empty packets of aspirin and out-of-date cold sore cream she found a half-used tube of Savlon.

'I changed the plaster this morning,' she said.

The tube of cream was missing its cap and there were congealed lumps around the nozzle. Lilly grabbed a piece of kitchen roll and wiped it clean. The smell of antiseptic hit the back of her throat.

Jack took the tube. 'Like I say, it looks a bit inflamed.'

Lilly was still cursing herself as she arrived outside the Grove. Why had she tried to hide the fact that David was staying? She should have just told Jack what was happening. Instead, the situation had put her on the back foot.

She glanced at her mobile, abandoned in the central console. Should she call him? Try to clear the air? Then again, why should she? They were finished. Over. Not long ago it had mattered to her what he thought. Then he'd started something with a cute little teacher from South Africa. All slender legs and smooth blonde hair. He said he hadn't slept with her, and Lilly believed him. Or at least she wanted to. But ultimately it didn't matter. While she'd been swollen and irritable with pregnancy, Jack had been sneaking around, enjoying dinners out and secret texts. That was enough for Lilly.

She turned off her phone and slid it into her jacket pocket.

The Grove had an impressive red-brick facade, the gaping entrance flanked by white columns. Built at the turn of the nineteenth century, it was impeccably maintained, swallowing government funding like a frog swallows flies. Its beauty had seen off numerous attempts to shut it down and replace it with a site built for purpose and efficiency.

Lilly grabbed her bag, locked the Mini and strode inside with more confidence than she felt. She absolutely detested hospitals, and if forced to come within spitting distance of one would start to sweat and shiver as if she had flu. It had been this way since her mother had died slowly and painfully when Lilly was twenty-one.

She fiddled with her top button and plastered on a grin, telling herself that this was different. This was a facility providing mental health care and conducting research. No one was dying.

By the time she approached the reception desk, her cheeks were beginning to ache with the width of her grin.

'Can I help you?' The receptionist wore a jersey wrap dress, pearl droplet earrings and a smile.

'I'm here to see Lydia Morton-Daley,' Lilly replied.

Before the receptionist could answer, a nurse, who had been ferreting in a drawer, interrupted. 'Visiting hours are not until two.'

'I'm a solicitor,' Lilly told her. 'I have an appointment.'

'A solicitor?' the nurse asked.

Lilly didn't let her smile fade. 'That's right.'

'You'd better call Doctor Piper,' the nurse told the receptionist.

The receptionist nodded and swivelled her chair so that her back was to Lilly, then she spoke quietly into a telephone. At last she replaced the receiver and came back to Lilly.

'Take a seat.'

The two women spoke in hushed tones as Lilly did as she was told, tucking her ankles under the chair, scanning the room. To her left was a low table scattered with leaflets. She picked up the brightest, shocking pink letters screaming at her to 'Spot the signs of an eating disorder'. As she read through the ten most common ways to identify anorexia, she noticed someone had scrawled a tiny message in biro: 'Fuck food'.

'Miss Valentine?'

Lilly looked up at a man in his mid-forties, eyes dark brown and accentuated by laughter lines, a smattering of grey at his temples. The nurse pounced on him and hissed something Lilly didn't catch. The man tapped her shoulders with the blades of his hands three times. Chop, chop, chop. Then moved towards Lilly.

'Harry Piper.' He held out his hand to Lilly. 'I've taken over Sheba's patient list while she produces the next Nobel prize-winning psychotherapist.'

Lilly shook his hand. The grip was firm, the skin of his palm smooth against hers.

'Our guest says she's a solicitor,' the nurse told him.

He turned to her. 'It's fine, Elaine. We're expecting her.'

The nurse gave Lilly a final look and left.

'Don't mind Elaine.' Piper bent his head towards Lilly. 'She's very suspicious.'

'Of what?' Lilly asked.

Piper laughed. 'Everything.' He gestured to a side door. 'Shall we?'

Lilly nodded and let him lead her through to the corridor beyond.

'Have you ever been in a mental hospital before?' he asked.

'No.'

'It's not how most people imagine,' he said.

'What do most people imagine?' Lilly asked.

There was a twinkle in his eye. 'Oh I don't know. A cross between *One Flew Over the Cuckoo's Nest* and *Jacob's Ladder*. Lots of blood and screaming into the night.'

Actually Lilly had pictured it as pretty calm. The patients koshed by antipsychotic medicine.

'I don't have any preconceptions,' she said.

Piper laughed and wagged a finger at her. 'So what did Sheba tell you about Lydia?' he asked.

'Not too much. She got nicked for stealing a car and driving under the influence,' said Lilly. 'And she was exhibiting symptoms of mental illness.'

Piper nodded. They had reached the end of the corridor and he began to tap in a code to open the next door, the pad of his finger met by a sharp bleep.

'What do you think?' Lilly asked.

The door lock released and he held it open for her. 'I haven't had a chance to spend too much time with Lydia yet, but I'd say Sheba is spot on. She usually is.'

'What's your diagnosis?'

'Too early to say. But there's a hell of a lot going on,' he said.

'What sort of thing?'

'She switches between being very angry and destructive to being indiscriminately affectionate. She's very manipulative and tells whopping lies. But she's also brutally honest about some things, inappropriately so.'

'Do you think she'll respond to treatment?' Lilly asked.

He stopped at yet another door, his fingers on the handle. 'Why don't you meet her and tell me what you think?'

When he opened the door a gush of hot air hit Lilly. Like being blasted by a hairdryer. Lilly felt sweat prickle in her armpits.

'Lydia hates to be cold,' said Piper.

Lilly entered the room and clawed at her collar. In the far corner was a girl. She was tiny, almost birdlike. Her bare arms shockingly snappable. She didn't look at them, instead she kept her gaze fixed on the wall.

'Lydia, this is Miss Valentine, a solicitor Sheba arranged to visit you,' said Piper.

'What happened to the fuckwit that came to the police station?' The girl's accent was cut glass, the voice clear.

'We thought you needed a specialist,' said Piper.

She kept her eyes firmly on the wall. 'Do my parents know?'

'Not yet,' said Piper.

A smile spread across the girl's face and she hooted with laughter, rocking back and forth until she broke down into a hacking cough. At last she looked at Lilly. The right side of her face was bathed in yellow, the remnants of a huge bruise fading into the skin.

'My parents are going to be fucking furious.'

'I'm a big girl now,' said Lilly.

Lydia stopped laughing and stared. 'They don't like being told what to do.'

'Nobody does,' Lilly replied, dropped her bag on the table and sat down.

'Right then,' said Piper. 'I'll leave you to it. Shout if you need anything, Miss Valentine.'

His eyes flicked to the panic strip running the length of the room. One touch and the cavalry would come running. Lilly gave a tight nod and he left.

'I need to ask you some questions about the night you were arrested,' said Lilly, taking out paper and pen.

'Not much to tell. It was a crap party.' Lydia yawned without covering her mouth and ambled to the table. She slid into the chair as if she were liquid.

'What did you do?' Lilly asked.

'Nothing.' Lydia bent forward and put her forehead on the table.

'You must have done something,' said Lilly.

'Just the usual stuff.'

'And what is the usual stuff?'

Lydia tapped her head gently against the wood. 'Drank a bit, danced a bit. You know how it goes. Oh and I sucked some boy's cock. I can't remember his name.'

Lilly gulped.

'He wanted to fuck me but I wouldn't let him. Later on I felt sorry for him so I gave him a blow job. He got a bit pissed off though because I wouldn't swallow.' Lydia looked up at Lilly. 'There isn't any pleasing some people.'

Lilly didn't respond but kept eye contact with her client. The girl wasn't smirking and her eyes were wide.

'I don't like the taste of spunk. Do you?'

Lilly didn't blink. 'How much did you drink?'

Lydia sat up in one long movement, like a cat. She took a deep breath and exhaled it to the ceiling.

'Did this boy give you the alcohol?' Lilly asked.

A smile broke across Lydia's face like a gash. 'I can almost hear your brain going into action like the good little lawyer that you are.' She leaned over and tapped Lilly's temple. 'Tick tock, tick tock. Did the nasty boy get Lydia drunk and force himself on her? Is this mess his fault?'

'Well, is it?'

'Sadly not. I was pretty sober when I did him. I found the vodka later.'

'Where did you find it?' Lilly asked.

Lydia sniffed and wiped her hand across her nose. 'In a cupboard. The parents had obviously stashed it there out of the way of the kiddies.'

'So you took it?'

'Oh yeah.' Lydia inspected the shiny streak of mucous on the back of her hand and Lilly tried not to gag. 'I drank about half of it and decided to go home. It really was a crap party.'

'And you stole the Mercedes?'

'I wasn't going to keep it.' Lydia was affronted. 'I mean, we've got better cars than that at home.'

'But you didn't have permission to take it?'

Lydia giggled. It was a high-pitched and girly sound. 'Obviously not. I mean I was as pissed as a fart and I don't have a licence.'

'Why did you do it?'

'I was bored.' Lydia elongated the last word in a tortuous whine. 'Just like I'm bored now. Can we go get a drink or something?'

Lilly looked around her. Were they allowed to just leave the room?

'This isn't a fucking prison,' said Lydia. 'I'm not under house arrest.'

With that, she went for the door and disappeared outside. Lilly bundled her things back into her bag and hurried after Lydia. From behind, the girl seemed skeletal, skinny jeans accentuating the lack of flesh on her bones, shoulder blades protruding around the straps of her vest. She seemed to walk with a slight limp, as if she were throwing one of her tiny hips to the side.

When she got to the door she wanted, she was greeted by a chorus of shouts. Lilly followed her into what could have been a school common room. Teenagers sat around chatting and drinking cans of Coke. One girl was painting another's toenails a lurid green. In the corner, two boys were playing pool, teasing one another after each shot. They might have been any normal kids but for the ladder of cuts and scars tracing the inside of their arms.

From the far side a girl let out a shriek and waved. She was enormously overweight, folds of skin and fat sitting one on top of the other as though she were encased in a pile of tyres.

'Lydia,' she screeched again.

Lydia leaned in to Lilly. 'That's Chloe. She's completely off her rocker.'

The girl bounced over to them sweating and panting. 'Where've you been?' she stuttered.

'I told you, I had to see my solicitor,' Lydia answered.

'Is this her?' Chloe's eyes moved wildly between her friend and Lilly. 'Is this the one?'

Lydia rolled her eyes. 'Yes, Chloe, this is the one.'

'Is she going to help?' Chloe struggled to catch her breath and batted away a trickle of perspiration running from her hairline to her cheek.

Lydia put a hand on her shoulder. 'For fuck's sake, calm down. Let me fetch you a drink.' Then she moved towards a fridge and began to rummage through the contents.

With her friend gone, Chloe stepped towards Lilly, a wave of body odour radiating from her.

'Are you going to help?' Chloe whispered, the words strangulated in her throat.

'I'm going to try,' Lilly replied.

'Thank you.' The girl's eyes glittered with tears. 'Thank you so much.'

Then she pulled at the elasticated waist of her trousers and thrust her hand down the gap, extracting a piece of paper.

'Take it,' Chloe hissed.

Lilly was horrified, but the girl pressed it into her hand. It felt hot and moist and Lilly had to check the urge to retch. Then without another word Chloe ran to her friend and whispered something into her ear.

Gem stands outside Ali's house waiting for someone to answer the door. On the street outside two dogs are humping. Gem looks away, her breath white in the cold.

When she was little, she used to pretend she was smoking. She'd go outside with her friend Adrianna, and they'd stand there with their fingers apart, sucking on their pretend fags, laughing their heads off before Adrianna's mum would call them in for something to eat.

'You want sandwich, Gem?' she always asked.

'Only if you're making some,' Gem would reply.

'Of course,' Adrianna's mum would say. 'I was just about to make it for myself.'

Same every time, which were a bit daft, 'cos Gem always wanted a sandwich and Adrianna's mum knew she did. But it were like a little game they played so as Gem wouldn't feel embarrassed or nothing.

Gem don't see Adrianna no more. Her nan got sick and they had to go home to Poland to look after her. Gem used to wonder when they'd be coming back, but now she knows they ain't. Who'd want to come back to this shithole?

At last the door is opened by Herika. She's wearing a turquoise scarf on her head that looks like it's made out of that really soft wool. Gem wishes she could touch it. Course she don't do it, 'cos that would be well weird.

'Is Ali in?' she asks.

Herika shakes her head.

'Shit.' Gem really needs to get some clean nappies for Tyler. 'Do you know when he'll be back?'

'Long time,' says Herika.

Gem pulls her coat around her. She's going to have to go over to Fred's. When she looked at Tyler's bum this morning there was fresh blood.

'Sorry,' says Herika.

Gem's shoulders sag. Why does it always have to be this way? She turns to leave, a flake of snow landing on her nose.

'Wait.'

Gem looks back round at Herika who is still in the doorway. The woman holds up a hand to her. 'Stay.' Then she disappears inside. In a couple of minutes she returns with a ten pound note and holds it out to Gem who fishes in her pocket for the razor blades she's come to sell. Herika ain't normally allowed to do any business without Ali but Gem ain't about to argue is she?

Herika waves away the packets of Gillette and Gem doesn't understand.

'For baby,' says Herika, pushing the tenner at Gem.

Gem don't need to be asked twice and grabs the money.

'Thank you,' she says.

The snow is coming down harder now, sticking in her eye-lashes, making her blink.

'Take.' Herika holds out a crumpled brown envelope towards Gem. It's the sort that bills come in and make Mum cry. 'Take.'

Gem ain't sure what to do. Money's one thing, but what's this?

'Take.' Herika makes it clear she ain't asking and Gem does as she's told.

When she looks, there are some numbers scribbled on it in red biro. It looks like it could be a phone number.

'For help,' says Herika and closes the door.

Gem's fingers are starting to sting so she pushes them deep into her pockets, the tenner in one hand, the envelope in the other.

The snow was big and weightless, huge feathers tumbling from the sky.

Jack pushed Alice's furry hat down over her pink ears but he was fighting a losing battle against the curls which twanged ever upwards. She had Lilly's hair for sure.

'What do think of this then?' He rolled a snowball and threw it against a tree.

Alice gurgled.

'Will we build a snowman?' he asked. 'A huge guy with a carrot for a nose?'

Kate soon joined them, stamping her feet and rubbing her hands together. 'It's brass monkeys out here,' she said.

'Och, you southerners. You've thin blood.'

'Whereas you lot from over the water are made of sterner stuff, I suppose?'

'Absolutely,' said Jack.

'We'll soon see about that.' Before he knew what she was up to, Kate scooped up a handful of snow and shoved it down the back of his neck.

'Mary, Mother of God.' Jack leapt a foot into the air. 'You'll pay for that, woman.'

He grabbed a fistful of snow himself and chased her with it, until she slipped and landed on her back. Then he pounced on top of her, a leg on either side of her and dangled the snow inches from her face.

'What do you think, Alice?' Jack turned to his baby. 'Shall I do it?'

Alice clapped her hands together.

'Think of the sisterhood, Alice,' Kate shrieked. 'The oppressed sex have to stick together.'

'Oppressed sex my arse-cheeks,' he said and crumbled the snow gently, letting it fall onto Kate's delicate features.

She smiled and flicked a glance at their position. 'While you're there . . .'

'Don't tempt me, woman.' He kissed her nose and got up. 'About this snowman.'

Half an hour later they had built a beauty and Jack held Alice, helping her wrap an old scarf around his neck.

'What shall we call him, eh?' asked Jack, wiping the dribble from Alice's chin. 'How about Frosty?'

'Blimey,' said Kate. 'If ever you get bored of the job, there's a career for you in writing children's books.'

'Okay, J. K. Rowling, what do you suggest?'

Kate stood back to admire their handiwork, stroking her chin in mock concentration.

'Bob.'

'Bob?' He raised his eyebrows. 'And you say I'm lacking in imagination?'

Kate was about to answer him back when Alice made a sound that stopped them both in their tracks.

'B . . . b . . . b.'

Jack held his breath. Alice had never made any attempts to speak before.

'B . . . b . . . b,' Alice repeated.

'See,' said Kate. 'She thinks Bob is a great name.'

Jack almost burst into tears. 'Woman, you are a bloody genius.' He leaned over and kissed Kate on the mouth. 'I've got to call Lilly and tell her.'

I watch Jack tell his ex all about the baby's attempt at speech. The light in his eyes is a cut as deep as bone.

I don't know why I want him, but I do. I've wanted him from the first second I met him. He barely noticed me at the nick. Maybe that's what appealed. A far cry from other men who always seem so very keen to please me.

Whatever the reason, I'm certain that Jack and I should be together.

He laughs at something the ex is saying and my legs feel bloodless. I'm young and beautiful and toned. Everything the ex isn't. But still I can't seem to compete.

Jack looks over and I smile back at him. I whitened my teeth this morning and they're as bright as the snow on the ground. He looks away.

The problem is the baby of course. It's the glue that keeps Jack attached.

A single flake of snow lands on the back of my hand. It isn't cold. I watch it melt against the heat of my skin, then suck up the drop of water left in its place.

Lilly hung up and punched the air. Alice had spoken. Well, not quite spoken but almost there. Hadn't she told everyone there was nothing to worry about?

When the mobile rang again she grabbed it and answered.

'See, Jack, I told you that these bloody doctors don't know what they're talking about.'

'Wow.' The voice was like oozing honey. 'That's not the usual impression I try to make.'

It wasn't Jack.

'Doctor Piper?' she said.

'Didn't we agree that you'd call me Harry?'

'I don't believe we discussed it.'

'Okay then,' he said. 'Miss Valentine, I'd much prefer it if you would call me Harry. Everyone does.'

'Okay, Harry.'

'And what about you?' he asked. 'Any preference as to how I address you?'

'Lilly's fine,' she said.

'Lilly.' He let her name hang in the air as if admiring something exotic. 'Well, Lilly, you left the Grove without telling me what you thought of my patient.'

'Your gatekeeper said you were in an important meeting and couldn't be disturbed.'

In fact the nurse had been snotty with Lilly, pointing out, unnecessarily, that Doctor Piper was a very busy man. Lilly had wanted to inform her that she wasn't exactly a lady of leisure herself, but thought better of it.

'Elaine does like to look after me,' Harry chuckled, 'but I would like to pick your brain if you have the time.'

'Pick away.'

'I have to do the rounds in a second,' he said. 'How about we have a chat after that?'

'Sure.'

'Over lunch? I don't know about you but I'm usually famished by one o'clock. I was always the naughty little boy who opened his sandwiches during morning break.'

Lilly laughed. She'd been on free school meals and had spent her mornings so hungry she'd had to stop herself from eating the desk lid.

'Shall I swing by your office around twelve thirty?' he asked.

'That would be lovely,' Lilly replied.

The answer machine winked and there were over thirty unanswered emails for Lilly to attend to but she didn't have time for that now. Instead, she set off in search of comb, perfume and lippy.

With her curls tamed into a vague approximation of real hair, and her throat and wrists dabbed with Chanel No. 5, Lilly felt almost human. Just a slick of mascara and she'd be ready for action. A rummage at the bottom of her bag revealed only a set of broken headphones and a pair of Alice's socks so she patted herself down and delved into the detritus collected in the nether regions of her pockets. As she pulled out the revolting wad of tissues and biscuits she didn't find mascara, but she did discover the piece of paper Chloe had forced upon her.

The thought of where it had been prior to its handover made Lilly shiver and she leaned to the bin and let it fall. But as she turned away, she stopped. Chloe had been so very insistent. There had been something very specific in her actions. Sure, Chloe was an inpatient in a mental facility where unusual behaviour wouldn't be, well, unusual, but Lilly recognized desperation when she saw it.

She bent over and retrieved the paper with her finger and thumb. Then she placed it on her desk and smoothed it open, ignoring the faint smell of sweat and worse.

There were three words scrawled in pencil. They were smeared and smudged, but still legible.

Please Help Us.

'You smell wonderful.' Harry Piper closed his eyes and inhaled. 'Chanel. My first wife never wore anything else.'

Lilly felt embarrassment splash her cheeks like an experimental artist as she took a seat across from him in the restaurant.

'First wife,' she said. 'Have there been many more?'

He held up three fingers. 'Not a great track record, I must concede.'

'Mine's not exactly sparkling,' Lilly replied.

'Then that's something else we have in common.'

The directness of his gaze matched that of his observation and Lilly wilted under both, taking refuge in the menu.

'On a day like today we need carbs,' Harry declared. 'Tell me you're not one of those awful women who only eat fruit and vegetables.'

Lilly raised her eyebrows at him. Did she look like she lived on lettuce?

'How about steak and chips?' she said.

'And sticky toffee pudding to follow.' Harry rubbed his hands together. 'It is snowing after all.'

When they'd ordered their food, which frankly took far longer than need be as the waitress giggled and fawned over every word Harry uttered, he poured them both a glass of Châteauneuf-du-Pape.

'Why don't you tell me what you thought of Lydia?'

Lilly took a sip. The wine tasted expensive. She hoped Harry was paying.

'Attention-seeking. Compulsive. No filters.' Lilly paused. 'And deeply, deeply unhappy.'

He smiled, the wine leaving a small stain on his bottom lip. 'You're good.'

'To be honest it wouldn't take Freud to work out that the girl's got problems.'

'Will she go to prison?'

'That depends on what you tell me about why she did it,' Lilly said.

'I haven't a clue why she did it,' Harry said. 'What did she say about it?'

Lilly shrugged. 'Not much. She was drunk and didn't know what she was doing. But I sense there's something more complicated at the back of it.'

'I'm sure you're right,' said Harry. 'There usually is.'

Lilly had met a lot of damaged kids in her time, their back stories all different yet violently familiar. Poverty, family break-down, drugs and despair. But what about Lydia Morton-Daley? Lilly wasn't naive enough to believe a privileged lifestyle pro-tected kids like that from every sling and arrow. Something had sent a girl with everything to live for on a downward spiral of alcohol, sex and self-destruction, but it would be a lot harder to pinpoint why.

What led a person from anger, frustration and sadness to full-blown mental collapse? Why could some kids hold on and others, like Lydia and Chloe, were unable to stop themselves falling off the edge?

The thought of Chloe's sweat-covered face, the manic look in her eyes as she passed the note made Lilly take a long gulp of wine. The thought of what the note said made her take another.

Harry topped up her glass. 'Are you okay?'

Lilly nodded. 'I met another patient this morning,' she said. 'A girl called Chloe.'

'What did she tell you?' Harry asked.

'What makes you think she told me anything?'

Harry smiled. 'Chloe always tells people things. That someone's poisoning her food, or that the nurses have put the evil eye on her. She's delusional and, sadly for her, those delusions are mostly negative in ideation.'

'Would it make any difference if they were positive?'

'I think so, don't you?' said Harry. 'If I could make my imaginings reality, I'd rather they were deliciously in my favour. I could quite enjoy my life as King of England or winner of *The X Factor*.'

'But it's not like that for Chloe?' asked Lilly. 'She's paranoid?'

'Utterly,' said Harry, then his face lit up as their food arrived.

★   ★   ★

45

Gem calls in the fish shop on the way home and orders a bag of chips. It's cheaper to buy a bag of frozen but you have to factor in money for the meter as well. And that thing eats money. It's a lot cheaper if you pay the bill directly, but Mum keeps forgetting. Or they never have enough. So some men came round and fitted the meter and the fucker swallows pound coins like a slot machine.

She's waiting for the fresh batch of chips to fry, listening to the crackling sound of the oil, when some bloke comes in and asks for fish, chips, a battered sausage and mushy peas.

'You hungry, Ted?' the owner asks.

'Marvin Hagler,' the man called Ted replies.

Gem watches him putting a stiff ten-pound note on the counter and pocketing his bit of change. Imagine spending all that lot just on one meal. The bloke don't look rich, but he must be loaded. Or stupid.

She takes her packet of chips, the heat burning her fingers through the paper and breathes in the smell. It'll feed them all with a few slices of bread. Tyler loves a chip sandwich with plenty of red sauce. It'll keep him full all day.

When she gets home, she's already peeling the paper open before she gets through the door.

'It's me,' she shouts. 'I've brought some chips.'

No one answers.

In the kitchen, Gem looks for clean plates but Mum ain't washed up from last night. Swearing, she runs them under the tap and flicks the grease away with her fingers 'cos there ain't no Fairy Liquid.

'Mum,' she calls over her shoulder. 'Come and get some food.'

There's still no reply so Gem heads through to the other room, her hands still wet. When she opens the door she stops in her tracks. Mum is stood by the window, holding Tyler, trying to stay as far away as possible from two men sat on the settee. The men are both bald, their heads shiny boiled eggs. They turn to Gem at exactly the same second, like they're keeping time.

'We've been waiting for you,' says the one nearest to Gem. He's wearing a fat gold chain around his fat white neck, and fat gold rings around his fat white fingers.

Gem don't move. She just stands in the doorway, her hands dripping water down her sides.

'Your mum tells us you've got something for us,' the man says.

Gem wraps her arms around herself. There's no way she's giving them the money. No fucking way.

The man holds out his hand. 'Give.'

Gem shakes her head. 'I ain't got nothing.'

'Gem,' Mum warns.

'I ain't lying,' says Gem. 'Ali weren't in.' To prove her point, Gem pulls out the packet of razor blades. 'See.'

'Shit,' Mum whispers. 'Why didn't you go to Fred's?'

'I was gonna but I brought some chips home first,' says Gem.

'There you go.' Mum smiles at the men. 'She'll get straight off, be back with some money in less than an hour.'

The men stand up together, like they're doing some dance routine. They're both massive and seem to take up all the air in the room. It makes Gem feel dizzy.

'You've wasted our time,' the man tells Mum. 'And we don't like anyone wasting our time.'

Tyler begins to whine and Mum jiggles him against her hip. He don't like it and stretches out a hand to Gem.

'Shut up,' Mum hisses, but that just makes him cry harder. When he won't be quiet she pinches his lips together.

'We'll have to charge you for this wasted visit,' the man says. 'Do you understand?'

Mum nods, trying to stop Tyler from thrashing his head about.

'I think an extra ten pounds should cover our time,' he says.

Gem opens her mouth to tell them they can't do that but Mum flashes her eyes. It ain't worth arguing with men like these. Not if you value your teeth.

They wait for the men to leave, and when they hear the door slam Mum throws Tyler onto the settee, where he goes stiff and screams.

'Fuck,' Mum howls. 'Why didn't you just give them the money?'

'I told you Ali was out.'

'So where did you get money for chips?'

Gem tries to think up a lie. She could try to make out she got them for free. But what's the point? No one gives away anything for free, do they?

'His wife gave me something so I bought chips.'

'Then why didn't you hand over what's left? That way he might not have added another tenner to what I owe. Honestly, Gem, where do you think we're gonna find another tenner?'

'I couldn't hand it over,' says Gem.

'Why the fuck not?'

Gem points her finger at Tyler who is curled into a little ball, sobbing his heart out. 'He needs nappies, Mum. You said yourself, that if the social worker comes round they'll take him into care. I can't let that happen, can I?'

'Oh fuck.' Mum sinks to the floor, tears pouring down her face and thumps the side of her head. 'Why the fuck does this keep happening to me?'

Gem don't know what to do. It feels like someone is pushing on her shoulders, trying to force her down. She'd love to sit and cry like Mum and Tyler, but she can't, can she? She's got to keep fighting.

'You feed the baby,' she tells Mum. 'I'll go to the shop for nappies.'

Mum looks up, eyes swollen and snot running down her lips. 'Have you got enough for that cream we used last time?'

Gem nods and leaves. The lift's out of order so she takes the stairs two at a time. When she gets to the bottom she turns right towards the shops, but at the last second takes a sharp left and almost runs to the phone box. A couple of local dealers are usually holed up inside, waiting for their skinny punters. Sometimes there's a queue of crackheads waiting their turn, hopping from foot to foot, desperate to get to the front of the line. But today it's free. Maybe dealers don't like snow. Maybe they got nicked.

She squeezes into the box and pulls out the envelope. Gem learned years ago that you can't trust nobody. People don't help you unless they want something in return. Is it possible Herika's different? She didn't have to give Gem the money, did she? There was nothing in it for her. Gem's pretty sure that if Ali found out he'd be well pissed off, but Herika risked it all the same.

Gem takes a deep breath and punches the numbers.

'*Selam.*' It's a woman's voice.

Gem nearly hangs up.

'Hello,' the woman says.

There's a pause. 'Hello,' Gem says at last.

'Can I help you?' The woman's accent is just like Ali's.

'I don't know,' says Gem, because she doesn't know.

'How you get this number?' the woman asks.

'Ali's wife gave it to me.' Gem runs her finger along the crumpled envelope. 'She wrote it down for me.'

'Herika?'

'Yes,' says Gem. 'Herika.'

'And what she tell you?'

'Nothing,' says Gem. 'She didn't tell me nothing. She just said to call for some . . . help.'

She realizes how pathetic that sounds. She's called a total stranger asking for help, when the truth is she has no idea herself what she even needs. The woman probably thinks she's lost the plot. She should hang up and get herself off to the chemist, then hightail it over to Fred's to see what he'll give her for the razor blades. She's wasting precious time when she could be out grafting, getting whatever she can to pay off Mum's debt.

'Okay,' the woman says.

'What?'

'Okay, I help you,' says the woman. 'Do you know Dirty Mick's?'

'Yeah.'

'I see you there in one hour.'

Lilly yawned as she put her key in the lock of the office door. A huge lunch with wine had left her content but knackered. She slid into her chair and shut her eyes. A ten-minute kip couldn't hurt.

When her mobile rang she was sorely tempted to ignore it.

'Lilly Valentine.'

'Ah yes, hello,' said the male voice. 'Paul Santana here.'

The oil slick.

'I'm assuming you received the case file,' he said.

Case file seemed a grand term for one document, but maybe that was how these commercial lawyers rolled. If you made everything sound meatier and more important than it actually was, you could get away with charging a million quid an hour.

'I got the arresting officer's notes.' Lilly stifled another yawn. 'I'm assuming that's everything.'

Santana coughed. 'That's why I'm calling, Miss Valentine. I did discover one more document. It was in my secretary's filing tray, tucked at the bottom. You know how these things are.'

Lilly glanced around the office. Every flat surface was littered with folders, books and letters. If this was supposed to be the paperless age, someone had forgotten to send the memo to her clients. God, she needed some help at work.

'Yes, I know how these things are.'

'Good, good, good,' said Santana.

'Why don't you just mail it to me?'

Santana coughed again. 'Indeed I will, but it's from the court, so I thought I should call you too.'

Lilly sat up. She hadn't yet had a chance to tell the court she had taken over Lydia's case.

'What is it?'

'Ah well.' Santana paused. 'It has the official number and heading on it.'

Bloody hell, he didn't know what it was, did he? He'd been a solicitor for how many years and didn't know what a court document looked like?

'Is it a notice of hearing?' Lilly asked.

'Yes.' Santana sounded relieved. 'It states that Lydia's case is going to be heard at Luton Youth Court.' He laughed. 'Rather you than me, to be honest.'

Lilly snorted. She spent half her professional life hanging around in youth courts, knee deep in empty crisp packets and swearing kids and she certainly couldn't picture the Oil Slick on those sticky seats.

'When is it listed?' she asked, reaching for her diary. She flipped the pages, hoping it wasn't next Monday as she already had two cases listed that day. With a fair wind and some luck, she could manage to run them back to back. A third case would prove impossible to juggle.

She tapped the end of her biro on Tuesday. That would work nicely. The page was currently empty and it would give her plenty of time to see Lydia again and prepare what exactly she was going to tell the court.

Santana coughed again. Lilly was tempted to recommend a spoonful of Buttercup Syrup.

'Sorry,' she said. 'I didn't catch the date.'

'Today,' he said.

Lilly dropped her pen. 'Today?'

'Yes. This afternoon at 3 p.m.'

Lilly checked her watch. It was half past two.

'I really am most dreadfully sorry,' said Santana. 'It won't be a problem, will it?'

Lilly didn't answer. She was already halfway to the door.

Chapter Three

Psychological Evaluation of Mary-Ann Yates

Purpose of Evaluation

Mary-Ann Yates was referred for an evaluation by her solicitors following her conviction at Luton Crown Court on 11 June 2004, in order to assess her cognitive abilities.

Background

Mary-Ann Yates is 34. Originally from Liverpool, she has been living in the Luton area with her sister Sinead Talbot, and her brother-in-law George Talbot, for over twenty years. She is currently in custody at HMP Highpoint.

Mary-Ann left school at fifteen. She has never been assessed before and has no major medical conditions.

Test Session Behaviour

Mary-Ann was dishevelled but clean during the test session. She appeared oriented to time, place and situation. However, she appeared confused as to the whereabouts of her sister and persistently asked the guards if she could see her soon.

General Intellectual Ability

Mary-Ann's thinking and reasoning abilities are mixed. Her non-verbal reasoning abilities are higher than her verbal reasoning to an extent that is unusual.

Verbal Comprehension

Mary-Ann's verbal abilities are below average. She would have difficulty keeping up with her peers in situations requiring verbal skills. This would impact upon her ability to function in normal social settings.

Perceptual Reasoning

Mary-Ann's non-verbal reasoning skills are above average, although her scores in these tests were not consistent. In some she scored very highly indeed, in others her scores were very low. Again this is an unusual outcome.

Working Memory

Mary-Ann's ability to sustain attention, concentrate and exert mental control is average, although once again her scores were inconsistent. In some tests she exhibited high ability to remember and retain. In others she exhibited a weakness in mental control that would make processing of information extremely time-consuming.

Summary

Mary-Ann's test scores showed inconsistencies not only between her verbal comprehension (which was low) and her perceptual reasoning (which was high) but also inconsistencies within her perceptual reasoning itself.

Similarly, her working memory appears to function well in certain circumstances but poorly in others.

These differences in cognitive abilities are indicative of a learning disability, although the assessment undertaken would be insufficient to ascertain the exact nature or extent of such a disability.

Lilly burst through the main entrance of the Magistrates' Court, and stamped the snow from her shoes.

'I'm late,' she told the lone security guard. 'Can I just go straight through?'

The guard raised an incredulous eyebrow, as if she'd suggested riding naked on an elephant to her hearing.

'They'll be waiting for me,' she pleaded.

He sniffed and tapped the conveyor belt of the x-ray machine. Lilly sighed and tossed her bag on. Were they expecting a terrorist attack on a cold afternoon when everyone else had gone home?

She growled to herself when he barely glanced at the monitor as her overstuffed bag passed through and snatched it up at the other side before racing up the stairs. Why did people have to be so bloody difficult? Could they not step outside of their box even in an emergency?

When Lilly threw open the door to the advocates' room and found Kerry Thomson hunched over her files, she knew she had the answer; some people couldn't manage a toe outside their little box.

Lilly pasted a smile onto her face. 'Hello, Kerry.'

'Hello.'

Lilly tried humour. It had never worked before on Kerry but there was a first time for everything. 'Fancy seeing you here.'

'I'm a Crown prosecutor and this is a court, it can't be too much of a surprise.'

Lilly sighed. Over the years she had tried to be nice to Kerry. When all the other lawyers sniggered behind her back, calling her The Whale, Lilly had resolutely refused to join in. And when Kerry had begun to slowly but surely lose weight, Lilly had always managed a supportive comment. None of it had made the slightest dent in Kerry's cast-iron dislike of Lilly.

'I'm here for Lydia Morton-Daley' she said.

'Your name's not on the notice.' Kerry pulled out a sheet of paper. 'It's some bloke called Paul Santana.'

'He's transferred the case to me,' said Lilly.

'You didn't let anyone know,' said Kerry.

Lilly pursed her lips together. She didn't want to say anything she might regret. 'I'm letting you know now, Kerry.'

Kerry placed the paperwork carefully back in its file. 'I know it's old-fashioned to consider such small things important.'

Not old-fashioned, just tediously pedantic. It could not matter one jot to Kerry who was representing Lydia.

'Do you have anything for me?' Lilly asked. 'I've only received the arresting officer's notes.'

'Speaking of which,' said Kerry and beckoned to a police-woman hovering outside the door. 'This is WPC Knight.'

Lilly smiled at the young woman whose pretty overbite seemed vaguely familiar, but she didn't have time for small talk to place her.

'Any more documents?' Lilly asked. 'I know it's old-fashioned to consider such small things important.'

Kerry slid a sheaf of paperwork across the desk. Lilly scooped it up. By the thickness of it, Lilly guessed it contained a transcript of the interview with Lydia at the police station. God only knows what the kid had said.

She pushed the door open with her foot. 'It's a pleasure doing business with you.'

He hasn't told her about me.

He hasn't said he's told her, or that he hasn't. It's one of those things we don't discuss. But I know he hasn't said anything by the way she doesn't give me a second glance.

I've seen her before of course. At the police station. But I didn't know then that she was of any importance. If I had known, I would have paid closer attention.

Once I understood her relevance, I did my research. I've read every-thing on Google. All those articles when her cases hit the headlines. Which they seem to do with uncanny regularity.

'If anyone likes more attention than Lilly Valentine, I've yet to meet them.'

I'd forgotten the fat woman was in the room.

'Everything she touches becomes a three-act drama,' the prosecutor continues.

I raise an eyebrow as if I can't quite believe it of her.

'Don't let the suit fool you,' the woman snorts, a drop of mucus fly-ing from her left nostril. 'Carnage follows her wherever she goes.' She pushes herself to her feet with a grimace. 'And men follow along behind that.'

'Men?'

'Wraps 'em round her little finger.' She holds up, not her little finger, but her index, the nail square and acrylic. 'She made a real fool of that poor policeman she was with.'

I hold the door open for her, taking care not to breathe in as she passes through.

'Then there was Jez.'

'Jez?' I ask.

'Jez Stafford. A barrister. Way out of her league if you ask me. Then some interpreter and it wasn't long ago there was some black guy hang-ing around. Apparently he was working for her, but I don't know any other solicitors that have secretaries with a six-pack, do you?'

I say nothing.

'God alone knows what they all see in her.'

I let her waddle ahead of me, shocked at my error. Clearly I've under-estimated Lilly Valentine.

Lilly was still fuming over Kerry's pettiness as she checked outside courtrooms three and four for Lydia.

The afternoons were usually reserved for a handful of trials or any case requiring an expert, and even those were finished by this time. Only one young woman remained, seated in the far corner, mumbling to herself and scratching her hand with enough violence to draw blood. When she caught sight of Lilly, she made a noise an animal might make if it were cornered.

Lilly put up a hand to show that she meant no harm and the woman turned her back, keeping up her whispered litany.

Lydia was lucky to be safe in the Grove. Far too many of the mentally ill ended up in the criminal justice system, spending terrified hours in police custody or prison. Too long for comfort, but not long enough to receive any useful help.

Lilly wasn't surprised not to find Lydia. The Oil Slick wouldn't have thought to inform the staff at the Grove that she needed to attend court. Hell, he probably thought personal embossed invitations were sent from the magistrates, together with spacious transport.

It wasn't ideal, but once she had an opportunity to explain what had happened, it shouldn't cause any real problem. She stopped at the courtroom door to wait for Kerry and caught the WPC staring at her. The young woman blushed and quickly looked away. Lord knows what Kerry had been telling her. Probably that she was the worst solicitor on the local circuit.

'After you.' Lilly held the door open and let the other two women pass. The WPC smelled of lemon, Kerry of damp jumpers.

They took their positions at the front of the courtroom. Lilly and Kerry alongside one another, though ten feet apart, the WPC just behind. It was usual for the advocates to chat while they waited, but Lilly really had nothing to say to Kerry.

The silence was broken by the opening of the inner door between the magistrate's chambers and the courtroom.

The usher came through it. 'Court rise.'

Lilly got to her feet, grateful to get things moving. She was less grateful when she saw the magistrate shuffling into court. Andrew Manchester. He looked as old as Yoda and as bony as Gollum. His dislike of the young people that came before him was matched only by his dislike of their solicitors.

'Miss Thomson.' He gave Kerry a small nod. 'Miss Valentine.' He gave Lilly only a cold stare and sat down. Then he turned to his clerk. 'I cannot help but notice that we are missing someone.'

The clerk handed Mr Manchester a sheet of paper.

'Do you have anything to say, Miss Valentine?' He tapped his ink pen against the paper. 'A reason why I should not sign this warrant for your client's arrest?'

'Indeed, sir,' Lilly replied.

'Then please address me. I am, as they say, all ears as to what could be more important than attending court.'

'I'm afraid she is in hospital, sir,' said Lilly.

'And what is wrong with her?' Mr Manchester's tone made it clear that he would take a dim view of anything less than a terminal complaint.

'She has been sectioned under the Mental Health Act,' Lilly told him.

That made the old bugger sit up straight. He even put down his pen.

'Following her arrest, my client's parents sought psychiatric assistance for their daughter,' said Lilly. 'It was decided that Lydia should be kept at the Grove hospital for her own safety.'

Kerry let out a curdled sigh.

'Problem?' Lilly asked her.

Kerry pulled herself to her feet. When her arse left the plastic chair it made a sound like a soft fart:

'A rich girl steals and crashes a car, putting goodness knows how many lives at risk, and suddenly she needs urgent help,' said Kerry. 'No doubt paid for by her parents.'

'Are you suggesting the psychiatrist in charge of Lydia's care has behaved unethically?' Lilly asked.

Mr Manchester put up a finger. 'Miss Thomson has done nothing of the sort. She has simply showed a degree of scepticism at the timing. A scepticism which frankly I share.'

'I'm sure I can provide the court with confirmation from the Grove that Lydia's current stay in their closed unit has everything to do with her mental health and nothing to do with avoiding a court attendance,' replied Lilly.

'Why did you not provide such confirmation in advance?' Mr Manchester narrowed his eyes. 'A lot of time has been wasted today.'

Lilly knew she had to be honest. 'I would have informed the court as to my client's whereabouts had I known about today's hearing, but unfortunately it was only brought to my attention —' Lilly checked her watch '— less than an hour ago.'

'Less than an hour ago?' Mr Manchester shouted. 'This case was listed in December.'

Lilly opened her arms. 'That may be so, sir, but when it was listed I was not representing the defendant. The notice was sent to Lydia's previous solicitor.'

The magistrate shot a look at his clerk, who ran her finger down her case file, before nodding that Lilly's assertion was correct.

Once again Kerry got to her feet. 'If Miss Valentine had served the paperwork informing us all of the change in representation things might have moved a little more smoothly.'

Lilly refused to even look at the other advocate. There was absolutely no reason for Kerry to land her in it. She was point-scoring to no other purpose than scoring points. Jesus, she really must hate Lilly.

Instead, she focused on Mr Manchester and awaited the inevitable tirade, but as the old man prepared to crank himself up to cataclysmic proportions, a noise from the back distracted them all as someone entered the court and gave a polite cough.

'This is a closed session,' Mr Manchester growled.

Lilly turned to discover Harry stood in the doorway.

'Huge apologies for the interruption, sir.' Harry held up a hand to the magistrate. 'I need to speak to Miss Valentine urgently.'

Lilly's mouth fell open. Kerry couldn't contain a snigger. All holy hell was about to break loose.

Mr Manchester thumped his desk. 'We are in the middle of a case!'

'I'm aware of that, sir,' said Harry.

'Then wait outside before I have you removed.'

Harry took a step into the courtroom. His voice was a study of calm and authority.

'I'm Lydia's psychiatrist and I have information that pertains to this case, sir. Information that needs to be conveyed to Miss Valentine immediately.' He paused. 'If this were not an emergency I wouldn't have left my patients.'

Mr Manchester was still incandescent with rage, but Harry's demeanour brooked no argument. Reason and intelligence oozed from him. The two men stared at one another for a moment, Harry still smiling, the magistrate almost purple.

'Very well.' Mr Manchester waved a dismissive hand. 'I will adjourn for five minutes.' He pointed at Lilly. 'Then we shall proceed come what may.'

Lilly nodded as Mr Manchester left for his chambers. She caught Kerry rubbing her hands with glee. The WPC, who frankly she'd forgotten about, had her head cocked to one side as if Lilly were something quite unfathomable. She ignored them both and grabbed Harry's arm, pulling him into the corridor.

'I've no idea what you're doing here, Harry, but you saved my arse,' she told him. 'I could cheerfully kiss you.'

He held her gaze for a second too long, until Lilly felt the heat of embarrassment seep up her throat and had to look away.

'How did you know I was here?' she asked.

'A Mr Santana called the Grove,' he replied.

'Wow,' said Lilly. 'The Oil Slick wasn't as useless as I thought.'

'What?'

'Lydia's old solicitor.' Harry clearly had no idea what she was talking about. 'Never mind.'

Harry put a hand on Lilly's arm. 'There's no other way to tell you this,' he said. 'So I'm just going to come out with it.'

'Come out with what, Harry?'

He was still touching her, but lightly, so she could hardly feel the weight of his fingers. 'Lydia is dead.'

Gem don't know what she's even doing here.

The café is virtually empty. A couple of black girls from the Clayhill are in the corner, all tongue studs and hair extensions. One of them is flicking her lighter against the bottom edge of the menu, making the plastic coating go black.

'Carry on with that and you're out,' says Dirty Mick, from behind the counter.

The girl kisses her teeth at him and gives him the finger.

'Don't think I won't call the police,' he says.

'Fuck you,' says the girl, but she throws down the lighter.

Some old boy on the next table shakes his head in disgust as he makes his way through a plate of food, cutting through each chip with his knife and putting one half into his mouth. Then the next. He'll be there all bleeding week.

Apart from that, the place is empty and Gem takes a table in the window.

'What can I get you?' Mick shouts.

Gem's stomach growls. 'A Coke.'

'That it?'

Gem nods and sits down. Whatever happens she's got to get Tyler's nappies. Mum will have a fit that Gem took this long.

Mick slams the Coke on the table. 'Last of the big spenders.'

She pulls the ring on her can and takes a drink. Five minutes and she'll leave. She was a total mug for coming in the first place.

She's almost ready to leave when a woman comes in. Her skin is toffee-coloured like Herika, but she ain't wearing one of them scarves on her head.

She stands by the table. 'You Gem?'

Gem nods.

The woman sits down. She's got a silver ring on every finger. Even her thumbs.

'You hungry?' the woman asks.

Her accent makes the 'h' sound more like a 'j'.

Gem tries not to think about the chips she left at home.

''Course you are,' says the woman. 'Teenagers are starving all day long, no?' She grabs the menu, flicks it over, then flicks it back again. 'Burger?' she asks.

Before Gem can answer she turns to the counter and waves at the owner. 'Burger, chips, cup of tea.' She checks what Gem's drinking. 'And another Coke.'

The man nods. Considering he's not overrun with paying customers he's not exactly friendly.

'I'm Feyza,' says the woman.

'Hello,' says Gem.

The woman drums her fingers on the tabletop. The rings flash like little fish. It reminds Gem of them foot spas where people put their feet in a tank full of them and they nibble off all the dead skin and that. Proper gross if you think about it.

The man arrives with the food and plonks it down in front of them without a word.

'Eat,' says Feyza.

63

Gem tries to eat as slowly as she can. She doesn't want Feyza to think she's a pig with no manners. But she's so hungry, it ain't easy.

Feyza pours some sugar into her tea and stirs it slowly. Round and round. Then she brings the cup to her lips. But she don't drink. She just lets it hover there, her mouth millimetres from the dark brown liquid, watching Gem.

'You in care?' Feyza asks.

Gem shakes her head.

Feyza frowns and puts down her cup. She still ain't even taken a sip. 'But you need money?' she asks. 'You need to earn money, yes?'

Gem swallows her last chip. She was right. Nobody gives something for nothing, but earning it is different. 'You're offering me a job?' she asks.

The woman gets up and makes her way to the counter to pay. She hands over a ten-pound note. 'You won't speak to me, but you take my money, hey?' she asks Mick.

He grunts and slams down her change.

'You are prick,' Feyza tells him and slides the coins into her purse.

She doesn't go back to the table, but makes for the door. For a second, Gem thinks she's going to leave without her, but then she turns and puts one hand on her hip.

'Come,' she says to Gem. 'I show you what we do.'

The warmth of Lilly's blushes evaporated, replaced by a chill that made her shudder. 'Dead?' she asked.

'You're shaking,' Harry said. 'Come and sit down.'

Lilly allowed Harry to lead her to the nearest bench and flopped into it.

'What the hell happened?' she asked. 'Did she kill herself?'

A place like the Grove would be careful. Suicide was something about which they were mindful. All drugs were carefully locked away. Belts were removed. Yet for patients as damaged as Lydia, there was always a way.

'We don't know what happened,' said Harry. 'The police are at the unit now. I should be there, but I thought you needed to know and I wanted to tell you in person.'

'That was kind,' said Lilly.

He gave a rueful smile. 'I wanted to get out of there too, so not entirely selfless.'

Lilly nodded. Harry was clearly dedicated to his patients. A failure like this would be painful.

'You can't blame yourself,' she told him.

He gave her hand a squeeze, then left without another word. Lilly watched him go, knowing there was nothing she could say to make it better. Today another young life had been wasted.

Back in court, Mr Manchester was waiting for Lilly with a grim expression. 'I trust the vital information that could not wait has been passed to you, Miss Valentine.'

Lilly sighed. She didn't have the energy for more fighting.

'I trust also that while you had your client's doctor here, you obtained written confirmation that she is unable to attend court.'

Kerry stood. 'As should have been provided beforehand.'

Lilly didn't rise to it. The stuffing had been knocked out of her.

'Perhaps you'd like to hand it over.' Mr Manchester held out his skeletal fingers.

'No.'

Mr Manchester let his hand fall with a slap. 'No?'

'No.'

'Miss Valentine, there had better be a very good explanation for your behaviour because you are very close to being put in the cells for contempt of court.'

Lilly closed her eyes. People like Manchester and Kerry had no idea. They sat in their little ivory towers making judgements about the lives of others, but what did they know? Their lives were bound up in this tiny corner of the universe, light years away from whatever tortured a child like Lydia until she felt there was only one escape.

'Miss Valentine,' the magistrate bellowed. 'You are this close.' He held his thumb and index finger a centimetre apart.

Lilly opened her eyes. 'There is no point in providing anything to the court.'

Mr Manchester was now so angry he could not speak, but he didn't scare Lilly. Let him throw her in the bloody cells.

'There is no point, sir.' She fixed him with the coldest of glares. 'Because Lydia Morton-Daley is dead.'

Jack was mightily pissed off.

He wasn't a man prone to the excesses of ego, not up himself in the slightest, he'd like to think, but Mary, Mother of God, this was a joke. He was an officer in the MCU, and shouldn't be dealing with suicides.

He'd only allowed himself to get sucked into this one because the woman on control had no uniform in the vicinity of the Grove.

'Please, Jack,' she'd said. 'It'll be a five-minute job, straight in and out.'

A soft touch, that was his trouble.

He stalked his way down the corridor to the room where he'd been told he would find the body. A young nurse hovered in the doorway, passing in and out like an agitated insect.

'I'm afraid I can't let anyone in.' She pushed a flustered hand against the pink spots appearing on each cheek. 'Not until the police arrive.'

'I am the police,' Jack snapped, immediately sorry for his tone. It wasn't this poor woman's fault that he'd been sent on an errand like a rookie two weeks into the job.

'Sorry . . . I didn't . . . you're not . . .' She waved a hand at his jeans and leather jacket.

'No worries,' he said.

The truth was the task wasn't the only thing affecting his mood. There was also the Grove itself. A mental institution. A loony bin. And memories of his youngest sister Teresa, being dragged away screaming.

'Jack.' She'd held her arms out to him. 'Tell Mammy I don't want to be here.'

Everyone said it was the best place for her. That she'd soon get better. But she hadn't, had she? And neither had the wee girl lying on the other side of the door.

'Who's in charge of the wing?' Jack asked the nurse.

'Doctor Piper,' she said.

'And where is he?'

The nurse scrabbled for her pager. 'I don't know. I bleeped him ages ago.'

'Never mind,' said Jack. 'Let's crack on.'

As he entered the room, what hit him first was the deep sense of peace. The room was bare and silent and cold. The girl in the bed could have easily been asleep, her eyes closed, her mouth relaxed, her duvet pulled up to her chest.

'What's her name?' Jack turned to the nurse.

She took a tentative step over the threshold, one foot in the room, the other still outside. 'Lydia,' she said. 'Lydia Morton-Daley.'

Double-barrelled surname. Expensive haircut. Posh kid, Jack guessed.

He skirted round the body to the bedside table. There were some white pills scattered around.

'Do you know what these are?' he asked.

'Probably her prescription,' said the nurse. 'I think she was taking Xanax.'

'How many would it take to kill a girl this size?' he asked.

'I'm not sure. Depends what they're mixed with.' The nurse frowned. 'I don't know how she had access to medication. Everything's locked away. We're very careful to only give out one dose at a time.'

Jack shrugged. 'I'd say someone wasn't careful enough.'

He looked on the table for a note. Nothing. He checked on the floor. Nothing.

'So, Lydia, did you leave us any clue as to why you did this to yourself?'

The nurse coughed. 'Obviously she wasn't well or happy.'

'Obviously.' Jack moved back to the bed. 'Could you come here, nurse?'

Her eyes shot open but her feet didn't move.

'First time?' Jack asked.

The nurse nodded.

'Sorry,' he said. And he was. You never forgot your first. It made its indelible mark on you. 'I want to lift the cover and I'd like you to witness me doing it.'

'Why?' The nurse sounded aghast.

'Allegations are sometimes made about theft or other matters. Just a precaution to protect Lydia and me.'

'I meant why do you need to lift the cover?' asked the nurse.

'Oh right,' he said. 'Some suicide victims die with a note in their hand.'

It happened often actually. The dead clutched their last words to their heart, as if to emphasize their importance.

'Okay then,' she said.

Jack wondered if he should warn her about the smell. At the moment of passing, a body released more than its spirit. He decided against it, what with her being a nurse.

Gently, he took hold of the duvet and peeled it backwards, revealing the tombstone pallor of Lydia's skin. Her shoulders so white they were almost blue.

'She was a very beautiful girl,' said the nurse.

Jack could see that must have been true. Even now, with her life force drained, she drew his eyes in. Like an exquisite statue. As he uncovered the rest of her upper torso, they discovered her naked breasts, partially hidden by crossed arms.

The nurse gasped. 'She looks like an angel.'

Jack nodded. The girl did look angelic, but there was no note in either hand.

'Let's just check down by her sides, then we'll leave her be,' he said.

He rolled back the duvet to the top of Lydia's pubis and stopped in his tracks. The room seemed to tilt and he had to clutch the fabric so as not to drop it. Neither he nor the nurse breathed. Open-mouthed, they looked at one another in horror.

Suddenly there came a sound at the door. A good-looking man in his mid-forties breezed in. 'Sorry I wasn't here to meet you, officer.' He extended a hand towards Jack. 'I'm sure Georgia here has taken good care of you.'

'Could you stay where you are, sir,' said Jack.

The man pursed his brow. Clearly more used to giving the orders around here. 'Is there problem?' he asked Jack.

Jack looked back at Lydia, where there was a very big problem indeed.

When Lilly collected Alice from nursery and headed home, David was already there. Her face must have told a thousand words.

'Rough day?'

Lilly let a stream of air reverberate across her lips. 'You could say that.'

'Want to talk about it?' David asked.

Lilly wrinkled her nose so David ushered her through to the kitchen, switched on the kettle and dropped a four-finger KitKat into her lap.

'I'll make supper,' he told her and buried his head in the fridge, raking through the vegetable tray at the bottom.

'No salad, please,' Lilly begged.

'Wouldn't dream of it.'

Lilly sipped a cup of Earl Grey and watched him chop mushrooms, peppers and cabbage.

'Got any soy sauce?' he asked.

Lilly leaned her chair back on two legs, as she was forever telling Sam not to do, and reached into the cupboard for the bottle.

'Have you spoken to Cara today?'

David poured a generous glug of sauce over the sizzling vegetables. A cloud of salty steam hit the air.

'I sent her a text this morning.'

'Saying what?' Lilly asked.

'Saying I'd like to see Flora.'

Deftly, he tossed the pan, the ingredients dancing in the air, before falling back into the heat.

'And what did she say?' Lilly asked.

'She said I should get my stuff by tomorrow or she's taking it to the tip.'

Lilly hid a smile. Cara was used to getting her own way. 'So what are you going to do?'

David threw a handful of noodles into the mixture and Lilly's stomach growled. She really fancied stodge. A nice chicken pie. With mash.

'Find a flat.' He gave a sneaky grin. 'Find a good solicitor.'

Lilly rolled her eyes. 'This is serious, David.'

'I know, I know. I'll go over there first thing and collect my stuff, then I'll find somewhere to stay.'

'And tonight?'

David turned back to his cooking. 'I wondered if I could crash here again.'

Lilly rolled her eyes again. His bashful routine was a bit ridiculous considering he was already here. She was about to tell him so when the doorbell rang.

'I'll go.' David almost ran out of the kitchen, presumably glad to avoid further discussion. When he returned, Jack was in tow.

'I explained that now wasn't a good time,' said David. 'But Jack insists it's urgent.'

Jack narrowed his eyes. 'I don't insist anything. It is what it is.'

Lilly groaned inwardly. Please let this not be about Alice's arm. She'd checked and double-checked it. She'd covered the puncture mark in Savlon. What more could she have done?

'We're about to have dinner, Jack,' she said.

Jack sniffed at the pan of stir-fry. 'Very nice.'

'Not really,' said Lilly. 'David made it.'

'Hey,' shouted David in mock indignation.

She had hoped it would break the tension but Jack's face was rigid.

'I hear you repped Lydia Morton-Daley,' he said.

Lilly nodded. 'I was in court this afternoon.' She held up a hand. 'Before you mention anything about further charges let me give you a heads up; she's dead.'

'I know,' said Jack.

'Then what's this about?' asked Lilly. 'Even the MCU can't push a case where the defendant's pegged it.'

Jack didn't answer.

'It's game over, Officer McNally. She topped herself.'

Jack appraised her coolly. Whatever had been between them was long gone. He looked at her as if she were a stranger to him.

'Actually, we don't think she did top herself,' he said.

Lilly sat up straight. 'What?'

'We don't think that Lydia killed herself,' he said.

'I don't understand.' Lilly shook her head. 'Harry said it was an overdose.'

'Harry?'

'Harry Piper, her therapist,' said Lilly. 'He came to court to tell me himself.'

Jack raised an eyebrow. 'So that's where he was. We were all wondering what was so important when one of his patients had died.'

'He thought I needed to know . . .' Lilly let the words trail away. 'What did she die of?'

'Drug overdose.'

'I thought you just said it wasn't suicide.'

Jack cocked his head to one side and something in Lilly's brain clicked.

'You think someone deliberately gave her too much.' She pointed at Jack. 'You think she was murdered.'

'We both know it can happen,' said Jack.

Lilly tapped her forehead with her fingers. Not long ago, when she had been pregnant with Alice, they'd been involved in a case where a girl had her drink spiked with drugs purchased from the internet. For all intents and purposes it had looked like suicide, when in fact it had been an honour killing.

'Something like that has got to be rare, Jack. Is there anything else to indicate murder?'

Jack reached into his jacket pocket and pulled out an A4 manila envelope. 'I'm just back from the autopsy. This is a photograph of what we found on Lydia's stomach.' He pulled out a glossy sheet and laid it on the table in front of them. Lilly gasped. David gagged.

The photograph showed her young client prone on the mortuary cot. Her skin was the matt alabaster of the dead, but across her stomach were cuts of the deepest crimson. Someone had cut into the body, spelling out two words.

Help us.

Chapter Four

**Transcript of Interview Conducted by Luton
Social Services on 15 June 2004**

Those present: Selima Begum (Head of Child Protection
Team), Sarah Hind (Child Psychologist), Terrence De Souza
(Luton Police).

Interviewee: Phoebe Talbot (date of birth unknown).

Selima: Hello, Phoebe. My name's Selima and I'm a social
worker. Do you know what that means?

Phoebe: Why is you wearing a scarf on you's head?

Selima: [laughs] Haven't you seen ladies wearing these
before?

Phoebe: No.

Selima: It just means I'm a Muslim, okay? Do you know what
a Muslim is?

Phoebe: No.

Selima: It means I believe in God and I call him Allah.

Phoebe: I believe in God.

Selima: And what do you call him?

Phoebe: God.

Selima: [laughs] That's nice and simple [pauses] so can you
tell me your name?

Phoebe: You's already said it.

Selima: I just want to check I've got it right.

Phoebe: It's Phoebe. P.H.O.E.B.E.

Selima: Excellent.

Phoebe: Not phobia. P.H.O.B.I.A. That's when you's scared of stuff.

Selima: That's great spelling, Phoebe. Who taught you to do that?

Phoebe: Gigi.

Selima: Your big sister?

Phoebe: She teached me to read as well but it's shhhh.

Selima: You're putting your finger on your lips, Phoebe. Does that mean it's a secret?

Phoebe: Yes.

Selima: Do you and Gigi keep any other secrets, Phoebe?

Phoebe: She make me nice cards for birthdays.

Selima: Oh that's nice isn't it? And do you know how many birthdays you've had, Phoebe? [pause] You're holding up six fingers, Phoebe. So you're six years old?

Phoebe: Yes but we's don't tell when it's a birthday.

Selima: Why is that, Phoebe? Why don't you and Gigi tell anyone it's your birthday?

Phoebe: I don't know. Gigi says it me. I don't think she wants them to have a party.

Selima: Why not?

Phoebe: They might invite other peoples.

Selima: Gigi worries that Mummy and Daddy might invite other people to the party?

Phoebe: Maybes.

Selima: And why would Gigi worry about that? Doesn't she like the people Mummy and Daddy might invite?

Phoebe: None of us like the peoples.

Selima: Why is that Phoebe?

Phoebe: We's just don't like them.

Selima: What do they do, Phoebe? What do they do to make you feel like that about them?
Phoebe: They do . . . [pauses].
Selima: Go on, Phoebe, you can tell us what they do.
Phoebe: They just do whatever they like.

Lilly opened the curtains to a fresh snowfall that had covered the garden in a white rug at least ten inches deep.

'School's closed,' Sam sang out from his laptop.

'Great,' said Lilly.

'You'll never get the Mini off the drive,' said David.

'Excellent,' said Lilly.

There was a meeting with Lydia's parents scheduled at the Grove and Lilly had intended to call in and speak to the pathologist beforehand.

David handed her a coffee. 'I'll take you in my car.'

'What about work?' she asked.

'No one will bother on a day like today.'

Lilly eyed him over the rim of her mug. 'What about Cara?'

'I'll head over there this afternoon.' David rummaged in the fridge. 'Then I'll pop into the local estate agent's for details of rentals.'

Lilly was unconvinced as she watched him juggle a block of cheese and a tomato, whistling as he thinly sliced them onto some toast. If he thought he could stay in the cottage indefinitely he had another thing coming.

As David's Range Rover powered through the country lanes, passing countless cars abandoned in snowdrifts, he gave Lilly a sneaky sideways look.

She pretended she didn't know what was coming. 'What?'

'Not so bad now, is she?' He patted the steering wheel. 'The old Chelsea tractor.'

Lilly pulled a face. She had indeed criticized the monster four-by-fours the Manor Park yummy mummys used for the school run and a weekly shop at Waitrose. She had also, on more than one occasion, described David's enormous beast as his 'penis extension'.

'You can't justify the amount of fuel this thing guzzles because it's proved useful one day of the year,' she said.

'You're welcome to walk,' he said.

She sniffed imperiously as she turned on the seat heater and stretched out her legs, watching the landscape pass as the car powered through snow and ice. When they arrived, Luton was eerily deserted. This early in the morning the street lights were still lit, casting the yellow light of a town across the snow-covered roads, making them seem sickly and wrong.

'Over there.' Lilly pointed to an unobtrusive brick building.

'Doesn't look much, does it?' said David.

'What were you expecting? Something out of *CSI*?'

'Er . . . yes.'

They both burst out laughing as David pulled over and Lilly was still chuckling as she jumped out of the car and crunched her way to the foyer. Once inside, however, the smile slid from her lips. This place pressed down on her shoulders.

With more purpose than she felt, Lilly strode down the corridor. When she reached Lab 3, she peered through the small round window in the door. Inside, Phil Cheney, a pathologist she'd known and liked for years, was bent over a cadaver. Meticulously, he moved across the dead man's forehead with a tiny pair of tweezers, breaking every few moments to drop his quarry in a clear evidence bag. When he appeared to be finished and Lilly couldn't wait a second longer, she tapped on the glass and Cheney turned. He recognized her and smiled, holding up five gloved fingers.

Shit. Lilly would have to spend even longer in this godforsaken place. She gave a shudder and began to pace.

At last Cheney appeared. 'You'll wear away our Persian rugs.'

Lilly was about to laugh but stopped in surprise. 'What happened to you?'

She gestured to his face. Normally adorned with multiple piercings, not just in his ears, but a ring in each eyebrow and a stud in his nose, lip and tongue, it was shockingly metal-free. And his NHS specs, held together with sellotape, or sometimes a plaster, had been replaced by a pair of rimless glasses that looked as if they had cost a small fortune.

'My new image,' he said. 'You likey?'

'It's certainly different,' Lilly replied.

Cheney grimaced. 'To tell you the truth I feel naked, but my new girlfriend insisted. It was either her or them.'

'What about the ink?' Lilly pointed to the sleeves of his lab jacket, which she knew covered tattoos from his wrists to his shoulders.

'We've agreed on an armistice. I won't get any more and she'll try to ignore the ones I've already got.'

'It must be love.'

Cheney sighed. 'I suppose it must be. Speaking of which, has McNally come to his senses?'

Jack and Cheney went way back. Old drinking buddies and general partners in crime.

'I told him he was making a big mistake,' said Cheney. 'You are the best thing that ever happened to him.'

Lilly smiled. Jack had obviously told Cheney he had left her rather than Lilly asking him to move out. Probably a male pride thing.

'Let's get down to business shall we?' she said. 'Lydia Morton-Daley.'

'Ah, yes.' Cheney rubbed his hands together.

His obvious enthusiasm might be disconcerting to normal folk, but Lilly was glad that the dead had someone on their side who gave a toss. He dived back into the lab and Lilly held her nose until he returned waving the autopsy report.

'Can you give me the edited highlights?' she asked.

'Blood levels indicate a large amount of benzos.'

'Enough to kill her?'

'On their own, probably not,' he said. 'But mixed with the zopiclone we found as well, very likely.'

'Could it be accidental?' Lilly asked. 'A mistake by one of the staff?'

'It would be some mistake. They're contraindicated.' He leaned towards Lilly and fingered through the report in her hand. 'And there's this too.' He pulled out the photograph that Jack had shown Lilly the night before. 'Makes me think this is no mistake.'

Lilly glanced down at it, sickened by the size of each word and the depth of each wound.

'No chance she did that herself?'

'Not unless she was able to withstand the pain of carving each letter into her own flesh and still manage to do it perfectly upside down and back to front.'

Cheney acted out writing across his own stomach and Lilly could see that to make it legible to an onlooker would be difficult with a pen, let alone with a knife.

'Then there's the small matter that she was dead at the time,' he said.

'Dead?'

Cheney nodded breezily. 'Post-mortem wounds, I'm afraid.'

Lilly groaned.

'Does it matter?' Cheney asked.

'It will to the girl's parents,' said Lilly. Suicide was one thing, but murder and mutilation were something else entirely.

She smiles at me from across the room. Her teeth are uneven and the hem of one leg of her navy trouser suit has been sewn up with black cotton. But I mustn't allow these details to cloud my judgement.

Watching her in court yesterday afternoon was very interesting. The fat prosecutor, who smells so bad I almost gagged, tried to attack her. Like a wasp she went for her again and again. Buzz, buzz, buzz. But Lilly Valentine swatted her away with the back of her hand.

Same with the magistrate. The poisonous little hobgoblin went for it. Full charge, head down. But she held her ground.

I've learned my lesson. If I'm going to win, I will need different tactics. A frontal assault will just strengthen her resolve. She's stubborn though. And that will be her undoing.

Lilly stood at the far edge of Harry's office and chewed her cuticles. She felt the sting as she bit too far.

'That's a bad habit,' said Harry.

Lilly looked down at her hands. The nails were down to the quick, the cuticles ragged and bloody. When had she started doing that? At four in the morning of course, when Alice was screaming as if the Hounds of Hell were on her tail.

He gestured to one of the chairs placed around his desk.

She sidled over to the seat furthest from Jack's. He was already in his place, speaking in hushed tones to the WPC at his side. Lilly recognized her from yesterday's hearing. She was the one who had arrested Lydia. Lilly caught her staring and the WPC looked away. No doubt she thought Lilly had made a spectacular idiot of herself in court.

Jack was nervous, endlessly smoothing down his tie. He almost never wore one and when he did, it was an instant giveaway as to how stressed he was feeling. The WPC leaned in to ask him something and he almost jumped out of his skin. Lilly couldn't blame him. None of them were looking forward to meeting Lydia's parents.

A small knock came at the office door and Lilly went rigid.

She noticed that Jack and the WPC straightened their backs too. Only Harry kept his relaxed appearance and opened the door.

'Mr and Mrs Morton-Daley.' Harry spoke to a point outside the office. 'Please come in.'

Lilly gulped. Waited.

At last the couple entered. Lilly noticed that despite flawless highlights and an unnaturally smooth forehead that screamed Botox, Mrs Morton-Daley looked significantly older than her husband. Perhaps the death of her daughter had aged her. Lilly knew that if anything ever happened to Sam or Alice she would look a hundred and eighty overnight. And she wouldn't give a shit.

Harry made the introductions. 'This is Officer Jack McNally of Luton MCU.'

Jack jumped to his feet and held out his hand. 'I'm so sorry for your loss.'

Mr Morton-Daley shook his hand but his wife just gave Jack an awkward nod.

'This is my colleague, WPC Kate Knight,' said Jack.

The WPC was about to speak, no doubt to offer her own condolences, when Mrs Morton-Daley narrowed her eyes.

'You were at the police station the night Lydia was arrested.'

'That's right,' said the WPC.

'Then why are you here?' asked Mrs Morton-Daley. She turned to Harry. 'Why is she here?'

Mr Morton-Daley gave three little staccato coughs.

'What?' Mrs Morton-Daley asked her husband. 'I'm not allowed to ask any questions?'

Harry moved forward in a seamless movement and placed a hand on her arm. 'You can ask as many questions as you like, Mrs Morton-Daley. We're all here to help in any way we can.' His voice was soft but the pressure he exerted on the woman must have been firm because she melted into a chair without argument. Her husband sat next to her.

'And this is Miss Valentine,' Harry gestured to Lilly. 'Lydia's solicitor.'

'I can't imagine how you feel,' Lilly said.

Mrs Morton-Daley blinked in surprise. 'At least that's honest.'

'At a time like this what else is there?' Lilly asked.

Mrs Morton-Daley stared at Lilly for an uncomfortable moment that turned the contents of Lilly's stomach to slush. Then she snapped her head towards Harry, who had taken his place behind his desk. 'How on earth could this happen?'

'Jennifer!' Her husband put a hand on her knee.

'For God's sake.' She threw his hand off. 'Don't you want to know? Or are you just . . .' She didn't finish her sentence, but shook her head and looked back at Harry expectantly.

'We all want to know what happened, Jennifer,' said Harry. 'May I call you Jennifer?'

Mrs Morton-Daley shrugged.

'Thank you,' said Harry as if she had granted him a huge privilege. 'That's exactly what the police are here to do, isn't that right, Officer McNally?'

'Absolutely,' said Jack. 'As soon as we suspected Lydia had been killed by someone else, we brought in a team. Every single person who was at the Grove yesterday is being interviewed as we speak. Their stories are being checked and double-checked.'

'Will that do any good?' asked Mrs Morton-Daley.

'I think it will,' Jack answered. 'In a place like the Grove, we can ascertain fairly easily who came in and who came out. We know who had access to the drugs cupboard and who didn't. We're talking about limited opportunity and that helps us.'

'You think you will catch the person who did this?' she asked.

'I give you my word that I will not rest until I do,' said Jack.

An oppressive silence fell on the room and Lilly prayed Harry would wrap the meeting up, but before he could do so, Mr Morton-Daley turned to her.

'When you last spoke to Lydia how did she seem?' he asked.

Lilly thought back to their meeting. How Lydia had told her about the events of the party the night she was arrested.

'Did she seem happy?' His wife sighed, but he continued nevertheless. 'Or, if not happy, at least at peace with herself?'

Lilly remembered Lydia. She had seemed angry and damaged and depressed.

'We hoped that this time and this place might do the trick,' he said. 'It was the last chance, you see, for all of us.'

Lilly didn't know what to say. How could she tell him the truth? Yet was it right to lie? Thank God Harry came to her rescue.

'Lydia was responding to treatment. Obviously it was very early days and the road ahead was long, but I was confident we could make a real difference.'

'Thank you.' Mr Morton-Daley's voice was filled with so much gratitude that Harry looked down at his hands. 'Thank you so much.'

Mrs Morton-Daley groaned, got to her feet and left the room. Her husband rose and regarded the open door.

'I must apologize for Jennifer,' he said. 'She's so very upset.'

'We completely understand,' said Lilly.

He moved towards the door, but hovered, uncertain. 'Do you?'

'Of course,' said Lilly. 'You should go after her, make sure she's okay.'

He gave a tight smile and went to find his wife.

Harry exhaled loudly. 'Well done, Lilly. You handled that like a pro.'

Gem strips the bed like Feyza showed her, pulling the top corners out and throwing them in the middle, then doing the same with

83

the bottom corners. That way she can pick the sheet up without touching the bit that anyone has been on.

Same with the bin. Pick the bag up by the handles and don't even look at the stuff inside.

'What's the matter?' asks the girl whose room it is. 'Worried about catching something?'

She's gluing on false eyelashes at the dressing table, a cigarette clamped between her teeth. Her name's Misty. Well that ain't her proper name obviously. None of the working girls use their proper names. Which seems a bit weird 'cos they don't keep nothing else private, do they?

She stubs out her fag, the lipstick-rimmed dog-end ending up in an ashtray overflowing with 'em.

'You scared of catching Aids?'

Well of course she is. And hepatitis. Or herpes. But Gem don't think Misty would take too kindly to her saying that. So she says nothing.

Feyza makes it clear that part of Gem's job is to keep her mouth shut.

She pulls a clean sheet from the cupboard in the corner and throws it over the bed, tucking the edges in nice and tight. Feyza only had to show her once and Gem could tell she was pleased. She's always been a quick learner. Everybody says so. She was in all the top sets in year seven and eight. Not any more. She don't go into school enough. But she bets she could learn it all if she started going again properly.

'Don't forget the pillowcase,' Misty tells her, but Gem is already changing it.

Misty's dressing gown falls open and Gem can see her black bra and a red love bite.

'Fuck's sake.' Misty checks it in the mirror and rakes through her make-up bag for a tube of thick concealer. She squeezes a blob on her finger and pats it over the bruise. It works like a dream. Gem's seen her using it on some pink scars she's got around her lips. Even up close you can't see them when she's wearing it.

'Hurry up,' Misty says. 'I've got a punter waiting.'

Gem puts the pillow on the bed and heads for the door with the dirty sheet and bin bag, while Misty throws her dressing gown over a chair. They look at each other for a second, Misty in a black thong that cuts between her arse cheeks, and Gem with her stash of spunk-filled condoms.

'Go on then,' says Misty. 'Fuck off out of it.'

Gem scurries away past reception. There's a sad sack in there, picking the dirt out of his nails, waiting his turn. His hair is grey and looks like it ain't been washed for weeks. Gem supposes she should feel sorry for Misty but frankly it ain't her business.

Lilly was attempting to make a quick getaway from the Grove and had sprinted halfway down the corridor, when Jack called after her. Her heart sank.

'Could I have a word, Lilly?'

She plastered on a smile and turned. 'Of course.'

He caught up with her, the WPC following just behind.

'What can I do for you, Jack?' asked Lilly.

He tilted his head at the WPC. 'Give us a moment, Kate.'

The WPC's face froze but she quickly recovered, plastering on her own smile before stalking away in the other direction.

'I'd say you just pissed someone off,' said Lilly.

Jack looked shocked. 'Kate? Why do you say that?'

'Being sidelined by your male boss is never pleasant for a woman,' Lilly told him.

Relief swept over his face. 'I'll square it with her later. Back at the station. Obviously.'

He was wittering now. Clearly she'd hit a nerve. She'd almost feel sorry for him, but she was starving and David would be waiting for her outside.

'You wanted a word,' she prompted.

He nodded, clearly glad to be on safer ground. 'I just wondered about David.'

'David?'

'He's staying at your place.'

'Only for a couple of days,' said Lilly. 'Silly bugger's been kicked out by Botox Belle.'

'It's not permanent then?'

Lilly laughed. 'I don't think my fifteen-year-old couch is comfortable enough for that.'

'He's on the couch then?' Jack looked at his feet.

'Of course he's on the bloody couch.' Lilly shook her head in disbelief. 'We're divorced.'

'People get back together,' he said.

'I can assure you that that is not on the cards for me and David.'

Jack shuffled from foot to foot. 'Does he know that?'

For God's sake. She had had some ridiculous conversations with Jack over the years, but this one was a classic.

'He dumped me for a dumb blonde, remember. The men in my life have a habit of doing that.'

If she could have sucked the words back in she would have, and then sewn her lips together for good measure. She didn't want to rehash old arguments with Jack any more than she did with David. She steeled herself for his defence, but it didn't come. Instead, he stared off down the corridor and spoke over Lilly's head. 'I'll be with you in a moment.'

Lilly glanced around and saw the WPC gliding towards them, hands behind her back. She didn't slow her pace when Jack spoke.

'I said I'll be with you in a moment.'

If the WPC noticed the tinge of irritation in Jack's voice she disguised it well. 'I think you're going to want to hear what I've got to say, Jack,' she said.

He folded his arms, an implicit sign that this had better be good.

'I've just spoken to the guys who have been searching the scene,' she said. 'They've found something.'

'What?' Jack asked.

The WPC kept a straight face but there was a twinkle in her eye as she brought her left hand into view. In it she was holding an evidence bag. Inside the bag was the unmistakable shape of a blood–stained knife.

I feel distinctly odd.

Like I'm having an out-of-body experience.

The way Jack dismissed me, I thought he was joking at first. When I realized he wasn't joking, I had to force myself to slip away. It didn't feel like me doing that.

Thank goodness that PC found the knife. I knew Jack would want to see it immediately.

We're walking towards the room where it was found now. Jack's talking but I only know that because his mouth is moving. I can't hear a word he's saying. It's like being deep under water. Or deaf. Yes, this is what it must be like to be deaf.

As I say, it's distinctly odd.

Jack grabs my arm and I try to focus. His voice is so quiet. Like he's at the other end of a long tunnel.

'Do you know whose room this is, Kate?'

I shake my head.

He looks puzzled and I resist the urge to trace my finger down the sweet little wrinkles in his forehead.

'Are you okay?' he asks, his voice still far away.

I nod and smile. How can I even begin to explain?

As we get to the right door, Jack checks up and down the corridor. The PC who found the knife is talking to the shrink. I don't like that one at all. The way he looked at Lilly was transparent. Dirty old man.

Jack stands with his feet apart and his fists balled. That's how I know he's shouting.

'Can someone tell me whose room this is?'

The shrink comes over and answers Jack, then he leaves to check the room.

Lilly was at the exit when she heard someone calling her. She stopped, hand still outstretched for the handle. Would she ever manage to leave this bloody place?

She turned and saw that this time it was Harry hurrying towards her.

'Shall I bring a sleeping bag next time?'

'Sorry?' Harry asked.

'Maybe a change of knickers and a toothbrush?'

She waited for him to get the joke but his eyes remained serious. Clearly her gallows humour was out of place.

'What's up, Harry?' she asked.

He scratched his scalp with both hands and exhaled. This was the first time she'd seen even a crack in his ice-smooth carapace.

'The police have found a knife,' he said.

'I know,' Lilly replied. 'They'll send it to forensics and hopefully they'll get a match.'

'I don't think they need forensics,' he said.

'No?'

He closed his eyes, fingers no longer clawing but remaining in his hair. 'I should have seen this coming. I should have known where this was leading.'

'What should you have seen coming?'

His eyes were still closed. 'The signs were there. You noticed them.'

A heaviness descended on Lilly, like a cloak weighted with stones. 'Harry.' She enunciated each word clearly. 'What did I notice?'

When he opened his eyes, they were bright with tears and regret and the cloak dragged her down with slow inevitability. She didn't need him to say the words, did she? She knew.

'Chloe Church,' said Harry. 'They found the knife in Chloe Church's room.'

Lilly didn't reply. Instead she chased an image around her brain. A hugely overweight girl, thrusting a soggy note into her hand. The note Lilly had discarded together with her concerns. Could it really be a coincidence that the words of that note had been the same ones carved into Lydia's cold white flesh?

'If I'd just listened to you,' said Harry.

Lilly's mouth went dry. Everything about that note had screamed of something being very wrong. Why had she done nothing about it?

'You can't blame yourself, Harry,' she said.

He sighed and gave the weakest of smiles. 'You're a good woman.'

Right now Lilly didn't feel remotely good.

'What's going to happen?' Harry asked.

'I can't say for sure,' Lilly told him. 'I'd imagine Chloe will be arrested and taken down to the station for questioning.'

'Absolutely not.' Harry's regret and uncertainty vanished. 'That cannot happen.'

'You can't stop it, Harry. Unless you're saying she's unfit.'

'I will most definitely say that.' Harry held his head high. 'Chloe is very ill.'

Lilly couldn't disagree with that. If Chloe had really killed Lydia and then cut a message into her dead body, that alone seemed conclusive proof.

'Jack won't be happy about it,' she said.

Harry shrugged. 'That's hardly our concern, is it?'

Lilly winced at the word 'our'.

'The important issue is that we protect Chloe,' Harry continued. 'Don't you agree?'

Lilly ran her top teeth over her bottom lip, worrying a piece of dry skin. 'I'm afraid I can't get involved, Harry. I worked for Lydia, not Chloe.'

Harry put his hand on Lilly's arm. 'I don't want to state the obvious but Lydia doesn't need you any longer.'

'There's still the potential for conflict,' said Lilly.

Potential! That was the understatement of the year. Or the decade. Chloe's note was a big fat screaming reality. When Jack found out about it he'd think all his Christmases had come at once.

'There would only be a conflict of interest if you took on Chloe's case,' said Harry. 'All you need to do right now is talk to the poor girl, explain what's happening. Then we can go and set out our position to Jack. If he arrests her, I dread to think what might happen to her.'

Lilly wavered. Her gut instinct was to walk away from this case as fast as she could. But Harry was right, Chloe did need help.

'I can see you're uncomfortable with this,' said Harry. 'In different circumstances I'd let you run straight out of that door and call someone else, but by the time I do that and another lawyer battles through the snow, it will be too late for Chloe.'

'You can tell Jack that Chloe's not fit for interview,' she said.

Harry snorted. 'I'm not convinced he'll take my word for it.'

'What makes you think he'll listen to me?'

'Oh come on, Lilly,' said Harry.

Lilly blushed. Did Harry know that she and Jack had been an item?

'Don't be embarrassed,' said Harry. 'Sheba told me you were the best in the business. I'm certain you can make Jack see reason.'

Lilly gave a weak smile. He didn't know about Jack and made everything sound so straightforward. And yet the tap, tap, tap of doubt was like a teaspoon against a hard-boiled egg.

'Whatever the rights and wrongs of this mess,' said Harry, 'Chloe needs our help.'

Lilly shuddered at the word 'help'. Hadn't Chloe already begged for that? And hadn't Lilly ignored her? Could she really do that a second time?

'Fine,' she said. 'Let's do it.'

Harry beamed. 'I knew you wouldn't let her down.'

He had no idea how spectacularly she had already done just that.

They scooted back up the corridor, Lilly chasing Harry as he led her through a myriad of security doors. If ever she needed to find her way out in a hurry, she'd be toast. As they passed a room with the door flung wide, Harry peered inside. Lilly followed his eye line and saw Jack and the WPC deep in conversation with a uniformed officer. Jack looked up and they exchanged a glance.

'We need to be quick,' Lilly hissed at Harry. 'Jack will want to know exactly where and how the knife was found, but that isn't going to take much longer.'

Harry led her back to his office. 'I told Elaine to put her in here.'

He opened the door and the nurse looked up. She was in the chair where Mr Morton-Daley had sat. Next to her, in Lilly's seat, was Chloe. Hunched over, her head in her chest, arms over her head. A sweat-soaked T-shirt had ridden up, revealing a ring of wet fat. Like lard in a hot frying pan.

Harry nodded to the nurse. 'Thank you, Elaine.'

It was clearly a signal for the nurse to leave, but she didn't seem keen to do so. Instead, she hovered in front of the door.

'We need to talk about this,' she said.

'We will, Elaine,' said Harry. 'We will.'

The nurse shot Lilly a look that she couldn't figure out. Frankly, there wasn't time.

'I really need to speak to Chloe,' she said. 'In private.'

The nurse gave a tight nod and left. Gingerly, Lilly took the empty place and placed a hand on Chloe's back. Instantly, she regretted it. She could feel hot damp flesh through the fabric of the T-shirt.

'Chloe,' she said, praying that the girl would sit up and she could remove her palm. 'I need to speak to you.'

The girl didn't budge and Lilly watched her hand rise and fall with Chloe's laboured breathing. She looked to Harry for help and he squeezed himself between his desk and Chloe, crouching at her bare feet, which still bore the deep red marks of whatever shoes she had previously been wearing.

'Chloe.' Harry's voice was gentle yet firm. 'We don't have much time.'

When she still didn't budge, he removed her arms one at a time, allowing them to flop towards the ground, and reached under Chloe's chin, pushing it up.

'This is Lilly Valentine.' He looked intently into Chloe's face. 'She's here to help you.' He cupped Chloe's chin and forced her head to the left. 'Do you remember Lilly?'

Lilly smiled in encouragement but Chloe's face was blank, eyes unfocused, mouth gaping, tongue lolling.

'We met in the common room,' Lilly told her, but there was no sign of recognition, only the wheezy breaths that puffed out the smell of onions into Lilly's face.

'She came to help Lydia,' said Harry and something skittered across Chloe's face. 'Now she's going to help you.'

Chloe's pupils fought to pinpoint Lilly as if she were a figure on the distant horizon.

'The police want to speak to you, Chloe,' Lilly said. 'But I'm wondering if you feel well enough for that.'

A string of saliva dripped from Chloe's tongue, stretching and stretching until it snapped and came to rest on the front of her T-shirt. Lilly glanced at Harry. There could be little doubt that this girl was unfit to be interviewed.

'To be honest, Chloe, I think I agree with Lilly that you're probably not well enough to speak to anyone right now.' Harry rubbed the girl's knee, making it shake visibly beneath her trousers. 'I think it might be better if you got some rest. Somewhere nice and quiet and dark.'

Without warning Chloe's head snapped back and she let out a terrified scream.

'It's okay,' said Harry, jumping to his feet. 'We're here for you, Chloe.'

Chloe screamed again, and reared away from Harry, tipping the chair back until it collapsed, spilling Chloe onto the floor.

'What's happening?' Lilly shouted as Chloe began to writhe, her eyes rolling back in her head, her arms and legs flailing. All the while screaming, like a pig being led into the abattoir.

'She's fitting,' said Harry, trying to reach over her mass to her face, but being batted away by Chloe's meaty fists. One caught him squarely in the eye and he reeled backwards with a cry.

'What shall I do?' Lilly yelled.

'Hold her down,' Harry replied.

Lilly leaned over Chloe who was now convulsing with such violence her head crashed against the floor, the skull making a sickening crack. An arm flung out at Lilly's chest, winding her.

'Hold her.' Harry had crawled up the right side of Chloe's body and pressed down onto her upper torso.

Lilly struggled to catch a breath and threw herself onto Chloe's left shoulder, trapping her arm beneath her. The girl heaved furiously, her arms pinned outwards as if she were crucified. She

HELEN BLACK

bucked with such force Lilly knew she couldn't hold her for much longer.

'Now what?' she shouted.

Then the door burst open and Jack's face went white as he took in the scene. 'What the hell's going on?' he asked.

'Get a nurse,' Harry told him. 'We need emergency sedative.'

Jack was so shocked he didn't move.

'Now,' Harry ordered and Jack retreated.

Lilly held on with all the strength she could muster until the medical team arrived and plunged a syringe into Chloe's thigh.

Chapter Five

Mr George Talbot
HMP Belmarsh
Prisoner number 50321/V   3 September 2004

Dear Mr Talbot,

Expiry of Public Funding Certificate

Further to your recent telephone calls to this office, it is with regret that I must inform you that Miss April Cash will not be able to make any further visits with you at HMP Belmarsh.

As has been explained to you, both by your barrister, Mr Wade, and our Miss Cash, your conviction at Luton Crown Court on 11 June is unappealable. An appeal against conviction can only be pursued where there was an error made during the trial or where new evidence has been brought to light. Neither of which applies to your case.

Similarly, you have been advised that there is no possibility of an appeal against the sentence passed down by the court on 26 July. Given the serious nature of the offences involved, a term of twelve years is highly reasonable, particularly given the ages of the victims and the fact that you did not plead guilty which, as Judge

Wilkes pointed out at some length, meant the witnesses were all put through an 'almost unbearable' ordeal. He stated that your actions have impacted upon everyone who had to read or hear about these crimes, including the jurors and legal teams.

I know that both Mr Wade and Miss Cash have advised you that you were fortunate to escape a life sentence and I completely agree.

Whilst I understand that you find yourself in a position you would not wish to be in, I recommend that you attempt to come to terms with the situation and the first step is to accept that your court case is now over. Indeed, the public funding certificate which covered the costs of your legal help has now expired. Therefore, I must make it plain that this firm is no longer representing you. I have instructed Miss Cash to make no further visits and to refuse all telephone calls from you. If you write to Miss Cash again, the letters will be returned to you unopened.

I trust that the position of this firm is clear to you.

Yours sincerely

Christopher Walters

Senior Partner at Walters, Radison and Daley

Lilly hurried through the dark to the Range Rover. The windows were steamed up but Lilly could make out David leaning back in his seat, eyes closed, hands behind his head, his lips moving as he sang along to whatever he was listening to. Lilly would bet Janis Joplin.

She tapped on the glass and he opened his eyes, smiled at her and bent forward to release the central locking. Lilly jumped in out of the cold. She'd been right about Janis.

'Thanks for waiting.' She held her hands over the heater.

'No worries.' He tapped the clock on the dashboard. 'We'd better shoot over to the nursery to collect Alice.'

Lilly checked the time. Five to six. Even if David barrelled it, she'd be late. Again.

'Don't worry,' he said. 'The weather will catch out lots of the parents.'

She wasn't sure he was right, but was grateful all the same.

'Everything okay?' he asked and indicated to pull out into the empty road.

Lilly fingered the place on her chest where Chloe's fist had caught her. She'd have a hell of a bruise tomorrow.

'The police found a knife in a patient's room. A girl called Chloe.'

'Bloody hell. How on earth did she get hold of a knife in somewhere like that?'

Lilly shrugged. 'Lord only knows. Jack thinks she killed Lydia.'

'Jack?'

'He was at the meeting with Lydia's parents,' she said. 'I expect this will become his case now.'

David turned his head towards her. 'Tell me you're not involved.'

'I'm not.' He narrowed his eyes at her. 'I'm not,' she told him. 'I just happened to be there when they found the knife. Jesus Christ, David, I didn't plan this.'

He went back to watching the road. 'Did Jack arrest her?'

'No,' said Lilly. 'She had some sort of fit.'

'Very convenient.'

Lilly shook her head. 'No way. This was for real, believe me, like something out of *The Exorcist*. She had to be sedated.'

'So what happens next?'

'Harry will sort out a new solicitor in the morning.'

'Harry?'

'The girl's shrink. He runs the unit.'

'That's an end to it then.' David sounded pleased but there was a jumpy feeling in Lilly's stomach.

She looked out of the side window, watching the rooftops all blanketed in snow, imagining the families inside, cosy and content. Tomorrow they might build snowmen or take their kids sledging. Lilly on the other hand would have to deal with the letter. Which meant that this wasn't the end. It meant this was only the beginning.

Gem thinks she's doing a good job. All the beds and bins are clean and she's done all the washing-up in the kitchen sink.

'It always go quiet now,' Feyza says. 'It pick up again after seven.'

'Even in the snow?' Gem asks.

Feyza laughs. 'It take more than bad weather to keep punters away.'

Gem imagines them trudging their way through the snowdrifts, just so they can get their end away. And pay for it.

'Shall I make the girls a cuppa?' she asks.

'Sure,' Feyza says, a funny look on her face.

Gem opens the cupboard and pulls out five mugs. One each for Amber, Loretta, Sapphire and Misty. And one for Feyza. Gem don't much like tea. She prefers Coke and Fanta and that.

Feyza must have told them 'cos they soon come out of their rooms for their tea, leaning against the counter in their dressing gowns.

'Where's Misty?' Gem asks.

Amber makes a sound like 'pffft' and stretches her legs out. There's a tattoo of a snake all the way from her ankle to her knee, winding round and round her calf. Its forked tongue points upwards like an arrow leading the way for the punters.

'She's in a mood, innit,' says Amber. 'Again.'

'Why?' Gem asks.

'Who knows, baby.' Amber winks. 'Maybe she's got PMT.'

The other girls laugh.

'Shall I take it to her?' Gem picks up the mug of tea. 'It's getting cold.'

'Why not?' Feyza says. 'Maybe she cheer up.'

Gem wanders off to Misty's room and taps on the door gently.

'What?' Misty shouts from inside.

Gem opens the door, the drink held out in front of her like a peace offering.

'What do you want?' says Misty from the chair at her dressing table.

'I brought you a cup of tea,' Gem replies.

Misty sighs and turns back to the mirror. Gem don't know if that means she wants it or not. But it seems a shame to waste it, so she scuttles over and puts it next to Misty with a smile.

Misty looks at her in disgust. 'What have you got to be so fucking happy about?'

Gem shrugs. She's just happy to be here, earning money. Feyza said she'd pay five pounds an hour so Gem should have enough for nappies, food and fags at the end of today.

'Don't be so horrible,' says Feyza from the doorway.

'I didn't hear you knock,' says Misty.

Feyza steps inside and closes the door behind her, arms folded over her chest. 'We need a chat, yes?'

Misty sniffs, picks up a bottle of cleanser and squeezes a big blob onto some cotton wool. She's forever taking off all her make-up and then redoing it all over again.

'Wipe frown from face too, you understand me?' says Feyza.

Misty rolls her eyes and aims the used cotton wool at the bin. She misses and it lands with a plop on the floor. Gem bends forward and collects it up, careful not to touch the orange stain of Misty's foundation.

'Customers want to see happy girls,' says Feyza. 'Not miserable bitches.'

'Customers don't care,' says Misty.

Feyza says, 'Don't push me.'

'Why?' says Misty. 'What're you going to do?'

'I put you out of here and you take your chances with all the rest.' Feyza jabs her thumb over her shoulder. 'On street.'

Misty slams down the bottle of cleanser and refuses to even look at Feyza.

'You know you on to good thing here,' says Feyza. 'Don't fuck up.' Then she leaves, slamming the door behind her.

'Fucking Turkish slag,' says Misty. 'On to a good thing? I make her more money than all the rest of the girls in here put together.'

Gem wonders if that can be true. Misty is busier than the other girls, but she'd have to be four times busier than them, wouldn't she? For every one customer they did, she'd need to do four. And though Misty is good at getting them in and out, even she ain't that quick.

'I could go to any of the Russians and they'd beg me to work for them, I'm telling you,' says Misty. 'Fucking beg me.'

She reaches for her fags and lights one. Gem notices that her hand is shaking.

'What are you staring at?' Misty shouts at her. 'Stop fucking staring at me.'

'Sorry,' Gem mumbles and gets out of the room before Misty really loses the plot.

Lilly woke in a better mood than the one that had dogged her at bedtime. It had snowed again and she made the decision then and there that she wouldn't wake Sam or Alice. They were having the day off and would spend it having snowball fights, interrupted only by disgustingly huge cups of hot chocolate. With whipped cream. And marshmallows.

As she plodded past the sofa, David stirred, his face buried in the pillow she had tossed to him the night before. He had, after all, played chauffeur all day.

'Tea?' she asked.

'If you're making,' he said.

She didn't bother asking if he wanted toast and shoved in another slice alongside her own. While she waited for them to pop she looked out of the kitchen window. Dawn was sneaking up on the fields beyond her garden, inching cautiously across the horizon.

'I always loved this view,' said David.

Lilly almost snorted tea through her nose. 'You did not. You said it reminded you of the dark side of the moon.'

He laughed and as the toast popped caught both slices in mid-air.

'You are such a lawyer,' he said. 'You hang on every word as if it were testimony at the Old Bailey.'

'I do not.' Lilly reached for butter and jam. 'I just hate bullshit.'

He slid two plates across the work surface and they sat down to eat in companionable silence. Lilly mused over what she would say to Jack about Chloe's letter. She decided to be brisk and businesslike. If she stuck to the facts, it was up to Jack to draw his own conclusions. Torturing herself about ignoring the letter was helping no one, least of all Chloe. Anyway, by the look of her yesterday it was unlikely a case would ever come to court. She was surely insane and incapable of facing trial. A lifetime in mental institutions beckoned, and might that not be for the best?

The phone rang and Lilly snatched it up so it wouldn't wake the kids. 'Lilly Valentine,' she said.

The person at the other end didn't speak. All Lilly could hear were deep rasping breaths. Jesus, dirty calls at this time!

'Who is this?' she demanded.

Still the caller didn't speak.

'Listen to me, sunshine,' she said. 'I'm tracing this call, so I'd get lost now if I were you.'

Only the rattling sound of breathing responded and she was about to slam down the receiver when the noise changed momentarily. It caught. Like a small sob.

'For God's sake, what do you want?' Lilly asked.

'I need . . .' The caller's voice choked into more crying. 'I need to speak to you.'

'You are speaking to me,' said Lilly. 'Why don't you start by telling me your name?'

There was a silence punctuated by a couple of sniffs.

'It's me,' said the caller. 'It's Chloe.'

Lilly's hand flew to her breastbone and the spot where Chloe had hit her. She glanced down her pyjama top but the bruising was yet to come out. Nevertheless, it hurt. Like a tiny jet of viciousness under her skin.

'How did you get this number, Chloe?'

'What?'

'You're calling me at home,' said Lilly. 'I'm wondering where you got the number.'

'I'm not sure.' Chloe paused as if trying to remember. 'Someone gave it to me. I think they said you'd written it in the book when you signed in.'

Lilly frowned. She could have sworn she'd given the office number. But it wasn't beyond the realms of possibility she'd made a mistake. She had just met with Cheney and was dreading the conversation with Lydia's parents.

'Okay, Chloe, what can I do for you?'

The girl began to sob once more. Lilly worried she might have another fit.

'Calm down, Chloe,' said Lilly. 'Take some deep breaths.'

The girl did as she was told and eventually the howling subsided. 'I need to talk to you,' she said.

'That's fine, Chloe, talk as much as you need to.'

'No,' said Chloe. 'Not on the phone. I need you to come here.'

'I can't do that I'm afraid,' said Lilly. 'I'm sorry but it's not possible.'

'You have to.' Chloe's voice dropped to a whisper. 'You have to help me.'

Lilly closed her eyes. She couldn't allow herself to be drawn in.

'You're the only one I can trust, now Lydia's gone,' said Chloe. 'Please.'

She sounded so very frightened. Like a girl much younger than she was. Lilly imagined what it must be like to be trapped in your own reality. Terrifying.

'Help me.' Chloe's voice was muffled as if she had her mouth pressed into the handset. 'Please help me before they come for me.'

Lilly sighed. 'Give me an hour.'

David parked the Range Rover outside the Grove.

'Thanks for this,' said Lilly. 'Again.'

'Are you sure you want to do this?'

Lilly looked over her shoulder at Alice strapped in the back in her car seat. She absolutely did not want to do this, but she knew she absolutely had to.

'You be very, very good,' she told the baby.

'She'll be fine,' said David. 'We'll head back now and drag Sam out of bed. Call me when you're done.'

She waved them goodbye and headed into reception to the visitors' book, checking yesterday's entry. There, scribbled under her name, was her number. Her office number. The inner door burst open and Harry strode out, his left eye puffy and purple.

'Did you give Chloe my home number?' Lilly asked.

'No.' Harry shook his head. 'I don't have it. Why?'

'She said someone gave it to her,' said Lilly.

He looked puzzled but just shrugged.

'It doesn't matter really,' Lilly continued. 'How is she?'

Harry see-sawed his hand. 'Still a bit spaced-out from the sedative, but very anxious. I tried to convince her to use a different solicitor, but she was adamant she wanted to speak to you.' He led Lilly through the warren of corridors to his office. 'The police are due to arrive in half an hour, so time is of the essence.'

Christ, it was like Groundhog Day.

'I'll do my best,' Lilly said.

Jack is in the shower, singing. He always sings in there. Sometimes old Irish folk songs, sometimes eighties pop numbers. All belted out, all completely out of tune.

I used to have a room-mate in college who was just the same. But it used to carve me in two every time she cranked up. In the end I just couldn't stand it a moment longer. What can you do?

It's different with Jack. It just makes me giggle. I suppose that's what love is: you just like everything about the other person, even the stuff that would ordinarily set your teeth on edge.

It's one in the face for those who said I couldn't experience love, isn't it? Those that said I couldn't form the necessary attachments. Didn't know half as much as they thought they did. Maybe I'll invite them to our wedding. Ha. That would be something, wouldn't it?

Jack's towelling himself off now, his howling reduced to a cheerful humming.

'What?' he asks. 'Why are you looking at me that way?'

'It's nothing,' I tell him. 'I'm just glad you're happy.'

'I am happy,' he says, wrapping the towel around his waist like a sarong.

He's been in a great mood since yesterday evening when we left the Grove. Like all decent coppers he loves a juicy murder, especially one where a good result looks likely. Also, though he'd never admit it, he was relieved when the ex confirmed that she was bowing out. He won't say so, but he loathes it when she's representing the defence, fighting him at every turn. And boy does she fight!

If he can keep her at arm's length, he's content and can remain civil, but if he's forced into her buffer zone he reacts badly.

Which is why I feel a tad guilty. I mean I don't want Jack to be unhappy, of course I don't, but I do need to finish off his relationship with her once and for all. And the best way to do that is to collide their worlds together. Give them no alternative but to fight.

That's why I gave the mad girl her number. I slipped it into her fat sweaty hand and told her that she was going to need a good solicitor.

I suspect Lilly will already be at the Grove when Jack arrives. It will ruin his day. But I'll be here to administer a bit of TLC.

As a plan it's quite brilliant. Minimal involvement on my part. Lilly's inability to back down will do the work for me.

I smile, feeling like a bomber who has just lit the touch paper.

Most of the chairs had been removed from Harry's office. Only one behind his desk and two in front remained. Chloe was sat in one of those, watching Harry's empty seat nervously. She looked around as Lilly and Harry entered but quickly returned to her anxious vigil.

Lilly slid in across the desk. Harry took the place next to the patient.

'How are you feeling?' Lilly asked.

'Better,' Chloe replied.

She certainly seemed much improved. She smelled faintly of coconut and her hair was wet as if she'd just had a bath. Her eyes, though heavy, were focused.

'We need to talk about what's going to happen,' said Lilly.

'The police are on their way, aren't they?'

Lilly nodded. 'They want to speak to you about Lydia's death.'

'Not here though? They want to take me to the police station?'

'That's right,' said Lilly. 'They want to interview you formally.'

'Yes.'

Lilly bent forward and placed her hands, palms down, on the desk. 'I'm not personally convinced that that's the right thing for you.'

'But I have to go, don't I?' Chloe scooted her chair towards Lilly. 'There's no choice.'

'We might be able to convince them that you're not well enough, Chloe.'

The girl's arm shot out and she grabbed Lilly's hand in her own. 'I need to tell them some things.' She held Lilly's fingers tightly. 'I need to tell you some things.'

Lilly could feel Chloe's flesh getting hotter as she increased the pressure.

'I need to explain.' Chloe's voice began to rise. 'I need to explain it all.'

'Now now.' Harry reached over and tried to remove Chloe's hand. 'Let's try to keep calm.'

But Chloe didn't let go, her grip becoming vice-like, her eyes wide and wild. 'I need . . .' Her words were lost somewhere in her throat.

Lilly put her free hand on Chloe's and stroked it gently. 'We are going to discuss it right now, okay? Me and you.' She looked at Harry. 'Could you give us some privacy?'

Harry frowned.

'It's completely fine, Harry,' Lilly told him. 'If it looks like Chloe might get ill again, I'll shout.'

He sent her a look that said it wasn't Chloe he was worried about. But Lilly gestured to the door. She'd spent a lot of her working life in the company of criminals and had been fearful of her safety only rarely. Besides, after a particularly nasty case where she'd been kidnapped, Lilly had learned some martial arts.

'I'm Chloe's solicitor now,' Lilly told him. 'And she has every right to speak to me in confidence, the same as any other client.'

Reluctantly, he stood and left the room. As the door shut behind him, Chloe let go of Lilly's hand.

'Thank you,' Chloe said.

'Not a problem,' said Lilly. 'I want you to feel comfortable. I want you to feel that you can tell me anything, but bear in mind that once you've told me something, you can't untell it.'

'I understand,' said Chloe. 'You'll be with me at the police station.'

'Like I say, I'm not certain I should agree to let them take you,' said Lilly. 'They don't just want a chat, Chloe. You're a suspect, in fact you're their main suspect.'

'I know.'

'They're going to ask you if you killed Lydia.'

'I didn't.'

'Then they're going to ask you if you carved some words onto her stomach.'

'I didn't.'

Lilly pictured how heated it would get in the interview room, with Jack putting the allegation to her again and again. How long before Chloe's fragile mind collapsed under the pressure of an interrogation?

'Then they're going to point out that a bloodstained knife was found in your room.'

'It wasn't mine,' said Chloe. 'It was Lydia's.'

Lilly shook her head. 'There's no way she could have done that to herself. I checked.'

'Then someone else did it,' Chloe panted. 'We can tell the police that someone else did it.'

'They won't believe you,' said Lilly.

'Do you believe me?'

Lilly took a deep breath. What she did or didn't believe was beside the point. Her job right now was to protect Chloe both from the police and from herself. 'You have to trust me, Chloe.'

'I do.'

'That's good,' said Lilly.

'That's why I gave you the note.'

Lilly stopped short. This was the one thing that wouldn't go away. However much she wanted it to.

'Help us,' Lilly repeated what it had said. 'You wanted me to help you. Then those same words were cut into Lydia's body.'

Tears glittered in Chloe's eyes. 'I just want you to take me to the police station. That's all I ask.'

There was a knock at the door and Harry poked his head round it. 'The police are here,' he said.

Lilly and Chloe stood up together.

'You stay here and I'll go and speak to them,' said Lilly and pressed Chloe back into her seat. 'You told me you trusted me, didn't you?'

'Yes.'

'Then let me do my job, okay?'

When Jack clocked Lilly, his face fell. She'd hoped Harry might have mentioned to him that she was here. Clearly not.

'I thought Chloe was getting a new brief,' he said.

'That makes two of us,' Lilly replied.

'Let me guess.' There was more than a hint of sarcasm in Jack's tone. 'She begged you to come over.'

Lilly pinched her lips together. The way he put it made the situation sound ridiculous. She was a grown woman and could have refused. Given the facts as they were, most would have refused.

'Problem?' asked Harry.

'No,' Jack and Lilly answered simultaneously.

'Excellent.' Harry rubbed his hands together. 'Then I'll be in with Chloe while you two . . .'

They watched him slip back into his office and waited until the door shut before speaking.

'I sometimes wonder if you do this on purpose,' Jack hissed.

'Do what?'

'Get yourself instructed on my cases.'

'Your case?' Lilly shook her head. 'I was already here when all this kicked off if you remember. I was already on this case.'

'You were here to have a quick word with the dead girl's family,' said Jack. 'You were here for Lydia, not bloody Chloe. Yet here you are this morning slap bang in the middle of my case.'

Lilly tried to hold back her anger. Yes, she had become involved in an unusual way, but the insinuation that she had wriggled her way into it was nonsense. And the idea that she had done so because of Jack was outrageous.

'Don't flatter yourself, Jack.' Her voice was cold. 'Chloe had already asked for my help while Lydia was still alive.'

'What?' Jack gave a mirthless laugh. 'You expect me to believe that?'

'I may be many things Jack, but a liar is not one of them. Lydia introduced me to Chloe and she asked for my help. Sorry to disappoint you but I was involved in this case long before you arrived.' She narrowed her eyes at him. 'Now, if you'd like to discuss the case or the evidence then be my guest, otherwise I'll go back in to my client.'

She watched Jack's Adam's apple bob as he swallowed down the information she'd just delivered.

'Why don't you wait here while I get the statement of the officer who found the knife?' he said.

'I think I can do that,' she answered.

★ ★ ★

Jack wasn't even sure he had a copy of PC Waterman's statement in his briefcase. He didn't need it anyway and could tell Lilly pretty much word for word what it said. But he needed a minute away from her. Mary, Mother of God, that woman had always had a way of crucifying him and today was just one of many where he made a complete and utter twat of himself trying to argue with her.

If he'd learned one thing over the long years he'd known her, it was that she would never, ever back down.

And what in the name of all things holy had he been doing accusing her of dishonesty? Lilly was the most honest person he had ever met. How many times had her brutal need to tell the truth cut him to the bone?

He didn't even try to find the statement but threw himself into the nearest toilet. He shouldn't let her get to him like this and he certainly couldn't let her see the effect she was having on him. He ran the cold tap and splashed his face repeatedly. If she saw this chink in his armour, she would use it to Chloe's advantage, no doubt about it. He had to act as he would to any other solicitor.

The paper towel dispenser was empty and he was forced to wipe his face with toilet roll, which left a grainy residue around his mouth. He picked off the white flecks with his thumbnail and went to speak to Lilly.

He found her, still outside the shrink's office, pinning her hair up, a grip in her mouth.

'I'm afraid I don't have the statement,' he said. 'Sorry about that. I'll make sure it's mailed to you as soon as.'

She spoke around the grip. 'No worries.'

'And I'm sorry about before.' He spoke slowly and clearly. 'I was just shocked to see you here. No excuse for rudeness.'

Lilly nodded, but there was still a tightness around her mouth even after she removed the grip and slid it into her curls.

'We're both professionals,' he continued. 'We've worked to-gether many times without any problems, haven't we?'

Lilly looked puzzled. They had worked on the same cases before but they both knew it had always caused problems.

'Business is business,' he said and clapped his hands together to signal that the matter was at an end. 'Let's get to it.'

I watch the chief superintendent shut the door behind him. He keeps him- self holed up in there like an animal hibernating in winter. I wouldn't be in the least surprised to find his desk drawers full of nuts and berries.

I bumped into him on one of his rare forays to the toilet and asked after his health. Only good manners. When he asked me how things were going, I told him about the dead girl, and the fat girl. And, of course, Jack.

'Tell him to give me an update,' he said and went back to his cave.

I pull out my phone and send a text:

To: Jack
From: Kate
Just spkn to CS and he was very interested in your case. Get you, Mr Big Shot. Expect u have it und contrl and will be promoted this time next wk.

'Shall I give you the gist about the knife?' asked Jack. 'Do you need to grab a notebook?'

Lilly watched him carefully. He'd moved from Mr Angry to Captain Reasonable in moments and she didn't know which one she liked least.

'We should get the prints back within the hour,' he said. 'But we're pretty certain they'll be your girl's, seeing as how the blade was found hidden among her clothes.'

Shit. There was the evidence stacking up.

'I think it might make more sense to discuss whether she's fit to be interviewed first,' Lilly said.

He looked like he was about to speak and she was anticipating an argument when his phone beeped.

'Excuse me,' he said and slid his phone from his pocket. As he read a text, a hint of laughter crossed his face. 'Sorry.'

'Something funny?' Lilly asked.

'Not funny . . .' He searched for the right word. 'Nice.' He reread it and slipped the phone away. 'Where were we?'

Christ, bring back Mr Angry, all was forgiven.

'Fitness for interview,' Lilly prompted.

He nodded. 'Right. Right. I'm assuming you don't think she is. Fit that is.'

'I'm not a psychiatrist.' Lilly shrugged. 'But I'd say it's definitely an issue. Well, you saw the state she was in yesterday.'

'I suppose our resident shrink backs that up?'

'He's adamant,' said Lilly.

'I'll have to talk to her at some stage,' he said.

'Maybe,' Lilly agreed. 'But in the meantime you know she's not going anywhere. She's held here under a section after all.'

Jack sighed, but it wasn't the sound of frustration, more that he was weighing his options. Lilly wondered, if this was an act, just how long he could keep it up.

'I'll tell you what, Lilly. Let's have a quick word with Chloe and see how the land lies.' He could not have sounded more reasonable. 'Then I can judge for myself.'

'Okaaaayyy.'

He nodded politely, almost a bow, then pushed open the office door. As one, Chloe and Harry looked up. At the sight of Jack, Harry's face darkened. In contrast, Chloe's seemed to light up.

'Are you the police?' she asked.

Jack allowed Lilly to step into the room before him then addressed the girl. 'That I am.'

'At last,' said Chloe.

'I don't think you should say anything.' Harry placed a cautionary hand on her arm and Chloe looked down at it as if she had never seen anything like it.

'I need to ask you a few questions Chloe,' said Jack. ' I just need to be sure whether today is a good time or not.'

Chloe looked up slowly, the radiance replaced by a thunderous desperation. 'And is it?' she whispered.

'Your doctor says not.' Jack jerked his head towards Harry. 'And your solicitor says the same.'

'Then surely that's an end to it?' said Harry.

Jack smiled. 'Not exactly.'

'You're not going to overrule my expert opinion?' Harry stood and stepped behind Chloe, hands placed firmly on her shoulders. No doubt he meant it to be comforting but Chloe cringed. 'You're not a doctor after all.'

'Just a lowly copper, I'm afraid,' said Jack.

Harry threw Lilly a searching look.

'Though Jack will take your view and mine into account, the final decision rests with him,' she said.

'That's preposterous,' said Harry.

'That's the law,' Jack replied.

The two men stared one another down. Harry outraged, Jack looking faintly amused.

'Look, Jack,' Lilly interjected. 'No one is trying to undermine your authority here.' She shot Harry a glare. 'I just think that given how ill Chloe was yesterday and the fact that she is still under the influence of a huge amount of medication, it would be better not to interview her today. We should at least wait until the prints on the knife come back from the lab; it's not as if she's going anywhere in the meantime is it?'

It looked as if Jack might agree when there was the sound of a slap. Like the smack of meat on a butcher's counter. Again and again.

It was Chloe, hitting her cheeks with her open palms. First one side and then the other. 'No, no, no,' she groaned, the intensity of each blow increasing.

Harry tried to grab her hands. 'I warned you, but you wouldn't listen,' he spat at Jack. 'This child is not well.'

Chloe dodged Harry and lurched forward towards Jack, flinging herself at him. He was much leaner these days, and her weight knocked him backwards, but he was also much fitter and agile, soon recovering and twisting Chloe's arm behind her back, bending her forward from the waist.

'What the hell are you doing?' Harry roared.

Jack ignored him and concentrated on Chloe. 'What's the problem here, Chloe?'

'The problem is you are assaulting one of my patients.' Harry's voice rang out.

Jack didn't look at the other man, instead his own voice dropped. 'Can I let go now, Chloe?'

The girl nodded and Jack released his hold, spinning her gently so she was facing him. Lilly could almost see the heat coming from her, like a cloud of yellow steam.

'Okay?' Jack asked.

Chloe looked up at him, her mouth slack. 'Please take me to the station.'

'What?'

'I want to go to the police station,' said Chloe. 'I want to go now.'

Chapter Six

Fact Sheet For Those Involved in Care Proceedings

Q: What is Cafcass?

A: The Children and Family Court Advisory Service.

Q: What does it do?

A: It safeguards and promotes the welfare of children involved in court proceedings, making sure their voices are heard and their needs met.

Q: What is a Children's Guardian?

A: A Children's Guardian is the person appointed by the court to represent the children when Social Services have applied to place the children into their care.

Q: Are they independent?

A: Yes. They do not work for Social Services or the court.

Q: What do they do?

A: The Children's Guardian represents the children during the court proceedings. They do this by instructing a solicitor who specializes in this type of case, by advising the court what the children need, by visiting the children regularly, and by writing a report saying what would be best for the child.

Q: Does the Children's Guardian always recommend what the child wants?

A: The Children's Guardian will always listen to the wishes

of the child and will inform the court about them. However, their report will say what they think is best for the child. This is not always the same as what they want.

Q: Is information given to the Children's Guardian confidential?

A: Any information given to the Children's Guardian may be included in their report and passed to the court and all the other parties.

Following Chloe's outburst, Jack had decided to take her into the police station and called for a squad car to do the ferrying.

'I'll meet you there?' he asked Lilly.

She was about to admit she didn't have her car with her and face the embarrassment of being forced to cadge a lift, when Harry suggested they go together. She was grateful to be spared the twenty-minute journey with Jack either chatting inanely or scowling ahead in silence.

They slogged their way across the car park, Lilly's feet sinking deep into the fresh snow. As the cold hit her ankles, she wished she'd worn boots.

'You okay?' Harry laughed as Lilly lifted her feet high, like a dressage pony.

'We need a bloody sledge,' she said, and he laughed again until he reached a silver Porsche Cayenne and pointed his keys to unlock it. What was it about posh boys and four-by-fours? Did they all have one in case of emergencies?

Inside smelled of clean new leather and Lilly grimaced at the thought of the puddle that would be forming at her feet, as the ice that was stuck to her socks melted.

'They might not let you in, you know,' she told him.

Harry gunned the car forward. 'Let me in where?'

'The station,' she said. 'Usually no one's allowed in the custody area except lawyers and job.'

'There's nothing usual about this situation though is there?'

'No,' Lilly agreed. 'But I've never known a suspect's doctor get access.'

Harry smiled. 'Then you've never met a doctor as persuasive as me before.'

Lilly smiled back. Harry was certainly persuasive and, as far as policemen went, Jack was on the reasonable end of the spectrum, but this was a murder investigation.

'Why do you think Chloe asked to be taken in?' she said.

Harry's smile slipped. 'She's in a very confused state of mind.'

'She seemed very clear about it,' said Lilly. 'She told me before that she needed to explain something to the police.'

'Did she?'

Lilly nodded. 'She was adamant. When I was on my own with her, she begged.'

Harry contemplated Lilly's words, clearly marshalling his thoughts. When he spoke his tone was measured. 'It's possible she feels she should be punished for what happened to Lydia.'

'She says she didn't do it,' said Lilly.

Harry pulled up outside the station. 'Do you believe that?'

'What I believe is neither here nor there.'

Harry saluted and dropped into a fake German accent. 'I am just following ze orders, commandant.'

Lilly punched him gently on the shoulder. 'It's not like that and you know it. I just can't afford to get caught up in maybes. If Chloe says she didn't do it then that's good enough for me. Right now my only job is to stop a vulnerable girl digging herself into a hole she can never get out of.'

Jack was waiting for them in reception. He looked Harry up and down.

'Where's Chloe?' Lilly asked.

'She's with the custody sergeant being processed,' said Jack.

'You've arrested her?'

Jack shook his head. 'No, no. I wanted to wait for you to get here to explain the caution to her. Just to be safe.' He meant he didn't want his main suspect admitting to anything he couldn't use against her at a later date. 'The sarge said he'd rustle up a uniform to sit with her in a side room until you got here.'

He moved towards the security door but stopped, hand over the keypad. 'I'm afraid you'll have to wait here,' he told Harry.

Lilly turned to Harry, she had told him to expect this, but his face gave nothing away.

'I think you need me in there,' he said.

'A kind offer, but I'm told Chloe was perfectly calm on the way over here,' Jack replied. 'And we have an FME at hand if there are any problems.'

'Nothing altruistic about my offer,' said Harry. 'In fact, it's not an offer.'

'No?' Jack narrowed his eyes.

'More a statement of fact,' said Harry. 'You need me in there with Chloe.'

Jack gave a polite nod. 'I'm afraid I have to decline that offer.'

'As I say, it's not an offer.'

Lilly had to hand it to Harry, he was persistent. In other circumstances she would have sat back and enjoyed the show, but she needed to speak to Chloe. She needed to impress upon her that she must say absolutely nothing to the police.

'Perhaps you could stay out here for now, Harry?' she said. 'If there's any suggestion that Chloe needs medical attention, we could call you through.'

'Sounds like a plan,' said Jack.

Harry rubbed the edge of his scalp with his thumbnail. 'I'm obviously not making myself clear here, which is probably my fault, but the fact remains that I have to be given access to Chloe. The law is very straightforward in this regard.'

Lilly sighed. She'd advised Harry that the law stated doctors had no right to be with their clients. She understood how protective he felt about Chloe, but he needed to let this go and allow her to do her job.

'I think Lilly and I are fairly au fait with the law in this regard,' said Jack.

Harry clicked his finger and pointed at Jack. 'Then you'll know Chloe is a minor and as such requires an appropriate adult. You can't speak to her without one.' He opened his arms wide. 'And here I am in all my appropriateness.'

Jack didn't miss a beat. 'The custody sergeant will be ringing Chloe's parents as we speak. I'm sure one will arrive soon.'

Harry threw back his head and laughed. 'Good luck with that.'

'What?' Jack asked.

Harry shook his head as if it were one of the funniest jokes he'd ever heard. 'Chloe hasn't had any contact with her parents in years.'

Lilly snapped up her head. In all the furore, she hadn't had any time to discuss Chloe's background. She'd assumed there would be a family worrying about her, much like Lydia's.

'Who looks after her?' Lilly asked.

'We do,' Harry replied. 'A social worker might visit her every six months, but I've never met the same one twice.'

Lilly felt her throat constrict at the thought of a child with no one in the world to rely on except doctors and nurses. How lost must the poor kid feel? Her nightmare was interrupted by Jack's phone, which he snapped open.

'Sarge,' he said.

She couldn't hear what was being said, but assumed by Jack's expression that what Harry had told them was true. When he hung up, he didn't speak to Harry but punched in the code and gestured him and Lilly through, before marching off ahead of them to the custody suite.

'Is he always such a charmer?' Harry whispered.

Gem pulls a clean pair of trousers over Tyler's bum. He smiles up at her, jam round his chops.

'You're a messy little beggar.' She tickles him, making him scream and laugh and hiccup all at the same time. 'Do you hear me, messy beggar?'

'You'll make him sick,' says Mum, searching through her dressing gown pockets for a fag. 'Anyway, why aren't you in school?'

Gem don't answer and fishes through a pile of socks for a pair, then she smoothes each one over the baby's little toes, rubbing them, making him laugh again. They both know Gem ain't going to school today and they both know Mum ain't really bothered. It's just something she says 'cos she thinks she should. Like when she says she'll take Tyler to the park. Just stuff they talk about at Sure Start.

'School's closed,' says Gem. 'Too much snow.'

Mums nods.

It ain't Mum's fault she's like this. She ain't like a normal person. It's like she's only half there, like a bit of her brain's missing or something.

When Gem got taken into care the second time, some doctor wrote a report about Mum for the court hearing. She weren't supposed to show it to Gem, but she did anyway, at the contact centre. It was pages and pages long, and Gem didn't understand a lot of it, but basically the doctor said Mum had something called attachment disorder on account of what had happened to her when she were a kid. He said she can't help being the way she is, but that she should never have had any kids.

Mum hates people like that. Doctors, social workers and what have you.

'Think they're so clever with their qualifications,' she says. 'Let's see how clever they'd be living here. Their bits of paper wouldn't do 'em any good in this shithole, would they?'

Mum talks a lot of rubbish, but she's right about that. None of 'em would last five minutes on the Clayhill.

When Gem gets over to the house, Feyza buzzes her in. She's already on the phone to a punter.

'We got lovely girl in today,' she says. 'Very pretty. Genuine sixteen years old.' She gives a raspy laugh, like a witch cackling. 'I don't bullshit, sir. This girl just have her birthday.'

On and on she goes, telling him whatever it is he wants to hear. Gem goes to the cupboard and pulls out a clean sheet and towel so she can do Misty's room before she gets in. The less Gem sees of Misty's miserable mug the better.

She lets herself in and chucks the sheet at the end of the bed. The whole place stinks of stale fags and Gem sees the overflowing ashtray on the dressing table. Misty must smoke a hundred a day or something. She dumps the dog-ends into the bin and reaches over for a can of deodorant and sprays it into the air. It don't make much difference so she searches through the other stuff for some perfume. There's mousse, hairspray, dry shampoo and endless tins of spray-on tan, but no perfume. She opens the top drawer and rummages through it. There's condoms, half-used tubes of lube and four or five dildos.

'What the fuck are you doing?'

Gem nearly jumps out of her skin and spins round on her toes. Misty is stood in the doorway, a proper scowl on her face.

'Nothing.' Gem pushes the drawer shut with her arse. 'Just cleaning up and that.'

Misty takes a step towards Gem. Her hair is pulled back off her face and she ain't wearing any make-up. There are dark circles under her eyes and the scars around her mouth look ugly.

'You going through my shit?'

'No,' Gem answers. A bit too quickly.

'You'd better fucking not be.'

'I ain't.'

Misty takes another step closer and, by the look on her face, Gem expects a punch on the nose. Thank fuck for Feyza, who calls for her from down the corridor.

'What?' Misty shouts over her shoulder.

'Here,' Feyza shouts back. 'Now.'

Misty looks disgusted, but slopes away to find her boss, leaving Gem with her heart banging in her chest. She don't waste another minute and gets the sheet on the bed and the bin emptied in double-quick time, then she slings her hook before Misty can get back.

When she starts making up the next room, Gem's still shaking, and it ain't just because Misty is a pure evil bitch. There's also what she saw at the back of Misty's drawer. Something anybody else might have missed. But Gem ain't anybody else, is she? She's lived her life on the Clayhill. And she knows a crack pipe when she sees one.

Chloe looked up from the table in the interview room, her facial muscles relaxed, her forehead free of sweat. Lilly had never seen her look so composed.

The WPC who had been at the Grove was sat opposite. She pushed a cup of tea across the table towards Chloe. 'Drink up now,' she said and stood to leave. 'Can I get anyone else a drink?'

'A jug of water and some glasses would be great,' said Lilly.

The WPC smiled. Her lips were very plump, as if she rubbed

them frequently with balm. Lilly ran an embarrassed finger over her own chapped mouth.

'Water it is,' said the WPC and left.

Harry, Lilly noticed, lingered just a little too long over the sight of her disappearing backside, firm and peachy against the material of her regulation trousers.

'So.' Lilly clapped her hands to break the spell. 'Are you okay, Chloe?'

Her client gave a heavy-lidded nod.

'You gave us a bit of a scare back at the Grove,' said Lilly. 'I thought Jack was a goner.'

'I wouldn't have hurt him.' Chloe's tone was easy. 'I wouldn't hurt anyone.' She smiled at Lilly. 'I just wanted him to bring me to the station.'

'Why?' Lilly asked. 'I was trying to get him to see it wasn't in your best interests to leave the Grove, and I think I was getting somewhere.'

'I know it's all very confusing, Chloe,' said Harry. 'But you must believe that Lilly is trying to help you here.'

'Sorry.' Chloe put her hand on Lilly's, but this time there was no insistence in it, just a gesture of apology.

'That's okay,' said Lilly. 'I just wish I understood why you're so desperate to be here.'

Chloe looked up at Lilly and something in her eyes was so magnetic, so intense, that Lilly couldn't avert her gaze. Chloe wanted to tell her something. Needed to tell her something.

'Harry,' she said, her eyes still glued to Chloe's, 'could you chase up the water?'

'Water?' he asked.

'If you wouldn't mind,' said Lilly. 'I'm absolutely parched.'

'Okay,' he said, and she felt rather than saw him get up and leave the room.

As the door closed behind him, Chloe let her head droop, and she melted forward until her face was pressed into the plastic of the table.

'Why did you want to come here, Chloe?' Lilly asked.

The girl's cheek spread like a melting snowball and she closed her eyes, so that her face seemed to become featureless.

'I need you to explain,' Lilly said.

Chloe didn't move or speak.

'Please tell me you're not intending to confess to Lydia's murder,' said Lilly. 'Because I won't let you do that.'

Chloe's eyelid fluttered, like ripples moving across surface water. 'Why would I do that?' she murmured.

'I dunno.' Lilly shrugged. 'I'm wondering what other motive there could be.'

'I didn't kill Lydia,' Chloe said. 'So I wouldn't say I did.'

Lilly blew air through her mouth. If Chloe didn't want to spill her guts to the police, what were they all doing here? Then again, maybe she was approaching this from the wrong angle. Maybe Chloe didn't want to be at the station.

'Okay, I get it,' she said. 'You were just determined to get yourself out of the Grove, and here's as good a place as any.'

Chloe gave a long slow sigh of relief. Satisfied that, at last, someone understood.

'Are you going to tell me why?' Lilly asked.

The moments fell away and Chloe didn't flicker. Lilly thought she could hear a clock tick, but knew it was her imagination.

'I can understand you're bored in there,' said Lilly.

'I'm not bored,' Chloe whispered into the table.

'Then what?' Lilly tried to disguise her impatience.

At last Chloe raised her head. Haltingly, she drew her body upright, like a crane dragging a shipwreck from the depths. 'Are you sure you want to know?' she asked.

'Of course,' Lilly replied.

Chloe waited as if unconvinced.

'Tell me why you wanted to get out of hospital,' said Lilly.

Chloe waited three beats, giving a small nod at each as if in time to her internal rhythm. 'They come for us at night,' she said.

'What?'

'When everyone is supposed to be asleep, they come for us.'

Lilly felt a prickle of apprehension. It started at her jawline and seeped down her throat towards her chest.

'They wait until they know it's safe, then they creep into our rooms.' Chloe walked her fingers across the table as if on tiptoe. 'Like burglars.'

'Who?' Lilly asked.

Chloe shook her head. 'Can't say. The drugs they give us make it blurry.'

'And what do these people do when they come into your room?'

'They take us away, probably in a wheelchair because you can't move your legs properly,' said Chloe.

The prickle spread throughout Lilly's body and she knew that under her clothes, every hair was standing on end. 'Where do they take you?'

'A small room, or a corner of a room, it's hard to know for sure but it's a . . .' Chloe tapped her forehead for the word. 'It's a dark space.'

Lilly didn't say anything more. Was this all just another one of Chloe's delusions? A hideous nightmare that seemed as real as skin and bone and dirt?

'I know you don't believe me,' said Chloe.

Lilly didn't know what to believe.

'I've tried to tell people before but they just told me it was all in my head. I explained to them that the pain was real, that it hurt.' Chloe slid a hand down her body so she was cupping her crotch. 'I even showed them the blood in my pants but they

125

said I'd done it to myself. I thought I must be going mad until I told Lydia.'

'What happened when you told Lydia?' Lilly asked. 'She said she believed you?'

Chloe nodded. 'She knew it was true.'

'How?' Lilly felt her blood fizzing in her veins as she waited for the answer. 'How did she know it was true?'

'Because they were doing the same things to her too.'

Lilly stepped out of the interview room and almost collided into Harry. Water sloshed out of the jug he was carrying, down Lilly's shirt.

'Sorry,' he said.

'My fault,' she answered, patting herself down for a tissue. She found one almost disintegrating in her back trouser pocket. She rubbed it against the wet patch across her chest, covering the area in white confetti.

'Let me.' He held out the jug for Lilly. 'I've got a clean hanky.'

Lilly took the jug from him and Harry pulled out a pristine square of white cotton. He moved towards her with it as if to dab the stain but as his hand almost touched her breast, he coughed and dropped his hand. 'Perhaps you'd better . . .'

Lilly swapped the jug for the handkerchief and tried to mop up her shirt. 'Remember when we went for lunch?' she asked.

'How could I forget?'

Lilly flushed. 'I asked you about Chloe, and you told me she lived in her own fantasy world, that she imagined people were doing terrible things to her.'

'What has she been telling you?' Harry asked.

Lilly looked around the custody suite. The sergeant was busy with paperwork and the only other person around was the WPC who was checking her phone. She took a step nearer to Harry.

'She says she's being abused in the Grove.'

Harry nodded. 'Poisoned? She often says she's being poisoned by one of the nurses. Or our pharmacist.'

'Not poisoned.' Lilly dropped to a whisper. 'She says she's being sexually abused.'

A shadow crossed Harry's face. He clearly hadn't seen that one coming. 'Chloe is very ill.'

'She says it's not just her. She says it was happening to Lydia too.'

Harry paused. This was a huge accusation. Unlikely to be true. And yet . . .

'If Chloe's telling the truth, it would give someone other than her a very big motive to murder Lydia,' Lilly said, as much for her own benefit as for Harry's. 'Did she ever say anything about it to you?'

Harry looked shocked. 'Of course not. She may be delusional, but I wouldn't simply dismiss an allegation like that,' he said. 'Patients like Chloe are vulnerable. We have to be careful.'

Lilly could have kicked herself. 'I didn't mean to be offensive. I'm just a bit rattled.'

'It's fine.' He smiled. 'Really it's fine. This is difficult for everyone.'

Lilly acknowledged his understanding with a grateful nod.

'Has Chloe named any names?' Harry asked.

'Nope. The details are very sketchy. She says she was drugged at the time.'

Harry exhaled through his nose. 'And Lydia can't exactly tell us much one way or the other.'

'Now that's where you're wrong.' Lilly took out her mobile and scrolled down her list of contacts until she got to Phil Cheney.

'Lilly.' Cheney answered on the first ring. 'You just can't get enough of the sound of my voice.'

'Sexy as your telephone manner is, Phil, this is about business.'

'I'm hurt and disappointed,' he said, but Lilly knew that dead bodies excited Cheney far more than flirting.

'Lydia Morton-Daley,' said Lilly. 'Was there any recent sexual activity?'

'Oh yes.' Lilly heard the thwack of his gloves as he pulled them off, then the tap, tap, tap of a keyboard as he accessed the file. 'Penetration front and back.'

'Consensual?' she asked.

'Tricky one to answer definitively,' he said. 'There were fissures but, if you'll pardon the pun, anal sex is a bugger for that even if you're happy to take part.'

'What if our girl was drugged?' Lilly asked. 'The muscles would be relaxed wouldn't they? Less likely to tear?'

'For sure,' he said. 'But the fissures were beginning to repair so they weren't inflicted at the time of death. More likely a day or so beforehand and there was no trace in her bloods of anything except the stuff that killed her.'

'But if she was raped a day or so before the murder, there are plenty of drugs that would have disappeared from her system,' said Lilly. 'Rohypnol for one.'

'Are you after my job?'

Lilly laughed. 'I think you're safe on that score, Phil. I find dead bodies a bit off-putting. You know, like any ordinary person.'

'I will take it as a compliment that you find me extraordinary,' he said. 'But you're right, Rohypnol and a few other suspects would have cleared from her system by the time of death and yes, they would have relaxed her enough for a rape to take place without too much physical trauma. So what are you saying? Someone drugs and rapes our girl, then comes back a day or so later and kills her?'

'Are you after my job?' asked Lilly.

'To be honest I find rapists and murderers a bit off-putting.'

'Touché.'

Lilly was still laughing when she hung up.

'Funny guy?' Harry asked.

'Oh yes,' said Lilly. 'Funny ha ha and funny strange.'

'You seem fond of one another.'

Lilly waved him away. 'We go way back, but, trust me, if I asked him out he'd run a mile.'

'I find that very difficult to believe,' said Harry.

There it was again, the familiar heat of a blush. God, Lilly was like a bloody teenager.

'So what did Romeo have to say for himself?' asked Harry.

Lilly nudged him with her elbow. 'That Lydia could have been raped. She'd certainly been having sex a day or so before she was killed.'

'Unfortunately, try as we might, we can't always prevent that sort of thing happening amongst the patients,' said Harry. 'Lydia was quite promiscuous. She used her sexuality as both a weapon and a way of punishing herself.'

Lilly recalled the conversation they'd had about the party on the night Lydia had been arrested and the casual reference to a sexual encounter that night. Harry's point was valid and a perfectly viable explanation, yet something inside Lilly wasn't persuaded. At least not totally.

'Don't forget Chloe came up with all this after Lydia was killed,' said Harry.

'She says she tried to tell people but they didn't believe her.'

'Well, she didn't say anything to me and I've worked very closely with her,' he said. 'She never gave any indication.'

Lilly looked at the floor. Perhaps Chloe hadn't asked for Harry's assistance, but she had certainly asked for Lilly's. Once again she thought of the letter. It had been a plea for help, but it was also a piece of evidence that gave her story a bizarre logic.

★ ★ ★

As I squeeze past Lilly and the shrink, they barely notice me. Too busy in their cosy little tête-à-tête.

He's actually quite revolting. A flirtatious remark here, a brush of the fingers there, but Lilly is lapping it up. At her age I suppose it must be pleasant to receive any attention, no matter its source.

Back inside the interview room, I put a glass of water in front of the fat girl.

'You must be thirsty?' I say.

Her face is so flat it seems almost deformed.

'Take a drink,' I say. 'They might be a while yet.'

There's a hint of suspicion in those piggy eyes, but she grabs the glass and drinks it down, the folds of her neck undulating as she swallows.

'I probably shouldn't say anything, being a policewoman, but Miss Valentine really is a very good solicitor.' I can still trace the girl's distrust. 'You should do everything she advises you to.'

She blinks at me like a confused puppy.

'The thing is, I wouldn't want to see someone like you go to prison for something they haven't done.'

I snake my fingers into my pocket and slowly reveal a bar of chocolate I bought from the vending machine. Uncertainty vanishes and the girl's eyes fill with want. Of course they do.

'Are you hungry?' I ask and carefully place the chocolate on the table between us, keeping my index finger on it.

The girl nods, every cell in her body focused on her desire to fill her stomach. If she wasn't covered in layers of blubber, you'd be able to see each sinew stretched towards the small red bar.

I tap it with my nail. 'Miss Valentine wants to protect you.' The girl's eyes are glued to the chocolate. 'So you must do what she tells you.' Saliva has started to collect in the corners of her mouth. 'Okay?'

She nods.

'Good girl,' I tell her and push the bar towards her.

She grabs it, unwraps it and crams it into her mouth. In less than three seconds it's gone and the girl looks at me, panting.

'Part of any good solicitor's job is to make things difficult for the police,' I say. *'If she wants to fight for you, she has to fight them. You understand how important it is that you let her fight them?'*

'Yes.' The girl's teeth are brown with chocolate. *'I understand.'*

Jack spotted Lilly striding across the custody suite towards him. She looked like she had something to say. That woman always had something to say.

'Can I have a word, Jack?' she asked.

'I was just about to check up on forensics,' he replied. 'See if the fingerprints match.'

'It won't take a second,' she said.

Lilly was like a train at full speed. Diversion from her course would only result in injury.

'Are you investigating anyone else for Lydia's murder?' she asked. 'Or is Chloe the only suspect?'

'We're keeping our options open at this point,' he said.

'So you've interviewed other people?'

Jack wondered where this was going. 'Like I told the Morton-Daleys, we're speaking to everyone who was in the Grove on the day she died.'

'You haven't brought anyone else to the nick though?'

It was true. They both knew it so he simply shrugged.

'Looks to me as if you've made up your mind,' she said. 'You've got your prime suspect and you're building your case around her.'

'I didn't put the knife in Chloe's room,' he said.

'Of course you didn't, Jack.'

'You're not suggesting the wee lad in uniform planted it?'

Lilly shook her head. 'I'm not suggesting a copper at all.'

'Then you've lost me, Lilly.'

'I'm suggesting that whoever killed Lydia could have easily placed the weapon in Chloe's room to make sure suspicion fell on her and not them. They knew that as soon as you found the knife you wouldn't look any further,' she said. 'And, let's face it, as a plan, it's certainly worked.'

Jack folded his arms. It was a classic defence tactic. Introduce a possible alternative suspect that the police had overlooked. Often called the SODDI. Some other dude did it. There was no way Jack was going to walk into that particular trap.

'And do you have any idea who might be responsible for this little piece of alleged handiwork? A name for me?'

'No name,' said Lilly.

Jack had suspected as much. It was just an attempt to muddy the waters.

'But you might want to have another chat with Phil Cheney at the lab,' she said.

'That's what I was trying to do when you stopped me,' said Jack. 'The fingerprints, remember?'

'While you've got him on the phone, you might want to ask him about Lydia being raped?'

'Raped?'

Lilly nodded. 'Cheney confirmed that Lydia had had sex a day or so before she died. He's not ruling out rape.'

Shit. If Lilly was trying to set up a SODDI, the introduction of a rape was like a gift. Who was more likely to have killed Lydia, a sex attacker or her wee friend Chloe? He could see Lilly in court now, painting a lurid picture of a maniac on the loose in the Grove, her client in the dock, hopelessness radiating from her.

'I need to make a call,' he said.

'I think you do,' Lilly answered.

Gem is counting out calling cards into piles of twenty and securing them with rubber bands, when there's a scream and a crash. The shock makes her drop a pile into the washing-up bowl.

'Fuck.' She fishes them out and tries to blow off the suds.

A couple of local boys collect them in the afternoons, to stick them up in phone boxes, newsagents and what have you. Feyza gives them a slap if they bend the cards because they cost a packet to print.

Gem's about to separate them out and borrow a hairdryer from one of the girls, when there's another crash and more shouting.

She sticks her head around the kitchen door. A few of the girls do the same from their bedrooms. Amber ain't wearing a top and she covers each boob with a hand. Everyone's looking down the corridor towards Misty's room.

Gem steps out of the kitchen and is almost knocked off her feet by Feyza flying past towards the commotion. Before she gets to Misty's door, it bursts open, hitting the wall behind. The punter backs out into the corridor, trousers round his ankles, bare bollocks swinging round like ping-pong balls in a pink sock.

Misty follows him, but she's limping badly 'cos she's taken off one of her shoes and is trying to hit the punter with it. He dodges the heel, which is a good thing. It's proper spiky and could do him some damage if Misty connects.

'Fucking bastard,' Misty is screaming at him. 'Fucking filthy bastard.'

Feyza manoeuvres herself between the punter and Misty, grabbing the shoe for good measure.

'What the hell goes on?' she shouts.

'She's mental, that one.' The man pulls up his pants. 'Off her rocker.'

'Mental?' Spit flies out of Misty's mouth. 'Mental am I?' She tries to reach round Feyza with her nails. 'I'll fucking show you how mental I am.'

Feyza gives Misty an almighty shove that sends her toppling backwards into her room. Then she gives the punter a more gentle push towards the kitchen.

'Put gentleman into free room, Gem,' she shouts. 'Get him drink and whatever else he needs.'

Feyza disappears into Misty's room and slams the door shut behind her. The man rushes away, tucking his shirt in and Gem leads him into one of the unused room.

'She shouldn't be working here,' he says. 'She needs locking up.'

Gem don't point out that she ain't in charge. Instead, she points to the bed she made earlier and pours some water from the bottle she leaves in each girl's room. It ain't new. She just fills the old ones up from the tap, but no one seems to care.

He takes the glass and sinks onto the bed.

'I've told you lot before about what sort of girls you can keep here,' he says. 'You don't get any bother as long as it's a quiet house. Do you understand?'

Gem don't understand, but she nods all the same. She glances at the door and wonders how long Feyza is going to be.

'So what's your name then?' he asks.

'Gem,' she says.

'And how old are you, Gem?'

'Sixteen,' she answers, quick as a flash.

He looks her up and down and laughs. She checks her jeans and trainers, wondering what's funny. They're old, but they ain't that bad. And anyway, once she's paid off the Slaughter brothers and bought a few things for Tyler, she's going to get a new pair from the market.

At last Feyza comes in.

'Bill, I so sorry about that. I don't know what comes over her,' she says. 'Misty one of our best girls.'

He sips the water and looks over the rim. 'Like I was just saying to this young lady here, you can't have nutters like that working here.'

'Come on, Bill.' Feyza gives a big fake smile. 'You know what working girls are like.'

'The mad, the bad and the fucking dangerous,' he says.

'Exactly.'

He drains his glass and hands it to Gem. 'Too much of the last one is bad news.' He nods at Gem. 'Even this one gets it.'

Feyza narrows her eyes. 'Put on kettle, Gem. Me and Bill talk business now.'

Gem doesn't need to be asked twice.

Lilly smiled at Chloe. There were a few stray crumbs on the girl's chin and Lilly fought the urge to brush them off.

'I've spoken to forensics,' she said.

'Who's that?' Chloe asked.

'People at the laboratory,' said Lilly. 'The place where they test all the evidence.'

'Like what?'

'The knife, for one thing.'

'It wasn't mine,' said Chloe. 'I didn't touch it.'

'They also look at dead bodies,' Lilly said. 'To see if they can find any answers that can help tell the police what they might have died of.' She paused to let what she was saying sink in. 'They also check what other injuries the person might have suffered, besides what killed them.'

'How?'

'What?'

'How do they check what other injuries the dead person has?' Chloe asked.

Lilly gulped. Incisions were made. Instruments inserted. Bodies butterflied like shoulders of lamb. It wasn't an image she wanted to conjure up for her client.

'I'm really not sure,' she said.

'Oh.' Chloe sounded disappointed.

'Anyway.' Lilly kept her tone bright. 'I spoke to them about Lydia and asked if she had been sexually assaulted.'

'I told you she had.'

'I know, but we need someone independent to back up what you've said.'

'Because I'm mad?' Chloe asked. 'No one will believe what I say because I'm mad?'

'This has nothing to do with your illness,' said Lilly. 'In serious cases like this, everyone needs to back up what they say. It's called corroboration.'

'Corroboration.' Chloe repeated the word as if it were in a foreign language. 'Corroboration.'

'Yup. Think of it this way, if two people say the same thing, it's a lot more likely to be true.'

'And did the people at the laboratory back me up?' Chloe asked.

Lilly pressed her lips together for a second. 'To an extent, yes. They confirmed that Lydia had definitely been having sex shortly before she was killed.'

'I told you.'

'They also confirmed that it could have been done against her will, especially if she had been drugged. Unfortunately, they didn't find any drugs in her system, but that's not too surprising. Some clear very quickly,' Lilly told her. 'What I'm hoping is that the police will at least accept that they need to look into the possibility of someone else being involved and release you in the meantime.'

Fear swept across Chloe's face. 'I'm not going back to the Grove.'

'I'll talk to Harry about what's best,' said Lilly.

'Where is he?'

'On the phone. He's taking what you've said very seriously and is looking into it right now.'

'Where will he send me?'

Lilly had no idea, but she couldn't let Chloe become distressed about that now. It was the last thing they all needed.

'I'm sure that's something else he's looking into right now.'

She was almost relieved when Jack poked his head around the door. 'Can I have a word, Lilly?'

Back in the custody area, they took up a seat on an empty bench, ignoring the flashing light behind the sergeant, alerting him to the fact that one of his prisoners was calling for attention. There was meant to be an alarm bell too, but the majority of sergeants disconnected them so they could at least hear themselves think. It was not unknown for junkies doing their rattle to press their call buttons all night.

'You've spoken to Phil?' Lilly asked.

'Indeed I have,' Jack replied.

'And he's told you that Chloe's story is not unreasonable?'

'He confirmed it's one possibility.'

Lilly sat on her hands so as not to punch the air. 'You'll release her on bail then?'

'No.'

The feeling of elation drained away. 'No?'

'Your client's made a huge allegation,' he said. 'I think it's only right that I ask her about it formally under caution. If this thing were to get to court we wouldn't want some smart-arsed lawyer saying I hadn't given her the chance to tell her side of the tale now, would we?'

Harry's eyes blazed as Lilly informed him of Jack's decision. 'It's outrageous,' he said. 'The man's a complete arse.'

Lilly hid a smile. 'To be fair, he probably should put the charge to Chloe, given she's raised a fairly spectacular defence.'

'But you know as well as I do that she can't stand up to an interrogation,' he said. 'She might say anything.'

'Agreed,' said Lilly. 'Which is why I'll tell her to answer "no comment" to every question.'

Harry shook his head. 'But won't that look odd? Wouldn't an innocent person want to set the record straight?'

'That's where you and I come in,' said Lilly.

Harry looked puzzled.

'We prepare brief statements and read them out at the top of the interview,' she said. 'You'll say how unhappy you are that she's being interviewed and I'll explain that she's not guilty, but I've advised her not to engage with the process.'

'And that will work?' Harry asked. 'Jack will accept it?'

Lilly laughed. 'Not lying down, no, but what's he going to do? Beat her until she squeals?'

'I get the feeling you've done this before,' Harry said with a smile.

'Maybe once or twice.'

They took up their places in an interview suite: Jack on one side of a table, Chloe on the other, flanked by Lilly and Harry. Frankly, it was a tight squeeze and Lilly tried not to jab her elbow into her client's doughy arm as she made notes of the date, time and those present.

The interview would be recorded by video, but Lilly liked to note what happened as it occurred. Old habits die hard.

'I'm sure your solicitor has explained that I'm taping this interview, Chloe?' Jack asked.

'No comment,' Chloe answered slowly and deliberately.

Jack laughed. 'We haven't started yet, Chloe. I just wanted to check you knew I was filming. Okay?'

Chloe's reply was mechanical. 'No comment.'

'Okaaaay,' said Jack. 'I think I can see where this is going.'

'No comment.'

'It wasn't a question, Chloe.' He looked at Lilly. 'Can I assume you've advised your client that I'm taping this?'

'You can,' Lilly answered.

'Then we'll get started.' Jack reached up and turned on the camera. 'My name is DCI Jack McNally and I'm here today to question Chloe Church in the presence of her solicitor.' He nodded at Lilly. 'For the benefit of the record, could you state your name?'

'I'm Lilly Valentine,' she said with a courteous smile.

'And, because Chloe is a minor, she is also accompanied by an appropriate adult,' said Jack and gestured to Harry.

'My name is Harry Piper.' Harry's voice was smooth. 'And I really must say at this juncture that I very much object to this interview.'

'I'm sorry to hear that,' said Jack, who did not sound in the least apologetic.

'Chloe, as you very well know, is extremely vulnerable.' Harry checked his notes. 'Her mental health is in such a fragile state I fear this interrogation could be very damaging. You have a duty of care towards her that you are breaching by insisting on this.' He waved a disgusted hand at the camera. 'Frankly, I'm shocked.'

Jack nodded his head. 'Thank you for your comments, Mr Piper.'

'Doctor,' said Harry. 'Doctor Piper.'

'Apologies, Doctor Piper.' Jack placed a loaded emphasis on the word 'doctor'. 'I've listened to your comments but feel I still have to proceed. Fortunately, from what I've seen today, Chloe is perfectly calm and lucid and she doesn't appear to be under the undue influence of any drugs, so I've decided it's safe to carry out this interview.'

'Based on what qualifications?' Harry demanded.

'Based on over twenty years in the police service and having carried out thousands of interviews.'

Harry rapped his finger against his notes. 'This is a travesty.'

'I'm sorry you feel that way, but I've run this past the custody sergeant and the FME.'

'FME?'

'Forensic medical examiner,' said Jack. 'Doctors who work for the police and check on our prisoners.'

'I see.'

'And he agrees with the custody sergeant that given the serious nature of the offence, Chloe should be given the opportunity to tell her side of the story.'

Neatly done, thought Lilly. Make it look like you're doing the suspect a favour.

Jack cleared his throat. 'Chloe, you do not have to say anything but it may harm your defence if you do not mention something which you later rely on in court. Anything you do say may be given in evidence.' He paused and watched Chloe. 'Do you understand what I'm saying, Chloe?'

Chloe opened her mouth, but Lilly jumped in.

'Before you begin, Officer McNally, I'd just like to get a few things clear for the tape. First, I have advised my client not to answer any of your questions. I've done this because I share Doctor Piper's concerns. He's eminent in his field and what's more he is Chloe's personal physician.' She smiled into the camera. 'I don't think any of us are in a position to overrule him. Secondly, I must say I'm disappointed that you have decided to centre your investigation around my client. Any evidence pointing to her involvement is purely circumstantial, and there are other more likely suspects that you seem determined to ignore.'

Jack looked at Lilly. Lilly looked at Jack.

'That it?' he asked.

'For now,' Lilly replied.

'Then let's kick off shall we?' Jack sifted through some papers on his lap. 'Chloe, can you tell me if you had anything to do with the murder and mutilation of Lydia Morton-Daley?'

Chloe glanced at Lilly who gave her a tiny nod.

'No comment,' said Chloe.

'Are you saying you did or you didn't?' Jack asked.

'No comment.'

'It's a big thing to be accused of, Chloe,' said Jack. 'I'm sure you want to tell me what happened.'

'No comment.'

Jack feigned confusion. 'See, I can't understand why anyone wouldn't give their side and I don't think a jury would be able to understand it either.'

Lilly coughed. 'If a jury ever watch this tape, and it's a big if, I'm sure they will be more than capable of understanding that I have advised Chloe not to answer these questions.' Lilly jabbed her chest with her thumb. 'My advice. If anyone wants further information I'll be only too happy to attend court and explain it.'

Jack stroked a finger down his tie. Lilly clearly had him on the run.

'So you didn't kill Lydia?' he asked Chloe.

'No comment.'

'And you didn't carve the words "Help Us" into her skin?'

Chloe gave a small groan. 'No comment.'

'You had nothing to do with any of that?'

'No comment.'

'What about the knife?' asked Jack. 'The one we found in your room?'

'No comment.'

'We know it was the one used to cut Lydia because the forensic team found traces of her blood and skin on the blade,' said Jack. 'Are you saying you didn't go near that knife?'

Suddenly, Lilly didn't feel so certain.

'No comment,' said Chloe.

'Are you saying you didn't touch that knife?'

Shit. Lilly had been too busy focusing on the sexual abuse angle.

'No comment,' Chloe replied.

'Because if you're saying you didn't touch that knife, I'm puzzled.' Jack whirled a finger around the side of his right temple. 'I'm puzzled because we found your fingerprints all over the handle.'

'No . . .' Chloe's eyes filled with tears. 'That wasn't a question was it?'

Chapter Seven

Case number 45701
In Luton Family Proceedings Court
Re: The Talbot children: Gigi (16), Oliver (13), Robert (11), Phoebe (6), Arianne (5), Nathalia (2) and Mimi (1).

Report of the Children's Guardian appointed by Luton Family Proceedings Court
My name is Patricia Lyons and I have been appointed Children's Guardian in respect of the above named family.

I have been asked to report back to the court in respect of the local authority's application for Care Orders for all seven Talbot children.

As part of my assessment I have read the Social Services files for and psychological reports of each child. I have also read the court transcript of the criminal proceedings against George Talbot, Sinead Talbot and Mary-Ann Yates. I have spoken at length with the children and their current foster carers. I have also had numerous discussions with the lead social worker in this case in respect of the Care Plans for each child.

I have also interviewed George Talbot and Mary-Ann Yates. The court will be aware that Sinead Talbot died days after she was sentenced at Luton Crown Court.

I should also say at this point, that this is an extremely difficult case; I have rarely come across children so badly and repeatedly abused over such a prolonged period of time.

Matters are further complicated by the number of children and the wide age gaps involved.

The view of the Local Authority is that all seven children should be made the subject of full Care Orders. Thereafter Mimi, Nathalia, Arianne and Phoebe should be freed for adoption. Robert and Oliver should be placed in a long-term foster placement, preferably together. Gigi will be seventeen next week and will thus no longer be the responsibility of the Local Authority. They have, however, confirmed that they will secure a package of support for her.

My main concern with the Care Plans as they stand is that the children will be split up. It is highly unlikely that the four youngest girls will be adopted as a sibling group and it may even prove impossible to keep Oliver and Robert together. For these children, who have suffered so much, this may prove the final straw for some of them. The girls in particular are extremely close and already look up to Gigi as their mother figure.

Since their release from the family home (which was to all intents and purposes their prison) they have lived together in a foster home. Whilst this has not been without problems, the children have derived some comfort from being together.

It has been said of course that some of the behaviours the children exhibit are exacerbated whilst they remain as a unit and a fresh start will free them of the temptation to repeat those behaviours. I cannot deny that this remains a concern. Patterns of behaviour have clearly been established by the children, especially the older ones, and these ingrained patterns are difficult to escape.

It has also been said that the children's parentage means

there is no necessity to keep them together. And it is true that DNA tests have shown that the Talbot children do not all share the same biological parentage. Gigi has George Talbot as a father and Sinead Talbot as a mother. Oliver and Robert both have George Talbot as their father and Mary-Ann Yates as their mother. Phoebe has George Talbot as her father but the mother is unknown. Arianne has Sinead Talbot as her mother but the father is unknown. Nathalia has Sinead Talbot as her mother but the father is unknown. Neither of Mimi's parents are known.

We have tried unsuccessfully to discover the identity of the unknown parents. There are no matches on the police databases. George Talbot informed me that all the adults in the house had numerous sexual partners, many of whom they barely knew. Mary-Ann mentioned a man named John who regularly visited and had sex with her but was unable to give further details.

When questioned as to how Mimi had arrived into the Talbot household, George stated that Sinead had said she was hers. Whether she did tell George this, I cannot say.

What I can say is that the mixed parentage of the Talbot children is a red herring. The bond they feel is strong and real. The fact that they are not all biological siblings is immaterial to them.

However, having balanced all the evidence, I have come to the opinion that although it is a far from perfect ending for these children, it is better if at least some of them have the chance to find forever homes through adoption.

I cannot express strongly enough that any adoption must not be closed. These children must be given the opportunity to have contact with one another. Without this opportunity it is my opinion that the Care Plans will be likely to fail.

* * *

'You lied to me,' said Lilly.

Jack had left the interview room looking very pleased with himself. And he had every right to be smug, didn't he?

'I'm sorry.' Fat tears ran down Chloe's fat cheeks. 'I didn't know how to explain it.'

'You said you had not touched that knife.'

'It's complicated,' said Chloe.

Though she was bigger than was normal, or indeed healthy, she seemed tiny, slumped in her chair.

'Try me,' said Lilly.

'It was Lydia's knife.' Chloe wiped her face with the heels of her hands. 'She asked me to hide it for her.'

'When?'

'I don't know.'

Lilly folded her arms, hoping she looked suitably unimpressed.

'A few days before she was killed, maybe,' said Chloe. 'She couldn't take it any more. She said she'd kill anyone who tried to touch her again.'

'So why would she give it to you if she needed it to protect herself?'

'Elaine kept doing spot checks on her room,' said Chloe.

'That's true,' Harry interjected. 'She had about three in the week before she died. Nurse Foley was worried about her behaviour.'

'But not your room?' Lilly asked Chloe. 'Your room didn't get checked?'

'Hardly ever.' Chloe looked to Harry for confirmation.

'She's been at the Grove so long,' he said. 'There've never been any problems.' He placed a hand over Chloe's. 'The worst we might find is a hidden biscuit.'

It was a plausible story. Sort of. It would certainly account for Chloe's fingerprints being all over the handle.

'Did you tell anyone else about the knife?' Lilly asked.

'No.'

'What about Lydia?'

'No.' Chloe sounded certain. 'She wouldn't.'

Lilly thought back to her meeting with Lydia. She had been an impulsive braggart, given to self-destruction. She glanced at Harry and his face said it all. It was highly likely that Lydia had told someone else about the knife.

'Why didn't you tell me any of this before?' Lilly asked.

'Because you wouldn't have believed me,' Chloe wailed. 'No one ever believes me because they think I'm mad.'

Lilly's reply caught in her throat. Chloe was right; no one ever believed her. Least of all Lilly.

In the custody area, Chloe leaned against the sergeant's desk while Jack charged her with murder.

'Do you have anything to say?' he asked.

Chloe glanced at Lilly.

'My client would like to confirm that she did touch the knife sometime before Lydia was killed,' said Lilly.

'Funny how she didn't mention that before,' he said.

'Well I'm mentioning it on her behalf now,' Lilly answered and turned to the sergeant. 'Bail?'

'Not a chance,' he said.

'Come on,' said Lilly. 'She lives in a mental hospital, she can hardly abscond.'

The sergeant shook his head and his careful comb-over began to separate. 'I'm not going to make that call.' He smoothed the greasy strands of hair back into place, putting Lilly in mind of Arthur Scargill. 'Leave it to the court, first thing in the morning.'

Lilly sighed and put an arm around Chloe's shoulders. 'Sorry, love, you'll have to stay here tonight.'

The look that crossed Chloe's face was easy to recognize: relief.

★ ★ ★

When they reached the narrow lane, Lilly pointed to her cottage. 'That's me,' she said.

'How utterly charming,' Harry replied and pulled over.

Lilly smiled. It did look chocolate-box perfect covered in snow, icicles hanging from the roof of the porch. Underneath was a less appealing assortment of cracked tiles and peeling paint.

'Hungry?' she asked.

'Famished,' Harry replied.

'You're welcome to stay for dinner,' she said. 'If you don't have to rush back home.'

Harry smiled and slid out of the car. 'I think the cat can manage without me.'

Once inside, they were greeted by a scarlet-faced David frantically rocking Alice who was howling like wolverine. Lilly took her from him and reached over to the dimmer switch; as the room darkened, Alice began to calm.

'I think she's part vampire,' Lilly laughed.

When David had recovered himself he raised his eyebrows at Harry.

'Oh, sorry,' said Lilly. 'This is Harry. He works at the hospital where my client was killed. Harry, this is David.'

Harry held out his hand and David quickly checked his own and wiped it down his jumper before taking it. Posh boy meets posh boy, thought Lilly.

'Pleased to meet you,' said Harry. 'You must be Lilly's husband.'

'Ex-husband,' said Lilly.

'Ah,' said Harry.

Lilly heard herself explaining the situation. 'He's staying here for a few days. While he sorts out somewhere to rent.' Clearly, Harry's opinion of her mattered.

David bobbed his head from side to side. 'All a bit complicated.'

'Not really, Dad.' Sam mooched into the room holding a sandwich so big he needed to tilt his head to get purchase. 'Your girlfriend kicked you out 'cos she thinks you've got a bit on the side.'

'Thanks for that, Sam,' said David.

Lilly fought back laughter and nudged her son with her hip. 'Plate.'

Sam cupped his free hand under the hunk of bread as a makeshift crumb-catcher.

'Is it like this in your house?' Lilly asked Harry.

'Sadly not,' he replied.

She led Harry through to the kitchen, leaving Sam and David playing on the Wii. With Alice under one arm, she foraged in the fridge.

'Can I help?' Harry asked.

Lilly gestured towards a bottle of Cabernet Sauvignon on the counter. 'Why don't you pour us both a glass?'

She pulled out chicken, yoghurt and a fat green chilli pepper from the fridge and plopped Alice in her high chair with an obligatory breadstick.

'You don't mind spice?' she asked.

Harry pulled the cork from the wine bottle with a flourish. 'The hotter, the better.'

'Do you want a glass of vino, David?' she called into the sitting room.

David let out a grunt Venus Williams would have been proud of. Sam was no doubt thrashing him at virtual tennis. Honestly, it was impossible to say which one of them was the more mature.

'In a sec,' he shouted back.

Lilly pulled out the coffee grinder and threw in ginger, shallots, coriander, cumin and half the chilli. Then she whizzed it all to a paste. When she removed the lid, the air filled with the smells of South East Asia.

Harry handed her a glass of wine and took a sip of his own. 'Just what the doctor ordered.' He grinned. 'After a day like today I think we deserve it.'

'Abso-bloody-lutely,' said Lilly and took a huge glug.

She scraped the aromatic paste into a hot frying pan and began chopping the chicken. The knife needed sharpening and it took some effort to cut the whole way through the raw flesh. She banished all thoughts of Lydia's injuries from her mind.

'I'm going to say this now, while I'm still sober and you don't think it's the alcohol talking,' said Harry. 'You were fabulous today at the police station. The way you handled the interview was better than watching the telly.'

Lilly pushed the meat into the hot spice mixture and stirred. 'It wasn't entirely successful, was it?'

'Not your fault,' he said.

Lilly supposed he was right, but it didn't make her feel any better about what had happened.

'What about tomorrow?' he asked.

'The Magistrates' Court has no jurisdiction over murder cases so it will be transferred to the Crown Court.' The chicken had browned nicely so she opened a can of coconut milk and poured it in. The sweet, oily scent was heaven. 'The most important thing for us tomorrow is the question of bail.'

'Will Chloe get it?'

'She's got a pretty good chance.' Remembering cardamom, Lilly tossed two pods onto the chopping board and reached for a potato masher. 'If you can give me as many details as possible about security at the Grove, how few patients have managed to escape and what have you.'

She smacked the pods with the masher and Alice screamed. Harry leaned over and cupped his hands over her ears. Lilly gave another whack but this time Alice only whimpered.

'She has your eyes,' said Harry.

'And her temper.' David strolled in and poured himself a glass of wine. 'Something smells good.'

'Malay curry,' Lilly told him.

David patted his stomach. 'If I stay here any longer I'll be the size of a house.'

'You know where the door is,' Lilly replied.

An hour later, everyone had had at least two platefuls of curry and rice and Sam and David sloped off for a round of virtual golf.

'They shouldn't leave you with the mess,' said Harry, collecting up the plates and scraping the almost non-existent leftovers into the bin.

'I'm just glad to see them getting on so well,' said Lilly. 'There was a time when his dad was so caught up in his new relationship Sam hardly got a look in. I think David's learned his lesson.'

'I'm impressed with how healthy things are between you and David,' he said.

'Healthy?' Lilly began filling the dishwasher. 'Bonkers more like.'

Harry slid a plate into the same rack as Lilly and their fingers brushed. 'If you saw how I got on with my ex-wives, you'd know the real definition of bonkers.'

'Not good?'

Harry laughed. 'To put it mildly. Then again we didn't have any kids to bind us together. Having Sam and Alice must be a huge driver for harmony to reign.'

Lilly was about to tell him that Alice wasn't David's, but stopped herself. He might ask who Alice's dad was and then what would she say? Oh, you know that nice copper you met earlier . . . she settled for a smile and diversion.

'Something that has occurred to me about Chloe is that even if I do get bail for her, she won't want to go back to the Grove,' she said. 'Given what she's told us, we couldn't put her at risk, could we?'

Harry nodded. 'I've been thinking about that too. I could put in place a closed facility.'

Lilly shrugged to show she had no idea what that was.

'Nice word for keeping her locked up,' he said. 'She would be moved to a secure room, accessed only by a code. I would ensure that only an extremely small and select group had the code. Staff who I would trust with my life.'

'Sounds like it could work,' said Lilly.

'We tend only to use it for dangerous patients, but there's no reason I can't implement it for Chloe if she agrees.'

'Twenty-four bang up,' said Lilly. 'Not much different from prison.'

'Oh, I won't keep her a prisoner,' he said. 'If she wants to attend therapy sessions or eat in the dining room or just hang out with her friends, I'll personally supervise her.'

'Isn't that a huge commitment?'

Harry nodded gravely. 'Frankly, Lilly, I've already let Lydia and Chloe down so badly that right now nothing is too much trouble.'

I watch Jack slurp a bowl of tomato soup, blowing on each spoonful before gulping it down with undisguised relish. He loves the stuff.

Funny, but I've never been interested in food. Even as a child I just ate enough fuel to keep me going. Crisps and sweeties held no allure. I remember one Easter I received five chocolate eggs. I worked out the cost of those foil-wrapped eggs and what I could have bought with the money. I was furious.

My parents never made that mistake again.

'Bread?' I offer a roll to Jack.

He smiles but shakes his head. A few months ago he read that eating carbohydrates after six o'clock is a sure-fire way to get fat and since then he's stuck to soup and salad.

'How did it go today?' I ask.

'Could have been worse, I suppose.'

'*The forensics are pretty damning, aren't they?*' I ask. '*I thought the girl's fingerprints were all over the knife?*'

Jack finishes his soup and puts down his spoon. '*You always want a confession if you can get one,*' he says. '*It seals the deal.*'

'*What did she say in the interview?*' I ask.

'*Not a single thing.*' Jack leans back in his chair. '*No comment, no comment, no fecking comment.*'

I open my eyes wide. '*I thought a girl like that wouldn't have been able to help herself.*'

'*Me too,*' he says. '*She got good advice and followed it to the letter.*'

I cock my head to one side. '*You've got enough evidence for a conviction,*' I say. '*Confession or no confession.*'

He nods. '*Her prints are on the knife and the knife was in her room. Then there's the so-called defence which she didn't mention until after the shit hit the fan.*'

'*A jury are going to find that very suspicious,*' I say.

'*You can't count your chickens with juries, Kate,*' he says. '*And Lilly can be very persuasive.*'

'*Oh Jack.*' I slide round the table and sit on his knee. '*I've seen you in court. You have the whole place eating out of the palm of your hand.*'

'*Really?*'

I put my arms around his neck and kiss him. He smells sweet and salty at the same time.

'*You don't know how good you are at your job, Jack.*'

He gives me a shy smile so I kiss him harder.

'*Now take me to bed,*' I say. '*And show me just how persuasive you can be.*'

The next morning Lilly came downstairs in her smartest black suit and high heels.

David let out a wolf whistle. 'Very nice, Ms Valentine.'

'Shut up and pour me some coffee,' she said.

He poured boiling water into a cup and slipped a slice of bread into the toaster. 'Shall I take you to court?'

'No thanks.' She took the steaming mug from him. 'Harry's picking me up.'

'Mr Keen Bean,' he said.

She took butter and marmalade from the fridge. She'd been both surprised and pleased when Harry offered to collect her as he left the previous evening. 'Don't be ridiculous,' she said.

'He's very attentive,' said David. 'Clearing up, offering lifts.'

Lilly shook her head and busied herself with buttering her toast.

'All that smiling and touching you is just business is it?' asked David.

'It's just his way.' Lilly took a bite. 'He's like that with everyone.'

'You mean he's a dreadful flirt?'

'That's exactly what I mean.'

David laughed and peeled a banana. 'Shall I look after the kids?'

'Are you sure you don't mind?'

'Not at all.' He looked out of the window. The snow was still deep and unyielding. 'They're better off at home, don't you think?'

'That's really good of you, David.'

He looked at her, suddenly serious. 'Just trying to help out. I do realize how good it is of you to have me here, Lil.'

Actually, she thought, after the initial shock, it wasn't working out badly. David was showing willing in a way he had never done when they were married. And Sam obviously loved having his dad under the same roof.

'Just don't get too comfy,' she said, nudging him with her elbow.

Lilly hopped through the snow like a robin and bounced into Harry's car.

'Good morning,' he said.

154

'Hi.'

'Sleep well?'

'Not bad.' She laughed. 'You?'

'Like a baby.' He pulled off. 'I really must thank you for last night. Terrific curry.'

'You're welcome.'

'How about I reciprocate this evening?' he asked. 'Cook for you?'

Lilly considered. Alice was going to Jack's and Sam would be more than fine with his dad. 'I'd love to,' she said.

Harry beamed at her. 'I can't promise you that my food will be a patch on yours. In fact I can promise you that it won't be a patch on yours, but I can say hand on heart that none of my ex-wives will be present.'

Lilly threw her head back and laughed. 'I'm sure I'd get along with them just fine.'

'No doubt about that. In fact I'm sure they'd all love you to bits,' he said. 'It's me they can't stand.'

Gem gets up late 'cos she don't feel right. It ain't that she's been sick or nothing, it's more that she's in a bad place in her head.

It's that punter who's done it. Bill. He made her feel proper uneasy with the way he looked at her. Like she weren't a person. Not a somebody but a something. Gem ain't a big fan of Misty or nothing, but she ain't surprised she lost the plot. Who wouldn't with him coming at you with his balls swinging around?

Mum's watching telly with Tyler on her lap. He's laughing at some cartoon.

'All right, love?' she asks Gem.

'I might go into school today,' says Gem.

Mum's face drops and she pushes Tyler onto the sofa beside her so she can get some fags from the table.

'I thought you said it was closed.' Mum lights up.

Gem shrugs.

'Anyway,' says Mum. 'I don't want you here when the Slaughter boys come round.'

'They're coming round today?' Gem asks. 'You never said.'

'They don't exactly make appointments.'

Gem puts a hand to her stomach. There's a fluttery feeling inside. Like a bird trying to escape. She thinks about the money in her jeans pocket. If she gives a tenner to Mum to pay off the Slaughters and buy food and fags and nappies, there ain't going to be nothing left tomorrow. Then this whole shitty circle will start all over again.

'It ain't for you to sort out this family,' says Mum. 'That's my job.'

Gem goes to get dressed. School can wait another day.

The entrance to the courthouse was cold and dark.

'Power's gone off,' said the security guard, blowing on his hands.

'What about the hearings?' Lilly asked him.

'We've been told to tell anybody who arrives that they're bailed for a week, but to be honest most of 'em haven't turned up,' he said. 'I mean they don't turn up at the best of times, do they?'

'What about defendants being brought over from the nick?' she asked.

The guard shrugged. 'Probably being sent somewhere else. You'd have to check in the cells.'

'Thanks,' said Lilly and headed to the stairs, past the silent X-ray machine, Harry close behind.

They strode down the concrete steps and pressed the buzzer to the custody area. There was no answer.

'Do you think it's electric?' Harry asked.

'Could be,' Lilly replied and hammered on the metal door with her fist. 'Hello,' she called out, without any idea whether her voice could carry through five solid inches. 'Anyone inside?'

At last there was a clicking sound and the door was opened by a man in his fifties, his teeth the dirty yellow of a committed smoker.

'Is Chloe Church here?' Lilly asked.

The guard pulled a piece of lined paper from his back pocket and carefully checked the three scribbled names.

'Computer's down,' he said, as if the lack of technology might set the process back by hours.

Lilly pointed to the second name on the list of three. 'That's her.'

'Right.' The guard took out the pen he had clipped to his breast pocket and put a tick next to Chloe's name.

'Can we see her?' Lilly asked.

The guard blew hard. 'Trouble is there are only the two of us here. No one else managed it. By all accounts, Jim tried to walk, but slipped on some black ice and did for his hip. He'll be off sick for weeks.'

Lilly hoped her face didn't disclose her impatience or lack of interest in Jim's injury.

'You can imagine it's a bit tricky,' said the guard.

Lilly nodded that yes she could well imagine the sheer complexity of the situation.

'We couldn't quite decide on the best course of action,' said the guard. 'I mean the handbook was no use at all. In the end it was Mike who decided what to do and I've gone along with it. Well, someone had to make a decision, didn't they?'

'And what did Mike decide?' Lilly asked.

The guard gave a shake of the head and a smile that displayed gums stained a similar hue to the teeth. 'We've put all three of them in the same cell, that way we can watch 'em more easily.'

Lilly wondered why three prisoners couldn't be watched perfectly well from three cells, given they'd be locked in them.

'The trouble is of course, now we've got 'em in together, it's a bit of a risk getting them out,' said the guard.

'Why's that?' Lilly asked.

'Think about it,' said the guard. 'If we open the door to release one of them, there's nothing to stop the other two rushing out as well. We'd be outnumbered, see.'

'Right,' said Lilly.

'Thinking about it, banging them up together might not have been the best idea,' he said. 'But there were no guidelines see. Nothing in the handbook.'

'Could I at least speak to Chloe through the grille?' Lilly asked.

The guard paused for a second, clearly weighing up the risks involved. 'Give me a mo.'

With that he clanged the door shut, leaving Lilly and Harry in the semi-darkness.

'Do you think he's gone to check the handbook?' Harry's shoulders were heaving with laughter. 'Maybe there's a section devoted to the opening of security flaps in inclement weather.'

'Stop it.' Lilly jabbed him with her elbow.

'Section thirty one, subsection six and I quote, where a power cut or similar act of God prevents a solicitor or other adult from having an interview with their client in the allocated facility, said interview may take place through the security flap of the cell providing the solicitor or other adult stands at least twelve point five centimetres from the cell door.' They were both cracking up now. 'However, if at any time the officer feels security is being in any way impaired he may terminate the interview at his discretion and without consultation with Mike or indeed Jim.'

When the door clicked open once more, Lilly gave Harry another dig in the ribs and straightened her face.

'We think it should be safe enough for you to have a chat through the flap,' said the guard. 'Providing you keep a reasonable distance from the door.'

'Twelve point five centimetres,' Harry whispered in Lilly's ear.

Lilly followed the guard into the custody area, ignoring the sniggering behind her. Once inside the main area, it became substantially lighter and she noticed the overhead strip lights were working.

'Emergency generator kicked in,' the guard told her and led her to the desk where a second man, presumably Mike, was nursing a bottle of Lucozade. Without a word he thrust a sheet of paper at Lilly.

'Put your details on there,' said the first guard. 'Plus your time of arrival.'

Lilly did as she was told and slid the sheet back to Presumably Mike.

'This way,' said the first guard and led them to a cell at the far end of the corridor. Lilly couldn't begin to understand the thought processes that hadn't chosen the nearest cell. 'Number nine,' he said, pointing to the number painted on the cell door.

Lilly nodded her thanks and put out her arm to open the security flap.

'Not too close now,' said the guard. 'Can't be too careful.'

It occurred to Lilly then that perhaps there was a dangerous offender in there. The sort that might make a grab for her hair or face. In which case she needed to get Chloe out ASAP.

Nerves began to kick in as she unlocked the hatch and lowered the flap.

When she looked inside the cell, her reaction was instant: laughter. Chloe was seated on the bed to the left-hand side, listening intently to the man perched next to her. He was at least eighty years old in his stockinged feet and hadn't a tooth in his head.

'My piles are the size of cherry tomatoes,' he told her with a gummy grin.

At their feet, another octogenarian had made a nest out of scratchy police-issue blankets and was sound asleep. She snored loudly, her lips reverberating like an engine. Perhaps she had heard the old guy's tales one too many times.

'Husband and wife team,' said the guard, as if he were describing Bonnie and Clyde.

'So I see,' Lilly replied.

God alone knew what they'd been picked up for, but whatever it was, Lilly was pretty sure that neither one of them was about to make a desperate bid for freedom. Frankly, Lilly doubted either of them could make it to the door unaided.

'Hi, Chloe,' she called through the hatch.

Both girl and man looked up. The old woman didn't stir so Chloe struggled to her feet and stepped over her. If she slipped, the woman would be crushed.

'How are you?' Lilly asked.

'Fine,' Chloe replied.

'Did you get any sleep last night?'

'Oh yes.'

Lilly appraised her client. She definitely looked rested and at ease.

'I'm going to try to get you out of here,' Lilly said.

Chloe's face tightened. 'I don't want to go back to the Grove.'

'I know.'

'You can't let them take me, Lilly.'

Ignoring the guard's warning, Lilly stepped up to the plate. 'It's going to be okay, sweetheart. I've spoken to Harry and he's got a plan to keep you safe.'

'No,' Chloe shouted. 'I won't be safe at the Grove.'

'I know you're frightened, but hear me out, Chloe.'

The girl's eyes were wide with fear but she nodded.

'You can be moved to a locked room and no one except Harry will have the code,' said Lilly.

Chloe shook her head. 'What if they guess the code?'

Lilly looked to Harry for help and he moved next to her.

'I'll make it impossible to guess,' he said.

'Like what?' asked Chloe.

'I don't know,' he replied. 'How about the date of birth of Lilly's baby? No one at the Grove even knows she has a baby.'

Chloe leaned forward so that her face filled the gap. A rectangle of pink flesh, with eyes.

'I promise I will keep you safe,' said Harry.

Chloe gave a solemn blink of acceptance.

Gem dragged the Hoover down the hallway. Feyza calls it Henry and it's got a face. Gem supposes it's meant to make cleaning up fun or something.

Somebody's brought a load of crap in on their boots and tramped it into the carpet so Gem has to move the handle as fast as she can.

Gem don't actually mind. It ain't like it's hard work, is it? And it's nice to see dirty things come up clean. If only everything in life were that simple.

'Can I have word, Gem?' Feyza shouts from the desk at reception.

Gem knocks off Henry with her foot and looks up at her boss. She's counting up a wodge of twenties, licking her finger between each crisp note. There's got to be hundreds of 'em in the pile.

'Come over here, Gem,' she says, placing the money in a metal box.

Gem leaves the Hoover and wanders back to reception.

'Sit down.' Feyza nods to the sofa that the punters wait on. It's squashy from all them fat arses.

Gem sits down and Feyza locks the box with a key she keeps on a long chain around her neck and tucked inside her blouse.

'You like to work here?' Feyza sits next to Gem.

'You ain't sacking me, are you?' asks Gem.

'Don't be silly.' Feyza pats Gem's hand with the tips of her fingers. 'Why I do that?'

Gem shrugs. People don't need proper reasons to do shitty stuff, do they?

'You welcome here as long as we open,' Feyza tells her. 'How long we open, I can't say.'

Gem don't know much about business but she don't think Feyza needs to worry. Plenty of punters. Plenty of cash.

'You see, Gem.' Feyza stretches out her legs. 'What we do here not legal.'

Gem nods. Well, she ain't stupid. Everyone knows brothels ain't legal.

'Police leave us alone because we don't cause problem out on street.' She points vaguely at the door. 'And we let those boys have free service here sometimes. Understand me?'

Gem nods.

'Bill here yesterday for this,' says Feyza.

Gem ain't that surprised. A slimeball like Bill would make a good copper.

'He not happy with Misty, I tell you,' says Feyza. 'Which very bad. He can make lot of trouble for us if he want.'

'Does he want to?' asks Gem.

Feyza pats her hand again. The nails are painted with black and silver crackle. 'Lucky for us, no. He just want free service.'

Gem looks down at her own nails, bitten so short they often bleed. 'Not with Misty, though,' she says.

Feyza snorts. 'Misty must stay well away from Bill.'

'Who then?' Gem don't know why she's asking. She knows the answer.

'He want you, Gem,' says Feyza, confirming what Gem already knew.

'I ain't a working girl,' says Gem.

'I know this,' says Feyza. 'I not even ask you if it was other punter. I just tell them piss off. But . . .'

But it ain't anyone else is it? It's Bill.

'Before you say yes or no, Gem, there is one thing for you to know,' says Feyza.

Somehow Gem thinks she knows everything she needs to know about fat, ugly, filthy Bill.

'What?' she asks.

'He not want full service,' says Feyza. 'He just likes girl to stand and watch while he give himself hand job.'

'Why?'

'Who knows?' Feyza gives one of her cackles. 'What is it you say? Be grateful for small mercies.'

What with the nails and the horrible laughing, Feyza could pass for a witch. Even her nose is a bit pointy, Gem notices for the first time.

'So, darling, you do this for me?' Feyza smiles. 'Small favour?'

Gem doesn't answer.

'One little favour,' Feyza says. 'And I don't ask you anything no more.'

Lilly and Harry went up the stairs to the courtrooms. They found the entire floor deserted and in darkness. Without any windows it was impossible to see anything but the faintest of shapes looming at them.

'Hang on,' said Harry.

Lilly heard a rustling sound and the chink of coins.

'Here we go,' he said and pointed a thin beam of light in front of them.

'A torch?' Lilly was gobsmacked.

'It's on my key ring.' Harry waved what looked like a pen at her. 'For emergencies.'

'Quite the little Boy Scout.'

'Dyb, dyb, dyb.'

Harry cast the torch around the foyer, but it was quite clear that there was no one around. 'What now?' he asked.

Lilly was about to admit that she had no idea when she caught sight of a yellow glow at the far end of the corridor.

'Over there,' she said, and they made their way as carefully as they could to the source of the light.

Halfway across, Lilly banged her knee against a bench. 'Shit.' The metal gave a clang.

'Okay?' Harry grabbed her arm. 'Have you hurt yourself?'

She rubbed her leg. 'I'll live.'

They went the rest of the way arm in arm, until they were in front of a door, weak light seeping under it.

'The advocates' room,' said Lilly and pushed open the door.

Inside, the room, though not bright, was bathed in the muted glow from the street lamps outside and Kerry Thomson stood next to the floor-to-ceiling window, holding a file next to the glass. Everything, including the prosecutor, had an unhealthy sepia colour, like an old and fading photograph.

'Lilly Valentine,' said Kerry. 'Of all the solicitors who would make it to court on a day like today, I'd have put money on you.'

'I'll take that as a compliment,' said Lilly, though she doubted it was meant as one.

'Let me guess who you're here for.' Kerry put a mock puzzled finger to her chin. 'Is it Mr and Mrs Wright charged with stealing a carton of drinking chocolate and four litres of milk?' She raised an eyebrow. 'Or is it Chloe Church charged with a nice, juicy murder.'

Lilly just smiled.

'I don't know how you do it,' said Kerry. 'You seem to have a nose for every decent case in Luton.'

'I could say the same about you,' said Lilly.

Kerry nodded at a tottering pile of files on the table in the middle of the room. 'I just deal with the cases I'm handed.'

'As do I,' Lilly replied.

'Of course you do.'

Lilly wanted to defend herself, but what was the point? 'Shall we crack on?' she said.

'How can we?' Kerry asked. 'We don't have a magistrate.'

'Not one?'

Kerry shook her head. 'We've been told to bail everyone.'

'Excellent,' said Lilly.

'Though obviously not your client.' Kerry smirked. 'I'm not going to agree to give your client bail, am I?'

'I don't see what choice you've got,' said Lilly. 'The police can't extend custody now she's charged and you certainly can't deny bail.'

Kerry's face dropped. 'She's on a murder rap.'

'So what?' Lilly shrugged. 'You have no authority whatsoever to keep her. If you try to, I'll bet she'll sue.'

'That blob of lard? Don't make me laugh.'

Lilly narrowed her eyes. Until very recently, Kerry had been a similar size and shape to Chloe. Frankly, she was no supermodel today. Where did she get off being so derogatory? Fortunately, Harry stepped forward before Lilly said something inappropriate in response.

'Chloe is in my care and I can assure you that if Miss Valentine advises me that she has a legal case, then I will pursue it on her behalf.' His voice was measured, but the threat clear.

'For God's sake,' Kerry muttered.

'Is there any rule against getting a magistrate to hear a bail application on the phone?'

Everyone looked up and found Jack in the doorway, a large torch in his hand. 'Well is there?' he asked.

'No,' said Lilly.

'Then why don't we do that?' asked Jack. He gave Harry a hard stare. 'Then there will be no need for petty threats of legal action, will there?'

'Great idea, Jack,' said Harry and snapped off his key-ring torch.

Jack found a phone that could take a conference call and plugged it into the landline by the table. While they waited for Kerry to find the magistrate's number, Lilly and Harry peered out of the window at the world below. Everything had disappeared. The snow had swallowed it all. Light, colour, noise. Everything.

'It's like the end of the world,' said Lilly.

'I know exactly what you mean,' Harry replied.

From the table where he was now seated, Jack sniffed.

'What?' Lilly turned on her heels.

Jack shook his head with a rueful laugh. 'You always were melodramatic.'

'I don't know what you're talking about,' she said.

'I'm sure.'

Lilly stared at him, but he busied himself with the phone, pretending to check for a dialling tone. At last, Kerry returned, huffing and puffing, a piece of paper in hand.

'I could only find Andrew Manchester,' she said.

Lilly stifled a groan. Another round with the poisonous dwarf. The hits just kept on coming. She watched Kerry dial the number with a sense of diminishing optimism.

'Hello.' Manchester's voice croaked out at them. He sounded as if they'd woken him. That should put him in a good mood.

'Mr Manchester.' Kerry leaned towards the telephone, unnecessarily. 'Kerry Thomson here from the CPS. I'm sorry to bother you at home, sir.'

'What do you want?' he asked.

'Well, sir, I'm at court and unfortunately there are no magistrates here,' she said.

'We bailed everyone for a further week,' he replied. 'Didn't you get the message?'

'Yes, sir, and we have bailed as many defendants as we can, but there is a problem with one of them. The solicitor is threatening to sue unless we have a hearing.'

'What?'

Lilly raked her cheek with her nails. That was not what she had said. At all.

'I have her here.' Kerry could barely contain her smile. 'Perhaps you'd like to speak to her.'

'Indeed I would,' said Manchester.

Lilly took a deep breath. 'Good morning, sir, it's Lilly Valentine here.'

'Oh, it's you.'

Lilly kept her voice as light as she could manage. 'Indeed it is.'

'What's this nonsense about suing the court?'

'I'm afraid Miss Thomson is over-egging the pudding there, sir. I simply pointed out that my client cannot be kept in custody without a court order to that effect and if the police or prison service or the prosecution attempt to do so they are entering into very sticky territory.'

Mr Manchester gave a small humph, which Lilly hope meant he took her point. 'And what is this defendant charged with?' he asked.

'Murder.' Kerry's voice was filled with relish. 'And a violent one at that.'

Lilly wondered if a murder could ever be non-violent but guessed now wasn't the time to ask the question.

'You'll appreciate that in the circumstances I can't just let this defendant walk out of court to offend again,' said Kerry. 'She's a dangerous person, sir.'

'You'll appreciate that in the circumstances I can't just let the defendant be carted off to prison,' said Lilly. 'She's fifteen years old, sir.'

Lilly and Kerry glared at one another across the table.

'Well, this is highly irregular, but there seems to be no alternative than to hear this application over the telephone,' said Manchester.

'Thank you,' said Lilly.

'Don't thank me yet, Miss Valentine. It is very far from being conducive to your application, isn't it now?' He didn't wait for Lilly to reply. 'Miss Thomson, please set out the facts.'

Kerry reached for the file and flicked it open. Chloe's mugshot stared up at her and she gave Jack an amused smile. Lilly wanted to knock it off her face and balled her fists under the desk.

'It's a sad case, sir,' Kerry told the magistrate. 'The defendant's victim was only fifteen years old herself. She was also highly vulnerable and suffering from mental illness.'

Lilly balled her fists tighter still. It was only days ago that Kerry had been arguing that Lydia was feigning her issues in order to avoid the charges against her.

'The Crown will say that the defendant murdered Lydia Morton-Daley at the Grove Hospital by way of poisoning. Then, not content with having killed her victim, she mutilated her body.'

'What is the weight of evidence against the defendant?' asked Mr Manchester.

'The knife used was discovered in the defendant's room and her fingerprints were found on the knife. Fairly conclusive, sir,' said Kerry. 'In the circumstances there is no way this prisoner can be allowed out on bail. She is clearly a very dangerous individual.'

'What say you, Miss Valentine?' asked Manchester.

'Well, sir, I'd first like to point out that apart from the connection to the knife, there is no other evidence whatsoever against my client,' said Lilly. 'And she has given an explanation as to why her fingerprints are present.'

'Only after the police discovered them,' Kerry interjected.

Lilly ignored her. 'Second, the description of the victim given by Miss Thomson could adequately describe my client also. A child and highly vulnerable. The suggestion that my client is predatory could not be further from the truth. In fact, having met both girls, I can tell you which of them is the most at risk and it's not Lydia.'

'That would be because she's dead,' said Kerry.

Lilly splayed her hands on the desk in front of her. 'Chloe is a very ill girl. She has been sectioned under the Mental Health Act for a number of years, remaining resident at the Grove. All I'm asking is that while this case is ongoing, she remains there. I'm not suggesting she be free to wander around Luton town centre, I'm simply asking that she stay in the secure ward of a mental facility rather than be sent to prison.'

'There is provision for the mentally unstable in custody,' said Kerry.

'Oh come on,' said Lilly. 'We all know that's not true. Last year there were sixteen attempted suicides at Highpoint and almost all of those women had issues with their mental health. The prison officers do what they can, but they're fighting a losing battle. The care and, more importantly, the security of a prison simply doesn't compare to a facility like the Grove. If you don't believe me you can go directly to the horse's mouth; I've brought the senior psychiatrist here to court.'

She nudged Harry, who gave a tight smile.

'Good morning, sir.' Harry's voice was pure public school. 'Harry Piper at your disposal. May I reiterate how dreadfully sorry I was to interrupt you the other day.'

'The situation was a difficult one, Doctor Piper,' said Manchester.

'Indeed it was.' Harry let Lydia's death hang in the air.

'You're a psychiatrist at the Grove?' Manchester asked.

'For my sins,' Harry said. 'I'm the senior clinician and I also have personal responsibility for Chloe.'

'What do you say on the subject of bail, Dr Piper?'

'As Miss Valentine rightly pointed out, what we're asking for is hardly bail in the strictest sense. Frankly, Chloe will be held securely on the wing, she won't be free to come and go as she chooses, far from it,' said Harry. 'She will however be safe and cared for, which is my priority.'

Kerry sniffed. 'What about the other patients? Will they be safe with the defendant in situ?'

'You could say the same of the detainees in prison. Or don't they count?' said Harry. 'At least at the Grove we can keep her behaviour monitored at all times, ensure her medication remains stable. I don't think anyone can argue that for a girl like Chloe, a high dependency mental unit isn't the appropriate place.'

Suddenly the power came on and the overhead strip lights flickered into action. The brightness was overwhelming and Lilly had to shield her eyes with her hands.

'In the circumstances I don't think I have any choice,' said Mr Manchester. 'The defendant must be allowed to return to the Grove.'

Lilly blinked into the glare, trying to rid black spots from her field of vision. When at last she could see, the first face that came into view was Harry's.

'You did it,' he said. 'You bloody well did it.'

Chapter Eight

From: Tinaoliver@lutonsocialservices.org.uk
To: Selimabegum@lutonsocialservices.org.uk
Subject: Phoebe, Arianne, Nathalia and Mimi Talbot
Hi Selima,

As you know, I visited Karen and Stu Bryson today to try to get them to change their minds about placing the girls back into care.

To say I found them in a distressed state would be an understatement. Karen in particular is at the end of her tether and Stu is worried she may have a complete breakdown if things carry on as they are.

The main problem, as we always knew it would be, is Phoebe. We all hoped that in the months following the adoption, her behaviour would settle down, but sadly that isn't the case. If anything it has got worse. Her destructive outbursts now take place at least once a day and whilst I was at the Brysons' house I saw one episode in full flow where she threw a cup from one end of the kitchen to the other, narrowly missing Mimi's head. Stu took her outside into the garden in an attempt to calm her but she was soon banging on the window with such force I was concerned she would put her fists through the glass.

Karen is terrified she is going to seriously injure one of the other girls or herself. She feels powerless to control the situation and Stu can't have any more time off work. He is already on a final warning.

When she was finally quiet enough for me to talk to, Phoebe told me she felt very angry with herself for hurting Karen and Stu, but that she doesn't believe they really want her living with them. She seems to want to test their commitment to her and is taking it to the very brink.

During a long discussion with Karen and Stu they were adamant that the adoption of the girls has broken down. However, after much begging on my part, they have agreed to wait another month during which time we can put in place more support. I suggested that we double the number of sessions the girls have in play therapy and that we set up counselling for Phoebe as soon as possible. I know we've been down this road before and she was completely resistant, but I think we need to try again, as much for Karen and Stu's sakes as Phoebe's.

Finally, I had to make a concession about Gigi. I know we promised Pat, the guardian, that we would promote contact between the girls and Gigi, but Karen and Stu are convinced that she is one of the main triggers for Phoebe's behaviour. They say that whenever Phoebe speaks to or sees her elder sister, she becomes unmanageable.

I know this is going to break Gigi's heart, but frankly, I didn't think I had a leg to stand on. It was either stop contact or lose the entire placement. I should probably have checked with you first, but Karen and Stu were so desperate I felt I had to give them the assurance on the spot.

Though I'm not looking forward to it, I'll tell Gigi what's happened in person. I owe her that much. Then

I'll sort the extra support. After that, I think the best we can do is keep our fingers crossed and hope for some improvement.

If you want to speak to me about this, I'll be in the office on Thursday.

Regards

Tina.

Lilly threw the directions to Harry's place into her bag and slid on a pair of heels, trying to ignore David's pointed look.

'You look nice,' he said. 'Hot date?'

'Don't be daft,' she replied. 'I'm meeting Harry to chat about the case.'

'And you need red lipstick for that?'

'Am I not allowed make-up at my age?' she asked. 'Maybe I should get a perm and dentures.'

He didn't answer but dug into his back pocket, producing the keys to his Range Rover 'You'd better take these.' He tossed them to her. 'The Mini will never make it.'

'Thanks.'

'Shall I wait up?' David asked.

Lilly just laughed and left him to it.

When she pulled up outside the address Harry had given to her, she wasn't surprised to find a smart apartment block with a concierge service.

'I'm here to see Harry Piper,' Lilly told the man in a grey uniform.

'Fifth floor.' He gestured to the lift. 'The penthouse suite.'

The penthouse suite. It had to be, didn't it?

Harry greeted her at the door with a smile. 'Wow,' he said. 'You look fabulous.'

Lilly thrust a box of chocolates at him.

'Come in, come in.' He led her into the open-plan apartment that spanned the entire top floor. The walls and furniture were all white, a shocking contrast to the black sky that filled the vast floor-to-ceiling windows.

His socks made a swishing sound against the tiles that seemed to stretch endlessly, the stone impossibly smooth. Probably imported from somewhere like Tuscany or Morocco. Lilly wondered if she should take off her shoes. She never bothered at home as there was little damage she could do to the battered and pock-marked floorboards that had been there as long as the cottage itself. But some people were more careful, weren't they? Especially with things shipped in at the cost of a family car.

'Drink?' Harry opened an American-sized fridge and pulled out a bottle of Dom Perignon.

'Just half a glass,' said Lilly. 'I'm driving.'

He nodded, poured the champagne and handed a flute to her. Lilly knew she should hold it by the fragile stem to keep it cool, but worried she might drop it. Torn between giving the impression she was a pleb and smashing a crystal glass on those priceless tiles, plebdom won out.

'Sit.' Harry pointed his flute to a sofa. 'Make yourself at home.'

Lilly perched at the very end, terrified her dress might somehow bleed colour onto the white cushions.

'It feels like we've seen a lot of each other, yet know very little,' he said.

'I suppose that's how it is when people work together.'

'Let's rectify that,' he said. 'Tell me about yourself.'

'Nothing much to tell.'

'How can that be true?' Harry slid onto the sofa next to her, one arm draped across the back, one foot crossing the other knee.

'For a start where do you come from? What was Lilly Valentine like as a child?'

Lilly sipped her drink. 'Well, I grew up in Yorkshire on a big council estate and my mum brought me up on her own after my dad left us.' She laughed. 'I'm making it sound so grim but it really wasn't. I had my mum and nan to myself and they adored me.'

'I was sent to boarding school at seven,' said Harry. 'Trust me, your childhood doesn't sound grim at all.'

'David wants to send Sam to boarding school,' said Lilly. 'He says it will turn him into a man.'

Harry drained his glass. 'I hear time and hormones tend to do a reasonable job.' He refilled his glass and put a splash more in Lilly's. 'Did you always want to be a lawyer?'

'God no. I wanted to marry Adam Ant like everyone else.'

'So what changed?'

Lilly paused. She remembered the exact moment when her world had turned on its head.

'I was arguing with Mum as usual about school because she made me go to one on the other side of town and I just wanted to go to the comp with all my mates from the estate.' Lilly could still smell the cigarette smoke from the two bus rides she had to take each morning and evening. 'She told me to stop bloody shouting and that she was taking me to her work. In the days she did piecework in the sewing factory, but in the evenings she cleaned offices, so off we went, her in her overalls, me sulking for England.'

'I can imagine.'

Lilly laughed. 'Anyway, we stopped outside a firm of solicitors and she let herself in. I'd never been anywhere like that before so I was a bit intrigued, though I'd never have let on to Mum, of course.' Lilly recalled the vase of flowers in the reception, how she'd touch them to see if they were real. 'At the back of the building was the secretaries' pool, all fax machines and typewriters and I stopped to have a nosey. The chairs looked super comfy and the desks all clean and neat. I knew how horrible the sewing factory was, the fibres in the air, how it made all the women cough their guts up and I said "Look, Mum, I get it. I know why you've brought me here. You don't want me to end up like you when I can get a nice office job like this."'

'And what did she say?'

'Oh my God, she gave me such a look. I mean she could always turn things to stone with one of her specials, but this was a look I'd never seen before. She grabbed my hand.' Lilly could feel Elsa's grip now. 'And she dragged me away from the typewriters and up the stairs to the managing partner's office. He had a sign outside with his name on. "Mr Vinter", it said, and she threw open the door and pushed me inside.'

Lilly stopped as if she still couldn't believe what she'd seen.

'The room was huge, or at least it seemed that way to me,' she said. 'There was this vast wooden desk with a glass paperweight at each end and the wall behind the chair was covered in photographs of his family. Children in their posh blazers, him and his wife in tennis whites, a bloody horse . . .' Lilly finished her drink, hoping she wouldn't cry.

'Your Mum knew you could do it,' said Harry.

'Oh, she was bloody convinced,' Lilly replied. 'Based on no evidence whatsoever she was adamant that I'd be a great solicitor.'

'Seeing you in action, she was right,' said Harry. 'She must be very proud.'

'She's dead.' Lilly gulped. 'She died before I even qualified.'

Harry put his hand on hers. 'Doesn't matter. She knew exactly how it would pan out.'

Lilly could see how Harry's patients put so much trust in him. His empathy was flawless.

'What about you?' she asked. 'How did you get interested in the inside of people's heads?'

'Everyone I knew at home and school was completely screwed up,' he said. 'I wanted to figure out why.'

'And did you?'

Harry let his head fall back. 'I guess so. I mean, you get some answers, but you also get a lot more questions, if you see what I mean.'

Lilly did know what he meant. How many times had she thought she had her life worked out, only to find more complications lurking in the shadows?

Gem crunches her eyes shut against the pain.

'For fuck's sake.'

She tries to open them, but it just hurts too much.

'If you don't look at me, this won't work.'

Gem knows she's got to and squeezes one open. Misty's hand is inches from Gem's face, tweezers opening and closing like an evil silver fish. What do you call them ones that eat people?

'Keep still and it'll be quicker,' says Misty and attacks Gem's eyebrows.

Ever since she came in to work and Feyza told her what was happening with Bill, Misty's taken it upon herself to help Gem get ready. She ain't exactly being nice, Misty don't do nice, but she ain't being her usual bitch-self either.

'There,' she says and pushes Gem in front of the mirror. 'What do you think?'

Gem checks her reflection. Her eyebrows look like two black caterpillars in a sea of raw red skin.

'Ice cubes are good for making them settle down. Or frozen peas,' says Misty. 'But we haven't got any.'

Gem don't point out that there's six foot of snow on the pavement or Misty will probably drag her down there and shove her face in it.

'What colour?' Misty asks and brandishes four lipsticks at Gem who just shrugs. Misty takes the top off the first one, screws it upwards and draws a fat pink line of it on her hand. Then she does the same with the second. 'I know you don't think any of this matters, that the likes of Bill don't give a shit what you look like.' She holds her hand out to Gem who taps the second line. 'But it's not about that.'

'No?'

Misty plants one hand at the back of Gem's head and holds her firm while she does Gem's mouth. 'No. It's about putting on a front and playing the part.' She steps back to admire her handi-work. 'Like Feyza's wig.'

'Feyza wears a wig?'

Misty bursts out laughing. 'What are you like?'

There's a tap on the door and Feyza lets herself in.

'Jesus Christ, Misty,' she shouts. 'She look like the Bride of Dracula.'

Misty pulls a face. 'A girl needs her armour.'

'A girl need give punter what he want, and get it done quick too,' Feyza replies.

'Easy for you to say.' Misty grabs a can of Elnett and sprays Gem's hair, making her cough. 'You're not the one with some dirty old copper wanking in your face, are you?'

Feyza waves her hand. 'We all must do some things in life that don't make us so proud. It called survival.'

'Yeah, well some of us need more help to survive than others,' says Misty.

'No more talk now. Find clothes for Gem,' Feyza orders.

Misty scowls at her but does as she's told and pulls out a suit-case from under the bed. She crouches and rummages through, muttering to herself.

'You be okay,' Feyza tells Gem.

Gem nods. She's been with some boys before, done some stuff

she didn't like. When she was in care she used to let this boy called Sean touch her up. All the girls let him. It were like some rule that weren't written down but everybody knew about it. If you didn't let him cop a feel, he'd mess with your stuff, or tell the other boys you were queer. And then your life wouldn't be worth living.

'If he tries anything funny, just scream,' says Misty.

'No more screaming here,' says Feyza. 'You make this fucking fuss remember? Now we in position like this.'

Misty slams the suitcase shut and throws some black lacy underwear at Gem. 'If that bastard had stuck to the script, I wouldn't have had to.'

Gem looks at the knickers she's meant to wear. They ain't really big enough to cover her arse. But that's the point of 'em, she supposes. The bra is a bit frayed around the edges.

'What size shoes to do you wear?' Misty asks.

'Five,' Gem replies.

'These are a six, but they'll do.' She holds up a pair of high heels. 'What about your name? What are you going to call yourself?'

'I already told him my name,' says Gem.

'Your real one?'

Gem nods.

'Shit,' says Misty.

'It not matter,' says Feyza and stands to leave the room. 'It really not matter.'

Misty looks away. Obviously it matters a lot to her. Like the make-up and the clothes and the wigs. Like what she keeps at the back of her dressing-table drawer.

Lilly slipped off her shoes under the table. She couldn't remember when she last felt so relaxed. Harry popped his iPod into the nearby dock and the sound of jazz filled the room. Lilly sighed.

'Everything okay?' Harry asked.

Lilly wiggled her toes. 'Everything's perfect.'

He gave her a smile and cut up a loaf of hot ciabatta.

'I know the circumstances are a little odd to say the least.' He poured olive oil onto a white plate then dribbled balsamic vinegar across the sparkling green puddle. 'But I'm really glad to have met you, Lilly.'

He offered her a piece of bread and she anointed it with the oil and vinegar.

'I'm glad too,' she said, taking a bite.

'You're different to most of the women I meet.'

'What with me being sane and all,' she said.

He laughed. 'There is that. But there's also the fact that you're quite remarkable.' He took a bite himself. 'A bit of a one-off.'

Lilly flashed a wicked grin. 'I bet you used to say that to wives one, two and three.'

'How can you say such a thing?' He placed a hand on his heart as if he'd been shot. 'I'm deeply wounded.'

Lilly took the last disc of bread and Harry cleared the plate away. 'Actually, I'm sure I did say that.' He dished out chilli con carne into bowls and sprinkled them with chopped coriander. 'The funny thing is, none of them were a one-off at all. They were all pretty similar.'

'In what way?' Lilly asked.

Harry took a pensive mouthful and chewed slowly. 'Pretty rich girls without much up top.' He tapped his temples. 'You'd think I'd learn, wouldn't you? Being looked up to and adored gets dull after a few weeks.'

'I wouldn't know,' said Lilly.

Harry wiped his mouth with a napkin. 'Oh come on, I'm certain you've had your share of fans.'

Lilly thought about David and Jack. She was sure that they'd loved her once. But fans? She didn't think so.

'The trouble is, men are intimidated by you,' said Harry.

Lilly nearly spat out her food. 'Intimidated by me? Don't be ridiculous.'

'Of course they are,' Harry roared. 'You're one of the most determined and single-minded people I've ever met. For most men that's quite a heady combination.'

'Is it?'

'You can bet on it, Lilly Valentine.'

'How come you're not intimidated?' she asked.

He winked. 'I don't scare easily.'

They laughed and finished the chilli. Harry picked up the bottle of red wine he'd opened and held it over her glass. 'Just a drop?'

'I'm driving home remember.' She placed her hand over the rim.

'You don't have to,' he said.

'I'll never get a taxi in this weather,' she said.

He held her gaze. 'I wasn't suggesting a taxi.'

Lilly gulped. He looked entirely unembarrassed. Brazen even. And why not? They were both single adults. Alice and Sam were safe with their respective fathers, and she could sneak in before dawn so Sam need never know. David might catch her, but so what?

People had sexual encounters all the time. It didn't have to be complicated, did it? Just honest and mutual attraction.

Did she dare?

She removed her hand from the top of her glass without taking her eyes off Harry and he filled it up to the brim.

Gem sits on Misty's bed, like a piece of meat on a chopping board.

The dressing gown she's borrowed is too big and the underwear beneath is scratchy and uncomfortable.

181

Before she left, Feyza had poured a slug of vodka into a cup of coffee and pushed it into Gem's hands. 'Do what you need for speed him up,' she said and disappeared.

Gem don't have a clue how she's meant to do that so she sips the coffee. It gives her a warm tingly feeling.

There's a knock at the door and Gem sits bolt upright, like they're supposed to when the headmaster comes into the room at school. Only nobody ever does. Bill lets himself in. He looks fatter and balder than before.

'All right, darling?' he asks and sits next to her, his knee touching hers.

Gem nods.

'Good girl,' he says. His voice sounds all raspy like he's been smoking too many fags. 'Has Feyza told you the score?'

Suddenly Gem feels sick. And scared. This ain't like them other times. This is with some bloke who could be her dad or her grandad. She should have told Feyza to fuck off. So what if the house gets shut down? Gem can go back to thieving.

'That fucking Turk would sell her baby for a couple of quid,' says Bill, as if that's a good thing.

Gem don't know what to do, so she don't do nothing.

'Stand there, darling.' Bill points to the spot in front of him, about a foot away, but Gem can't move. 'Don't piss about, darling, we haven't got all night, have we?'

He shoves her by the arm, off the bed, to the place where he wants her. She wobbles in the high heels that don't fit.

'Take the gown off,' Bill tells her.

Her hands are shaking so much she can't undo the belt.

'For fuck's sake,' says Bill and undoes it for her.

The gown falls open.

'That's right, Gemma, that's right,' he says.

She lets it fall off her shoulders and then to the ground.

'Beautiful, Gemma,' Bill says. 'You know what to do.'

She watches his hand go to his flies and wants to tell him that it's Gem, not Gemma, and that she doesn't know what to do. Then she stops short. She thinks about what Misty told her. How this is all about putting on a front. Playing a part. She looks down at the body that don't look like her own in the skimpy underwear, and she knows that it don't belong to Gem. It belongs to Gemma. And that Gemma knows exactly what to do.

She lets her fingers run between her chest and down her stomach, letting them rest on the seam of her knickers.

Bill is in full flow now, his hand moving up and down like a piston, grunting like a pig at an abattoir.

'Yes, Gemma.' Spit flies out with his words.

And Gemma does what she needs to do to speed things up.

Lilly felt dizzy as Harry kissed her throat, opening one button of her shirt with a steady hand.

She hadn't even finished the glass of red wine he'd poured for her but her head was spinning. She felt drunk and reckless.

'Would now be a good time to suggest moving to the bedroom?' Harry asked.

This was the moment for Lilly to change her mind. For her to fasten her top and head home. That was the sensible thing to do.

'I think now would be a very good time,' Lilly replied.

He stood in front of her and held out a hand. She took it and he pulled her to her feet and into a tango embrace, leading her from the sofa, cheek against hers, arm outstretched.

When they reached the bedroom door, giggling like children, he spun her around and kicked it open with his heel.

'*Olé.*'

'Don't you need a rose in your teeth?' Lilly asked.

'All out of fresh flowers.' Harry patted himself down, found a pencil in his back pocket and stuck it in his mouth sideways. 'Any good?'

'You might get lead poisoning.'

He took it from his mouth and threw it over his head, behind him. 'Let no one question the lead in my pencil,' he said.

Lilly kissed him. A man who was sexy and funny had walked, quite by chance, into her life. That the same man seemed to fancy the pants off her seemed pinch-point lucky. But here she was, a foot from his bed.

Suddenly, he swept his arm under her and scooped her off the floor.

'Put me down,' Lilly screamed.

'Who says romance is dead?'

'You'll break your back,' Lilly laughed.

He took a step forward. 'My lady is as light as a feather.'

'My lady weighs not much less than a donkey,' said Lilly. 'Now put me down, you daft sod.'

Undaunted, Harry staggered forward, Lilly kicking her legs. When he reached the bed he dropped her unceremoniously, where she landed with a bounce and collapsed into another fit of giggles.

'And you call me a one-off,' she said.

He crouched beside her, his face serious. 'That's because you are.'

'Thank you,' Lilly answered softly.

They looked at one another for a second and, as he moved towards her, Lilly closed her eyes.

Then his mobile rang.

Lilly opened her eyes.

'I'll ignore it,' said Harry.

'Okay,' said Lilly.

But they both knew what one another were thinking. What if something was wrong? What if there was a problem with Chloe?

The ringing stopped and Harry smiled. 'Obviously wasn't important.'

The mobile rang again.

'I think you'd better take it,' said Lilly.

Harry pressed his lips together and answered. 'Harry Piper. This had better be good.'

Lilly watched him as he listened. His face remained impassive, giving nothing away.

'I see,' he said a number of times. 'I understand.' Then he put his phone away.

'Everything all right?' Lilly asked.

Harry smiled, but this time there was no certainty in it. 'I don't think it is, Lilly,' he said.

'Chloe?'

Harry nodded. 'She's had a complete breakdown and had to be sedated.'

'What happened?'

Harry exhaled and looked away. 'She's saying that someone came into her room after lights out.' He shook his head as if he couldn't believe it. 'She's saying she's been attacked.'

As Lilly pulled up in the Range Rover outside the Grove, she put her hand on Harry's arm.

'We don't know the full story yet,' she said.

Harry's face was stony. 'I told her I would keep her safe. I made a promise.'

They got out of David's car and hurried through the snow, Lilly wobbling in her high heels. Once inside, they were met by Elaine Foley.

'How is she?' Harry asked.

'Not great,' Foley replied.

'Do you think she's telling the truth?' Lilly asked.

Foley looked her up and down with a knowing smile. Lilly's pencil skirt and heels told the nurse what she needed to know.

Lilly jutted out her chin, determined not to worry about the judgement of others. 'Could it be a delusion?'

'It could be,' said Foley.

'I need to speak to her.' Harry's tone was urgent and he swept away, up the corridor.

Lilly tottered after him, cursing her shoes. Finally, he stopped outside a door and punched in a code. Inside, Chloe was on the bed, lying on her side, one arm dangling, motionless, over the side. Though she was wearing a T-shirt and hoody, her bottom half was naked. Mountains of white dimpled fat, punctuated by a flash of black pubic hair.

'Talk to me, Chloe.' Harry crouched down beside his patient. 'Tell me what's happened.'

Chloe didn't reply but blinked her recognition that he had spoken.

'Chloe, it's me, Harry,' he said. 'Tell me you're okay.'

She blinked again and this time a single tear coursed down her cheek.

Lilly entered the room, her heels clicking an annoying rhythm. She kicked them off and padded her way to Chloe. At the bottom of the bed was a discarded sheet, which Lilly retrieved and placed over her client.

'Thank you,' Chloe whispered.

'You're welcome.' Lilly kept her voice soft. 'Do you need anything else? A drink?'

'Water.'

Lilly nodded and went to the sink to fill a plastic cup.

'There you go.' She held the cup to the girl's lips and let her take a mouthful. 'Enough?'

When Chloe nodded, Lilly removed the cup and wiped the girl's chin with her finger.

'Please tell us what happened, Chloe,' Harry said, his voice jarringly loud.

Chloe just shut her eyes, so Lilly went back to the sink, poured away the remaining water and waved Harry over.

'I don't think Chloe is going to want to discuss this with you,' she told him.

He looked shocked. 'I'm her doctor.'

'You're also a man,' said Lilly. 'Think about it.'

He opened and closed his mouth, then looked back at Chloe on the bed. 'Do you think she'll talk to you?' he asked.

'I'll certainly try my best,' Lilly replied.

He went back to the bed and took the limp arm in his hand. 'I'm going to leave you with Lilly. You can trust her.'

When Chloe didn't answer, he held her hand a little longer, then left them alone. Without Harry, the room seemed empty and when Lilly spoke she half expected an echo.

'I need to ask a few questions, okay?'

Chloe nodded.

'Did you tell Nurse Foley that someone came into your room after lights out?'

'Yes.'

'And is that true?'

Chloe's voice was small but clear. 'Yes.'

'Who was it?'

'I don't know,' Chloe said. 'It was dark and they drugged me.'

'How did they drug you?' Lilly asked.

Chloe pushed back the sheet to reveal the flesh of her thigh and tapped her finger. There amongst the pockmarked skin was a red dot. It was fresh.

'What happened then?' Lilly asked.

Chloe shook her head. 'It's hard to remember.'

'Just try.'

Chloe pushed the bridge of her nose with her thumb as if she were trying to force her memory to work. 'They definitely took me somewhere.'

'Where?'

'I don't know. It was pitch-black and small and smelled like something.'

'Like what?' asked Lilly. 'What did it smell like?'

'Soap.'

It was a hospital, the whole place smelled like soap.

'What next?' Lilly asked.

'It's all jumbled up,' said Chloe. 'There was something cold against my face. Then my arm was pulled tight behind my back.'

'Go on.'

'Then something was inside me, stretching me, pulling me.'

Lilly kept her words deliberate. 'Are you saying you were raped, Chloe?'

'I thought I would break in two.'

'Can you be sure?' Lilly asked. 'You said yourself that it was confusing.'

Chloe sucked in a breath and hauled herself up, so that she was sitting on the bed, her legs over the side, covered in the sheet. Slowly she removed the sheet and opened her legs. The smell of sweat hit Lilly. Along with the smell of blood. And the smell of sex.

'It hurts,' Chloe said. 'It really hurts.'

Jack's mobile woke him. He checked the time. Who in God's name would ring at this hour? He checked caller ID and panic gripped him. It was Lilly.

'What's wrong? What's happened?'

Kate sat up in bed next to him, her eyes full of concern.

'Nothing's wrong,' said Lilly. 'At least not with me.'

188

'Do you know what time it is?' Jack asked.

'Did I wake you?'

Irritation gave way to the old-fashioned feeling of being mightily pissed off. 'Of course you bloody well woke me!'

He waved at Kate to go back to sleep and got out of bed.

'I need to talk to you about Chloe,' said Lilly.

Jack closed the bedroom door behind him. 'You've got to be kidding me.' He realized he was shouting and dropped his voice. 'You're calling at four in the morning to chat about a case.'

'Not exactly.'

'Not exactly,' Jack hissed. 'Then what exactly? Because this can't go on, Lilly.'

'I don't know what you mean.'

'I mean you and I are no longer together, that there is nothing between us.'

There was silence on the line.

'We have a daughter between us,' said Lilly at last.

Jack groaned in frustration. 'Yes, we do, but that is all. The rest is over. You ended it remember?'

'As I recall, you had some part in it,' she said.

Jack snapped his mouth shut. He refused to be drawn into another discussion as to what he had supposedly done. He hadn't got anywhere during the eight hundred other similar discussions, had he? He was sick and tired of defending himself.

'Ancient history, Lilly,' he said. 'Doesn't matter who said what and who did what, we've both moved on.'

'I know that, it's just—'

He interrupted her. 'Why on earth are you calling, Lilly? I'm a copper and you're a defence lawyer so we can't have cosy chats about our cases. Especially not in the middle of the night.'

There was a pause and when Lilly spoke again her voice was cold and distant. For once it didn't sting.

'I was calling to inform you about something urgent,' she said. 'Something that couldn't wait for you to get your beauty sleep.'

'Such as?' Jack snapped.

'Chloe has been raped.'

It was a sucker punch. Full-fisted.

'You're joking,' he said.

'Don't be ridiculous, Jack. Chloe was drugged and sexually assaulted, so I suggest you get yourself and a rape team down here pronto.'

She hung up, leaving Jack shivering in the shadows.

I creep back to bed, forcing a smile away. Honestly, I have to push the corners of my mouth down with my fingers, like I used to do to my baby sister.

Everything is working out beautifully.

When Jack comes back into the bedroom, his face is white.

'Is there a problem?' I ask.

'I need to get over to the Grove,' he says, pulling on the T-shirt he discarded earlier. 'Chloe's been raped.'

'Oh dear,' I say.

Jack's face tells me I didn't get that one right. 'Sorry,' I say. 'Bit disorientated.'

His face softens and he touches my cheek. 'Is it okay to leave you in charge of Alice?'

'Of course it is.'

When he leaves, I snuggle into his pillow and inhale him. It's a bit disappointing that she actually did have a genuine reason to call him, but it's his reaction that matters. And Lilly's reaction to his reaction.

I think I can safely predict that by the end of today they will wish that they had never met.

★   ★   ★

190

Lilly's head whirled. It was imperative that she concentrate on Chloe, but she was still reeling from her conversation with Jack. Yes, it had been difficult to navigate their separation, but she'd always assumed that whatever happened, they'd retain their respect for one another.

The door to Harry's office opened. It was the man himself.

'Did you call the police—' He stopped mid-sentence. 'You look awful.' When Lilly didn't answer he rushed to her side. 'It's a shock, I know.'

She couldn't tell him it wasn't just the rape that was making her spin. 'I'm fine,' she murmured.

He took her face in his hands, pushing her hair back from her forehead. 'We'll get through this.' He looked into her eyes. 'All of us.'

She grabbed hold of his waist and held on tight as if the world had begun to crack beneath her feet and she were afraid of falling through the fissures.

'Listen to me, Lilly.' He made her name sound like a musical note. 'If we stick together, we can do this.'

He was right. Let Jack think what he liked. She didn't need his good opinion.

'I have to get myself together before the rape team arrive,' she said. 'Splash my face with cold water and what have you.'

Harry nodded and released her. When she got to the door, she turned and found him watching her.

'You, me and Chloe,' he said.

'You, me and Chloe,' she repeated.

In the ladies' room, Lilly cupped her hands under the tap and brought water up to her face. Then, her cheeks still dripping, she leaned against the sink.

Her reflection in the mirror made her grimace: skin winter-pale, eyes ringed with smudged mascara. With her untamed hair, she looked like the Joker from Batman. As for the outfit, could anything be less appropriate than a pencil skirt and heels?

'Pack it in,' she told herself. This was going to be hard enough without worrying about how she looked. Harry understood. They had to batten down the hatches and pool their energy.

Outside the toilets, Lilly bumped into Jack.

'Good morning,' he said.

Politeness stiffened Lilly's mouth. 'Good morning. What did you do with Alice?' she asked.

'I left her alone with a bottle of bleach and a packet of matches,' he replied.

Lilly sighed and they walked together towards Chloe's room, where the rape team were waiting.

'This is Doctor Hicks,' said Jack.

Lilly shook hands with a woman in her fifties, grey hair cropped in a boyish style.

'And DI Crofton,' Jack continued.

The second woman was younger, her handshake less firm, the palm clammy. Probably nervous.

'Lilly Valentine. I'm Chloe's solicitor.'

'Can I verify the details?' Hicks pulled out a notebook and Crofton scrambled to follow suit.

'Chloe is a patient here,' said Lilly. 'She's held under the Mental Health Act and has been for some time.' She let the women write it down. 'A few days ago she informed her doctor and I that she and at least one other patient were being habitually abducted from their rooms and raped.'

'Why didn't you call us then?' Hicks asked.

It was a question, not an accusation, but it stung all the same.

'Chloe isn't well,' she said. 'She sometimes says things that aren't true. I didn't believe her and I let her down.'

'But you're in no doubt this time?' asked Hicks.

Lilly shook her head.

Hicks put away her notebook and picked up the small plastic case at her feet. It was time.

Lilly knocked on the door and they entered. Chloe was lying on the bed, clutching the sheet under her chin.

'This is Doctor Hicks and DI Crofton,' Lilly told her, then she shut the door on Jack. 'They're here to gather any evidence they can about what's happened to you, Chloe. They want to try to find out who did this.'

'Hello, Chloe.' Hicks's voice was professional but not intimidating. 'I'll explain what I'm doing as I go along, but if at any time you need to stop or ask a question please do.'

When Chloe didn't answer, Hicks bent to her suitcase, unsnapped the locks and brought out white forensic gloves for herself and Crofton.

'Let's start with your hands,' she said. 'Do you know if you scratched your attacker?'

Chloe gave a shrug.

'She thinks she was drugged,' Lilly explained. 'She remembers very little.'

'Not a problem.' Hicks moved seamlessly to the bed. 'Forensics can fill in lots of gaps.' She took Chloe's right hand. 'Let's cut the nails and swab the fingers. If there's anything there, I'll find it.'

'Like what?' Chloe asked.

'Skin, hair, blood.' Hicks brandished a pair of nail scissors and Crofton moved forward to catch the clippings in an evidence bag. 'You name it, I can trace it.'

Hicks stopped and let out a little puff of air. Chloe's nails were already bitten to the quick. No chance of finding anything under there.

'We'll scrape instead.' Hicks slid away the scissors and produced a wooden stick, which she used to scrape around the nail and cuticle of each finger, dropping it into the bag when she was finished. Crofton immediately sealed the bag and labelled it.

Armed with a cotton bud, Hicks then wiped each finger from tip to knuckle. The room was so silent Lilly could hear her own breathing. At last Hicks finished and the bud was bagged away.

When Hicks next spoke, it seemed impossibly loud, though Lilly knew she was keeping her voice deliberately low. 'If you're ready, I'll begin the intimate samples.'

Chloe didn't reply.

'Do you understand what I'm going to do, Chloe?' Hicks asked.

Lilly felt sick. Chloe was a child. This was all very, very wrong.

'Let me explain,' said Hicks. 'First, I'll wipe the whole area, then I'll comb through your pubic hair. Finally, I'll take a vaginal swab as gently as possible.'

Lilly inhaled through her nose in an attempt to quell her nausea. It didn't work.

'Is that okay, Chloe?' Hicks asked.

When no answer was forthcoming, Hicks moved forward to peel away the sheet, but Chloe clung to it.

'What's wrong, Chloe?' Hicks asked.

Chloe gulped, her throat bobbing. 'I've wet myself,' she whispered.

'Not an issue,' said Hicks. 'I've seen a lot worse.'

Chloe didn't move but hung on to the sheet.

'Can I hold her hand?' Lilly asked.

'Of course,' Hicks replied.

Lilly prised away one of her client's hands and threaded her fingers through. The girl held on tight.

'It's going to be just fine,' Lilly told her.

Chloe nodded but her grip told Lilly she didn't believe it. It tightened again as Hicks finally removed the sheet and got to work. Lilly tried not to look too closely. It was enough to see

Hicks dropping bloodstained wipes and swabs into evidence bags with alarming efficiency.

'Almost there, now,' Lilly said, as much for her own benefit as for Chloe's.

At last, Hicks straightened. 'Vaginal exam complete.'

Chloe allowed herself a tiny sigh. But Lilly had caught the look on Hicks's face. There was a but. And a big but at that. A but as dark and as ominous as a rain cloud.

'But looking at the tissue damage, I should do an anal exam too,' said Hicks.

Bile filled Lilly's throat and she fought to swallow it.

'I'm so sorry, Chloe,' said Lilly. 'I'm so very sorry.'

Chapter Nine

Transcript of 999 call made from 077231823471

Date: 28 August 2007

Time: 15.30

Operator: Emergency services. Which service do you require?

Caller: Help me.

Operator: I'm going to do all I can to help you, madam. Can you . . .

Caller: Please . . . [begins to cry].

Operator: Can you tell me where you are, caller?

Caller: 62, Longdale Avenue in Luton.

Operator: Thank you and can you tell me your name?

Caller: Debs, I'm called Debs.

Operator: Okay, Debs, just try to stay calm and tell me what you need. Police, fire or ambulance?

Caller: Police. No, ambulance. I . . . [crying].

Operator: That's okay, Debs, I'll get both for you. You're doing really well. Now can you tell me what's happened?

Caller: I don't know. I got back home and let myself in and there's just so much blood . . .

Operator: Are you hurt, Debs?

Caller: No.

Operator: Is anyone else hurt, Debs?

Caller: I can't . . . [groans] . . . Oh my God, I can't . . .

Operator: Listen, Debs, officers will be with you any moment, so just take a deep breath and tell me what you can see.

Caller: Blood. I can see blood on the floors and walls and kitchen cupboards.

Operator: Can you see where it's coming from, Debs?

Caller: There's no one down here.

Operator: Should anyone be home, Debs?

Caller: The kids . . . [crying] and my husband. He was supposed to be looking after them. Oh God, where are they?

Operator: Can you see them, Debs? Can you hear them?

Caller: I need to check upstairs.

Operator: It might be better to wait for the officers to do that, Debs.

Caller: They might need me . . . [sound of footsteps].

Operator: Debs?

Caller: . . . [sound of breathing].

Operator: Debs, can you still hear me?

Caller: . . . [screams].

Operator: Debs, can you speak to me? Can you let me know you're okay?

Caller: It's the dog.

Operator: What about the dog, Debs? Has he hurt someone?

Caller: . . . [crying].

Operator: Has the dog attacked anyone, Debs?

Caller: No . . . [crying] . . . She's killed him. She's killed the fucking dog.

The cottage was empty.

Lilly thanked her lucky stars and chucked her keys onto the kitchen table. What she wanted more than anything was to rid herself of the stupid skirt and take a shower.

She poured herself a large glass of orange juice and headed upstairs, turning on the jet of water with her free hand. When it was as hot as she could stand, she chugged down the juice, stripped off her clothes and dived in.

She stood there for a few moments, hoping to scald away her inertia, but she was bone-tired and her neck could barely take the weight of her head. She felt sapped of everything. Energy. Concentration. Hope.

When had the world become such a terrible place?

Her work had always brought her into contact with people who lived in the shadows. Those who saw the vulnerable as fair game. But in all her years, she hadn't seen anything like this. A child without a home or parents. A child with a fractured mind. A child no one would believe. Who would target such a child? Who could be that manipulative?

The thought of such a person made Lilly want to vomit, so she opened her mouth and let it fill with scorching water.

The things that had been done to Chloe were unthinkable. Lilly spat out the water at her feet.

How dangerous would someone like that be? Dangerous enough to kill?

Her questions were interrupted by a thud outside the bathroom. Lilly froze. She listened. Apart from the hiss and fizz of water and steam, there was nothing. Her imagination was playing tricks on her. No great surprise in the circumstances.

Thud.

Lilly held her breath. No mistake this time. Someone was in the cottage. In Lilly's bedroom.

She looked around for something with which to protect herself. The side of the bath was littered with empty shampoo bottles and small slivers of soap welded to the enamel. Around the rim of the sink were some discarded balls of cotton wool, a toothbrush and a half-used tube of cream that was supposed to work miracles on cracked heels. As makeshift weapons went, none seemed promising.

Shit.

Lilly grabbed a towel. Whatever she was going to do, she wasn't going to do it naked.

Thud.

This time Lilly jumped. The chill of fear rippled across her hot pink skin.

Maybe she should stay in the bathroom? The intruder would soon work out that there was nothing worth nicking and leg it. Then again, maybe he hadn't come to steal. Maybe he knew she was alone. She gulped down her panic. Maybe she should run at him? Hopefully he would be terrified and make his escape. What would be best? Lilly's mind screamed and her chest constricted; all the while, the noise outside the bathroom got louder.

Jesus, she had to do something. It might be the wrong something. But it was better than nothing.

She tucked the towel under her arm, swallowed and launched herself at the door.

'Aaaaggghhhh.'

'Aaaaggghhh,' Sam screamed back.

The towel fell at Lilly's feet.

'OMG, Mum.' It wasn't clear whether Sam's disgust was in respect to Lilly's sudden appearance or the sight of her naked body.

'Sam?' Lilly scrambled to cover herself. 'What are you doing here?'

He waggled a bare foot at her. 'Looking for socks.'

'You scared me to death.'

'Why?'

'I didn't think anyone was in.'

Sam scratched his head and sniffed. 'So, can I borrow socks or what?'

Lilly nodded and made for the bed. Her knees were shaking so much she had to support herself against the wall.

'Where's your dad?' She sank onto the bed. 'Where's Alice?'

Sam opened her bedside drawer and rummaged through the mismatched knickers and bras.

'Jack brought her back not long ago,' said Sam.

'Did Jack say anything to Dad?'

'I answered the door,' said Sam, holding up a fishnet stocking and raising an eyebrow. 'Dad's taken her for a walk in the snow.'

Lilly snatched the stocking from him. 'That's nice of him.'

'It's extremely nice of him,' Sam said. 'Considering.'

'Considering what exactly?' She was in no mood for one of Sam's observations about his baby sister's 'crazy ways'.

'Considering that Alice isn't his daughter,' he replied.

Lilly gave a nod. David didn't have to do anything with Alice if he didn't want to. That said, she didn't have to let him crash on her sofa.

At last Sam found a pair of socks. Well, not a pair, but one black and one navy were as near as damn it in the Valentine residence.

'It doesn't matter how much he tries, does it?' Sam sat next to Lilly with a plop. 'You'll never forgive him, will you?'

'I forgave him a long time ago, love.'

Sam shook his head. 'Not properly.'

'He'll always be your dad, nothing can change that.'

'But you'll never let him be a part of the family again.'

'He has a new family now,' said Lilly.

Sam pulled on the first sock. It had a hole in the heel and Sam's skin peeped through. A spud, Lilly's dad used to call them.

'He's not living with them,' Sam pointed out. 'He's living here.'

'Only until he sorts himself out,' said Lilly. 'He doesn't want to be here permanently.'

Sam pulled on the other sock and looked at his mum sideways. 'You sure about that?'

'Yes.'

He smiled, patted her on the arm and left the room, abandoning Lilly to wonder what the hell all that was about.

Gem checks her reflection. There ain't a full-length mirror in the flat. Only half on Mum's wardrobe door. The top bit's missing so she has to bend down to see her face. It got broke when they had to move last time. A midnight flit 'cos of the rent arrears. Mum paid two blokes from down the hallway to move their stuff. They didn't have a proper van or nothing, just one of them cars where you can lay the back seat flat. Well, what can you expect for twenty quid?

Gem told 'em they'd never fit the wardrobe in there, but they were having none of it.

She kneels down and examines the skin on her cheeks, her neck and her chest.

She don't look no different.

To be honest, she don't feel no different.

Mum stirs in the bed. 'What you doing?' she asks Gem.

'Nothing.'

Mum leans over the side of the bed and fingers through an ashtray until she finds a dog-end worth lighting.

'Where's the baby?'

'Watching telly,' says Gem.

Mum lets herself fall onto her back, takes a mouthful of smoke and blows it up at the ceiling. 'Is it still snowing?' she asks.

'Yeah,' says Gem.

'I might take Tyler up the park later,' says Mum.

Gem looks at her Mum smoking her fag, then back at herself in the mirror.

Nothing's changed. Nothing at all.

★ ★ ★

Lilly was still rattled as she made herself a cup of tea. She wrapped her dressing gown even tighter, as if the fabric itself were holding her together. She supposed she should finish her shower and wash her hair, but right now her bones felt as if they'd been replaced by lead piping.

She heard the door open and David speaking softly to Alice, telling her to slip off her boots so she wouldn't tread snow through the house. Despite the fact she couldn't yet walk. One of Cara's legacies. Botox Belle kept a wooden cupboard in the hallway, which housed sets of slippers. You took a pair and put your shoes in the space. Like a bowling alley. If you had an umbrella, Cara would roll it and place it neatly at the base of the coat stand. Lilly had only ever had a coat stand once, but Sam mostly ignored it and threw his school blazer over the banister. And Jack owned his leather jacket and nothing else so it had stood there resentfully half used, like a tree towards the end of autumn knowing the next strong wind would see it entirely bare.

When David arrived in his socked feet, he was holding Alice on his hip.

'Hello, Mummy,' he said, waving her hand up and down.

Lilly took her daughter from him. 'How was your walk?'

'Great.'

Lilly spotted the encrusted snot around Alice's nose and knew that it had probably been mixed at best.

'How was your hot date?' he asked.

Lilly sighed and rested her chin on top of Alice's head. 'We had to leave before pudding to go and see Chloe.'

David's eyes widened.

'Turns out she was telling the truth,' said Lilly. 'There is a rapist at the Grove.'

'Oh my God,' said David. 'Is she all right?'

Lilly pictured her client on the hospital bed, her skin quivering while Dr Hicks tried to collect samples from her vagina and anus.

202

'No, she's not all right at all.'

'You can't start blaming yourself, Lilly.'

'Can't I?' Lilly's eyes filled with tears. 'If I'd just listened to her in the first place . . .'

'Stop.' David's voice was firm.

'You don't understand.'

'Yes I do,' he told her. 'I understand that when you take on a case you give your all to your clients and that's always been one of the things I admire most about you.'

Lilly let out a hollow laugh. 'I can't even remember the number of times you've told me to pack my job in.'

David sank into the chair next to hers and took her hand. His skin felt cold. 'I only ever told you that because it doesn't make you happy, Lil.'

'Of course it does.'

David shook his head. 'No it doesn't and it never has. Look at you now. You're drained and miserable.'

'I'm not.' Lilly forced a smile. 'I'm just knackered because I was up all night and then Sam scared the crap out of me when I was in the shower.'

'It's okay, Lilly, you are who you are and I get that now.' His tone was sincere. 'Better late than never, eh?'

They sat for a second, hand in hand, as they had done years ago, when Lilly had thought she had found the man who she would love for the rest of her life. The man who changed the lyrics of songs to fit her name. The man who once gave her a piggyback down Boulevard Saint-Germain in Paris because her feet were killing her.

'One good thing to come out of this,' said David, breaking the spell.

Lilly removed her hand and picked up her tea. 'What's that then?'

203

'You can now prove Chloe didn't murder that other girl,' he replied.

Maybe it was lack of sleep, but Lilly couldn't follow his thread.

'Think about it,' said David. 'You've been saying that the most likely killer is the person attacking the patients, but the police didn't buy that because there wasn't anything tangible to prove there even was an attacker.'

The light bulb went on in Lilly's brain. Jack had all but dismissed Chloe's account as a convenient fiction invented after the event. But now there could be no argument. Chloe had been telling the truth all along.

The incident room was quiet. Most of the team were out taking statements and the couple of bodies who had stayed at the nick were methodically inputting data into the computer system.

Jack tried to do the same. He needed to log the notes he'd taken earlier, particularly Dr Hicks's preliminary findings, but he just couldn't settle.

He looked up at the whiteboard covered in scribbles, arrows and photographs. Bang in the centre was one of Lydia Morton-Daley. It was a holiday snap given to Jack by her parents. She was wearing denim shorts and a bikini top, shielding her eyes from the sun, half smiling into the camera.

Next to it was a mugshot of Chloe, her face round and white like a mound of dough waiting for the oven.

Jack had been certain she'd killed Lydia. Sure, she'd come up with the story about a mystery rapist, but not until after he'd found the knife with her prints all over it. And where had he found it? Hidden in Chloe's bedroom, for the love of God. He'd looked at the evidence and come to a rational conclusion. The same conclusion any copper would have come to.

So why did he feel so bad?

He went back to his notes and began to type half-heartedly with two fingers until Kate passed the open door and mouthed the words 'you okay?' at him. Though most of the nick knew they were together, they'd agreed not to make it obvious in work.

Jack shrugged so Kate came in, checking around, ensuring the other officers were busy.

'Is it true then?' she whispered.

'Depends what you're talking about,' he replied.

'That Chloe was raped last night.'

Jack rubbed his face. He needed a shave.

'It's true,' he said.

'Shit.'

Yup. That about summed it up. Not only had he arrested the wrong person for Lydia's murder, he'd also allowed the real perp to swan around until he struck again.

'We're lucky she's not dead.'

Kate cocked her head to one side. She always looked sweet when she was perturbed. 'I don't think you can make that leap of faith, Jack,' she said.

'No?'

'No.' She splayed her hands on the desk. Her fingers were long and slender, the nails short and clean and perfectly round. 'Just because it transpires that Chloe was telling the truth about the rapist doesn't mean she was telling the truth about killing Lydia.'

'From where I'm sitting it's the most logical explanation.'

Kate pressed her lips together. They were covered in something with a slight sparkle that caught the light. God, he wanted to kiss her.

'You only think that because you're upset,' she told him. 'You're looking for reasons to blame yourself.'

'Wouldn't anyone?'

Kate hesitated as if choosing her words with care. 'Initially, they would, yes, but then they'd start to reassess the evidence.'

'Don't you think I've been doing that all morning, love?'

She gave him a small flash of the eyes at his familiarity but he was past caring.

'Sometimes it's hard to see the wood for the trees,' she told him. 'Especially when you haven't had any sleep.'

He smiled at her and opened his palms, indicating that she should carry on.

'The sad fact is that girls like Lydia and Chloe are abused all the time. I bet you could go into any mental hospital, prison or drugs rehab and find a victim of rape.'

'You reckon?'

Kate nodded her head. 'There are people who take advantage of the weak.'

Jack knew it to be true. Half the working girls in Luton had been lured onto the game by nasty bastards looking for easy pickings in the care homes.

'But murder?' Kate continued. 'That's a world away from having sex with someone just because you can.'

'Maybe whoever killed Lydia did it to avoid detection for the rape,' said Jack. 'Maybe it was just a straightforward cover-up job.'

'It's possible,' said Kate. 'But it was hardly straightforward, was it? I mean, why would you carve a message into her?'

'To fit Chloe up?' Jack suggested. 'You kill Lydia then carve her up so you can plant the knife.'

Kate rolled her eyes. 'Isn't the most likely scenario that it was Chloe who killed Lydia? She's extremely ill and volatile, who knows what goes on in that mind of hers.'

'But what about the rape? I mean, we know it did happen.'

'Unconnected,' said Kate.

Jack exhaled. 'You really think so?'

'I really do,' she said. 'It's a red herring. Obviously the defence will seize on it, but it's a red herring all the same.'

'So where do we go from here?' he asked.

'You're the senior officer in the case.' She winked at him. 'But if it were me, I'd demand Chloe's records going back to the year dot, then we can all see how crazy this girl is.'

'I bet they'd make interesting reading.'

'Too right,' said Kate. 'Oh and I'd also haul in that shrink of hers for questioning, insist he stop protecting Chloe and start explaining what exactly is wrong with her.'

At last Jack smiled. Harry Piper was just the type of man Jack detested. Smug and over-entitled. If he were a copper he'd be on the fast-track programme. Dragging him into an interview room would give Jack great pleasure.

Standing in the reception area of the police station, Lilly was fired up.

After her conversation with David, she'd dashed back to the shower, then headed straight out to speak to Jack. She was determined to make him see that Chloe's rape proved beyond all doubt that she wasn't involved in Lydia's death.

'Can I help you?' asked the copper without any enthusiasm. Front desk duty was everyone's most hated job.

'I'd like to speak to Officer McNally,' said Lilly. 'He's with the MCU.'

The lad (and he was most definitely still a lad) ran his finger along a list of names and extension numbers.

'Is he expecting you?'

'Not exactly.' Lilly watched the finger hovering over the phone. 'We're working a case together and it's vital I see him.'

The lad sighed. He might only be seventeen, but he was clearly already weary of everyone and his wife declaring their case urgent.

'Tell him it's Lilly Valentine.' She slid her card across the desk. 'He'll want to see me.'

The lad gave a shrug and dialled the number.

'No answer,' he told her.

'He could be away from his desk,' Lilly pointed out. 'You should try his mobile.'

The lad sighed even more theatrically and punched in the number for Jack's mobile phone. As he waited for an answer, he picked at a scab on his neck until it began to bleed.

'Gone to voicemail,' he said.

Lilly tried to be patient and smiled. 'Could you call one of his colleagues and find out where he is?'

'I don't know who his colleagues are,' he said. 'It's a big station.'

Lilly bit her tongue. It was hardly Scotland Yard and it wasn't beyond the wit of man to try someone else in MCU. Was there any wonder so many people had no faith in the police if this disinterested teen was their first point of contact?

She was about to spell out what the copper should do when she spotted a WPC she recognized skipping through the snow outside the door. Lilly abandoned the extra from *The Inbetweeners* and headed after the WPC. Someone had tried to clear away a path outside but it had frozen over in the night and made the pavement more treacherous. Lilly cursed as she tried not to fall on her arse.

'Excuse me,' she called out to the younger woman who was moving with impressive speed towards the car park. 'Hello there.'

Damn, what was the WPC's name? Lilly had met her first in court and then again at the Grove when the knife had been found in Chloe's room. God, Lilly's memory was hopeless. And it should be easy to conjure up, because she remembered it rang a bell.

Kate. Lilly snapped her fingers. That was it. Kate.

'Hey, Kate,' Lilly yelled.

The WPC was almost at the entrance to the car park when she halted and turned. She squinted at Lilly and frowned.

'Sorry to bother you.' Lilly trotted towards her, slipping and sliding, her arms flapping. 'I don't know if you remember me.'

'Of course I do.'

'Oh good,' said Lilly. 'It's just that I'm looking for Jack McNally and I wondered if you might know where he is.'

The WPC didn't smile. 'You used my first name.'

'Sorry,' said Lilly, with a nervous laugh.

'How did you know my first name? Did Jack tell you?'

Blimey, this one was hostile. Lilly was used to it of course. As a defence brief she was rarely greeted with warmth. 'I think Jack used your name when we met at the Grove,' said Lilly. 'It kind of stuck in my mind.'

The WPC stared hard.

'I need to speak to him about the Chloe Church case,' she said. 'There have been some developments.'

The WPC folded her arms. 'You mean the rape.'

The way she said the words, so blunt and cold, made Lilly shiver.

'You think Jack should drop the charges against your client,' said the WPC.

Lilly folded her own arms and stared right back at the other woman. Being suspicious of the defence was one thing, but this was taking the piss.

'I think I should speak to the officer in the case about it,' she said. 'And that would be DI McNally.'

'He won't change his mind,' said the WPC.

'I beg your pardon?'

'Jack and I discussed it earlier.' She gave a smile. Well, not really a smile, more the pulling of her facial muscles into the facsimile of one. 'He's pushing on with the charges against your client.'

Lilly felt her jaw slacken and instantly clenched her teeth. Jack had been running it past this pair of frosty knickers? Why? She wasn't even on the team, was she?

'We're both in complete agreement about the fact that the rape is unimportant,' the WPC added.

'Unimportant?'

'I think Jack described it as a . . .' The WPC scratched her temple. 'Ah yes, now it's come to me. He described it as a red herring.'

Lilly was incredulous. Jack was one of the most intelligent and thoughtful coppers she had ever met. It was the thing she most loved about him. Or had been. The old Jack would never have used any of those words about a brutal attack on a vulnerable child. Then again the old Jack would never have used this piece of stone as his sounding board.

'So where is he?' she asked.

The WPC gave that weird pretend smile of hers. 'I believe he's making an arrest.'

'Who?'

'I don't think I'm at liberty to tell you that.'

'Never mind, love.' Lilly caught sight of Jack's car pulling into the car park. 'I'll ask him my bloody self.'

I have to suck in my cheeks to stop myself laughing. When you know people are watching you have to react in a certain way. Like when Jack's looking at my mouth. I use lip balm so they'll stick together just a fraction of a second.

But this is all so funny that I'm struggling.

First of all the ex accosted me outside the station. She looked ridiculous tottering about in the snow. I thought she might fall at one point, which would put me in a difficult position, wouldn't it? Leave her in the slush or touch her.

DARK SPACES

I tried my utmost to explain to her that there was no point harassing Jack because he'd already made his decision about the fat girl, but some people just don't listen.

Then when Jack arrived, she almost leapt at him, making some very snide comments about me I might add. Apparently, he shouldn't be discussing the case with 'a junior officer'. He was about to put her firmly in her place when lo and behold she spotted the nasty little shrink in the car.

'Is this a joke?' she screamed.

'No joke,' Jack replied.

'Then do you mind telling me why the hell you've arrested Harry?'

Honestly, I thought she'd jump out of her (not very firm) skin.

'Perverting the course of justice,' said Jack.

Then she made this choking noise in her throat and for a second I thought she might have some sort of fit.

'And what exactly is he supposed to have done?' she yelled.

'I don't think this is the time or place to go into it,' said Jack.

'Fine.' She put her hands on her hips. 'I'll see you inside.'

Then she bent forward and spoke to the shrink through the car window. 'I don't know what this bullshit is about, Harry, but rest assured I'll sort it out.'

Like I say, too, too funny.

We watch her now, sloshing her way back to the station entrance, the bottoms of her trousers getting soaked through.

'Someone's very cross with you today,' I say.

'She's always bloody cross with me,' Jack replies.

'I don't understand it,' I say. 'You're just doing your job. It's nothing personal.'

He nods but carries on watching her receding figure.

'You'd better get His Lordship booked in pronto.' I nudge Jack with my hip and cock my thumb at the shrink still sat in the back of the car. 'We don't want Miss Valentine to blow a gasket.'

At last he turns and smiles at me. 'I suspect that horse has already well and truly bolted.'

He's correct of course. I've wound her up like a clockwork toy. Sorry, Jack, but it's for your own good.

Jack gave the custody sergeant Piper's details as quickly as possible. Piper wasn't making any problems but Jack wanted to get him out of the custody area sharpish, if only to get away from Lilly's eyes, which were boring into the back of his neck with the subtlety of a pneumatic drill.

She was too involved in this case. Sure, she always gave every client her full commitment, but this was worse than usual. It was as if she'd decided that Jack was the enemy, when all he was doing was investigating a crime. Nothing personal, Kate had pointed out, making it sound so sensible and reasonable. But Kate was sense and reason personified. Lilly on the other hand . . .

As the sergeant neared the end of the custody sheet, he looked up at Lilly with an innocent smile. 'You're Mr Piper's solicitor, I take it.'

'Yes,' she snapped.

Jack felt sorry for him. He'd schlepped into work despite the weather and was probably hoping for a quiet shift, only to be faced with the full force of angry Valentine.

'I have to check these things,' said the sergeant. 'Just in case.'

'Just in case what?' Lilly threw out her arms. 'I couldn't have exactly wandered in could I?'

'Well, no . . .'

'I mean I couldn't be on my way to the shops and have taken the wrong turn could I?' Poor guy. Lilly was on a roll now. 'Or maybe you thought I sneaked in, is that it?'

'Of course not . . .'

'I'm sure you must get that a lot? People sneaking in for a look at the secret workings of the custody suite?'

The sergeant went pink. 'You might be Mr Piper's appropriate adult.'

'Does he look under eighteen to you?' Lilly nodded her head towards Harry.

'Why don't you just give the sarge your details, Lilly?' said Jack.

Lilly glared at him, removed a card from her breast pocket and pressed it into the sergeant's hand. Why did she have to be like this? Why did she have to be so difficult?

'It would waste a lot less time if you just told the sarge who you are,' he said.

'Waste time?' Lilly shouted. 'You've arrested Harry on some ridiculous charge and you're lecturing me on wasting time?'

'It's not a ridiculous charge,' said Jack.

'Then tell me what evidence you've got because from where I'm standing it looks to me like the case against Chloe is collapsing and you're clutching at straws.'

Keep calm, Jack, keep calm.

'I asked Dr Piper for Chloe's medical records and he refused to furnish them,' he said. 'I also asked him some questions about his patient and he refused point-blank to discuss her.'

Lilly narrowed her eyes. 'That's it? That's all you've got?'

'The information is imperative,' said Jack. 'By refusing to cooperate, Dr Piper is deliberately hindering the police in their investigation.'

Lilly swivelled on one foot to face the custody sergeant. 'Can I use interview room three to speak to my client?' She didn't wait for him to nod, but simply took Harry's elbow and led him to the room in question. When she got to the door, she looked over her shoulder. 'I'd call up to the chief super if I were you and give him the heads-up that if this turns out to be as big a pile of shit as it sounds, he's about to have his arse well and truly sued.'

When the door slammed, the sergeant let out a breath. 'I bloody well hope you know what you're doing with this one, Jack.'

Jack let out a laugh. He was sure he knew what he was doing, wasn't he?

'My God,' said Harry. 'When you mean business there's no stopping you, is there?'

'He had no right to arrest you,' she said.

Harry shrugged. 'I guess he's just doing his job.'

'No way,' said Lilly. 'He has completely overstepped the mark here.'

Harry perched on the corner of the table in the middle of the room. Signs of tiredness were etched around his eyes.

'You don't have to discuss your patients with the police,' she said.

'I know.'

'In fact you shouldn't discuss them with the police.'

Harry smiled. 'I know.'

'Jack knows perfectly well that what he's asked you for isn't on,' said Lilly.

'Then what's he up to?'

Lilly held up her index and middle fingers. 'Two things. First and foremost, he's digging. He knows Chloe's case is on the skids and he's looking for anything that might prop it up.'

'And the second thing?' Harry asked.

'He's making this personal.'

'Why would he do that?'

Lilly's throat felt tight. She wanted to tell Harry the truth about her relationship with Jack, but she couldn't bring herself to do it. The fact that she hadn't mentioned it before would make her look like a liar. Which, she supposed, was exactly what she was.

'Jack and I go way back,' was all she could manage.

'You've battled it out on cases like this before?'

She should tell him. It was completely wrong not to tell him. 'Yes,' she said, sickening yellow bile of cowardice sweeping through her.

'And I'll bet you've beaten him too.' Harry leaned forward. 'You've got to understand, Lilly, that loss of pride and loss of face can be a very destructive force on the psyche. Especially in men.'

Lilly nodded and rushed from the room.

Outside the interview room, Lilly tried to keep the disdain from her voice. 'This is beneath you,' she told Jack.

'Just doing my job.'

'Carry on like this and you won't have one,' she hissed.

He looked as if she'd just shot him at close range.

'Don't give me the injured puppy routine,' said Lilly. 'You've dismissed the rape of a child as unimportant and now you've nicked her psychiatrist on some trumped-up charge when she needs him most.'

Jack smoothed his tie. 'That's just the way it's come out.'

Lilly shook her head. Once upon a time she wouldn't have believed this of Jack if the Pope himself had sworn it to be true.

'Who are you, Jack?' she said.

'A copper,' he answered. 'Nothing more, nothing less.'

'Well, I don't recognize you at all.'

Lilly and Jack glared at one another across the desk. The introductions had been made and he'd read the caution to Harry.

'I can see you're champing at the bit to say something, Miss Valentine,' Jack said.

'Not especially,' Lilly replied.

'Really?'

Lilly shrugged. 'Given how idiotic this whole situation is, I've told my client that he is well within his rights to refuse to answer any of your questions.'

'So he's going to give a "no comment" interview?' Jack let out a snort. 'Having failed to cooperate at his office, I can hardly say I'm surprised by that.' He poured himself a plastic cup of water. 'Though a jury might, of course.'

Lilly sighed. 'Who said anything about a "no comment" interview? I may have told my client that he doesn't have to say a word if he doesn't want to, but it transpires there are quite a few things he does have to say to you, officer.'

Jack took a sip of water and wiped his lips with his thumb. 'Excellent.'

Harry cleared his throat but Jack held up his hand.

'If I can just stop you there, Dr Piper,' he said. 'There's a time-honoured tradition in police interviews. I ask the questions and then you answer.'

'There's a time-honoured tradition of having evidence before making an arrest,' Lilly muttered.

Jack ignored her and smiled at Harry. Harry smiled back. 'Fire away.'

'A couple of hours ago I called you in your office at the Grove and asked if I could come and see you to discuss Chloe Church,' said Jack. 'And you agreed?'

'Of course,' said Harry.

'Yet, when I arrived and asked you to tell me about Chloe's condition, you declined to do so.'

'That's correct,' said Harry.

'And when I asked that you furnish me with a copy of her medical records you also refused.'

'Indeed.'

'Your actual words were . . .' Jack took out his notebook and began thumbing through the pages.

'Let me save you some time, Officer McNally,' Harry said. 'My actual words were "Over my dead body."'

Jack tapped his notebook with a nod. '"Over my dead body." Interesting turn of phrase wouldn't you say?'

'Not particularly.'

'Really? Given the circumstances involved?' Jack asked. 'One of your patients has been murdered, yet you refuse to help the police?'

Harry gave a laugh that turned into a groan, then morphed yet again into a sigh.

'Officer McNally, how long have you been in the force? Let me guess, fifteen years, maybe twenty? Either way, someone of your rank and length of service must have heard of the Hippocratic oath.' He didn't wait for Jack to reply. 'Let me refresh your memory. It's an oath that dates back to Ancient Greece and it sets out the ethics involved in being a medical professional. I will prescribe regimens for the good of my patients according to my ability and my judgment etcetera, etcetera. Ringing any bells now?'

'What do the Ancient Greeks have to do with the murder of Lydia Morton-Daley?' asked Jack. 'A girl who was in your care? A girl who was your patient?'

'Oh, but they have everything to do with my patients, officer.' Harry rubbed his scalp with his knuckle. 'You see the oath goes on to say a lot of things and it culminates in probably the most important promise a doctor can make. All that may come to my knowledge in the exercise of my profession or in the daily commerce of men which ought not to be spread abroad, I will keep secret and I will never reveal.'

Jack looked unimpressed.

'Patient confidentiality,' said Harry.

'Lydia is dead.'

'But Chloe is not.'

HELEN BLACK

Jack leaned forward on his elbows. 'Are you seriously telling me you'd put this oath before a murder?'

'Are you seriously telling me you've come across any doctors who didn't?'

'Lots of doctors provide information,' said Jack.

'Without their patients' consent?' Harry widened his eyes. 'I don't believe you.'

'Are you saying Chloe withheld her consent?'

'I'm saying I have no idea.' Harry threw his arms out to his side, catching Lilly's shoulder. 'You didn't give me any chance to discuss it with her, did you? You just waltzed into my office and demanded her notes.'

'I gave you notice.' Jack pointed at Harry. 'I called you before-hand, which would have given you ample opportunity to ask for her consent.'

'I had no idea you were angling for that,' said Harry. 'When you told me you wanted to discuss Chloe, I assumed you meant her rape. Stupid I know to think the police might just be interested in catching the person who did that, given how dangerous such a person would be and the fact that they are still at large. Instead you arrest me and drag me here.'

Lilly decided it was time to draw matters to a close. 'I think, Jack –' she lowered her voice to the volume she used on Sam when screaming and wailing were having no effect '– that you need to take some advice from your superior officer.'

When Jack left the room, Lilly let out a gasp of delight. 'And you say I'm good.'

'Was I okay?' Harry asked.

'Okay? You were bloody fantastic,' she laughed. 'When you said you thought the police might just be interested in investigating the rape, I could have kissed you.'

Harry took her hand. 'Well, don't let me stop you.'

Chapter Ten

Form C15
Application for contact with a child in care.
Section 34(2) and (3) Children Act 1989
Date Issued: 02/01/2008
The Court: Luton County Court   **Case Number:** 139 65 08
**The full name(s) of
the child(ren):**   **Child(ren)'s number(s):**
Phoebe Talbot   6012-6015
Arianne Talbot
Nathalia Talbot
Mimi Talbot

Your relationship to the child(ren):
Sister
**The order applied for and your reason(s) for the
application.**
**(If you are relying on a report or other documentary
evidence, state the date(s) and author(s) and enclose a
copy.):**
The applicant Gigi Talbot seeks an order for contact with her
sisters.

On 17/02/2004 the applicant and her siblings were
removed from their parents and placed into the care of the

local authority. A full care order was made on 4/12/2004 and the care plan provided by the local authority confirmed that the children would be allowed to continue to see one another.

However in May 2006 the applicant was informed by Social Services that contact with her younger sisters had been suspended in order to facilitate their foster placement.

Since then she has not been allowed to see or speak to them despite the fact that the adoption placement in question has broken down, as did the subsequent foster placement and that the girls are now separated, with Mimi and Nathalia living in a placement in Wales, Arianne in a placement in Brighton and Phoebe currently in a specialist unit in the Bedford area.

It is the applicant's contention that having no contact with her has not helped, that in fact it has hindered their ability to make proper attachments. Phoebe in particular has deteriorated to the point that she is now considered a danger to herself and others.

The applicant believes that the mental health of all concerned will benefit from regular contact and attaches the report of Dr Piper dated 28 December 2007.

Lilly drove Harry home, pulling up outside his apartment block.

'Want to come in for a coffee?' he asked.

The twinkle in his eye told Lilly he was suggesting more than a hot drink, and after his performance at the station she was tempted.

'I think we both need some rest,' she said.

'We can drink it lying down,' he said.

Lilly laughed and gave his shoulder a playful punch. 'I have to get home to Sam and Alice,' she said. 'David has been a godsend but I can't leave him in charge much longer.'

Harry smiled, opened the door and slid out into the snow. His breath turned the air white. 'Sure?'

'Get thee behind me, Satan,' she said.

He winked and headed off. When he reached the entrance, he turned and held his forefinger and pinky to his ear like a phone. Lilly nodded, waved and sped away.

It was idiotic at her age to be so excited that a man was going to call her. She should grow up. The trouble was, Harry was such an appealing man. The way he'd put Jack in his place. So calm and collected. A ripple of pleasure ran up her spine and she shivered. Bloody hell, she had got it bad. Time to get home and do some work on the case. That should cool off her jets.

Gem gives a massive yawn.

She's properly knackered. Bill has already been this morning and said he's coming back later. It ain't like she has to do that much, but somehow it takes it out of her.

She yawns again and goes back to the washing up, scrubbing at a lipstick mark on the rim of one of the mugs.

'You'd better start getting yourself ready, Gem,' Feyza tells her.

See, that's another thing. The getting ready for Bill. It don't take two minutes to get all the gear on. Though she's getting quicker with the slap that's for sure. But it still takes time that she should be spending doing the sheets and bins and that. The girls like it all cleared up as soon as a punter's gone and Gem don't blame 'em. When Bill shuts the door behind him, she runs to the sink to wash him off.

'I wish he'd only come once a day,' she says.

Feyza frowns. 'Be glad he keen.'

Gem don't answer. She's glad of the job, 'course she is. And the extra money Feyza gives her, Gem's well glad of that. Another twenty quid every time. She don't even have to since Bill ain't paying, but Feyza says it's only fair. She might be an old witch but she is fair.

'What you spend your money on?' Feyza asks. 'Clothes?'

Gem scratches the mug with her thumbnail. She ain't spent any of it yet. She's hidden it inside a sock in her bedroom and ain't even told Mum. She might start asking awkward questions. Well, she probably wouldn't seeing as she really don't even ask where Gem goes each day, but Gem ain't chancing it. Anyway, she'll only get it into her head that they need something: a new fridge or a bed for Tyler. To be fair, they do need a new fridge and a bed for Tyler, but not before Gem's paid off the Slaughter brothers.

Gem plans to go see the bald bastards tonight. She's gonna find out exactly how much Mum owes and if it's a hundred quid she's gonna give it to them then and there. Once that's all squared, Mum's nerves should get a bit better. Then they can sit down with some catalogues and look at fridges and beds.

'You know Bill say to me that you are first girl he like in long time,' says Feyza.

Gem nods and puts the mug on the draining board.

'He say to me you are special,' says Feyza.

'Special needs more like,' says Gem.

Feyza gives one of those freaky laughs and wags her finger. 'Funny girl.'

It ain't that funny, is it?

'Serious, Gem.' Feyza's face drops. 'You can make lot of money if you want?'

Gem frowns and wipes her hands on the tea towel. 'How many times a day does he want to come over?'

'Not just Bill,' says Feyza. 'He have lot of friends.'

Gem gulps. How many is Feyza talking about? Two or three? More?

'I wouldn't have time what with all the rooms to do and that,' says Gem.

'You give this up of course.' Feyza waves a hand at the sink as if she can make it disappear by magic. 'You work like other girls.'

Gem shakes her head. Letting Bill wank over her is one thing, but she ain't ready to become a tart.

'Good money.' Feyza rubs her thumb and finger together. 'Plenty of good money for girl like you.'

Gem shakes her head again and pushes her way out of the kitchen. 'I've got to get ready,' she mumbles.

Lilly needed socks and, like Sam that morning, she couldn't locate a pair, but her feet were too cold to care. She eventually pulled on one red fluffy ankle sock and one orange and black number that came up to her knee. She pushed it down, noting that she looked like a reject from *Fame*.

Alice gurgled at her.

'I know, I know,' said Lilly. 'Gok wouldn't be impressed.'

To be honest Gok probably wouldn't like her tracksuit bottoms either, with their ripped knee and pockets full of washed-in tissue rubble. Or her fleece for that matter. She'd bought it when she and David had taken Sam to Lapland. He'd been four years old.

'Still, you know what they say,' Lilly told her daughter. 'It's what's on the inside that counts.'

Alice blew a spit bubble and rolled over to the corner of the room where she began biting the edge of the carpet. Lilly moved to stop her, but Alice gave a pre-emptive shriek.

'Have it your way,' Lilly said and prayed there was nothing toxic in the underlay.

Why did babies like to suck and chew stuff? True, most favoured hands, fingers and dummies, but Alice lived to be different. She was her mother's daughter after all. Lilly wondered if she'd been awkward at Alice's age and felt the familiar stab of sadness that her mother wasn't around to share stories. How she would have loved to hear tales of how she used to rip up the Vinylay with her bare teeth.

The sound of canned TV laughter interrupted her thoughts as it seeped through the floorboards. David and Sam were watching back-to-back episodes of *Two and a Half Men*. Lilly had been tempted to join them but she needed to crack on with some work.

She opened an A5 notebook and began scribbling notes and thoughts in no particular order. First there was Lydia: a beautiful ball of self-destruction. Lilly could well believe that she would threaten to lift the lid on what was happening to the girls at the Grove with no thought for her own safety. Had she paid the ultimate price? It certainly looked that way. But who had killed her? Lilly had originally thought it must be someone with a link to the hospital: a worker, a visitor, a patient. But Chloe's rape, as horrific as it was, had narrowed the field of suspects significantly.

Someone had got into Chloe's room. Someone had got past Harry's secret code. How many people could have managed that? Not many.

She reached for her mobile and called Harry.

'Missing me already?' He sounded sleepy.

'No . . . I mean not . . . what I'm trying to say is . . .'

'Lilly,' he laughed. 'I'm teasing you.'

Lilly laughed back. Of course he was teasing her.

'So what can I do for you?' he asked.

'I was thinking about Chloe,' she said.

'Okay.'

'And I was thinking about who could have got access to her room.'

There was a pause on the line and Lilly could hear Harry breathing.

'You put a code on her room door, didn't you?'

'I did.'

'It was Alice's birthday, wasn't it?'

'Yes.'

'Then one of the people who knew the code must have attacked Chloe.'

There was another silence, but this time no breathing.

'How many people had the code?' Lilly asked.

'Three.'

Bloody hell. Lilly hadn't realized it would be so few.

'That's great, Harry.'

'Is it?'

'Absolutely,' said Lilly. 'If there are only three possible suspects, that's going to make it relatively easy to work out who did this.'

'Actually, there are two,' said Harry. 'The three includes me and I'm pretty convinced that I didn't do it.'

Two. Unbelievable.

'Who are they, Harry?'

He let out a sigh full of misery.

'Harry?'

'You have to understand Lilly, that these are people I trusted implicitly,' he said. 'If I had had any doubts at all, I would never have given them the code.'

'I know that,' said Lilly.

'I can't believe it of either of them, even now.' There was genuine pain in his voice. 'I can't even say their names.'

Lilly wished she were there to put her arms around him. 'Listen,' she said. 'You don't have to say their names. Just take a few minutes to yourself and then email me.'

Harry let out a noise somewhere between a cough and a sob. 'Lilly Valentine, you are one in a million.'

Jack stood at the chief super's desk. The office had been redecorated since he'd last been inside and the walls were now a quiet shade of duck-egg blue. The blinds were new too. Not the standard issue white plastic venetian tat that everyone else had to put up with, collecting dust on every slat, the strings broken and tangled so that half the rooms in the nick only ever got sunlight through a triangular-shaped gap to the bottom left-hand side.

There was a ban on uniformed overtime, but the chief needed his rattan blinds.

'What the hell is going on, Jack?'

'Sir?'

'Don't play silly buggers with me,' said the chief. 'I hear that the Morton-Daley case is going pear-shaped and that you've just arrested the most senior psychiatrist at the Grove.'

Jack licked his lips. The nick was half empty but someone had been telling tales out of the classroom.

'Take a seat, Jack.'

The chief super pointed to a chair tucked into the corner of the office. Why couldn't the man have it the other side of his desk like a normal human? It wasn't that it was heavy or difficult to move, it was just that Jack felt an eejit dragging it across the room. A scenery mover at the theatre, not one of the players.

He spent longer than necessary getting the chair into position. He wanted to make a point, though he wasn't sure what the point was. At last he sat down.

'Tell me what's going on, Jack.'

'Just pursuing legitimate lines of inquiry, sir.'

The chief put his elbows on the desk and steepled his fingers at nose height. A movement Jack had seen a hundred times and recognized as a prelude to a bollocking.

'You made an arrest on the Morton-Daley case, I hear,' he said.

'I did,' said Jack. 'Another patient at the Grove called Chloe Church.'

'Solid evidence?'

'Very solid,' said Jack. 'Morton-Daley's body was mutilated and we found the knife used in Church's room.'

'Prints?'

'All over it.'

'So why haven't you put this thing to bed?' asked the chief. 'Why isn't this thing on its way to trial?'

'We got delayed when the kid had some sort of an episode and had to be sedated,' said Jack.

'Sedation lasts twenty-four hours at the longest.'

The implication was clear.

'Unfortunately we hit another stumbling block,' said Jack.

'It had better be a concrete block to hold up a murder job.'

'The kid was raped,' Jack told him.

'What?'

'Someone got into her room at the Grove and raped her.'

'Was it a bad one?' the chief asked.

Jack wondered if there could ever be a good one. 'It was pretty bad, sir.'

The chief super exhaled, his breath making a slight whistle. 'That's rotten luck.'

Jack wasn't sure if he meant for Chloe or the investigation.

'And what about the psychiatrist?' The chief peered down at a solitary Post-it note stuck to his desk. 'Harry Piper?'

Someone had been telling very detailed tales out of school.

'He worked with Morton-Daley and Church,' said Jack.

'I know that.'

'I think he has a lot of information that could help this investigation,' said Jack.

The chief carefully peeled off the Post-it note, folded it into quarters, then placed it into his empty waste bin.

'Such as?'

'Such as whether Church has ever been violent before. Such as whether her condition makes her unfit to plead,' said Jack. 'Hell, we don't even know why she's in there. For all we know she's been fantasizing about all this for years.'

'You want her medical records,' the chief super said.

'Too right,' Jack replied.

'And this Piper chap refused?'

'He did.'

'So you arrested him?'

'I did.'

'He had his patient's consent, did he?'

Jack coughed and smoothed his non-existent tie.

'Tell me he had his patient's consent to release,' said the chief.

'There was a misunderstanding, sir.'

'God's teeth, Jack, why the hell did you arrest him?' asked the chief. 'He can't give you anything without consent.'

'All to do with Ancient Greece, I understand,' said Jack. 'If you want my opinion, it's a pile of shit. Doctors shouldn't be above the law.'

The chief closed his eyes and sighed. 'Tell me he's not suing.'

Jack remembered that Lilly had threatened exactly that.

'I'm telling you now,' said the chief, 'if he sues, your days as a DI are numbered and I won't be able to protect you.'

Jack couldn't think of a time the chief super had ever protected anyone but himself.

'Piper's not the type to sue,' he said.

'You'd better pray you're right about that,' said the chief. 'And you'd better pray he doesn't get himself a decent lawyer.'

'Yes, sir.'

'In the meantime get a court order for the medical records like you should have done in the first place,' said the chief. 'Then put this bloody mess to bed.'

Alice had fallen asleep on the carpet, saliva dribbling down her cheek and pooling in the fibres. Lilly toyed with putting her into her cot, but even the gentlest of touches could wake her, which would mean running the risk of an Alice-style meltdown.

Instead, Lilly left her where she was and draped a blanket over her. A social worker wouldn't approve, but they didn't have the devil child to deal with, did they?

She grabbed her laptop and tripped down the stairs in search of food. Sam was still glued to the television, but David was in the kitchen, rummaging in the fridge.

'I haven't managed to get to the shops,' she said. 'What with the snow and this case, there isn't a free minute.'

'I'm thinking it's got to be pasta,' said David, extracting a few puckered cherry tomatoes from the fridge, each a small, red kiss.

Lilly headed to the cupboard. It wasn't bare but it wasn't bulging Nigella style either.

'We've enough to cobble something together,' she said. 'Hopefully things will have calmed down tomorrow.'

David peered out of the kitchen window. Despite the hour, heavy-bellied white clouds bleached the sky. 'I wouldn't put money on it,' he said.

Lilly retrieved a jar of black olives and a bottle of extra virgin olive oil. 'Things should definitely be more quiet at work anyway. I've pretty much solved Jack's case for him.'

David poured boiling water into a pan and dropped in a few handfuls of spaghetti.

'How did you manage that little trick?'

Lilly sniffed a piece of Parmesan. It was past its best, but it would have to do.

'I've got the names of the only two people who could possibly have raped Chloe.' She glanced at her laptop. 'Or at least I will have any moment now. Then all Jack has to do is match up the DNA.'

'Will it really be that straightforward?'

Lilly reached for the cheese grater. 'I don't see why not.'

Right on cue, a ping sounded from Lilly's laptop. She opened the email from Harry. All it contained were two names:

1. Elaine Foley.
2. John Staines.

'Everything okay?' David asked.

'Yep,' she said and joined him at the window.

A wind had got up, haranguing the tree branches and rattling the cottage woodwork.

'There's a storm coming,' David said.

Gem pulls up her hood against the cold. The wind feels like there's ice inside it, jabbing at her cheeks.

She said she wouldn't be long, three-quarters of an hour tops, but it's going to take her longer in this weather. She hopes Feyza don't go mental at her. It ain't as if she's messing around or nothing, but it's really hard to even walk in this.

She fights her way through the Clayhill, to the address she's been given. It ain't far from their own block as it goes.

It weren't hard to find out where the Slaughter brothers lived. She just asked a few people on the estate. Nobody questioned why she wanted to know. People round here are always needing a bit of help to tide them over. It's not like they can just rock up at a cashpoint, is it?

Once, when Gem was in foster care, the woman used to do her big shop on a Saturday and on the way she'd stop at the bank to do 'business'. That made Gem laugh 'cos she thought it meant doing a shit. Thing is, she'd never been in a bank before. Turns out the woman meant paying in cheques and taking out some cash. Plus, she always got a statement. Gem remembers the look on her face as she checked the printout. Proper smug it was.

'There you go.' She used to shove it under Gem's nose and tap one of the numbers with her finger. 'My little gravy train is what you are.'

She was all right as it goes. Better than some of the others. At least she left Gem to get on with it and didn't keep asking her how she was feeling.

When she gets to the door, she suddenly feels nervous. The Slaughters ain't exactly friendly. Then again, she's come to give them money, so they shouldn't be too unhappy.

She knocks on the door and waits, moving from foot to foot because it hurts if she keeps them in one place for too long. She needs thicker socks. With no holes either. When she's sorted all this, she'll make a shopping list, maybe go into town tomorrow.

At last someone opens the door. It ain't either of the brothers. 'What?' he asks.

He's a small, black geezer with about twenty chains round his neck. There's no way they're real gold.

Gem pulls off her hood. 'I need to speak to the Slaughters.' The wind hits her from the side, making her ear throb.

'About?'

He's a proper cocky little arsehole, giving it the big 'I am', thinking he's hard because he works for the hard boys, when all he's doing is opening their door.

'I've got something for them,' she tells him.

Someone from inside the flat shouts, 'Shut the fucking door, will you.' It sounds like one of the brothers. 'You're letting all the fucking heat out.'

'Wait here,' says Mr Cocky and bangs the door in her face.

Gem blows on her fingers. She can't remember ever being so cold in her life and there's been a million times when they've had the gas and leccy cut off.

The door opens again and Mr Cocky nods his head for her to go in. He kicks the door shut behind her, like he's using some karate move. Gem walks down the corridor to the lounge. Their flat's got the same layout, plus the telly's on proper loud.

She opens the door and finds the brothers sat on a settee, smoking and watching porn.

'She says she's got something for you,' says Mr Cocky.

The younger brother looks up from the telly and frowns. 'Jesus fucking Christ, she's dripping every-fucking-where.'

Gem looks down at herself and the ice crystals falling off her coat onto the carpet.

'And she's got fucking shoes on,' the brother shouts.

'Take them off, you silly cunt,' Mr Cocky tells Gem.

'You're calling her a silly cunt?' The brother laughs. 'You're the silly cunt who fucking let her in.'

At least that's something Gem can agree with him about.

'Get 'em off,' Mr Cocky says, so she bends down and takes off her trainers, but they've already left two wet marks on the carpet.

'Look at that,' the brother snaps. 'Put them by the fucking door.'

Mr Cocky grabs Gem's trainers and scuttles away with them.

'You'll fucking clean that up as well,' the brother shouts after him. Then he turns to Gem. 'So, what do you want?'

Behind him, the other Slaughter brother hasn't even bothered to look at her. He's just staring at some girl on the telly while someone out of shot shoves a dildo up her arse.

'I don't know if you remember me,' says Gem.

''Course I fucking remember you,' says the younger brother. 'Do you think I've got fucking Alzheimer's?'

'I didn't know how many people you deal with,' says Gem.

'Too fucking many.'

Gem knows that as far as men like these are concerned, there can never be enough people borrowing money. If silly mugs like her mum dry up, they might have to get a job or something.

'So how much do you want this time?' he asks.

'I don't want to borrow any money,' says Gem.

'Then what the fuck are you bothering me for?'

'I've come to pay back what Mum owes early.'

Now both brothers look at her proper shocked. They don't say nothing so the room just fills with the sound of screaming from the telly.

'Oh, baby,' the woman shouts at the hand and the dildo. 'All the way, baby.'

It don't look to Gem like there's any further for the dildo to go.

'How much have you got?' asks the older brother.

'Enough,' says Gem.

He grinds his fag out in the ashtray on the coffee table.

'She borrowed forty didn't she?' Gem asks.

'That's right,' says the older brother. 'Plus the cost of our wasted visit.'

'Plus interest,' the other one chimes in.

Gem nods.

'It comes to a round hundred,' says the older one. 'You got that, have you?'

Gem reaches into her pocket, pulls out a roll of notes and holds it out. 'It's all there. You can check.'

The younger Slaughter takes the notes from her and counts them out. 'Fuck me.' He hands the cash to his brother. 'Where did a little fucker like you get that?'

'Don't matter,' says Gem. 'Just cross my mum off your list all right?'

They don't answer her so she turns to leave. When she gets to the door, Mr Cocky is waiting, her trainers in his hand, a stupid grin on his face.

'You'd better get in there and clean up the mess,' Gem tells him.

'And you better get back out there and do some more grafting,' he says.

'Ain't your business what I do,' she tells him.

He lets out a laugh and Gem can smell stale fags and beer on his breath. 'You're gonna need more cash to give us.'

'I ain't giving you nothing,' says Gem. 'I've sorted it.'

'Don't be fucking stupid,' says Mr Cocky and opens the front door letting in a blast of freezing air. 'You'll make your payments like usual.'

Gem tries to grab her trainers from him. 'I told you I've sorted it.'

Mr Cocky laughs again then with a swift jab that Gem ain't expecting he pushes her outside into the snow.

'Your silly slag of a mother came round earlier today,' he says. 'She needed a bit to tide her over.'

Gem shakes her head. 'You're lying.'

'Shut that fucking door,' one of the brothers roars from inside.

'You're lying,' Gem screams, her feet burning with cold.

Mr Cocky throws the trainers past Gem and over the balcony.

'Tell me you're lying,' Gem is crying now.

But he just laughs and shuts the door.

I pour Jack a tumbler of whiskey and dig out two ice cubes from a tray in the freezer. They stick to my thumb and burn the skin.

'Join me, Kate?' he says, when I hand him his glass with a chink, chink, chink.

I don't drink alcohol of course. I can't abide the sensation of being out of control.

'Just a small one,' I say with a cheeky smile and splash some in a glass for myself.

Over the years, I've learned to bring it to my lips when people are watching and spit it out when they're not. I love the subterfuge of it all, if I'm honest. A small thrill in a dull day. And so much better than explaining myself.

There have been a couple of occasions when I've thrown caution to the wind and knocked it back. Those occasions didn't end well.

Mummy used to call her evening glass of gin 'medication'. She thought that was funny. Oh, how we laughed.

I've had my share of medication. Thorazine, Mellaril, Risperdal. Tiny white and blue pills that steal away your life. Not in a dramatic whoosh, you understand, more a gradual unravelling. After a while you can only watch as who you are floats away like dead leaves in a slow-moving stream. At first they dance around in the water, just out of reach, but still in sight, until piece by piece you realize they've gone.

A girl with very long, very black hair taught me how to hide the pills under my tongue and spit them out later. I wonder what became of her?

'Did you sort out a court date for the medical notes?' I ask.

'Kerry's on it.' He means the fat prosecutor. They've been on the phone all evening. 'She'll let me know first thing.'

'I think the whole thing's ridiculous,' I say.

'Too right.'

'Since when were doctors above the law?' I say.

Jack waves his now empty glass in my direction, the ice cubes rattling at the bottom. 'That's exactly what I tried to explain to the chief.'

'What did he say?' I ask, giving him a refill.

'What do you think?' Jack takes a gulp. 'He told me I'd better pray Piper doesn't have a good solicitor.'

'Why?'

'In case he sues,' Jack replies, his voice slightly blurred around the edges.

I shake my head. 'I know you and Lilly have been having a few small problems . . .'

'Small?'

'Okay. I know you two have been having some pretty huge difficulties lately,' I say. 'But I don't believe she would ruin your career like that.'

'No?' He looks into his whiskey as if the answer might be hiding in there.

'No.' My tone is firm. 'You're the father of her child after all.'

235

He takes another long sad drink and I top him up again.

'Are you trying to get me pissed?' he asks.

'You look like you need it,' I tell him.

As much as I dislike drinking myself, I've always enjoyed watching others do it. That way you can retain control of yourself and take away the other person's. With men like Jack you don't even need to take it. They just hand it to you gladly.

'Look,' I say. 'I'm no fan of the way Lilly's behaved recently, but she wouldn't ruin your life to make a point. No way.'

Jack pats my leg. 'You always think the best of people, Kate.'

Chapter Eleven

Luton Express and Star
Date: 16/03/2008
Judge Attacked in Family Court

Police were called yesterday to an incident at Luton County Court when a twenty-year-old woman let off a fire extinguisher in the face of a judge.

His Honour, Hugh West, was hearing an application by the young woman to be allowed contact with her younger siblings who are in foster care, but when he explained that would not be possible she became angry.

'At first she was just shouting and swearing,' said Carlton Reed, who works as a security guard in the court. 'To be honest, I felt sorry for her because she only wants to see her family.'

Carlton confirmed that the young woman's solicitor tried to calm her.

'She gave her a glass of water and tried to make her see sense,' he said. 'The problem was some of her witnesses hadn't turned up to give evidence so the judge's hands were tied.'

Unfortunately, just as everyone believed the situation was under control, the woman grabbed the fire extinguisher from the wall.

'I thought she was going to throw it,' Carlton said. 'But she managed to get it working and fired it straight into the judge's face.'

Mr West was taken to hospital and, although shocked, has not suffered any lasting injuries.

The twenty-year-old, who cannot be named for legal reasons, was arrested and is due to appear in Luton Magistrates' Court today.

Lilly made herself a cup of tea and stretched her sleep-sodden legs. Today she was going to have a quiet one. She was going to play with Alice, take a walk in the snow, go out to the shops and cook for everyone. She thumbed through a cookbook, mentally tossing up between slow cooked beef and fish pie. Either would provide the rib-sticking comfort she craved this morning.

'You working today?' Sam looked over Lilly's shoulder.

'Nope,' she said.

'Amazeballs.'

'Is that even a word?' she asked.

'It is if you're under sixty.'

Lilly tried to bat him around the head but he ducked away.

'Have you seen your dad?' she asked.

'No.' Sam looked worried. 'Isn't he here?'

'I don't think so,' Lilly replied. 'He wasn't on the sofa when I got up.'

'What did he say last night?' Sam asked. 'Did he mention he was going out?'

Lilly laughed. 'I'm not his mum.'

'You don't think he's gone back to Cara do you?'

'I doubt it,' Lilly said. 'He's left his manky razor in the bathroom.'

Sam frowned, anxiety etched across his forehead.

'Would it be such a bad thing if he did go home?' Lilly asked. 'Little Flora needs her dad.'

'I need my dad.'

Lilly smiled at him. Sam had loved having David around. He'd been so much less moody with Lilly and much more accommodating of Alice. But would it hurt all the more when David did leave? Would it open up all those old wounds?

The unmistakable sound of a key rattling in the lock came from the front door, followed by David swearing as he tripped over the recycling.

'Dad?' Sam's face lit up. 'Dad, is that you?'

David ambled into the kitchen holding a supermarket carrier bag of food in each hand. 'Who were you expecting?' he asked. 'Still, I suppose it's possible anyone could turn up to see your mother.'

Lilly went to bat him around the head, and he attempted the same manoeuvre as Sam to evade her. But he lacked his son's speed and she managed to give him a smart clip around the ear.

'Is that any way to treat someone bearing gifts?' He held the bags aloft.

'Bloody hell,' said Lilly. 'You must have been waiting outside when the doors opened.'

David dropped his bags on the kitchen table and began to unpack. 'They said on the news last night that hardly any delivery vans were making it through to the shops so I thought I'd better grab what they had.' He picked up a bag of frozen cod fillets. 'Pretty poor pickings, I'm afraid.'

'No worries.' Lilly tapped her cookbook. 'I was planning fish pie.'

'See, Sam.' David rubbed his hands together with a grin. 'What a team your mum and I make!'

'You da' man,' said Sam holding up his palm.

'No, you da' man.' David high-fived him.

Lilly gave an indulgent sigh and opened her laptop.

'I thought you weren't working today,' said Sam.

'Just checking my emails,' Lilly replied.

In fact, she was looking for something from Jack, but there was nothing. The previous night she had sent him a note, informing him of the two names Harry had given her and suggesting he run them past the CPS. She'd kept the whole thing short and formal to avoid misunderstanding.

Jack was tired and hungover. He'd drunk far too much whiskey last night and hadn't been able to sleep. Every hour, on the hour, he'd got out of bed and reread Lilly's email.

Kate put an arm around his shoulders. 'You need something to eat.'

She was right. His gastric juices needed something to work on apart from alcohol and fury.

He put a slice of bread in the toaster and pulled margarine from the fridge, but when he removed the top, the sight of the oily softness turned his stomach.

When the toast popped, he took a bite and chewed the dry mouthful, fighting the urge to heave. Then he looked at the email once again.

To: Jack McNally
From: Lilly Valentine
Subject: Chloe Church

As you are aware, it is part of Chloe Church's defence that both she and Lydia Morton-Daley were repeatedly sexually assaulted whilst in the Grove. It is also her contention that the perpetrator of said attacks is likely to be the perpetrator of Lydia Morton-Daley's murder.

To this end, Dr Harry Piper has compiled a list of those individuals who had access to Chloe's room. It is fortunately a very small list and therefore it should be easy and quick to undertake the necessary forensic tests.

The names of the individuals in question are:

Elaine Foley.

John Staines.

I would urge you to contact your lawyer as a matter of the utmost urgency as we will be making an application to the court.

Jack swallowed the toast, gagged and ran for the toilet. With his head down the bowl, he cursed Lilly Valentine one more time. She was a prize-winning, grade-A bitch and he couldn't work out why he had never seen it before.

Poor Jack is in a dreadful pickle.

I can hear him vomiting in the toilet.

I admit I topped up his glass one too many times last night. Mea culpa. But in all honesty, the thing that's made him ill is the email from the ex.

Lilly Valentine really does have the most stupendous timing.

At four this morning, he finally showed it to me, convinced that it is confirmation that she's starting proceedings against him on behalf of the nasty little shrink. Well, of course the email doesn't say that, but Jack's vision has clouded. He appears, quite literally, unable to comprehend English.

I feigned shock and disgust in equal measure. It seemed the right thing to do.

Here he comes now, smelling of bile and mouthwash. Silly sausage.

'I can't believe she's doing this to me,' he says.

'Come on, Jack, she hasn't done anything,' I say. 'Yet.'

He flops into a chair at the kitchen table and I massage his shoulders. His skin feels clammy in my fingers.

'Do you know what the most ironic thing about all this is?' *His head bends forward in defeat.* 'I've bent the rules a million times for that woman. I put my head on the block like an eejit, but it looks like all that's been forgotten.'

'People have short memories,' *I say.*

This is true. It never ceases to amaze me how easily people erase their tiny minds and rewrite history to suit themselves. I never forget anything. Ever.

'When they move on they want to pretend the past never existed,' *I tell him.* 'Especially when there's someone new on the scene.'

Jack turns to look at me. 'Someone new?'

'Oh, ignore me.' *I carry on kneading his shoulders.* 'I'm probably reading too much into things.'

Jack catches my left hand with his right. 'Let me be the judge of that.'

I pause. I sigh. I pause again.

'Kate?'

'I could be completely wrong, but the way Lilly's behaving makes me wonder if she has a new partner,' *I say.*

'Who?'

I shrug. 'I don't know, Jack, it could be anyone. She seems pretty cosy with Harry Piper.'

Jack's body stiffens. 'That would make sense.'

'I could be way off here, Jack.' *I say.* 'I'm just thinking out loud.'

He nods, but I can see where his mind is leading him.

'She wants to play happy families with the head doctor,' *he says.* 'And I'm just a bloody inconvenience.'

'That would be one possible explanation,' *I say.*

He jumps to his feet. 'Alice is my daughter and if Lilly thinks she's going to push me out, she's got another thing coming. She thinks getting me the sack will help her do it, but she's wrong,' *He gives a hollow laugh.*

'Frankly, I'll have so much time on my hands I'll get more contact with Alice. Mary, Mother of God, I'll get her to move in.'

Suddenly, he turns green and sprints off to the toilet again. I'm not sure whether it's the sound of Jack dry retching, or the thought of Alice coming to live with us, but I give a shudder and have to sit down.

It's not that I dislike Alice. It's more that she's a baby and babies don't register on my radar.

Then again, if Alice did become a permanent fixture she would certainly cement things between Jack and I. We would be a unit. And Lilly would be nothing but a memory we could rewrite. Now I think about it, it's the perfect solution. A ready-made family.

I can't have children, you see. When I was fifteen I gave myself an abortion. It was a very simple procedure, actually. The foetus came out quickly and painlessly. But I didn't stop bleeding afterwards and had to have surgery. Everyone was completely melodramatic about it, particularly my mother, who sobbed and held my hand for days on end. I tried to explain that I didn't care, but no one believed me.

Jack comes back into the kitchen. 'Sorry, love. I'm all over the place and talking shite.'

'I don't think you are, Jack,' I tell him. 'I think we should have Alice come and live here.'

'What?'

'If we don't, it will only be a matter of time before Lilly stops you having any sort of relationship with Alice,' I say.

'I'm not sure she'd actually do that,' he says.

'I think she might,' I say. 'She already keeps you at arm's length and you've said yourself that her ex-husband hardly had any contact with his son.'

'David was a complete arse,' he says. 'He brought most of it on himself.'

'So Lilly told you,' I say.

'I dunno.'

He's wavering. Come on, Jack, pick up the pen and let's edit the history books here.

'And I'll be honest with you Jack,' I say. 'I've been really worried about Alice.'

'Worried?'

I take his hands in mine. 'We both know there's something wrong with Alice. She's a beautiful girl, utterly gorgeous, but something's not right. It may be a tiny thing that can be sorted out, but I don't think Lilly will ever allow her to access any help she might need.'

'She's in denial,' Jack says.

'Yes, she is, and that's understandable, but we have to put Alice's best interests above our own feelings and above Lilly's.'

He doesn't answer, just looks into my face.

'I love Alice like my own,' I say.

His eyes well with tears. 'Do you really think we could do this?'

'Yes I do,' I say. 'Now you get a shower and sort out an application for those bloody medical notes. The chief super will find it hard to sack anyone who's just caned a murder case.'

With that, I shoo him out of the room and log on to the internet to find a local family solicitor. I can't resist a laugh when the first entry is for a firm in Harpenden: Valentine & Co.

Lilly pulled on her wellies.

'Going out?' David asked.

Lilly nodded. 'Sam's cracking on with some work the school emailed, so I thought I'd take Alice out for a bit of fresh air.'

'Want some company?'

'Why not?'

They stepped outside the cottage, their boots disappearing in a snowdrift.

'Bloody hell,' Lilly laughed. 'We must have had another six inches last night.'

David scooped up Alice, put her on his shoulders and they set off. Lilly could feel wet snow sliding down the inside of her boot as they made their way up the garden to the fields beyond. There was no right of way across the farmer's land, but he was relaxed about Lilly hopping the fence every once in a while providing she steered clear of the crops.

'This always was a fabulous spot,' said David.

Lilly fought the urge to point out that he'd been quick enough to leave it when Cara caught his eye.

'We've been happy here,' she said. 'Sam and I.'

The rough track that divided two fields was lost, so they settled on a march in a straight line. It was hard going and Lilly's calves soon began to burn.

'I think Sam has enjoyed having me around,' said David.

'Of course he's enjoyed it,' said Lilly. 'He misses you something rotten when you're not around. I'm sure Flora is missing you right now.'

He nodded and kept on through the snow.

'You can't avoid Cara forever,' said Lilly.

'I know.'

'You have to sort something out for Flora's sake.'

'I just need some time to get my head straight,' said David.

'It doesn't work like that with kids. They need to know where they are and when they're going to see their parents, otherwise they get confused and sad.'

'Was Sam confused and sad when I moved out?'

Lilly wasn't going to lie. 'Yes, he was. He never knew when you were going to turn up or when you were going to cancel.'

They reached a high beech tree, its branches laden with snow, the boughs groaning under the weight.

'I'm going to make it up to him,' David told her. 'And to you, Lil.'

She turned, ready to explain that he should concentrate his efforts on his children and not worry about her, when a shout came from behind them and a figure stumbled in their direction.

Lilly cupped her hand over her eyes. 'Is that Sam?'

'I think so,' David replied.

Her son soon caught up with them, out of breath with trying to run in the impossible terrain.

'Where's your coat, Sam?' Lilly chided. 'You'll catch your death of cold out here without a coat.'

He shook his head at her in exasperation. 'That doctor.' He had to stop and swallow some air.

'You mean Harry?' Lilly asked.

Sam nodded.

Lilly felt her stomach muscles tense. 'What about Harry? Did he call?'

'He's at the cottage,' said Sam.

'Now?'

'Yeah,' Sam replied. 'I said you were out with Dad and Alice, but he wouldn't listen.'

'You weren't rude, were you, Sam?'

'No. I just tried to tell him that you weren't working today, that you were, you know, spending some time with your family. I mean it's not a crime, is it?'

''Course not,' said Lilly. 'But it's not Harry's fault if something important has come up.'

Sam shrugged. 'Doesn't matter anyway. He wouldn't leave.'

They trudged back to the cottage, Sam grumbling to his dad that Lilly never got any time off and Lilly trying to work out what might have happened. Please God it wasn't Chloe.

'I'm sorry to turn up on your doorstep like this,' said Harry.

He was literally on Lilly's doorstep. Sam hadn't let Harry into the house, but had left him freezing outside.

'Come inside.' Lilly gave Sam a withering look over her shoulder. 'You must be going numb.'

She led Harry through the cottage to the kitchen.

'I need to speak to you,' said Harry.

'And they don't have phones in Harpenden?' Sam muttered.

'Finish the work that school emailed,' she said.

'Done it.'

'Then go and watch telly,' Lilly told him.

He threw Harry a scowl before traipsing into the lounge and turning the television on so loud that Alice screamed.

'Sam!'

He reduced the volume to merely ear-splitting with a theatrical sigh.

'Kids,' said Lilly. 'If they told us how it was going to be, we'd have all bought goldfish instead.'

Harry gave a polite smile.

'So, what's up?' Lilly asked.

'I got a call from someone called Kerry Thomson,' he said.

Lilly felt light-headed. Jack must have passed on the list of suspects to the CPS. Kerry must have decided that there was no case for Chloe to answer.

'What did she say?' Lilly asked.

'She said I have to go to court tomorrow.'

'That's quick.' Lilly beamed. 'I thought they'd wait until forensics came back with a proper ID on the rapist, but the CPS must have decided they didn't want to waste any more resources on it. Cutbacks and all that.'

'I don't think it's got anything to do with cutbacks,' Harry said.

'Then it must be my legal genius.'

Harry didn't laugh. Was he pissed off that she wasn't giving him credit for his part?

'I know it was difficult for you to give me those names,' she told him.

His eyes clouded over.

'You're going to have to forgive yourself, Harry,' she told him. 'Yes, they're your closest colleagues, but one of them is a very dangerous individual.'

'I know that.'

'Then why so glum? Soon that guilty party will be in jail and tomorrow Chloe will be freed from this horrible thing hanging over her,' said Lilly.

Harry shook his head. 'I don't think so.'

'What?'

'I don't think the police have started making any investigations into the names I gave you. They haven't even been in touch,' he said. 'I don't think tomorrow's hearing has anything to do with dropping the case against Chloe.'

'Then why on earth is the case listed tomorrow?' Lilly asked. 'What does Kerry need you in court for?'

No sooner had the words come out of her mouth than Lilly knew the answer. The realization struck her like a hammer blow. 'Don't tell me,' she said. 'The CPS have applied for Chloe's medical notes.'

Harry nodded. Lilly had to sit down. Jack hadn't begun an investigation and Kerry hadn't decided to drop the proceedings. On the contrary, they were ploughing on with the case against Chloe. Disappointment flooded over Lilly.

'Will they get the notes?' Harry asked.

'Depends,' Lilly replied. 'Can you hand on heart tell the court that there's nothing in there that would support the prosecution case against Chloe?'

'I don't know.'

Lilly hid her face in her hands. Bang went her quiet day.

Gem turns the shower up as hot as it'll go and covers herself in soap, rubbing the bar directly over her skin, including her mouth.

There's a knock on the bathroom door and Misty walks in. She's smoking a fag, flicking her ash into the cup of her other hand. Gem feels a bit embarrassed in front of her, which is stupid if you think about it.

'You can't have a shower after each one,' she tells Gem. 'Your skin'll fall off.'

Gem don't care and carries on scrubbing.

'Just douche yourself,' says Misty. 'Get rid of the smell of johnnies and that.' She looks around for an ashtray. 'You are using johnnies aren't you?'

Gem's shocked she even needs to ask.

'Don't look like that.' Misty drops her fag end into the lav. 'That Turkish bitch will do anything for a few extra quid.'

Gem turns off the shower and starts to dry herself.

'You sore, are you?' Misty asks.

'A bit.'

Gem told Feyza last night that she'd start seeing some of Bill's friends and she's done three already today.

'Use plenty of lube.' Misty checks her reflection in the mirror, raking her fingers through her hair. 'Get them done as quick as you can.'

Everyone keeps telling her that and Gem does try, but the last one seemed to take an hour.

'Lie there like a piece of meat and they'll ride the fucking arse off you,' Misty says. 'Pretend you're enjoying it and talk dirty. Tell 'em you've never had a cock like it.' She leans closer to inspect the scars around her mouth. 'And if that don't work stick your finger up their arse.'

'What?'

Misty puts up her middle finger, the nail shorter than the rest. 'Give it a quick suck and get it right up there.' She shoves the finger in her mouth and pulls it out with a wet smack. 'And don't ask, just do it.'

Gem pulls on a pair of red knickers and a black bra; her hair's still wet and water trickles down her back.

'You done that one who calls himself John yet?' asks Misty.

Gem shrugs. Some of 'em tell you their names, some of 'em don't say a word.

'Mucky grey hair,' says Misty. 'Smells like a skip.'

Oh him. Gem had to hold her breath while she did him.

'I always use the finger on that one,' Misty says.

'Why are you telling me all this?' Gem asks.

Misty turns away from the mirror and faces Gem. 'I was your age once, started working straight out of care.'

'What happened to your mum?' Gem asks.

'Died.'

'How?'

'Long story,' says Misty. 'Now get your face back on, there'll be more punters this afternoon.' When she gets to the door, she stops. 'And keep a note of how many you do, so you know how much Feyza owes you.'

Gem shakes her head. She ain't likely to forget how many men she's doing it with, is she?

'Listen to me,' says Misty. 'You soon lose track.'

On the way to the Grove, Harry barely spoke and the inside of his car was oppressively silent and hot. The heater belted out like a hairdryer. Yet Harry still shivered every few minutes.

'You okay?' Lilly asked.

'Think I'm coming down with something,' he replied.

Lilly knew how he felt; despite the Saharan temperature in the car, Lilly's hands were clap cold.

When they arrived at the hospital he held each security door open for her, without catching her eye. Lilly felt more wounded than she knew was reasonable. He was a man who had found

250

himself in the eye of a perfect storm and had every right to retreat into himself. The trouble was she had got used to basking in the warmth of his attention and the lack of it bit her like the chill air in the streets.

She was in the middle of telling herself to grow up, when Elaine Foley walked into their path. Lilly stopped in her tracks and stared.

Foley gave Lilly an imperious glare. 'Problem, Miss Valentine?'

Problem? Of course there was a problem. Only two people could have killed Lydia and one of them was standing directly in front of her.

'No problem,' Lilly mumbled.

Harry opened the door to his office. 'Lilly and I have work to do.' He nodded for Lilly to hurry inside, which she did, feeling Foley's eyes drilling holes into her spine as she did so.

'She's still here?' Lilly hissed.

Harry shut the door. 'Of course she is, Lilly. I have no actual evidence that she's guilty of anything, do I?'

'But she had the code.'

'So what?' he said. 'The police clearly don't think there's anything in it, do they?'

'Tell me she doesn't have access to Chloe's room.'

Harry slapped his hand on his desk, making Lilly jump. 'I'm not a total idiot. I told her that there was bound to be an internal inquiry, and until then she shouldn't attend to Chloe. I told both of them the same thing.'

Lilly nodded. He was in an impossible situation. He could hardly start accusing people of rape and murder.

'Which one do you think might have done it?' Lilly asked.

Harry shook his head. 'That is a path I simply cannot go down.'

He was refusing to engage. Understandable really.

'Listen, Harry, I need to speak to Chloe before we get started,' she said. 'Why don't you take a breather? Get yourself a drink and sit down for five.'

'Thank you.' He still didn't look at her.

As soon as Lilly let herself out of Harry's office, she realized she would never find her way to Chloe's room. The labyrinth of corridors snaked out in all directions. She peered down each one in turn, feeling like a fly trapped at the centre of a spider's web.

'Can I help?' Foley had sneaked up behind Lilly. 'You shouldn't be wandering around on your own.'

The other woman was standing too close, her eyes too penetrating. Lilly took a step back.

'I need to see Chloe,' she said.

Foley stared for several seconds as if she thought Lilly might not be telling the truth.

'Follow me,' she said, snapping her head around and stalking away from Lilly.

'Thank you,' Lilly offered, falling into line.

As they passed through the arteries of the hospital, Lilly spotted a picture she recognized. Three dandelion clocks in a row. As a child, she had tried to blow away the seedlings, shouting the hour after each deep breath. When the stalk was bare she would watch them dance on the breeze like fairies.

Chloe's room was at the end of the corridor, but there was a man hovering outside, pushing a medication trolley. When he saw them approaching, he quickly moved on, nodding at Nurse Foley as they crossed, greasy grey hair hanging over his eyes.

'Who was that?' Lilly asked.

'What?'

'That man,' Lilly said. 'He was looking into Chloe's room.'

'I doubt it,' Foley replied. 'Just turning round his trolley. Those things have a life of their own.'

Lilly wasn't so certain. 'Do you know his name?'

Foley stopped at Chloe's door and pressed her face to the glass. 'Here she is.'

Lilly looked over Foley's head and could see a huge black mass lumbering towards them.

'Miss Valentine's here to see you,' Foley shouted.

There was a movement inside, then the door opened.

'Hey, Chloe,' said Lilly. 'How are you?'

'She's fine,' said Foley. 'Aren't you?'

Chloe opened her mouth as if to reply, but instead there came a gut-wrenching sob. Then tears came from a place deep inside her. A place Lilly knew she could never reach. Could anyone?

Lilly waited for Foley to say or do something, but she just watched Chloe, as if rooted to the spot. Disgusted, Lilly pushed past her.

'I'll take it from here,' she said and ushered Chloe back into the room, nudging the door closed with her arse.

When she got Chloe to the bed, she looked around for some tissues and saw the nurse's shadow still outside. Lilly knew she shouldn't start asking the question and that forensics would give the answer soon enough, but she couldn't help herself. Was that woman guilty? There was definitely something off-key about her. A coldness. A streak of cruelty even. Maybe Lilly was just reading too much into things?

'Come on now.' Lilly handed Chloe a box of man-size Kleenex. 'I'm here.'

Chloe took a tissue and wiped her face. 'I wish it would all end.'

'It will,' said Lilly. 'I promise.'

Chloe shook her head. 'How will it?'

'For one thing we'll catch the person who did this,' said Lilly. 'Then we'll make the police see that they have to drop the case against you.'

Chloe waited as if she were expecting much more, but Lilly didn't have a magic wand. She might be able to sort out some of the legal issues, but the damage had been done. Not just by recent events. Chloe's pain and suffering had started long ago.

'Chloe,' Lilly said. 'Why are you here in the Grove?'

'The judge said I had to.'

'No, I mean before all this,' said Lilly. 'Why did you come here in the first place?'

'I'm not well,' Chloe replied.

That much was patently true. But why? What had happened to Chloe? What had caused the disintegration of her mind?

'Do you remember arriving?' Lilly asked.

Chloe shook her head.

'Do you remember anything before you came here?'

Chloe was about to shake her head again, but stopped herself. 'I remember a dog.'

'A dog?'

'A big fluffy one,' said Chloe. 'Everybody loved it.'

'Was it your dog?'

'I don't think so.'

Lilly patted Chloe's hand. 'I always wanted a dog.'

'Did you get one?'

Lilly laughed. 'No. My mum said they were dirty and smelly.'

'They are.'

'I had a hamster,' Lilly told her. 'Now they *are* dirty and smelly.'

'What was its name?'

'Tammy. It used to run round and round on this wheel all day long,' said Lilly. 'Then I dropped it on its head.'

'Did it die?'

'Not straight away, but I don't think it ever recovered,' said Lilly. 'It didn't go on its wheel any more.'

'It lost the will to live,' said Chloe and closed her eyes.

Lilly watched her client. The poor kid. How long could she live like this? Locked in a cage, waiting to be hurt? Was there any chance she would ever get better?

'Can I look at your medical notes, Chloe?'

'Why?'

'First, I'd like to know a bit more about you,' said Lilly. 'Second, the CPS have asked for copies and I need to know what's in there in case I want to argue against it.'

'Fine,' said Chloe, with a sigh.

I know a lot of police officers detest solicitors, but I've never understood that. Most solicitors aren't that bright and they're easy to manipulate. I accept that my judgement may be coloured by the fact that my father was a tax lawyer.

Matthew 'call me Matt' Pickwood seems standard issue; suit from Marks and Sparks, shirt and tie given to him by his girlfriend for Christmas. The law books lining the shelves behind him all out of date, a hangover from his days at university.

'I must emphasize that winning residence of a child from their mother is going to be difficult,' he says. 'Especially where the mother has been the primary carer since birth.'

'Difficult, yes,' I say. 'Impossible, no.'

Matt looks at Jack. The poor man's so uncomfortable; given half a chance he'd run from the room never to be seen again.

'What Kate said,' Jack mutters.

I need to take charge and remind him exactly why we're doing this.

'You have to understand, Mr Pickwood, I mean Matt, that we have no desire to hurt Miss Valentine in any way, shape or form.' I take Jack's hand. 'In many ways she is a good person.' Jack nods and I give his fingers a little squeeze. 'But we have to do what's right for Alice. She's all that matters to us.'

Matt picks up his pad and scans the notes he's made. He wears a wedding ring made of dull silver.

'You say Miss Valentine is resisting any diagnosis or treatment for Alice's special needs?'

'She did take her to see a consultant recently,' Jack replies.

'That was only because the GP insisted,' I point out. 'You'd been asking to take her yourself for months, hadn't you?'

Jack looks down into his lap and nods.

'You also believe that Miss Valentine is attempting to sabotage contact between you and your daughter?' Matt asks.

'I used to be able to see her all the time,' says Jack.

'Now it's kept to a bare minimum,' I say. 'Miss Valentine decides exactly when Jack can have Alice and if he asks for any more contact he's turned down.' I lean forward so that Matt can see down my top. 'She wouldn't allow Jack to go to the hospital with her. We don't even know what the consultant said because she refused to discuss it.'

Matt lowers his pad and smiles at Jack. 'This is going to be quite a fight. Are you sure you're ready for that?'

Jack lifts his head and his eyes are shining. At first I think they might be filling with tears, but no, they're glinting with anger.

'I'm absolutely ready,' says Jack.

I want to clap and cheer for him, but I rein myself in and settle for leaning over and kissing him on the cheek.

When Lilly left Chloe's room, Harry was waiting for her in the corridor.

'I didn't think you'd find your way back,' he said.

'Thanks.'

He put a hand on her cheek. 'Sorry I've been so grumpy.'

'This is difficult for you, Harry,' she said.

'Shall we?' He gestured down the corridor.

Lilly nodded and they moved off.

'Why did Chloe end up in the Grove?' Lilly asked when they got back to his office.

Harry took the seat at his desk. 'Before my time, I'm afraid.'

'Nothing in the notes?'

'There might be,' he replied. 'I remember Dr Cromer, my predecessor, saying something about a psychotic episode but I don't recall the detail.' He began tapping on his laptop, fingers whizzing across the keyboard. 'She'd been in care from a young age so she probably suffered all manner of abuse.'

Lilly cringed. She knew too many children who'd been removed from neglectful parents only to find themselves being looked after by the brutal machine of the state. Out of the frying pan . . .

'She doesn't seem to remember much at all,' said Lilly.

'I know,' said Harry. 'Could be memory loss due to trauma, could be subconscious blocking.'

'Do you think it would help Chloe to remember?'

Harry paused. 'I used to think so, Lilly, but each time we tried Chloe would have an episode. If I tried again, I'm not sure she'd survive it.'

'Then how will she get better?'

He gave a sad smile. 'I think we're going to have to settle for functioning.'

Lilly tried to take it in. At fifteen years old, Chloe could never look forward to an ordinary life.

'Will she have to stay in hospital forever?' she asked.

'I hope not,' said Harry. 'I'd like to think that after all this is behind her, she could concentrate on getting well enough to try a supported placement.'

'And she has no family?'

Harry shook his head.

'No one's ever tried to get in touch?'

'Not to my knowledge.'

God, it was unfathomably sad. What a desolate life Chloe had led.

'Here you go.' Harry slid his laptop across the desk. 'Chloe's medical notes.'

'Right from when she first came here?' Lilly asked.

Harry pulled a face. 'It's quite vague to begin with. Dr Cromer was old school. Liked to keep it all up here.' He tapped his head. 'When he left I had to cobble together what I could.'

Lilly nodded. She'd worked for a fair few old codgers in her time. Some of them were unconcerned how anyone else would run their case files if they went on sick leave, retired or fell under a bus.

'I on the other hand have been meticulous,' said Harry. 'I could give you a run for your money.'

Lilly laughed. Meticulous was not a word that sprang to mind about the piles of notebooks and scraps of paper Lilly had in her to-do tray.

She opened the file saved, simply, as 'Chloe Church' and found herself looking at a document with hundreds, probably thousands, of entries. Each one numbered and divided into three columns. The first for the date, the second for the author and the third, fatter column, to record 'comments'.

This, Lilly could see at a glance, was going to be a slow process.

'Enjoy,' Harry told her with a mischievous wink.

An hour later, Lilly rubbed her eyes. It was obvious that when Chloe had arrived at the Grove she had been in the throes of a severe mental breakdown.

'Patient requires restraint and sedation'.

'Patient on suicide watch'.

Dr Cromer's notes were brief but clear.

'Patient prescribed Valium and temazepam'.

However, after a few days Chloe stablized and remained calm for several weeks with Dr Cromer recording nothing more remarkable than: 'Patient well'.

Then, out of the blue, she had another episode. No trigger was noted, but the symptoms were serious.

'Patient suffering suicidal ideation'.

'Patient delusional'.

Dr Cromer prescribed more drugs and the situation was once again brought under control – a pattern that persisted throughout his tenure and into Harry's, though his comments were more detailed.

'Chloe is in a state of high anxiety. She describes herself as very frightened and asks to move out of her room, which she fears is haunted. I have agreed that she can move to a different corridor and prescribed Xanax 100mg.'

'Chloe has made herself vomit twice this morning. She says JS is giving her the wrong medication, which makes her feel as if she is in a dream state. We discussed that this was known as disembodiment and a symptom of depression and anxiety.'

'Who's JS?' Lilly asked.

'John Staines,' Harry replied. 'He's a pharmacist. Worked here forever.'

John Staines. One of only two suspects.

'It says in the notes that Chloe thought he was messing with her meds.'

Harry nodded. 'What can I tell you? He's the person Chloe associates with medication, so any delusions about that would necessarily involve John.' He smiled at her. 'You'll probably find she accuses us all in there at some point.'

'He's on the list,' Lilly said. 'Your list.'

'Yes, he is.' Harry went back to his work, unwilling to discuss the subject further.

'What does he look like?' she asked.

'I've never given it much thought,' Harry replied without looking up. 'Fifties. Grey hair.'

'Scraggly and hanging in his face?'

'That's a touch harsh, but yes, I suppose sartorial elegance is not one of John's strong suits.'

It was the guy with the trolley. Had to be. Lilly shivered. He could certainly have drugged Chloe, and Lydia for that matter.

'Leave it to the police, Lilly,' Harry warned her.

She went back to the notes.

Two hours later, Lilly closed the laptop. 'Done.'

'What's the verdict?' Harry asked.

'There's nothing in there that even suggests Chloe has a propensity for violence,' Lilly replied. 'There are a few argy-bargies with staff, but that's when she's being restrained and she's frightened. No one's come away with worse than a few bruises.'

'Then there is no reason for the police to have access to them.'

'Probably not, and I'll argue that tomorrow,' said Lilly. 'But, to be honest, even if they win, these notes won't help their case. There's nothing suspicious in there.'

Chapter Twelve

Prisoner Location Enquiry Form

Your full name:
Phoebe Talbot
Your date of birth:
08/04/1998
Address line 1:
Hampton House, Locksford Way.
Address line 2:
Clayhill Estate
Town/city:
Luton
Postcode:
LU2 4TY
Telephone number:
01582 86222
Email address:
hamptonhouse@centralbedfordshire.gov.uk
Reason for enquiry:
I wish to find my sister who I have not been allowed to see
for two years
Full name of person you wish to contact:
Gigi Talbot

His/her date of birth:
Sometime in 1988

Lilly arrived at court early. It was quiet but at least the electricity was on.

She headed straight for the advocates' room where Kerry had already commandeered the table, spreading her papers around her.

'Nice to see you again, Lilly.' Kerry's voice dripped with sarcasm. 'No doubt you've got a set of medical notes for me.'

'Nice try,' said Lilly. 'But you'll have to get a court order if you want them.'

'That's what we're here for.'

Kerry bent her head and went back to her files, as if she had nothing more to say to Lilly. Bloody rude cow.

'Actually, that's not all I'm here for,' she said.

Kerry left her finger on the document she was reading so she wouldn't lose her place and looked up.

'I wanted your opinion on the list of suspects,' said Lilly.

Kerry sighed and glanced at the word her finger was marking as if it were far more important than anything Lilly might have to say. 'I don't know what you're talking about, Lilly.'

'That's strange,' said Lilly. 'Two days ago I sent an email to Officer McNally listing the people who had access to my client's room at the Grove. I assumed that those people would have been tested forensically by now to find out which one raped her.'

'First I've heard of it,' said Kerry.

'Very odd,' said Lilly. 'I advised him to pass it on to you as a matter of urgency. After all, you're going to look pretty stupid when I tell the judge that I want the matter set down for committal because there's no case to answer.'

'No case to answer? Your client's fingerprints were on the knife.'

Lilly opened her palms. 'What choice do I have, Kerry? You

262

know our defence is that the same person who raped Chloe also murdered Lydia, and I've provided you with a list of suspects. If the police refuse to investigate then what am I to do?'

'You can't expect us to launch some expensive operation on the whim of one of your client's wild fantasies.'

Lilly folded her arms. 'Chloe's rape was very real according to Dr Hicks. She took the usual samples. All you have to do is scrape the inside of two mouths to see who matches.'

'Two?'

'Two. You try telling the judge why you didn't bother and see how far you get.'

'And what if none of them match?'

'Then I'm a twat and your case just got a hell of a lot stronger.'

Harry was sat in the waiting area outside court, flicking through a copy of *HELLO!*, the heel of one foot resting on the knee of the other.

'I didn't guess celebrity gossip was your thing,' she said.

He laughed and put the magazine down on the seat next to him. 'Doesn't everyone need to know Jennifer Aniston's top tips for thick, shiny hair?'

Thinking of her own unruly mop, Lilly thought she probably did need to know those tips.

'I've already put a right royal rocket up the prosecution's arse about the list of suspects,' she replied.

Harry's face fell.

'I know you can't bear the idea that one of those people is guilty,' she said, 'But we have to know. For Chloe's sake.'

'You're right of course.'

Kerry and Jack approached. Kerry was hugging a fat file to her chest and Jack slouched next to her. He didn't acknowledge Lilly but threw a scowl at Harry.

'We're popular,' Harry whispered in Lilly's ear.

'Like Russell Brand in a convent.'

Jack's face darkened further at the sight of Lilly and Harry laughing. He needed to grow up.

'You give me the medical notes and we'll do the forensics,' said Kerry.

Lilly processed the offer. The notes weren't a problem and the court might well order their release in any event. 'When?' she asked.

'Straight after the hearing,' said Kerry. 'Jack will go with your man to the hospital and get it done.'

Jack worried the carpet tiles with the toe of his boot. Clearly he wasn't happy with the proposals. Clearly he had been given no choice.

'Fine,' said Lilly.

When Kerry and Jack were out of earshot, Harry grabbed her arm. 'I thought you were going to fight them about the notes.'

'Don't worry, Harry.' She put a hand over his. 'There's absolutely nothing in those notes that can hurt Chloe.'

Harry's face remained unconvinced and he dug his fingers further into her flesh.

'Trust me, Harry,' she told him.

The pressure he was applying was almost starting to hurt when he let go.

'Sorry,' he said. 'Of course I trust you.'

Kate was right. Lilly and Piper were having it away.

Jesus, how had he not seen it before? So bloody cosy. Like giggling kids. They'd probably set up the whole thing about the notes between them. Piper could easily have got his patient's permission, but Jack would bet his arse that Lilly had advised him not to, knowing full well that Jack would nick him. Then they could sue and ruin him. Get him out of the way.

Not bloody likely.

'Are you listening to me, Jack?' Kerry barked.

'Sorry,' he muttered.

'Why the hell didn't you send me the list?' she asked.

'It wasn't a priority.'

'Where Lilly Valentine is concerned everything is top priority,' said Kerry. 'You do not want to give her the upper hand. Ever.'

Jack nodded and followed the prosecutor into court. Lilly had already taken her place at the front, joking with the clerk as if she were in the pub. Then she turned and waved at her client, and the girl waved back. All smiles like she didn't have a care in the world. There was no way on God's green earth that the kid was innocent.

'My rule of thumb, is not to trust her,' Kerry hissed. 'She always has an agenda and she always has a plan.'

Jack knew fine well that Lilly had a plan. It was to replace him with bloody Piper. Well, she had better watch out because now he had a plan of his own.

When the hearing was over, Lilly gave Chloe a thumbs-up. She seemed much brighter today. Perhaps just getting away from the Grove cheered her up. That place would depress Jedward.

Whatever the reason, it was heartening to see signs of life in her client.

In stark contrast were Jack and Harry, who both had a face like a slapped arse. God knows what was wrong with Jack these days. He was beyond weird. At least Harry had good reason to feel sad. He'd been forced into breaching patient confidentiality, which he didn't take lightly, and he was about to find out which one of his most trusted colleagues was a rapist. Not to mention the recent death of a patient.

'It'll be all right, Harry,' she told him. 'You go back to the Grove and oversee Jack. I'll bob down to the cells and speak to Chloe.'

She watched him leave, resignation weighting his shoulders. Poor man. Could anything else go wrong for him?

'Put your tongue away, woman,' Jack snapped.

'I beg your pardon?'

'You're making a show of yourself.'

Lilly narrowed her eyes. 'There's only one of us here doing that.'

He shook his head in disgust and walked away. What the hell was all that about? Lilly decided she didn't have the time or the energy to care and headed down to the cells.

'Hello, Lilly,' said Chloe, tucking into a plate of mince and mashed potatoes. 'They brought me lunch.'

'So I see.'

'I wonder if there'll be any pudding.'

Lilly sat on the bed next to her client and smiled. 'You seem a lot more relaxed.'

'I am.'

Lilly watched Chloe chase the last spoonful of grey meat around the plate.

'Can we talk?' Lilly asked.

Chloe shrugged and smacked her lips.

'Tell me about Lydia,' said Lilly.

'She was my friend,' said Chloe.

'How close were you?'

Chloe smiled. 'She always said we'd already met in a previous life.'

'When she told you she was going to blow the whistle on the abuse did you believe her?'

'Oh yeah.' Chloe nodded vigorously. 'She couldn't deal with it at all.'

'I'm sure you both found it hard,' said Lilly.

'It was worse for Lydia though.'

'Why?'

The cell door opened and the guard stepped in with a bowl of Swiss roll and custard. Chloe's face lit up.

'Why was it worse for Lydia?' Lilly repeated.

'She'd been raped before.'

Chloe shovelled in almost half the bowlful, yellow custard collecting at either side of her mouth.

'It really screwed her up, you see.' She took another huge spoonful. 'Because it was her dad that did it.'

Gem checks the time on her phone. She's proper late for work and Feyza has texted her twice already.

She tries calling Mum again, but it goes straight to voicemail. Probably run out of charge. Mum ain't good at remembering to plug in her mobile at night.

Thing is, she's got no way of even guessing when Mum will come back. When she goes on the missing list like this it can be hours or days. And there ain't no way of telling where she's at.

Tyler starts coughing. He's woke up full of some horrible bug. Both his cheeks are bright red. There's no way Gem can leave him. Not even cuddled up on the settee in a pile of blankets.

Her phone goes again. Another text from Feyza: 'Where the fuck are you?'

She opens her arms and smiles at Tyler. 'Come on, mate.'

Normally he would jump at her like one of them baby monkeys you see on the telly, but today he just lets her pick him up, then lays his head on her shoulder. She pushes his hair off his face. It feels wet from where he's been sweating.

'I'm taking you out,' she tells him.

'Park?'

'Not right now, mate,' she says. 'Maybe later.'

He don't argue the toss, just gives another cough that sounds full of snot.

She pulls his coat off the peg by the front door. It don't really fit him no more and she has to fight to do up the zip. She'll get him a new one soon. He can't go through the rest of the winter without a coat that fits him, can he?

Once they're outside, Gem realizes she's going to have to carry him. It's hard in the snow, though, and he's heavy these days. She remembers the day he was born and how little he was. Mum had him in a cot at the side of her hospital bed and one of the nurses let Gem pick him up and hold him. His funny, baby fingers grabbed hers and she was surprised by how strong he was.

'Going to be a bruiser that one,' the nurse said.

She were right as well. He weighs a bleeding ton.

When they get to the house, she kisses his cheek. 'Listen to me, Tyler, you've got to be a good boy in here, all right? You've got to sit nicely and not make a fuss. Okay?'

He nods into her shoulder.

'I'll get you a drink and a bag of crisps,' she says. 'Then you can close your eyes and have a lovely sleep.'

He nods again. Maybe it ain't a bad thing that he's under the weather. At least this way he won't race round causing a riot.

When she gets inside, the other girls all start making a fuss of him, asking him his name and that. But when Feyza sees him, she's got a face on her like thunder.

'What time you call this?'

'Sorry,' Gem mumbles. 'My mum went out.'

'And what he doing here?' She points at Tyler.

'I told you. My mum went out.'

'You think he can stay here?'

'I can't leave him on his own,' says Gem.

Feyza shakes her head. 'For fuck's sake. Do you think this is nursery?'

'Oh come on, Feyza.' Misty steps forward. 'He's not going to do any harm, is he?'

'You stay out of this,' says Feyza.

'He can sit in the kitchen.' Misty pats Tyler's cheek. 'You'll be quiet, won't you, big boy?'

Tyler buries his head into Gem's neck. She can feel hot snot on her skin.

'Look at him,' Misty says. 'You won't know he's here.'

'And what will clients think, eh?' Feyza gives one of her laughs.

'You really think that lot give a fuck?' says Misty.

'Oh fine. Whatever.' Feyza walks away. 'But if he give me one problem, he must go.'

'Don't mind the nasty old witch,' Misty whispers to Tyler. 'We'll look after you.' She copies one of Feyza's laughs and that makes him look up and smile.

'Witchy,' he says.

'That's right.' Misty takes Tyler, pops him down on one of the chairs in the kitchen and nods at Gem. 'You get yourself ready. Bill is due here in ten.'

Lilly pulled up outside the Morton-Daleys' place. A large detached house with electric gates. There was only one car in the drive, which she hoped meant the husband was out at work.

She trudged over to the keypad and pressed the buzzer.

'Yes?' The voice was unmistakably that of Lydia's mother.

'Mrs Morton-Daley, it's Lilly Valentine.' Lilly bent to the intercom. 'I represented Lydia if you remember?'

'What do you want?'

Lilly recalled Mrs Morton-Daley's anger in Harry's office. It clearly hadn't subsided. In the circumstances why should it?

'I wonder if I can talk to you about Chloe Church?' Lilly asked.

'What's there to say? She killed Lydia. End of story.'

'The thing is,' said Lilly, 'I don't think she did kill Lydia.'

Laughter burst from the speaker into the cold air. 'So you're Chloe's solicitor now?' Mrs Morton-Daley shrieked. 'You lost one client so you quickly replaced her with another. Ah, well, we all need to earn a crust, don't we?'

'It isn't like that,' said Lilly.

'I'll bet,' said Mrs Morton-Daley. 'God, you people make me sick. Goodbye.'

A long mournful tone streamed towards Lilly. Then silence. The conversation was at an end.

Lilly headed back to the car. What had she expected? She patted her pockets for the keys and cursed her lack of realism. She should have known there was no way the dead girl's mother would want to speak to the lawyer of the murder suspect.

She unlocked the car and was about to get in when a creaking sound came from behind her. Lilly turned and saw the electric gates open. Beyond them, Mrs Morton-Daley stood in her doorway, pulling a black cardigan around her.

'You'd better come in,' she called to Lilly and disappeared inside the house.

Lilly trotted across the drive. Now all she needed to work out was how to bring up the allegation that this woman's husband had raped her daughter.

'Tea? Coffee?' asked Mrs Morton-Daley. 'Or something stronger?'

Before Lilly could answer, the other woman opened the fridge and pulled out a bottle of white wine.

'It's a bit early, even for me,' said Lilly.

Mrs Morton-Daley shrugged and filled her own glass to the brim.

The kitchen was a work of art. Stainless-steel cupboards and vast Perspex work surfaces. In the centre was an island constructed of grey brick. It put Lilly's higgledy-piggledy kitchen to shame, yet she got the sense that her own brought more joy.

'Sit.' Mrs Morton-Daley pointed to a high stool at the island.

Lilly lifted herself onto it. It was every bit as uncomfortable as it looked. Mrs Morton-Daley leaned against the fridge, glass in hand, eyeing Lilly.

'So what makes you think Chloe didn't do it?' she asked.

'A lot of things. She just isn't a violent person,' Lilly replied. 'And she loved Lydia. Apart from doctors and nurses, Lydia was the only person in Chloe's life. She has no family or friends.'

Mrs Morton-Daley took a gulp of wine. 'She's ill and people who are ill do unpredictable things. I should know.'

'That's true, but Chloe's illness leads her to be frightened and anxious,' said Lilly. 'She's never attacked anyone before.'

'Then get the doctors to say so.' Mrs Morton-Daley's glass was already half empty. 'It's got nothing to do with me.'

'I just wondered if you could tell me anything about Lydia? What sort of girl was she?'

Mrs Morton-Daley drained her glass and reached into the fridge for a refill. 'I'll tell you what sort of girl she was, Miss Valentine.' She raised her drink in salute. 'She was a fucking nightmare.'

Lilly almost laughed. When someone died, those left behind generally fell into platitudes. Mrs Morton-Daley's honesty was rare and raw.

'She drank, she smoked, she slept around.' The woman's lips glistened with moisture. 'She stole anything that wasn't nailed down.'

'What do you think was at the root of it all?' Lilly asked.

'A lot of things, but mostly it was down to the fact that she'd been abused by her father.'

Wow. Mrs Morton-Daley was a bit pissed, but, even so, Lilly hadn't expected such an admission. She recalled Mr Morton-Daley. Much younger. Fawning and nervous. His wife barely able to disguise her loathing.

'Why didn't you leave him?' Lilly asked.

'What?'

'Why didn't you leave Lydia's father if you knew what had happened?'

Mrs Morton-Daley stared for a second as if she couldn't follow Lilly's words, then she tossed back her head and hooted with laughter.

'Oh my God.' She staggered to the island, wine sloshing out of her glass onto the brickwork. 'Shit.' She looked around her for a cloth and, when she couldn't find one, mopped up the wine with the sleeve of her cardigan. 'Byron will go spare if that marks.'

Never mind the bloody bricks, Lilly wanted to scream, the man raped your daughter.

'I think you've got the wrong end of the stick, Miss Valentine.' Mrs Morton-Daley sniffed her sleeve and grimaced. 'Byron isn't, wasn't, Lydia's father.'

'Oh, I see.'

Mrs Morton-Daley struggled out of her cardigan and let it fall to the floor. 'Your face was a picture. You thought Byron raped Lydia and we all carried on. Business as usual.' She reached for her drink. 'I suppose you must see a lot of horrible things in your line of work.'

Lilly nodded. Sometimes she worried that her work made her expect the worst in people. The trouble was she was rarely disappointed.

'Lydia wasn't ours.' Mrs Morton-Daley swayed. 'I mean not biologically ours.'

272

'She was adopted?'

'We got her at seven,' said Mrs Morton-Daley. 'All pigtails and buck teeth. We thought we could offer her a home.' She waved her glass around the kitchen, spilling yet more wine, but this time ignoring it as if she'd given up. 'But the damage was already done, you see.'

'Did you know about her background?' Lilly asked.

'We knew there'd been neglect and we knew Social Services suspected worse, but they said it would be okay. They said that with the right strategies we could help her.'

'But you couldn't?'

Mrs Morton-Daley shook her head. 'We tried everything: firm boundaries, relaxed boundaries, play therapy, family counselling, you name it. For eight long years we tried every trick in the book.' Her eyes filled with tears. 'None of it made any difference, because she hated us.'

'I'm sure she didn't,' said Lilly.

'Yes, she did. She hated us and everything we stood for. Anything she thought we valued, she wrecked.' Tears streamed down the woman's face. 'Byron couldn't stand it. He said it was like living with the enemy. He wanted to give up and put her back into care.' She wiped her eyes with the back of her hand. 'But I couldn't do that, could I? She'd already been let down by her real parents and I refused to do it to her a second time.'

Lilly had come across lots of broken adoptions. Lives trashed. It was a lot more common than people realized. One of Social Services' dirty little secrets.

'I think you were brave to carry on,' Lilly told her.

'Or just fucking stupid,' Mrs Morton-Daley replied. 'Now does any of this make you think it more or less likely that Chloe killed her?'

'I'm going to be brutally frank,' said Lilly.

'I think I can take it.'

Lilly smiled. 'I think someone at the Grove has been taking advantage of the female patients.'

'You mean raping them?'

Lilly nodded. 'Exactly. I also think that person was able to get away with it until he picked on Lydia.'

'There is no way Lydia would have kept her mouth shut.'

'That's what Chloe told me,' Lilly said. 'Lydia was about to let the cat out of the bag when she was killed.'

Mrs Morton-Daley's hand flew to her mouth. 'You think she was murdered to shut her up?'

'Yes, I do,' Lilly replied. 'Did Lydia ever give you any indication about what she was going to do?'

Mrs Morton-Daley shook her head. 'Lydia never told me anything. Sometimes she would go weeks without saying one word to me.' Then she stopped and put down her glass. 'She did give me something though.'

Lilly's heart gave a quick skip under her breastbone. 'What?'

'It was the last time I visited her in the Grove. Just a second.'

Mrs Morton-Daley left the room, returning with a white padded envelope clutched to her chest.

'I thought it was just a load of old rubbish,' she said.

Lilly took the envelope and peered inside. It was full of documents. Many yellow and faded.

'She said they were important, but I didn't believe her,' said Mrs Morton-Daley.

'The important thing is that you kept them,' Lilly replied.

Gem rips off a bit of kitchen roll and wipes herself down. She wishes she could have a shower but there's another punter due in ten minutes and she needs to check on Tyler. Anyway, Misty was right; her skin's proper dry from all that soap.

She pulls on a dressing gown and races down the hallway. He's still in the kitchen, having a cuddle on Misty's knee.

'Has he been all right?' Gem asks.

'Poor love,' says Misty. 'He's under the weather.'

Gem leans over and touches his forehead with the back of her hand. He's proper hot.

'You got any Calpol?' Misty asks.

Gem shakes her head. 'I'll nip out and get some after my next job,' she says.

Tyler lets out a rotten cough.

'Get some Buttercup Syrup while you're at it,' says Misty.

Gem nods, takes hold of Tyler's hand and gives it a little squeeze.

'Where's your mum then?' Misty asks.

Gem shrugs.

'Drugs is it?' Misty asks.

'No,' Gem shouts.

'All right, keep your fucking hair on. It doesn't make much of a difference, does it?'

Gem takes Tyler from Misty and rests him on her hip. 'She'll be back soon. She never stays away for long.'

'If you say so.'

'I do.'

Misty gives her a look that would poison a snake and stands. 'Just make sure you get the poor kid some medicine.'

All the way home, Lilly wondered about the papers in the padded envelope. What had Lydia considered so important?

Most of all, she wondered if there was any confirmation in there that she had indeed been raped. If Lilly could prove that, she could surely make everyone see that the rapist and the murderer were one and the same.

By the time she arrived at the cottage, her head was throbbing with it. When she got out of the car she understood that it was more than the case making her ache. Every bone in her body hurt. As she stumbled inside, she was sweating and could hardly swallow.

'Blimey, Lil,' said David. 'Are you feeling all right?'

Lilly see-sawed her hand.

'I'm just about to make Sam a bacon sarnie,' he said. 'Would that hit the spot?'

She shook her head.

'God, you must be ill. Why don't you go and lie on your bed?' he said. 'I'll bring up a hot drink.'

She smiled weakly and did as she was told, rolling herself up in her duvet. The envelope was still in her hand. Sick or not, she needed to read its contents. When she pulled out the first document, she was shocked to find a printout of a BBC internet newsfeed from 2002. The story of George and Sinead Talbot rang a bell. Hadn't they been convicted of abuse on a football team of kids? As she read on, her memory was jogged further. Seven kids. Beaten. Starved. Raped. Despite her temperature, Lilly's blood ran cold.

'Put that away.' David was in the doorway, a steaming mug in his hands. 'You're too ill to work.'

'I'm fine,' Lilly said. Or would have said if her throat hadn't been packed with razor blades.

'Drink this,' said David, pushing the mug at Lilly.

She sipped the hot lemony liquid and was instantly soothed.

'Honey?' she whispered.

'And whiskey,' David replied. 'Get it down you and get some sleep.' He moved the envelope to the bedside table. 'This lot can wait until tomorrow.'

Chapter Thirteen

To: hamptonhouse@centralbedfordshire.gov.uk
From: prisoner.locationservice@noms.gsi.gov.uk

Further to your recent enquiry we confirm that Gigi Talbot is currently a serving prisoner at HMP New Hall.
Her prisoner number is HP341 992.

Lilly woke up wondering who had sneaked into her room during the night and beaten her with a cricket bat. It could be the only logical explanation for the pain in both her legs. When she forced herself out of bed, she feared they might not actually take her weight.

'You cannot be thinking of going to work,' said David, when she eventually made it downstairs.

'Just a cold,' she said, rifling in a drawer for painkillers. Why on earth did she keep all this crap? Yards of crêpe bandage that smelled faintly of banana, an empty packet of hay fever relief, an unopened tube of soluble vitamin C tablets. Was it too late for those? At last she found a stray paracetamol, blew the fluff from it and popped it into her mouth. She swallowed it down with a glass of water, each gulp a needle jab to the inside of her throat.

'You need to stay inside today and wrap up warm,' David told her. 'You don't want pneumonia.'

Lilly's mother had always warned her of the same thing. Though she'd also warned that eating too much sugar caused worms.

'I won't be much longer than an hour,' she said.

'Then straight back to bed?'

'Promise.'

When she opened the door, a man was making his way to the cottage, holding a brown envelope. He wasn't the postman.

'Lilly Valentine?' he asked.

Lilly nodded.

'Special delivery,' he said and handed her the envelope.

It looked like something official from the court. God knows why they'd sent it here, rather than to her office. She slung it onto the back seat with the padded white one given to her by Mrs Morton-Daley. She had to make time to read those documents today.

I measure the walls of the spare bedroom, almost giddy with excitement.

'What are you up to?' Jack asks.

'We need to make this room nice for Alice.'

'She won't sleep on her own,' he says.

I note down the numbers in inches and centimetres to be sure I have the right ones.

'She will when we get her diagnosed,' I say. 'When we can get her some treatment.'

'You think?'

I roll my eyes. 'When she comes to live with us we can make sure she sees the best specialist there is. We'll have her right as rain, you'll see.'

'She might not come to live with us,' he says. 'Lilly will fight us tooth and nail.'

The trouble with Jack is that he's a pessimist. He says real life has made him that way. Not me. I have absolute faith in my own abilities. I have never failed at anything in my life and I'm not about to start now.

'It needs a lick of paint,' I tell him. 'Definitely not pink.'

That makes him laugh. Alice is so not a pink and frilly kind of girl.

'We should go out to the shops,' I say. 'Order a little bed and a new duvet cover.'

'The town will be deserted in this weather.'

'Good,' I say. 'I hate crowds.'

'I don't much feel like shopping.'

I feel a tiny stab of impatience rise in my chest, but push it back down. Jack's not like me. Well, no one is really.

'Come on now,' I say. 'You can't sit around all day and mope while you wait for the DNA results to come back. The lab will call you.'

'That's what I'm worried about,' he says. 'What if they confirm one of those eejits on Piper's list did rape Chloe?'

I put down the tape measure and give him a hug, making sure my thigh slides between his.

'What if they did? It doesn't mean they killed Lydia, does it?'

'I guess not.'

'Now get your coat, we're going shopping,' I say.

He opens his legs a little and pushes into me. 'Can it wait half an hour?'

Eyes and nose streaming, Lilly pulled up outside the Grove. Why hadn't she packed any tissues? What person with such a foul cold wouldn't pack tissues?

She leaned over to the glove compartment. There was a tin of travel sweets and a glasses case. No tissues. Damn. She was certain David would have a handy pack. She opened the glasses case and there was a little cleaning cloth. She had no choice; it was either that or her sleeve.

She blew her nose three times into the cloth and stuffed it in her pocket. Then she took a sweet and began to suck, hoping it would ease her sore throat. She just did not have time to be ill.

She sat for a moment, psyching herself up, when two figures emerged from the hospital. They were deep in conversation, their exchange becoming more heated as they moved away from the building.

Elaine Foley and John Staines. Arguing.

Lilly watched them for a few moments, trying to hear what they were saying. Foley appeared to be counting, her fingers moving from one, then two, then three. Staines shook his head violently.

Abruptly, Foley stopped and put her hand on Staines's arm for him to do the same. She had spotted Lilly. They both stared at her and Staines whispered something to Foley who nodded. Then, as if by agreement, they scurried off in different directions like rats caught in a floodlight.

Lilly was shaking when she reached Harry's office.

'You're not well,' he said.

'I'm fine,' she answered. 'I just saw Foley and Staines in the car park and something was definitely going on between them.'

'I'm not surprised,' said Harry. 'Yesterday they were told they were rape suspects and had their DNA taken.'

Of course they wouldn't be pleased by that. One of them was about to be arrested. Or maybe both of them? They had certainly looked more than colleagues, and it would have been a hell of a lot easier to get into Chloe's room as part of a team.

'I'm shocked they're still at work,' said Lilly.

'Innocent until proven guilty, Lilly. It's the law, I believe.'

She smiled. Someone like Harry would never ride roughshod over the rules.

'I need to see Chloe,' she said.

'Everything okay?'

Lilly nodded. 'I paid Lydia's mother a visit yesterday.'

'Was that wise?'

'Probably not,' said Lilly. 'Turned out to be bloody interesting though.'

'Do tell.'

'First, Lydia was adopted, having been raped by her father,' said Lilly. 'Second, she gave me this.' Lilly waved the padded envelope. 'Lydia asked her mum to hang on to it.'

'What is it?'

'Documents,' said Lilly. 'Some of them going back years.'

'May I?'

Lilly handed him the envelope and he took out the first piece of paper. 'What's this all about?' he asked.

'I don't know,' she replied. 'I've hardly started on them. I just wanted to know if Chloe could cast any light on why Lydia kept them.'

'I doubt it,' he said.

Lilly retrieved the envelope and slotted the document back inside. 'Worth a try anyway.'

Harry led her through the corridors to Chloe's room. When she saw the picture of the dandelion clocks she almost tried to blow the time, then she waited for Chloe to answer the door.

Chloe's face was motionless. The brightness on display at court had evaporated. She shuffled back to her bed and lay down.

'I won't get too close,' Lilly laughed. 'I've a lousy cold.'

Chloe didn't answer, as if she didn't care one way or the other.

'I went to see Lydia's mother yesterday,' Lilly said. 'She gave me this.' She waved the envelope at Chloe. 'Apparently, Lydia had asked her to keep it safe.'

'So she gave it to you instead?'

'She did it to help you, sweetheart,' said Lilly. 'Lydia is dead but there might be something in here that will prove she was raped. If I can prove that, I'm a lot closer to proving you didn't kill her.'

Chloe turned over. 'I'm tired now.'

'Okay.'

Lilly watched her client breathe then left the room.

Jesus, but Jack hated shopping. Wasn't it the same for every man in the world?

His parents would always end up having a mighty row, then stop speaking to one another altogether.

His ma would turn to Jack and say, 'Would you ask himself if he likes these towels, or does he not care at all what the state of the house is?'

Only weird men liked shopping. Men like Piper. It was probably his main hobby, swanning round department stores, running his fingers over quilts and getting excited about cushion covers.

'What do you think about this one?' Kate asked, holding up a roll of wallpaper like a sceptre.

He knew what his response should be. 'It's nice,' he said. 'What do you think?'

'Bit girly perhaps,' she said.

'Well, you know, she is actually a girl,' he said.

'Yes, but we don't want her growing up all silly and incapable, do we?'

Jack hadn't known that wallpaper could have that amount of impact on a personality, but he wasn't enough of an eejit to say it out loud.

Two women walked towards them. One dark and dressed in bright red, the other had a baby in a sling. They chatted easily to one another. See, women could shop all bloody day and still not get bored.

'Jack?' The woman in red spoke. 'It is you, isn't it?'

Jack looked puzzled.

'It's me,' the woman roared. 'Sheba.'

The light dawned. Sheba. A shrink he and Lilly had worked with many a time.

'Do I look that bad?' she asked.

'Of course not,' he said. 'I was just away with the fairies. Shopping will do that to you.'

'I'm Kate.' Kate stuck out her hand. 'Jack's girlfriend.'

Sheba smiled. Her lipstick was as red as her coat. 'Nice to meet you, Kate.' She turned to the woman with the baby. 'This is my girlfriend.'

Jack spluttered. He couldn't help it.

'What's the matter, Jack?' Sheba asked. 'Never realized I batted for the other side?'

Jack was speechless. How did you answer a question like that?

'Don't worry,' she giggled. 'I'll take it as a compliment. So tell me, how's Alice?'

Jack tried to smile. 'Fine.'

'I saw Lilly at the hospital, did she tell you?' asked Sheba.

Lilly never told Jack anything, did she?

'She didn't mention it, no.'

'I suspect she was too upset,' said Sheba.

Kate snorted and Sheba narrowed her eyes.

'Lilly's not really worried about Alice,' Jack explained. 'She doesn't think there's anything wrong with her.'

Sheba pursed her lips. 'Of course she's worried, Jack. She's just trying to come to terms with it at the moment.'

'What do you mean?'

'It's very common indeed, especially amongst mothers.' Sheba's voice was gentle. 'Accepting your child may be disabled in some way takes time. It's a process, like a bereavement.'

'No one died,' said Kate.

Jack knew she meant well, but she sounded too harsh.

'What Kate means is that if Alice is disabled, she needs some form of treatment,' he said. 'We can't get any of that if Lilly won't come on board.'

Sheba took a step back and her voice took on a directness of tone. 'As I understand it, Alice has had all her physical checks, which have come up negative.'

'But what about other things?' Jack asked. 'What about autism? She shows all the signs and yet Lilly won't have her diagnosed.'

'Alice is far too young for such a diagnosis,' Sheba replied. 'No doctor would consider it at her age.' She gave him a hard stare. 'Frankly, Jack, I'm disappointed in you. I know you and Lilly have separated, but you owe her more respect and kindness than this.'

'Respect has to be earned,' Kate said.

Sheba looked at Kate as if she were a silly ten-year-old trying to pick a fight and gave a dramatic sigh.

'Has it come to this, Jack?' she asked. 'I really did think better of you.'

Back in the car, Lilly placed the padded envelope with the brown one given to her that morning. What was it? The forensic tests couldn't possibly have arrived so soon could they?

She grabbed it, but before she could tear the paper, her mobile rang. It was Sheba.

'Hey, yummy mummy,' Lilly said.

'You sound terrible,' said Sheba.

'Cold,' Lilly explained.

She checked the temperature gauge on the dashboard. Minus three. How could she still feel so hot? She opened her top two buttons.

'Lilly, I'll get straight to the point,' said Sheba. 'I met Jack earlier today in John Lewis and I didn't like what he had to say at all.'

'Oh yeah?'

'He was very critical of you and how you're dealing with Alice,' said Sheba.

Lilly was stunned. Jack had been discussing their business in a shop? With Sheba? He barely knew Sheba.

'The woman he had in tow didn't help either,' said Sheba.

Woman?

'When I say woman,' whispered Sheba, 'I should point out that she was half his age and a shit-stirrer to boot.'

Lilly couldn't speak. Her raw throat had closed up altogether.

'I don't know what they're up to,' said Sheba. 'But I wanted to give you a heads-up.'

Lilly ripped open the envelope and dragged out its contents. 'I know what the bastard's up to,' she said.

She slammed on the brakes and skidded three feet in the snow, smacking the pavement outside Jack's new place. Then she flew out of the car, leaving the door wide open, and hammered on his door with the side of her fist.

He opened it with the look of a rabbit who'd just seen the farmer. 'Lilly?'

'You bastard,' she screamed. 'You utter bastard.'

'Calm down now,' he said.

Lilly held the envelope in her fist. 'You send me this and then tell me to calm down?' She waved it in his face. 'You're trying to take away my girl.'

Hot tears dripped down her hot face, like they'd been doing from the moment she saw what was in the envelope: a letter from Jack's solicitor stating that he would be applying to court for custody of Alice.

'What on earth's going on, Jack?' A young woman appeared behind him, slender, in a denim miniskirt and knee-high boots.

'You?' It was the bloody copper from Jack's nick. 'You and Jack?'

'Go inside, Kate,' said Jack.

'Yes, go back inside, Kate,' Lilly shouted. 'This has absolutely nothing to do with you.'

'I suppose you've said the same thing to Harry Piper,' Kate said with a sneer.

'Harry Piper!' Lilly let out a hysterical laugh. 'I've been on one date with Harry bloody Piper, and it wasn't even that because we got called back to the Grove. Harry has nothing to do with me and my family, whereas you're planning to play mummy to my baby.'

Kate folded her arms.

'You're not denying it then?' Lilly shouted.

'Why should I?' Kate asked. 'You can't do it.'

Lilly stepped forward, fully prepared to punch the bitch in the face.

'Kate, go inside,' said Jack. 'Now.'

Kate scuttled away, leaving Jack and Lilly staring at one another.

'I won't forgive you for this, Jack,' Lilly told him. 'Not ever.'

'I know,' he murmured.

She balled up the envelope, threw it at his feet and staggered back to the car. She drove off as fast as she could, but stopped when she got round the corner, opened the door and vomited into the snow.

Gem staggers in to work, Tyler in her arms.

He ain't hardly slept all night. Coughing and crying, crying and coughing. When Mum still hadn't turned up by four o'clock in the morning, Gem started crying as well.

'This is joke?' Feyza screeches.

'He was fine yesterday, wasn't he?' Gem asks.

They both know full well that he lay down as quiet as a mouse all day long while Gem did eight punters.

'What if someone calls Social Services?' Feyza asks. 'Or police?'

'Who would do that?'

Feyza shrugs. 'A customer maybe.'

'Half the customers in here are the fucking police,' Gem says.

Feyza takes a step towards Gem. When she speaks her voice is quiet. 'Don't give me backchat.'

Gem bites her lip so she won't cry.

'You want work here,' says Feyza. 'You do what I say, yes?'

Gem nods.

'Now put baby in kitchen and get ready,' says Feyza. 'Lots of make-up. You look like shit.'

Lilly rested her head on the steering wheel.

She was spent. Didn't even think she had enough energy to get home. Her mobile rang and she answered it on autopilot.

'Lilly Valentine.'

'What's wrong?' It was Harry. 'Where are you?'

She looked up and down the deserted street. Doors closed to the elements. Families warm and safe inside.

'I'm nowhere, Harry. I'm bloody nowhere.'

'Hold on,' he said. 'I'm coming to find you.'

Half an hour later, Harry slipped into the passenger seat and let Lilly sob into his chest. He didn't say a word while she told him about Jack and Alice. And Kate! He just held her firmly, his arms strong, his breathing rhythmic. When she calmed, he wiped away her tears as if she were a small sad child.

'You must think I'm a complete nutcase,' she said.

Harry shook his head. 'You're just overwhelmed, Lilly, and that's not a crime. You need looking after.'

'I can look after myself.'

'Of course you can,' he said. 'But you've been doing it for too long. Isn't it about time you let someone else in?'

Lilly pushed her hair from her face. Some of the tendrils were wet and stuck to her cheeks. Letting someone in was hard. It made you vulnerable. Was it possible she was ready with Harry? She'd known him such a short time and yet he made her feel so secure.

'What a pair we are,' he said. 'Trouble follows us around.'

'Has something else happened at the Grove?'

'Elaine and John have gone,' he said.

'Gone where?'

Harry sucked air through his teeth. 'Good question. They left in the middle of a shift and won't pick up their phones.'

Here it was then, the answer they'd been waiting for. Foley and Staines were both guilty of the rape on Chloe and weren't going to stick around for forensics to prove it.

'I'd better tell . . .' Lilly stopped mid-sentence. There was no way she was going to call Jack. 'The police station is on my way home. I'll call in and tell them what's happened.'

Harry pulled her into his arms again. 'It's going to be all right, Lilly. It's all going to turn out fine.'

Gem feels fantastic.

Like she could kill a dragon. Like she could fly through the air. Like she could kill a dragon while flying through the air.

She collapses into a fit of giggles.

'Calm it down,' Misty tells her.

But Gem don't want to calm it down. She wants to feel like this for the rest of her life.

She flicks the lighter and puts it to the pipe, sucking in the smoke.

Wooooohoooo . . .

It rushes through her like a train. No, faster than a train, like a plane. Gem's never been on one, but she thinks it must feel like this, rushing through the sky, leaving one of them thin white lines trailing behind.

Who would believe that just a few minutes ago Gem was proper sick and tired? She couldn't see a way past all the shit, what with Mum gone and Tyler poorly. The thought of letting a bunch of old men fuck her made her feel suicidal. When she caught Misty having a rock, she begged her for a try. Now Misty ain't a bad person, but when push comes to shove she's a crackhead so when Gem offered good money, she took it.

'Thing is, Gem,' Misty tells her. 'You've got to ration yourself with this stuff.' She takes a greedy puff from the pipe. 'Otherwise you just end up working to buy more gear.'

Gem nods. She don't want to end up like them girls on the estate, skinny as twigs and covered in bruises, picking up johns in the street, doing them in the back of a car, then running to the dealer for a hit. All day long, that's what they do. Smoke, fuck, smoke, fuck.

Gem ain't going that way. She just needs something to ease it all along.

'Better get a shift on,' Misty says. 'You've got a punter.'

Gem finishes the rock. She's got one of Bill's mates waiting. Big fat fucker who takes too long. So far, she ain't tried Misty's finger-in-the-arse trick, but today she'll give it a go.

She pulls on a dressing gown to go check on Tyler.

Big Fat Fucker is already here, leaning in the kitchen doorway, sweating like a pig.

Gem flies down the corridor. 'What you doing?'

He turns and smiles. 'Hello, darlin'. You pleased to see me?'

'What you doing?' Gem pushes past him into the kitchen where Tyler's sitting up, sucking a lolly. 'Did you give him that?'

'What's up with you?'

'Did he give you that, Ty?' Gem asks the baby. 'Did that man give you the lolly?'

'Nice man,' says Tyler.

Gem pulls it from Tyler's lips and he bursts into tears. 'Why did you give him this?' Gem waves the lolly in Big Fat Fucker's face. 'What are you after?'

'Now just hold on here.'

Tyler screams at the top of his lungs.

'Did you touch him?' Gem shouts. 'Did you fucking touch him?'

Right on cue, Feyza appears. 'What's going on?'

'This one's lost the plot,' says Big Fat Fucker. 'She's only gone and accused me of being a nonce.'

Feyza turns and looks at Gem.

'He can't go round handing out sweets to kids,' says Gem. 'What sort of man does that?'

Before Gem can say anything else, Feyza has given her a slap so hard it knocks her to the floor.

'Shut up now,' Feyza tells her. 'And shut baby up too.'

'He shouldn't even be here,' says Big Fat Fucker. 'It's not right in a place like this.'

'I know,' says Feyza. 'He go now.'

'By rights I should call Social Services,' he says and takes out his mobile.

Gem feels like a nest of rats has been disturbed in her gut. Tyler can't go into care. It would break Mum's heart. And Gem's as well. They'll never get him back. Not after everything that's happened.

She won't let him make the call.

The air around her turns white and her ears ring as she jumps to her feet, throws herself at him and knocks the phone out of his hand. It arcs through the air towards Feyza. Big Fat Fucker stretches for it, misses and grabs a handful of Feyza's hair instead. It comes away in his fingers and he lets out a yell as he drops it to the floor.

Feyza screams and her hands fly to her head, now as bald as one of the Slaughter brothers. 'I fucking kill you,' she shrieks at Gem.

Big Fat Fucker looks at the wig lying on the carpet like a dead cat, then at Feyza. Then he looks at Gem. 'You're all finished,' he says.

Too late he notices that Gem isn't finished with him. When he sees her arm pulling back and the punch coming, it's already connected with his nose, making a proper ugly crunch as the bone breaks. Blood everywhere.

Wooohooo.

Chapter Fourteen

To: Head of Social Services
From: Patricia Lyons, Children's Guardian
Subject: Phoebe Talbot

Further to the meeting on 3 October 2009, I must reiterate
my grave reservations about not passing on the information
of her sister's whereabouts to Phoebe.

Keeping this from her will, I believe, only serve to exacer-
bate her feelings of abandonment and isolation. Her mental
health is already very fragile and I am of the opinion that
this step may prove to be one too far.

I wish for my opposition to be noted formally on Phoebe's
file.

Lilly parked outside the station. A swift recce of the car park told
her Jack wasn't around so she marched into reception and asked to
speak to someone from MCU.

'Officer McNally isn't here,' said the teen, who appeared to have
entirely forgotten their last encounter.

'I know,' said Lilly. 'Anyone will do.'

His hand hovered over the phone, clearly unsure what to do.
Lilly didn't have the patience for this, not now with her temperature soaring and her mind in free fall.

'Get anyone in the team.' She tried to keep her voice at a reasonable level. 'I really do not care who it is.'

When the lad's eyes still wavered, she slammed her hands on the counter. 'Just start at A and work through the list.'

He nodded and began to dial. Sometimes it paid to be unreasonable.

Finally, she was buzzed through to the custody suite where a DI Hammond was bringing in another prisoner. Apparently, he could spare Lilly a few seconds. That was fine by Lilly. All she wanted to do was pass on the information about Foley and Staines and get the hell out of there.

Once in the custody area things weren't so straightforward. Someone, who she assumed was DI Hammond, was chasing a young girl around the benches. The scene was almost comic in that the DI was at least seventeen stone and hardly nimble and the girl was wearing only knickers, bra, suspenders and stockings.

'Just sit down,' DI Hammond begged, his belly rolling from left to right under his shirt.

'Are you his mate?' the girl screamed. 'You lot are all his mates, aren't you?'

'Whose mate?' DI Hammond asked.

'Bill.' She pointed at the DI. 'And Big Fat Fucker and all the rest of them. Do they work here then, do they?'

The girl caught a glimpse of Lilly and darted behind her, holding Lilly in front of her for defence. Lilly could smell sweat and crack. And fear.

'Hold on a minute,' she told DI Hammond. 'Let's all just calm down here.'

The girl behind her was crying now, huge sobs from under her diaphragm.

Lilly took off her jacket and put it around the girl's shoulders.

'I wouldn't do that, miss,' said DI Hammond. 'We picked her up in a brothel.'

Lilly flashed him a look. 'And that means you can treat her as if she isn't human, does it? She's clearly underage and she's clearly very frightened, so can I suggest you stop looking at her as if she's something the cat dragged in and call a doctor.'

By now the girl had sunk to the floor, weeping and pulling her hair.

Lilly crouched next to her. 'Can you tell me your name, sweetheart?'

The girl looked up at Lilly, with eyes so sad and lost, it made Lilly shudder.

'Gem,' the girl whispered.

'I'm Lilly. Do you think you can come and sit on the bench?' Lilly smiled. 'I don't know how much longer an old woman like me can stay in this position.'

'You ain't old,' Gem said.

Lilly helped the girl to her feet. 'That's a matter for discussion.'

She led Gem to the bench where DI Hammond was waiting with a blanket from one of the cells. Lilly grabbed it and put it over the girl's thin legs.

'They've taken my brother,' said Gem. 'They've taken Tyler.'

'She had a little boy with her,' DI Hammond told Lilly.

She nodded as if it were an everyday occurrence that a child would be forced to work as a prostitute and take her younger brother with her. The fact was this was perfectly normal for kids like Gem. They had no choice.

'Where's your mum, Gem?' Lilly asked. 'Where can we find her?'

Tears welled in Gem's eyes once again and she let out a sound so desperate it was obscene. 'Please help us.' She clutched Lilly's arm. 'Please help us.'

The ex's cottage is all rather twee with gingham curtains and herbs growing in pots. I can hardly believe Jack lived here. He must have hated it.

My mobile vibrates in my pocket but I don't answer. It will be him. We've had our first fight, you see. After we bumped into that dreadful woman in John Lewis, the one with the ridiculous name and the baby so ugly I almost gagged, he told me I shouldn't have interfered. Then when Lilly came round to the flat, screeching like a banshee in labour, he was even more angry. He said I had 'made matters worse'.

Bless him.

Of course, I pretended to be hurt. I even managed a few tears.

He's calling to apologize, but I'm going to let him stew just a fraction longer.

Jack needs to understand that nothing else matters now. Just him and me and Alice. We have to finish what we started and can't be sidetracked by a few bumps in the road.

I move a pair of wellington boots from the step with my foot. They're garish yellow with lime green spots. What grown woman chooses something so revolting?

I plaster on a smile and ring the bell.

A man answers. 'Can I help you?'

He's well spoken and needs a decent haircut. This is going to be a breeze.

'WPC Knight.' I hold up my warrant card. 'May I come in?'

Lilly's new client was being seen by the FME. She almost laughed out loud at the situation. Only she could pick up a new case on a routine trip to pass on a message.

Still, what was the point of this job if she couldn't help a kid like Gem? If she'd learned anything in recent times, it was that when a vulnerable child asked for help, she should give it.

While she waited, she began flicking through Lydia's documents, hoping to find something that would help Chloe. After the news clipping of the Talbots' arrest there was a pre-sentence report on the mother, then a psychological assessment of the auntie. As

Lilly read, a story began to emerge. The Talbot children had been routinely and systematically abused, but sadly their torture didn't end with their removal from their parents. Damaged and angry, they ricocheted around care homes and foster placements, moved on and separated from the only thing that had sustained them: each other.

Phoebe Talbot, in particular, seemed to have been broken by this treatment, spiralling into self-destruction.

As fascinating and heartbreaking as all this was, it did beg an obvious question: why did Lydia Morton-Daley have these papers? What did it have to do with her?

Lilly ploughed on. Perhaps Lydia would be mentioned later.

When she reached an application by Gigi Talbot for contact with her younger sisters, she stopped short. There was no mention of Lydia but another familiar name caught her eye. In support of her application, Gigi had attached a report by a Dr Piper. Was that a coincidence? Could there be two Dr Pipers?

Lilly pulled out her mobile to call Harry, but she was distracted by the FME coming out of his room with Gem.

'How is she?' Lilly asked.

'I'd say she's suffering with stress and exhaustion. She needs rest and recuperation.'

'I know a good place,' said Lilly. 'If you can make the calls, doc, I'll drop her there myself.'

'Hold on a minute.' DI Hammond lumbered over. 'There's the small matter of an assault charge.'

'Do you really think the victim's going to give a statement?' Lilly asked. 'A customer in a brothel?'

'You never know,' said DI Hammond.

'I suspect he might be reluctant when he finds out she's fifteen,' said Lilly.

'What with him being a copper an' all,' said Gem.

DI Hammond sighed and his shoulders drooped.

'Bail her to the Grove,' said Lilly. 'We'll come back next week for a review.'

Lilly ushered Gem towards the entrance of the Grove. DI Hammond had rustled up a paper suit for her, but the temperature had dropped dramatically. Minus six and counting, according to the gauge on the dashboard. A fresh flurry of snow whipped round them.

'Don't worry, it's like a sauna inside,' she told Gem.

Despite the cold, Gem lagged behind, shivering into the wind.

Lilly took her hand. 'It'll be fine.'

'I'm not a nutcase,' said Gem.

'Of course you're not, sweetheart,' said Lilly.

Applying gentle pressure, Lilly pulled Gem inside and introduced her to the nurse on reception. While Gem was being processed, Lilly's phone rang. It was Jack so she ignored it. Wasn't it enough that he had accused her of being a bad mother and was threatening to take Alice from her? Did he have to argue with her about Chloe's case too? He must know now that Foley and Staines had done a bunk. He should be spending his time finding them, not harassing Lilly.

A bleep indicated a text. He was persistent if nothing else.

To: Lilly Valentine
From: Jack McNally
Results of DNA tests do not match either suspect.

Lilly stared in disbelief. No match? There had to be a mistake.

She swallowed her pride and her anger and called Jack. 'Are you absolutely sure?' she asked.

'Yes. If you want, you can check with Cheney,' he replied.

'I don't understand it. It has to be them.'

'It isn't,' said Jack. 'And no one else had access to Chloe's room.'

'No one except Harry.'

'Harry wasn't on the list.'

'Well, no,' said Lilly. 'I just assumed you'd test him anyway to exclude him.'

'Why would I do that, Lilly?' Jack asked. 'His name wasn't on the list and he certainly didn't volunteer when I was at the Grove taking samples.'

'Perhaps he didn't realize he needed to,' said Lilly.

'Or perhaps he didn't want to give a sample.'

'Oh come on, Jack, I know you don't like him but you don't think it was him, do you?'

'I don't know what to think, Lilly,' he said. 'I just know that he is the only other person who knew the code to Chloe's room.' He hung up.

The floor zoomed up towards Lilly and she had to put out her hand to steady herself.

'Are you okay, Lilly?' Gem asked.

'It's this cold,' said Lilly. 'It's making me light-headed.'

'Sit down here.' The nurse proffered her chair.

Lilly sat down and put her head between her knees. It couldn't be Harry. It just couldn't be. He was devoted to Chloe and his other patients. He was a man of integrity and honour. Wasn't he?

'I need some air,' she said and rushed from reception.

The night outside was bitter, but Lilly didn't care. At least she could breathe, let her mind clear. She leaned against David's car, her hands burning on the frigid metal, and pictured Harry. The way he wore coloured scarves that matched his eyes. The way he smiled at her. The way he made her feel.

This had to be a mistake. Someone else had got into Chloe's room. Maybe Foley or Staines had given the code to another member of staff. That would explain why they had run away. All

Harry need do was take the DNA test. That would prove he had nothing to do with it.

She was starting to feel better, when she saw the padded envelope on the back seat. It niggled her. Why had Lydia kept these papers? Why was Harry's name in there?

She opened the car door, reached inside and leafed through the file in the snow. Lydia's name didn't appear. Nor Harry after his brief mention. Perhaps it was just a coincidence?

She ploughed on, reading and searching.

When she reached the end, she froze. The last document hit her in the solar plexus. She looked up into the night, snowflakes landing on her face. When she looked back down, nothing had changed. What she thought she'd read was true. In 2010, Phoebe Talbot changed her name to Chloe Church. The magistrate who consented confirmed his 'sincere hope that this will allow Miss Talbot to put away her past and concentrate on her future'.

The documents weren't Lydia's, they were Chloe's. Her friend had probably agreed to keep them safe for her.

Harry must have known all this. If he'd been involved in Gigi's application for contact, was it possible that he didn't know Phoebe had later changed her name? Was it possible he didn't know who Chloe was? And if he did know, why had he denied any knowledge of how she came to be in the Grove? Why had he said no one had ever tried to get in touch with Chloe?

Lilly shook her head. She needed to sort out Gem then she would find Harry and ask him. No doubt he'd be able to explain everything. She stumbled inside to find the nurse alone.

'Where's Gem?' Lilly asked.

'I took her to her room,' said the nurse. 'It's a few doors down from Chloe. Can you find it? We're short-staffed tonight what with the weather.'

'I'll be fine,' Lilly mumbled.

After a couple of false turns, Lilly saw the picture of the dandelion clocks and knew she was on track. She peeped through the glass of the nearest door and saw Gem asleep on her bed. Smiling, she pushed it open as quietly as she could, intending to tuck her client in. A good night's rest would hopefully stave off some of Gem's fears.

She neared the bed and reached for a blanket, but didn't put it over Gem. Something didn't seem right. The girl's skin seemed deathly pale and her breathing too shallow.

'Gem,' she whispered, but the girl didn't stir. 'Gem.' She rubbed her client's cheek. It felt slack.

She wasn't asleep. She was unconscious.

Lilly turned in panic. She had to get help. How long would it take her to run to reception? Too long.

When she saw a figure outside, Lilly's heart leapt in relief and she flew to the door, throwing it open. The figure was Harry. Thank God.

'Harry,' she called.

He was outside Chloe's room now and turned to Lilly's voice.

'Come quickly.' Lilly ran towards him. 'There's something wrong with this patient. I think she's unconscious.'

'Oh my God,' he said. 'What's happened?'

'I don't know, she . . .' Lilly didn't finish her sentence. 'What's that?' She pointed at the syringe in Harry's hand.

'This?' He held it needle up, a drop of liquid swelling from the sharp point. 'Anti-anxiety meds.'

Lilly couldn't swallow. Couldn't breathe.

'I'm having to do the rounds,' said Harry. 'With John gone.'

That made sense. Didn't it?

'Did you give some to Gem?' Lilly asked.

Harry smiled. 'Don't worry, Lilly, it's completely harmless.'

'How do you know that's what she needs?' Lilly asked. 'You can't have assessed her yet.'

'The doctor from the police station called me,' said Harry. 'He gave me his diagnosis.'

Lilly exhaled. It was true the FME had said Gem was suffering with exhaustion and stress. Lilly was overreacting, being paranoid.

'God, Harry, I'm sorry,' she said. 'Everything's getting out of control what with Jack calling about the DNA testing.'

'Oh yes?'

'Turns out there's no match for Foley or Staines.'

'I see.'

'Someone else must have got the code,' said Lilly. 'Someone not on your list. I'm going to suggest to Jack that he tests everyone who works here.'

'Will he agree to that?'

Lilly see-sawed her hand. 'He's not going to be over the moon about it but I think I can persuade him, though you'll have to go first just to exclude yourself.'

Harry's smile didn't slip and that's when Lilly knew. This man she'd embraced. This man she'd kissed. This man she'd wanted to have passionate sex with . . . was Chloe's rapist.

The thought ran through her like a tidal wave and she bent from the waist and retched onto the carpet.

Her next thought was that she was in terrible danger.

Gem can hear screams from outside her room.

She tries to get up but it's proper hard. Like she ain't got no control over her arms and legs.

She bets that doctor is up to no good. The minute she set eyes on him, Gem knew he was a wrong 'un. She's met too many men like that over the years. Men what like young girls.

There's no way she's going to let him in here. She'll barricade herself in if she has to.

She puts all her energy into getting out of bed. She ain't letting that bastard beat her. Wobbling all over the shop, she makes her way to the door, but when she gets there she sees it ain't the doctor shouting, it's her solicitor, Lilly.

She's been proper nice to Gem. Not like solicitors she's had before, who write down every word you say but never look you in the eye. Lilly's different. She makes you feel like you matter. She told Gem not to worry about Tyler, that she'll try and get a placement for him and Gem together.

Gem opens the door to call to Lilly and sees the doctor dragging her down the corridor by her hair.

Lilly kicked out, her shoes flying through the air.

'Harry,' she yelled. 'Harry, stop this.'

He was tearing her hair from its root, the scalp on fire. She clawed at his hands, but his grip just tightened.

Jesus Christ, he was insane.

Pain seared through Lilly's skull and she cried out. 'Harry, please stop,' she begged. 'Let me go.'

Tears poured down her face. She knew he wouldn't let her go.

Out of the corner of her eye, Lilly caught sight of someone. It was Gem. 'Help me,' she screamed.

Gem was leaning heavily against the door frame to her room, her eyes heavy, her jaw slack.

'Gem, please help me.'

The girl gave a slow blink. A gesture Lilly had seen Chloe make a thousand times. Chloe who shut down her systems when Harry was around. Chloe who only came to life when she was away from the Grove. Why hadn't Lilly seen all this?

Gem swayed into the corridor, saliva trickling down her chin. What could she possibly do in that state?

'Please,' Lilly screamed.

Gem looked around her, then up and down the corridor.

'There's no one here,' Lilly shouted.

Gem took a step towards Lilly and stumbled. Then another step, as if in painful slow motion.

'Do something, Gem.'

Gem swayed from side to side then bent down and picked up one of Lilly's discarded shoes. She held it up to her face, turning it over as if she'd never seen anything like it before.

'Gem.'

The girl looked at the shoe, then at Lilly, then back at the shoe. At last she threw it at Harry. Her aim was so weak it barely glanced off him, but it was enough to distract him momentarily, giving Lilly a chance. She seized it, ripping his hands from her hair.

He lunged for her, but she was too quick, throwing herself out of his reach. He lunged again and this time she surprised him by throwing herself backwards, smacking the back of her head into his face. The sound of his lips bursting rang in her eyes.

She crawled a few feet away and jumped up.

'Run.' She grabbed Gem by the hand and half pulled, half dragged her down the corridor. But Gem couldn't run and fell off balance. Lilly hauled her back upright, but it was too late. Harry had bridged the gap. He grabbed Gem by the shoulders, spun her round and punched her in the stomach. The girl deflated like a day-old balloon.

'Harry, don't do this,' Lilly said to him.

He moved towards her, his face unrecognizable. Mouth and chin dripping with blood, eyes haunted. Harry Piper had gone. If he had ever existed at all.

Lilly backed away, until she hit the wall behind her. She put out her hands to stop him. He batted them away and pressed his body against hers, crushing her. She began to sob.

'You need help,' she told him. 'You're not well.'

His hands came up and he clasped her throat. Lilly's eyes popped open.

'You can explain to the police.' Lilly choked on her words. 'You won't go to prison.'

His hands tightened, the thumbs digging into Lilly's windpipe. She fought for breath, her mouth wide. Her airway was closed.

She pushed her arms out to the side, palms slapping the wall in terror. The end could be only seconds away. Her vision began to blur. Her arms went rigid, the left hand scratching against brick. The right against something smoother. What was it? She strained to look. The picture of the dandelion clocks. No breath left to blow them.

Harry bared his teeth at her as if he might bite. This evil man was going to rob her children. She refused to let his face be the last thing she saw and closed her eyes. Instead, she pictured those dandelion clocks in their glass frame.

Glass. The thought rocketed through her. Glass.

She balled her fist, drew her arm forward and punched backwards. The frame cracked but didn't break. She punched again. This time the glass shattered and she closed her hand around the nearest shard. It cut deep into her skin but she didn't care. She grabbed it and pulled it away from the rest. Her hand dripped blood as she brought her arm down to her side. It shook with anticipation.

Harry, she thought, what happened to you?

Then she plunged the shard of glass deep and low into Harry's gut.

He gasped, eyes open wide, but he didn't release his grip.

Lilly's hand was slick with both their blood. She almost dropped her weapon.

One last effort, Lilly, she told herself.

She pushed the shard deeper and drew it upwards, feeling skin and muscle tear.

For a second, Harry looked surprised. Then he smiled. 'Lilly?' he said. He coughed, a red smattering rattle. 'Lilly? Is that you?'

He released her throat and toppled back onto the carpet.

Lilly sat on the back steps of the ambulance, having her newly sutured hand bandaged.

'This needs proper stitches at the hospital,' said the paramedic.

Lilly nodded but her mobile rang.

'Ignore it,' the paramedic advised her.

'It's my son,' said Lilly.

The paramedic sighed, but waved at her to take it.

'Sam?'

'Mum, you have to come home now.'

'What's wrong?'

'It's Alice.' Sam's voice was frantic. 'She's gone.'

Lilly stood, pushing away the paramedic. 'What are you talking about, Sam?'

'This woman came to the cottage, saying she was something to do with neighbourhood watch.' He was crying now. 'She said she'd just look at the windows upstairs to make sure they were secure.'

'You let a strange woman into the house?'

'She was a policewoman, Mum. Dad checked her card and everything, but she left without telling us and when we checked on Alice she wasn't in her cot.'

Lilly's heart thumped in her chest. 'What was this policewoman called?'

'Kate something,' said Sam. 'I'm sorry, Mum, I'm so sorry.'

I don't know why the baby keeps howling.

I thought all children were supposed to like sitting in the front seat. The trouble is she keeps rolling about and hitting her head against the door. Presumably that's what those contraptions with the straps are for.

'Oh shush,' I tell her. 'You're giving me a headache.'

It's dark out now, and snowing hard, so visibility is poor. I need to concentrate on the road and can do without Alice breaking my brain in two.

My phone vibrates for the hundredth time. It's Jack again. I should call him back and put him out of his misery, tell him that I forgive him, that our little tiff is over.

When I get home, I think we're going to have some fun, making up.

Jack was waiting for Lilly outside the cottage.

'Where is she?' Lilly shouted.

'I don't know,' he replied. 'I've called and called Kate but no answer.'

'Where's Sam?' Lilly asked.

'Out with David, checking the streets.'

Right on cue, they rounded the drive and Sam ran to his mother, throwing himself into her arms.

'We'll find her.' Lilly kissed the top of his head. 'Don't you worry, we'll find her.'

'She can't have got far in these conditions,' said David. 'The end of the road to the left is impassable.'

'Then she's gone right,' said Lilly.

They all turned in the same direction. How far had Kate gone? Where was she headed?

'I'll see if I can catch up with her,' said Jack, heading to his car.

'Take mine.' David tossed his keys. 'It's much better suited to the snow.'

Jack nodded his thanks and jumped in. Lilly got in the passenger seat.

'Oh no you don't,' said Jack. 'You need to stay here.'

'You think I'm sitting at home while your mad girlfriend is out there somewhere with my little girl?'

Jack's face was grey but he gunned the engine and set off. They worked their way carefully through the snow, skidding occasionally. When they reached the village boundary, Jack stopped at the crossroads.

'Which way?' Panic made Lilly's voice shrill.

'Maybe up there?' Jack gestured to the left turn, snaking up to the Downs. 'It's a short cut back to mine.'

Lilly felt her chest constrict. 'It will be completely treacherous up there.'

'The trouble with Kate is that she thinks she's invincible,' said Jack, pulling left.

Lilly punched the dashboard and yelped as the pain bounced through the bandages.

'Are you going to tell me what happened?' Jack asked.

'Haven't you already heard through the police bongo drums?'

'Yes,' he said. 'But I thought it might be nice to hear it from you.'

'At a time like this you still want to score points?'

The car reached the top of the hill, and Jack slowed to make their descent down the other side. If the tyres lost their grip, it was a long way to slide.

'It's not about point scoring, it's about respect,' he said.

'Respect?' Lilly was incredulous. 'What respect did you show me when you threatened to take Alice?'

He didn't answer. Instead, he just stared down the hill. Halfway down, a car was overturned in the road.

'No.' Lilly jumped from the car. 'Alice?' She ran to the wreck. Jack caught up and checked inside. 'Empty,' he said.

'Jesus Christ.' Lilly looked around wildly. 'Where are they?'

The wind howled across the Downs, snow flaying their faces. How long could a baby in her pyjamas last in this weather? Lilly stumbled out into the dark night, calling her daughter's name. There was no one here. Just miles of rolling hills, all blanketed white.

Behind her, Jack called out, but she couldn't hear him above the wind. She backtracked towards him, using her footprints to ease her steps. After a few strides she groaned at her own stupidity. Lilly wouldn't be the only one leaving footprints. She screwed her eyes, trying to pick out a fresh track. There. Leading from the car, down a steep bank to the right. Lilly waded towards it, slotting her feet in the marks left by Kate. The other woman was younger and fitter, the prints wider apart, but Lilly followed them one by one until they led to a channel.

The going was hard and Lilly's legs turned to lead and her chest began to sting.

'Alice,' she called, but the blizzard threw the words straight back at her.

Up ahead was an ancient tree. Bare branches amputated to stumps. Lilly lumbered towards it, then leaned against its trunk to catch her breath.

What was Kate thinking, coming out here?

'Alice,' Lilly screamed again in desperation.

This time the tree seemed to provide her words with shelter and they weren't batted back at her. Instead, she heard a different sound. A cry. She listened harder. Definitely a cry. It had to be Alice.

Lilly let go of the tree and ran on, her feet in time with Kate's matching her, print for print.

The cries became louder and Lilly thought she saw a figure through the snow. She picked up her pace. Yes. Up ahead. A figure.

Kate was making her way across a ridge. The footpath was narrow. Below was a drop of a hundred feet, maybe more. Lilly felt her feet struggle for purchase.

'Kate,' she shouted. 'It's not safe.'

The figure up ahead lost its footing, putting out one arm for balance. Lilly screamed. If Kate fell, she would take Alice with her.

'Kate, please stop. You and Jack can have Alice, just please keep her safe.'

The figure stopped instantly. Waited. Then turned.

It was Kate, a smile on her face, Alice in her arms. The baby was soaking wet, hair plastered to her scalp, shivering.

'Take her home with Jack,' Lilly told her. 'Do whatever you want, just do it now.'

Kate cocked her head to one side like a bird. 'You'll give her up as easy as that?' she asked.

Lilly held out her arms, as if she could steady Kate from where she stood. 'Of course.'

'You won't fight for your daughter?'

Lilly began to cry. 'You win, Kate.' She sank to the ground. 'You and Jack have ground me down. He's back there if you want him.'

'We're going to be a family.'

Lilly nodded and buried her head in her hands, sobbing.

Kate inched her way back along the ridge. When she came alongside Lilly she paused. 'Actually, Lilly, I'm rather disappointed.'

Lilly looked up at the other woman. For the second time that night, she knew she was in the presence of sheer madness.

'Fuck you,' she shouted and circled Kate's legs, bringing her down onto her back like a felled tree. Then she pulled back her arm and punched Kate square in the mouth. Kate screamed and her hands flew to her face, releasing Alice.

Lilly grabbed her baby and held her close under her coat. Alice clung on for dear life.

'You hit me.' Kate sounded affronted. 'You actually hit me.'

'I didn't want to disappoint.'

★　★　★

Lilly and Jack sat in the back of a police car, while Kate was taken away. Neither could let go of Alice, who lay over both their legs, fast asleep in a blanket.

'I think I'm done with women,' said Jack.

'I know I'm done with men,' Lilly replied.

Chapter Fifteen

The following morning the sun shone. It was a perfect day for playing in the snow before it melted. Sam was outside with Alice, holding her up to an icicle, encouraging her to catch the drips with her tongue.

Lilly watched them with a smile and tried to wash a cup with the hand that wasn't bandaged. When she dropped it back in the soapy water for the second time, David took it from her.

'Cara's asked me to come home,' he said.

'What did you say?' Lilly asked.

'Nothing yet,' he said. 'I wanted to talk to you first.'

'Me?'

'I didn't stop loving you, Lilly, just because you kicked me out,' he said.

'I didn't kick you out,' she retorted.

He held up his hands. 'The point is I never wanted to leave and if you wanted me to stay now, I would.'

She didn't answer. David was a good man. A flawed man, but a good one. Not so long ago, he had made her heart skip a beat just by walking into the room.

It was going to break Sam's heart when he left.

Sheba met Lilly at the Grove. She looked incredible for a woman who had given birth so recently.

'You are looking at the new senior medic,' she told Lilly.

'Isn't it a bit soon?' Lilly asked. 'What about maternity leave?'

Sheba waved her away. 'Women like us need our work.'

'Speaking of which,' said Lilly. 'I need to speak to Chloe.'

'*Mi casa, tu casa*,' said Sheba.

Lilly made her way to Chloe's room. She hadn't put her hand up to knock when it opened.

'Lilly.' Chloe hugged her tight. 'Lilly, are you all right?'

Lilly laughed. 'I'll live.'

Chloe led her into the room by the hand. Sunshine streamed in. 'Is he dead?' she asked.

'No,' said Lilly. 'He's recovering in hospital. When he's well enough, he'll be charged with your rape.'

'Will I have to give evidence?'

'Yes.'

'Good,' said Chloe.

'And Jack's reinvestigating Lydia's murder,' said Lilly. 'You're still under suspicion, but he needs to be sure Harry didn't kill her.'

Chloe wandered to the window and traced a water droplet with her finger as it meandered down the pane. 'They won't find any evidence against him for that,' she said.

'No?'

'No.' Chloe turned around and smiled sadly. 'Lydia killed herself.'

'What?'

'We saved up our meds, hid the pills under our tongues,' said Chloe. 'It's easy if you know how.'

'Why did she do it?'

'She couldn't stand it, Lilly. Her dad doing those things to her,' she said. 'She wasn't as strong as me.'

Lilly imagined how hard that would be. How destructive it must have made Lydia feel. The girl had come to the end of her tether and looked to her friend for assistance.

312

'What about the words carved on her stomach?' Lilly asked.

Chloe lowered her eyes.

'You?' Lilly asked.

'I had to send a message somehow,' said Chloe. 'You didn't answer my first one.'

Lilly wondered if she had known all along. She rifled through her bag and pulled out the padded envelope. 'This is yours, I believe.'

Gingerly, Chloe reached out for it. 'Did you read it?'

'Of course.'

'That's my story,' said Chloe. 'My whole story.'

'Not quite,' said Lilly. 'I decided to contact your old guardian, Patricia.'

'She was always nice, Pat was.'

Lilly nodded. 'She kept an eye on you all, even when the case was closed. For one thing, she knew you were in here.' She paused. 'She also knows where Gigi is.'

For a moment, Chloe said nothing then she let out a noise that was a wail and a laugh all at the same time. She grabbed Lilly's arm.

'Lydia said we could trust you.' She smiled at Lilly. 'She said all along that you would help us.'

As Lilly made her way towards the exit, she wondered what Chloe's life might hold. There could be no happy endings, that was certain. Perhaps some peace after all these years?

She waved at the receptionist, who was caught in an argument with a young woman brandishing a bunch of garage carnations.

'No, I'm not next of kin, I'm a friend,' the young woman shouted. 'That a crime round here is it?'

'Everything okay?' Lilly asked.

The young woman spun to the sound of Lilly's voice, dirty blonde hair whipping her hollow cheeks.

'Well, fuck me sideways,' she said. 'If it isn't Lilly Valentine.'

Lilly smiled. It had been years since they'd last met, but she'd recognize that voice and those pink scars around her mouth anywhere.

'Kelsey Brand,' she said. 'How the devil are you?'

Kelsey shrugged. 'You know.'

'Kept out of trouble?' Lilly asked.

She'd represented Kelsey in a trial where she'd been accused of killing her own mother and hoped the poor kid's life had changed for the better after the 'not guilty' verdict.

'Misty!'

Behind them, Gem rushed down the corridor and threw herself at Lilly's old client.

'Misty?' Lilly raised an eyebrow.

'Don't ask,' said Kelsey and gave Gem a quick hug. 'Mind my clothes.' She pushed Gem away and thrust the flowers at her.

'You two know each other then?' Lilly asked.

'Misty's been looking out for me,' said Gem.

'Didn't do a very good job, did I?' Kelsey sniffed. 'Seeing as how you've ended up in the nuthouse.'

'I ain't going to be here for long,' Gem told her. 'I'm going into foster care with Tyler.'

'If Social Services can get a placement for you both,' said Lilly.

Kelsey nodded. 'Families should be together.' She pointed at a coffee machine. 'Come on, I'm gagging for a cuppa.'

Lilly watched Kelsey and Gem chat as they tried to work the machine. Two more girls she had tried to help. Two more girls for whom, like Chloe, there were no happy endings. Then she headed out into the cold, bright morning wishing life could be just a bit more straightforward.